What others are
about the Sun Coast

"I've read *Evidence of Mercy* ... my wife's
excellent ... A gain for the Christian community, a gain for the world. I
think Terri's going to have a great impact ..."

Marvin Sanders,
American Family Radio, on "Today's Issues"

"Terri Blackstock has much experience in writing fiction for the general market. The quality of her writing is evident in *Evidence of Mercy*, and her style of writing should appeal to both men and women who enjoy plenty of suspense, a touch of romance, and a thought-provoking example of faith in action. The Christian fiction community has reason to celebrate the arrival of this talented writer and to look forward to future installments of the Sun Coast Chronicles."

Christian Book Review

"A romance writer who is moving from the ABA to the CBA market with this work, Blackstock crafts a fine tale of intrigue and romance."

Library Journal

"Once again, Terri Blackstock has shown us what hard-hitting, suspense fiction is all about. *Justifiable Means* lives up to its billing. ... Is it pure entertainment? Hardly. Blackstock shows a struggling, vulnerable Christian dealing with the challenge of compromise, as well as the consequences of taking God's matters of justice into our own hands. Is it challenging? Of course. She knows right where to hit us. This one certainly has a 'male appeal.' Is it only for the choir? No way. This one is a good one for a gift to unbelievers. It doesn't threaten, but it doesn't shy away from the presentation of the challenging truth, either. Since it's baseball season, I'd say she knocked it out of the park!"

Harry Kraus, M.D.,
author of *Stainless Steel Hearts* and *Fated Genes*

"Terri Blackstock's Christian suspense novel, *Evidence of Mercy* (Zondervan, 358 pages) joins the ranks of powerfully written, 'gentler' fiction. ... It is well-written, skillfully tempered, and loaded with the elements needed to keep pages turning."

The Grand Rapids Press

"Readers will enjoy *Evidence of Mercy* by Terri Blackstock. Terri, who used to write secular romance novels until the Spirit of God spoke to her heart, has turned her talents to the field of Christian romance/suspense, and you'll love this thriller! I read it in a single evening, not because it was short, but because it was good!"

Angela Elwell Hunt

"Former Harlequin and Silhouette author Terri Blackstock has crafted a romantic, fast-paced thriller that illustrates the power of God's forgiveness. *Evidence of Mercy* will have its readers eagerly awaiting the second book in this Sun Coast Chronicles series."

Aspire Magazine

"*Evidence of Mercy*, by veteran writer Terri Blackstock, is strongly reminiscent of books by Robin Cook (in its use of 'soft' violence and multiple points of view) and Mary Higgins Clark (in its portrayal of the heroine and the romantic element). Unlike many recently released novels that kind of 'ambush' the reader with the surprise discovery well into the book that there's a Christian message, the element of faith is introduced early."

Release Ink

"Fast-paced and emotionally charged, this book is sure to leave readers eagerly awaiting the next release. Blackstock's characters are believable and contemporary. The message of God's forgiveness is beautifully presented as Lynda rediscovers the faith she's neglected over the years. The author's chilling insight into domestic violence touches a relevant social issue. Her well-researched scenarios provide the realism that accounts for the growing popularity of legal thrillers. While Blackstock may be a new name in Christian publishing, her secular romances have sold more than 2.5 million copies. Romance/suspense readers will applaud her move to the Christian market."

Bookstore Journal

"Terri Blackstock's writing in her first CBA novel, *Evidence of Mercy*, can be compared to ABA mystery writer Mary Higgins Clark's. Some similarities: Heroines are independent, professional women; villains stalk the heroine with building suspense; love interest develops gradually and is not the focus of the action; violence is not graphic. Be on the lookout for her future projects."

Christian Retailing

SUN·COAST 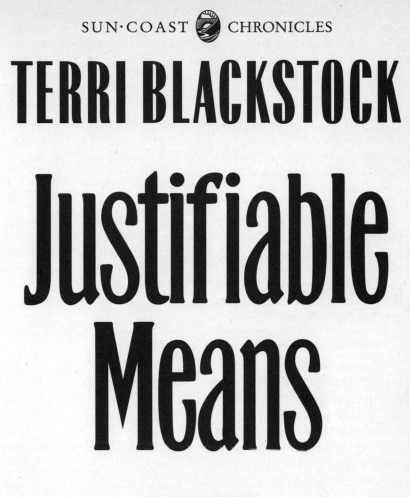 CHRONICLES

TERRI BLACKSTOCK

Justifiable Means

ZondervanPublishingHouse
Grand Rapids, Michigan

A Division of HarperCollins*Publishers*

Justifiable Means
Copyright © 1996 by Terri Blackstock

Requests for information should be addressed to:

📖 ZondervanPublishingHouse
Grand Rapids, Michigan 49530

Library of Congress Cataloging-in-Publication Data

Blackstock, Terri.
   Justifiable Means: a novel of suspense / Terri Blackstock.
     p.   cm. — (Sun coast chronicles ; bk. 2)
   ISBN: 0-310-20016-4
   I. Title.   II. Series: Blackstock, Terri, 1957–   Sun coast chronicles ; bk. 2.
PS3552.L34285J87   1996
813'.54—dc 20
                                   96-11939
                                     CIP

Published in association with the literary agency of Alive Communications, 1465 Kelly Johnson Blvd., Suite 320, Colorado Springs, CO 80920.

Interior design by Sue Vandenberg Koppenol

Printed in the United States of America

99 00 01 02 / ❖ DH/ 10 9 8

This book is lovingly dedicated to the Nazarene.

ACKNOWLEDGMENTS

Special thanks to all of my AOL friends who shared their expertise with me. I am so grateful for the help of Florida attorneys Michael Cohen, James Mays, Mike Gotschall, and a certain judge who wishes to remain anonymous. Also, many thanks to the cops who answered my endless questions—Lou and Pat and others who didn't want their names published. And a huge thank you to Cathy Logg, Washington state crime reporter, who continues to be a wonderful resource.

I also thank my children—Michelle, Marie, and Lindsey, for not taking it personally when my preoccupied "Uhh-hmms" don't really answer their questions—and my husband, Ken, for keeping the family going even when I'm buried in the pages of another world. Without his powerful prayers, his support, and his constant encouragement, I'd have found an easier job long ago.

But most of all, I thank the One who called me and set me apart, and turned my writing into something that has purpose. He truly is a God of second chances.

CHAPTER ONE

The lights from the squad cars were still flashing in the night, illuminating the modest apartment building in alternate shades of blue and black. Larry Millsaps pulled his unmarked Chevy to the curb and glanced at his partner. "So much for having a night off."

Tony Danks nodded bleakly as he scanned the crowd forming on the sidewalk. Officers were already questioning some of the neighbors, and other uniformed cops came and went through the building's front door. "This hasn't happened in—how long?"

Larry grabbed his windbreaker from the backseat and pulled it on over the 9 mm he had holstered under his arm. "Almost a year since the last one."

They got out of the car and pushed through the crowd, not bothering to flash their badges since all of the cops in the small St. Clair Police Department knew the two detectives by sight. They made their way through the crowd into the building. "One a year is too many for me," Larry said. He'd been plagued by the trauma on the young girl's face the last time. There was a look that rape victims wore, a waiflike, haunted look that spoke of violation and soul-deep despair. This one probably would be no different, and he started up the stairs reluctantly, past the other tenants who were watching the open door of the apartment with fascination and dread, waiting for bits and pieces of the drama to be revealed.

There were four cops inside the apartment, two with cameras and one with a camcorder, recording the crime scene just as they'd found it. Lamps were broken, tables overturned, glass shattered ...

Larry spotted the victim then, sitting alone on a chair in a corner, cocooned in a blanket, her blonde hair wet and stringing in her face and around her shoulders, her pale blue eyes raw and swollen from crying. One of the cops handed him a clipboard with her report on it, then turned his back to her and, in a quiet voice, said, "She showered before she called."

"Figures," Tony whispered.

Larry looked back at the young woman and felt that familiar, unwelcome stirring of frustration and compassion as she glanced hopefully up at him with big, blue, tearful eyes, as if he might offer her some comfort, some hope, some . . . *something*. Her showering would definitely make it tougher to get the evidence they needed, but Larry couldn't say he blamed her. She had been defiled, desecrated, dehumanized, and he couldn't imagine any victim of such abuse *not* wanting to wash the filth away.

"Is she hurt?" he asked.

The uniformed cop nodded. "He had a knife. She has a pretty deep cut on her leg. The ambulance should be here soon."

Larry stepped over the broken glass, the lamp shades on their sides, and skirted around the overturned table until he stood in front of the woman. "Hi, I'm Detective Millsaps." He glanced over his shoulder and saw that Tony was right behind him. "This is my partner, Detective Danks. Are you all right?"

She swallowed hard and whispered, "Yes."

Stooping down to get eye level with her, Larry glanced down at the report the other officer had handed him. "Your name is Melissa Nelson? May I call you Melissa?"

"Yes," she said again.

"Good," he said in a don't-spook-the-victim voice. "And you can call me Larry. He's Tony." He scanned the information the first cop to the scene had compiled, and saw that she was twenty-three years old. He looked into her face again. "Melissa, I know that you've already given your statement, but would you mind telling it one more time? Tony and I will be the ones trying to find the man who did this to you. We really need to hear it firsthand."

A stark, determined look filled her reddened eyes. "Yes. I'll tell it over and over until they catch him," she said through clenched teeth. "I don't care how many times I have to tell it."

"Good. First, could you start with a description of him?"

"I can do better than that," she said, smearing her tears away with a trembling hand. "I can give you his name."

"You know him?" Tony asked, sitting down on an ottoman near her chair.

"Yes. I work with him. His name is Edward Soames, and he lives in some apartments on Fresco Street on the north side of town."

Larry jotted down the street. "Have you given this information to anyone else?"

"Yes," she said. "The first officer I talked to is calling it in." A sob broke her voice, and she gave in to it, then tried to recover. "He probably thought I wouldn't tell anybody, that I'd be too ashamed. That I'd just sit here and deal with it."

Tony took his notepad out of his coat pocket and clicked his pen. "Was this someone you were dating?"

She shot him a disgusted look. "Of course not. I was just sitting here watching television, and he knocked on the door. When I opened it, he pushed his way in. He grabbed me, and . . . I started fighting him with everything I had . . . but it didn't stop him . . ."

"I understand he had a weapon?" Larry asked.

"Yes," she said. "A knife. A switchblade, I think." She opened her blanket, revealing the shorts and T-shirt she wore, and lifted the bloody towel she'd been pressing on her leg. "I thought he was going to kill me."

Larry winced at the sight of the cut. "That's deep. You're going to need stitches. The ambulance should be here soon."

"It just all happened so fast," she went on. "And then he was gone . . . and . . . I didn't know what to do. I was so disgusted, so repulsed . . . I didn't think about the evidence. I just wanted to wash it all away . . . but it's not going to go away . . ."

She was trembling, and Larry feared she was going into shock from loss of blood. He made her press the towel back over the wound. Outside, sirens sounded. He hoped it was the ambulance.

"He . . . he touched that table. His fingerprints are there. And they're on the doorknob. And he had my blood on his shirt when he left . . . it was a . . . a T-shirt with some cartoon on it. And if he's not home, if you need to identify him, there's a picture of him in his office at work. We both work at Proffer Builders, over on

Haynes Street. He has a recent picture of himself on his desk, catching a fish or something. You could use that to identify him. My boss, Henry Proffer, could let you in. He's in the book."

Tony jotted rapidly as she spoke, and Larry was amazed at how easy it was to get information out of her. Victims of such trauma were usually confused, disoriented, and too upset to remember details.

"Has he ever threatened you before?"

"No," she said. "Oh, he's come on to me, but I just blew it off. I didn't know he was capable of this."

They heard the paramedics running up the stairs. "Melissa, we'll talk to you later. You go get that leg stitched up and let the doctor examine you."

Larry started to stand up, but she grabbed his coat and looked up at him desperately. "You won't just let this go, will you? You're going to go pick him up, aren't you?"

"Of course. Someone's probably picking him up right now."

The paramedics hustled in, but she kept clinging to Larry's coat. "But what if he didn't go straight home? He probably wouldn't. He would know that someone might be looking for him. You have to find him! He's dangerous, and he'll come after me again."

"We won't rest until we have him behind bars," Larry assured her. "You have my promise. Now show them your leg. She needs stitches, guys, and she's lost a lot of blood."

"Let's get you onto the stretcher," one of the EMTs said, coaxing her out of her chair onto her good leg.

"But behind bars isn't good enough!" she pled through gritted teeth, eyes desperate, in obvious pain as she stood. "You have to keep him there. You have to get a conviction."

"We will."

She glanced frantically around the apartment as they tried to put her on the stretcher. "My word won't be good enough. You'll have to have enough evidence. You can't forget anything!"

Larry frowned. "Our police officers are trained, Melissa. They know what to do."

"But will they dust for fingerprints? Will they look for hair follicles, to prove he was here? They can't just stop with my identification of him!"

The paramedics began to carry her out, even though she hadn't yet lain down. "Please don't let them miss anything," she said. "Find the officer I talked to first. I gave him more details— you need to know them."

"We will, Melissa," Larry said. "Just try to relax. We'll talk to you after the doctor examines you. And I'll let you know the minute we pick him up."

But the look on her face as she finally lay down told him that she would believe it when she saw it. Larry watched the paramedics carry her out. Slowly, he turned back to his partner.

Tony looked pensive, perplexed. "Well, she sure came out of her shell. Coaching us on police procedure? That's a first."

Larry shook his head. "Maybe we just underestimated her because she looks so fragile. She's obviously pretty sharp. And let's face it—botched investigations make headlines. You can't blame her for being careful."

Tony stared at the empty doorway for a moment longer. "Yeah, but careful is one thing. There was something more than careful there. Doesn't feel right."

"You're not suggesting she's lying."

"No," Tony said thoughtfully. "Not exactly. I'm just saying that something doesn't ring true. It was all too easy."

"You could look in her face and tell she was raped," Larry said quietly.

"Unfortunately, facial expressions don't hold much water in court."

"Give me a break, Tony. Are we gonna make a broken, violated woman tap-dance and stand on her head to prove that what she described really happened? There's no reason anyone would want to put herself through all this if it didn't really happen."

"Put herself through what?" Tony asked.

"Through *what?* Are you kidding?" Larry asked. "You think this is fun for her? The interrogations of cops who don't believe her, lawyers who drag her through the mud—"

"Okay, okay," Tony cut in. "Maybe you're right. Obviously, there's plenty of evidence here."

"And there'll probably be a lot more when we find this guy."

"We'll see, buddy," Tony said. "I hope you're right."

Two hours later, after being photographed, stitched, examined, and interrogated by the doctors and social workers who claimed to want to help her, Melissa sat alone in the examining room. She had turned the lights off; now she watched frantically out the window into the parking lot for some sign of Edward Soames.

He's going to kill me, she thought miserably. *If they don't lock him up, he'll kill me.*

But they hadn't locked him up. So far, according to the social worker who'd made some phone calls for her, he hadn't even been picked up. He was still out there somewhere, driving around, no doubt looking for vulnerable women to attack.

She had begged the doctor not to release her—not until Soames was off the streets and in police custody. She was too terrified to stay in that apartment by herself, too plagued with memories—she would get no rest. If she could just stay here overnight, long enough for them to find him, then tomorrow she could face going home.

Reluctantly, the doctor had agreed, but told her that, before they admitted her, a police detective would need to talk to her some more. She didn't know why. She'd already given them more than enough information to find him and arrest him. She'd left nothing to chance. Instead of talking to her, they ought to be out looking for him.

She heard footsteps coming up the hall and looked toward the door. Her doctor ambled into the room, studying her chart. "Okay, Melissa," he said, still in the soft, cautious voice that made her want to scream. "We're going to move you to a room now. Are you sure you want to stay?"

"Will it have a guard?" she asked.

"I'm afraid not. But I'm sure you'll be safe here. They'll have this guy picked up in no time, and you won't have to worry."

She sighed and looked out the window again. A car had just driven up, and a tall, slender man was getting out. Was that him? No, she thought with relief. Not yet.

She stood up, wincing at the pain from the stitched gash on her thigh, and the doctor made her sit back down. "An orderly is bringing a wheelchair. You need to stay off that leg for a while. You don't want to break the stitches. Oh, and I've prescribed some-thing for pain, if you need it."

Her eyes strayed out the window again. "No, I don't want it. I need to stay sharp, just in case." The orderly wheeled the chair in, but she didn't take her eyes from the window. "Does that room have a window over the parking lot?"

The doctor glanced at the orderly. "I don't know. Does it?"

The orderly thought for a moment. "Yeah, I think it does. I can change her to a room that doesn't, if she wants—"

"No," she cut in, getting up on her good leg and transferring her weight to the chair. "I want to be able to see the parking lot. I need to see who's coming."

The doctor shot another look at the orderly. She realized that they thought she was suffering from paranoid delusions, but she didn't care.

The orderly wheeled her out, and the doctor stayed beside her. "Oh, Detective Millsaps called and said that he might not be able to come back by tonight. He said it might be morning before he could make it."

"No," she said quickly. "Tell him to come tonight. Please. I don't care what time it is. I don't think I'll do much sleeping tonight."

"We could give you something to help you."

"No," she said again. "I told you, I need to stay alert. Tell him to come no matter how late it is. Have they found Soames yet?"

"He didn't say."

Tears sprang to her eyes again, and she scanned the hallway as if he might jump out of one of the rooms at any moment. "He's still out there. He's too smart to get caught."

"If he's in St. Clair, they'll find him."

"And what if he's not? What if he's already left town?"

"Then you're safe. You don't have to worry."

But his logic was lost on Melissa, and as they pushed her onto the elevator, she tried not to panic. This was just the beginning, after all; it was too soon to jump to conclusions. Larry what's-his-name had seemed competent. Maybe he would catch him. Maybe Soames would finally be taken off the streets. Maybe women everywhere would be safe from his violence.

It had taken two hours to get the warrant they needed for Soames's arrest, as well as a search warrant to check out his apartment, car, and place of business. Though the paperwork had taken longer than he wanted, Larry had been confident that the uniformed officers would find and apprehend Soames even before the warrant was in Larry's hand. But Soames had managed to evade them so far.

As they walked rapidly between the police squad cars in the parking lot toward their own unmarked car, Tony said, "You have that look on your face, Larry."

"What look?"

"The look that says you know exactly where we're going to find Soames."

"Wish I did, pal. I was thinking we should probably go by his office first and get that picture Melissa told us about. Then we could start with the bars in town. See what turns up."

Tony climbed into the passenger seat and checked his notes as Larry started the car and pulled out into traffic. "Let's see. We have the name of the business owner. We could ask him to meet us there to let us in."

"That's what I was thinking. Meanwhile, if Soames is stupid enough to go home, we have people there waiting for him."

"Sure would help if we had a tag number."

"Yeah. Kind of weird, don't you think? A man that age not having a tag registered to him?"

"Maybe he uses somebody else's car."

"Or maybe he drives a stolen car."

Tony grinned and nodded toward a pay phone coming up on their right. "Pull over. I'll call her boss."

Larry watched, chin propped on his palm, as Tony made the phone call. He tried to calm the rising tide of urgency he felt. But that woman sitting with wet hair stringing around her shoulders, trembling as she hugged her bloody knees to her chest, had gotten under his skin, and he wanted, badly, to give her some peace—right now.

Tony got back into the car. "He said he'd meet us there. Sounded helpful. He said he had the guy's tag number in a file at the office, too."

"Great. Let's go."

CHAPTER TWO

Henry Proffer, a short man with Hulk Hogan arms and a ruddy complexion from years under the harsh Florida sun, was waiting when Larry and Tony reached the small office of Proffer Builders. "Is Soames all right?" he asked. "He didn't have an accident or anything, did he?"

"There was a rape tonight," Larry said as he followed the man in and waited for him to flick on the light. "Another one of your employees—Melissa Nelson. Edward Soames is a suspect."

The man's face drained of color. "Melissa—raped? When? Was it here?"

"No," Tony said. "In her apartment. She said there was a picture of Soames on his desk. We need to use it and look around a little."

Looking disturbed, Henry led them down the hall to a small office. He turned on the light, then stepped back as they walked into the immaculate room. "She said *Soames* raped her? You sure that's what she said?"

"Absolutely. When's the last time you saw him?"

"Well . . . today. Around 4:30 or so. It was just an ordinary day. He's my best architect. He's not a rapist!" Distraught, he watched as they took the picture, studied it, and deposited it in a paper sack.

"Can you tell us anything about Soames? What kind of man he is? Where he likes to go after work? Any abnormal behavior you've noticed with women?"

Henry lowered himself into a chair and raked a hand through his hair. "Well, he seems like a decent guy. He does good work. I've never gotten to know him that well, but I've had no complaints about him." He frowned as he looked up at them again. "Uh . . . what were the other questions? Oh, yeah. Women. Well, he was kind of a flirt. But then, so am I. No crime in that. I wouldn't think he'd have to force himself on anyone. I mean, he never had trouble getting a date. Women like him."

"What about Melissa? Did he ever show any interest in her?"

"Well, sure. I mean, so did I. She's a cute girl. A little too serious, sometimes. She's kind of hard to get to know. Doesn't talk much. Kind of high-strung. You know—jumpy. She's only worked here about a month, so none of us knows her very well."

"She get along with Soames?"

"Well, yeah. I mean, I guess so. I kind of thought she might have a crush on him, tell you the truth. She acted funny around him. You know, tense. Clumsy. That kind of thing."

Larry gave Tony a troubled glance. "You said you had his tag number?" Tony asked.

"Sure," Henry said. Popping out of the chair, he rushed down the hall. Larry followed him.

"This is too much," Henry said when he reached his own office. "I mean, what am I gonna do tomorrow? Is Melissa gonna be back? Is Soames? We're working on a big bid for a new office complex on Highland Drive. I can't do without either of them." He pulled out the file he'd been looking for and flipped through it. "Here it is." He got a pen and jotted the number down. "He drives a dark blue Cherokee. Couple of years old. Oh—and you asked where he liked to hang out. He has a favorite bar over on Triumph Street—you know, over by the Kash 'n' Karry. Steppin' Out, I think it's called."

"Thanks." Taking the paper from him, Larry hurried back up the hall to where Tony was still looking through Soames's things. "Come on, Tony," he said. "I think we've got him."

It took only a few minutes to run the tag number through the police computer.

"Edward J. Pendergrast?" Tony jotted the number down. "What do you think, Larry? Is it someone else's car, or did this guy change his name?"

Larry grabbed the radio mike. "Do me a favor, Jane," he told the desk cop who'd done the search for him. "See what you've got on that name."

The radio crackled. "Will do."

A few minutes later, Jane radioed back. "Hey, Larry. Are you ready for this?"

"Yeah, go ahead."

"Edward J. Pendergrast has a rap sheet. Two rape charges, as well as breaking and entering, and assault with a deadly weapon. In the first case, the grand jury acquitted him of all charges due to lack of evidence. The second one never even got to the grand jury because the judge released him on a technicality. Something about an illegal search and seizure."

Larry glanced at Tony. "You believe this?"

"He obviously changed his name. Got to be him."

"Let's get him," Larry said.

Steppin' Out was a popular bar where young professionals came to mingle and drink and dance after work each night. The parking lot was full of BMWs and Mercedes, Jaguars and Infinities. When they found the dark blue Cherokee, they checked the number. "That's it. That's the number," Larry said, trying to control his rush of adrenaline. "He's inside."

"Did you get a good enough look at that picture to recognize him?"

"I think so. Let's go."

They double-parked behind the Cherokee so that their suspect couldn't make a run for it, then went in and tried to blend into the crowd. The mingling aromas of two-hundred-dollar-an-ounce perfume, cheap aftershave, booze, and cigarette smoke wafted on the air, and the music from the band sent a deafening roar over the voices and laughter around them.

"And they really come here to relax after work?" Larry asked his partner facetiously as they wove through the crowd.

"It's really not such a bad place. You should try it sometime when you're not on duty."

"No, thanks, pal," Larry said. "I prefer to breathe clean air and have a little peace and quiet when I relax."

Tony grinned. It was no secret that Larry never darkened the door of any of the bars in town unless he was on duty and looking for someone. Tony, however, didn't mind stopping in now and then. "Great place to meet women."

"I meet plenty of women," Larry said.

"Right," Tony muttered with a smirk. "At church. That's a surefire setup for disaster. Get involved with Judy Churchgoer, and you've automatically got to start giving up stuff, making commitments, acting like the Pope. No, I'd rather meet someone in a place like this, where nobody really expects anything."

Larry had heard it all before. He concentrated on scanning the faces of the people at the bar.

"See anything?" Tony asked.

"Not yet. You?"

Tony shook his head, then checked the faces at the tables—men with their most seductive smiles, women with their faces tipped up in anticipation. A soft haze of smoke gently floated over their heads, as if it held some magic that would cast a spell on each of them.

"There." Larry grabbed Tony's arm and nodded toward the back corner of the room.

It was the face they had seen in the picture, though it wasn't as happy as it had been when photographed catching a twenty-pound bass. He seemed to be sulking as he sipped on his drink and watched a group of women at the bar. His striped pullover shirt was clean and freshly pressed, as were his khaki trousers. He'd obviously gone home to shower after leaving Melissa's—he must have been quick, since he hadn't been home when they'd tried to pick him up.

"Here goes." They wound their way between tables. Soames saw them coming toward him and straightened.

"Edward Soames?" Larry asked, extending his right hand as if to shake.

Soames looked from one man to the other, then accepted the handshake. "Yeah, that's me."

Larry snapped his handcuffs on Soames's wrist. "I'm Larry Millsaps, with the St. Clair Police Department. I have a warrant for your arrest. Would you come with us, please?"

Soames sprang out of his chair and tried to wrest his hand away. "For what?"

"You're being charged with the rape of Melissa Nelson. You have the right to remain silent . . ." As he rambled off the words that had become second nature, he jerked Soames's other arm in front of him and snapped the second cuff.

Even in the darkness, Soames's face was visibly reddening. "Wait a minute! I didn't touch her! What did she say?"

"If you cannot afford an attorney, one will be appointed . . ."

"This is crazy!" Soames shouted. "I never laid a hand on her! She invited me over, then changed her mind and said she was sick or something. I left! That's all there was to it!"

"That's not what *she* says, pal."

"Then she's a liar! I didn't *do* anything!"

The band stopped playing midsong, letting the chorus die a slow death. The crowd in the bar had already grown suddenly quiet. As Tony frisked him, Soames cursed and searched the faces around him. "Hey, McRae!" he shouted. "I need a lawyer, man! Help me!"

Larry groaned as Steve McRae, a lawyer he had had run-ins with before, hurried through the crowd. "I'm his lawyer. What's going on here?"

"They're arresting me for rape!" Soames whispered harshly. "*Do* something!"

"Do you have a warrant?" the lawyer asked the detectives.

"We sure do, McRae," Tony said, pulling it out of his pocket. "We also have one to search his car and his apartment."

"They're trying to pin a *rape* on me," Soames whispered so that the crowd wouldn't hear. "A rape that never happened."

McRae raised one finger to quiet him. "Don't say a word," he ordered. "Not one word. Calm down and just go with them, and we'll get this all straightened out."

Soames cursed again. His face reddened as they pulled him through the crowd, with McRae following.

"Put him in the car," Larry told Tony. "Radio it in, and I'll start searching his car." He turned back to Soames. "Give me your car keys."

"I'm not giving you anything!" Soames spat out.

"Fine. Then I'll bust a window and unlock it myself."

Soames kicked at some invisible object. "They're in my pocket," he said. "I'm cuffed, remember?"

But before Larry could reach into the man's pocket, Soames slid his own hand in, fished the key chain out, and flung it at him. "You're not gonna find anything in there," he said as Tony pushed his head down and guided him into the unmarked car's backseat. "I'm telling you, she's crazy. You'll find that out yourself. I didn't touch her, man. She started freaking out on me, even pulled a knife on me, and I got out of there."

McRae, the lawyer, leaned into the car. "If you want me representing you, Soames, you're gonna have to shut up, *now*! You and I will talk when you get to the station. You're not gonna tell them anything until I give you permission."

"But I didn't *do* anything, man. I have nothing to hide!"

"That shouldn't be too hard to prove."

Soames wilted back on the seat.

A squad car pulled up, and patrons of the bar spilled out onto the parking lot as Larry got his flashlight and began his search of the car. He checked the glove compartment, handed the registration papers to Tony, then released the trunk latch so that Tony could check inside. Then he bent down and shone his light under the seat.

"Bingo," he said. He stood up and pulled a pair of rubber gloves out of his pockets, slid his hands into them, then bent down again. "We've got something here, Tony."

"What is it?"

"Oh, just a bloody shirt," he said. "With a cartoon on it. And look. A knife."

Tony leaned through the back door, astounded. "You mean he just stuffed them under his seat?"

Larry opened the knife. "Blade's got blood on it. What do you bet it's hers?"

"Why would he be that stupid?"

"Maybe she was right. He banked on her being too ashamed to tell anyone." Larry dropped the shirt into a bag, then the knife into another one. "Is there anything back there?"

"No," Tony said. "The trunk's coming up empty."

Larry slid out of the car and went back to his own. Soames sat in the backseat, his teeth gritted, waiting. "Tell me something, Soames. Why would your car be registered under the name Pendergrast?"

Soames shook his head. "I'm not telling you a thing until I've cleared it with my attorney."

"Fine," Larry said. "Then I guess it's going to be a long night for all of us."

When Soames was booked and locked up, they headed for his apartment. Several tenants came outside at the sight of the fleet of police cars in the parking lot, and Larry assigned one of the officers to question them about Soames. They used his key to get in, then began searching for any sign that a rapist lived there.

The apartment was immaculate, with plush, unblemished furniture and cherrywood tables. Nothing was out of place. The bed was made, all the shoes were put away, and the bathroom was spotless. If there was anything telling here, it would be hidden, Larry decided.

He went through the drawers in the kitchen, looking for anything out of the ordinary. When he found a stack of snapshots, he flipped through them. They were low-quality pictures of women who looked as if they hadn't known they were being photographed, coming in and out of doorways, getting into cars—all photographed from a distance. Carefully, he studied them. A vague reflection on some of them made him wonder if they'd been taken from inside a car.

"Larry!" Tony called from the other room. "Come take a look!"

Larry found Tony in the bedroom closet, where the police photographer was taking pictures of something they'd found on the shelf. "What is it?" Larry asked.

"A bag," Tony said. "It has a pair of binoculars, another knife, and a camera with a night lens."

Larry brandished the stack of photos. "And here's what he was taking pictures of."

Tony glanced through the pictures and looked up at him. "His prey?"

"Could be. Found anything else?"

23

"Yeah. Our man seems to be into pornography. There's magazines up here that would curl your toes. And videos, too."

"Tag 'em. We'll take 'em all."

When they'd labeled everything that seemed to have any significance for their case, they talked to a few of the tenants standing outside. All of them considered Soames a quiet, secretive kind of guy who went out a lot at night and didn't come in until the wee hours of morning.

When they'd finished searching and removed all of the evidence, they drove back to the precinct. "You ready to hear what he has to say for himself?"

"Sure," Tony said. "This ought to be good."

CHAPTER THREE

Melissa didn't feel the pain in her leg until she got the phone call from Larry Millsaps, telling her that Edward Soames had been picked up, and that they'd found the bloody shirt and knife under his seat. They had also discovered, Larry said, that Soames had been charged with rape before, under another name. He wouldn't be going anywhere for a long time, Larry predicted.

Only then had Melissa been able to relax enough to notice the stinging pain of her cut and stitches, or to realize how her head hurt and how exhausted she had become. Even so, her mind was still reeling. What if something about the search had been illegal? What if they'd forgotten to read him his rights? What if the doctor's report was too ambiguous? What if some idiot judge let him out on bail?

She almost wished she had taken the painkiller or the sedative the doctor had offered so that she would be able to rest tonight and have her wits about her tomorrow, when she would need them. It wasn't too late—she could still call the nurse and ask for something. The social worker had urged her to take something to help her sleep, so that her mind could release what had happened. But Melissa couldn't afford to release it. She had to keep her facts lined up in her mind, like exhibits in a trial. She had to review them, over and over, so that she could make sure everyone else did their job. Otherwise, something might be overlooked. Someone might drop the ball.

Reluctantly, she moved away from the window, where she'd been watching the parking lot, and lay down on the bed. But sleep didn't come. Morning would be here soon enough. And then, maybe, she could breathe. Then she could make sure that morning was something Edward Soames would never again experience outside a jail cell.

W hy did you change your name?" Tony asked Soames, who sat slumped in a chair at the end of the table.

McRae nodded to him, and Soames said, "I didn't think I could get a job if someone found out about my record. I was falsely accused, and I was found innocent. But the stigma of the arrests would have followed me here."

"You weren't found innocent," Larry said. "You were never tried."

"If I wasn't found guilty, I was found innocent," Soames said. "It's in the Bill of Rights."

"You have an interesting history of similar false accusations," Tony said sarcastically. "What a poor, misunderstood guy."

Soames leaned on the table, intent on making them understand. "The first one was some married woman who had a crush on me, and when I rejected her, she came up with this crazy story to get attention. The second one was a girl I'd broken up with. She was trying to get even."

"And this one?"

His lawyer leaned forward. "Tell them what you told me about her invitation today."

Soames nodded. "It's weird. Most of the time, she acts like she doesn't even know I exist. Won't look at me, hardly answers me when I talk to her, gets real nervous around me—"

"A real challenge, huh?" Larry asked.

Soames ignored it and went on. "Today, after my boss leaves, she comes into my office and asks me if I'd like to come over for dinner tonight. She seemed real nervous, but I thought it was cute, you know? And I had plans, but I canceled them. I told her I'd come."

"*She* invited *you*," Larry repeated doubtfully. "You're sure about that?"

"She *did*, man. I was surprised."

"Were there any witnesses?"

Soames thought for a moment. "The bookkeeper in the office, Gretchen, was still there, but I don't know if she heard it or not. Melissa was talking real low, like she didn't want to be overheard."

Tony wrote the bookkeeper's name down. He couldn't wait to ask her. "So—what time did you tell her you'd be there?"

"I said seven. She said okay, and then went home. Then, I show up about 7:15 or so, and she meets me at the door looking real agitated, and tells me that she's not feeling well. She wants to cancel. I thought she was mad 'cause I was late, so I apologized, but she tells me to leave. I got a little ticked off, since I had canceled a date to come over there, and I thought the least she could have done was call—"

"Ticked off?" Larry cut in. "How ticked off?"

"Just a little hot. Hey, I didn't touch her! I just said something about her jerking me around, that I didn't appreciate it. Next thing I know, she's pulling a knife on me—one of those long carving knives like for a turkey—and waving it at me and screaming for me to get out. So I went. That's absolutely all there was. I never laid a hand on her. I didn't even come more than four feet into her apartment."

"Another false accusation?" Tony asked with mock sincerity.

"That's exactly what it is! And I have no idea why she's out to get me. Why she'd call the police and lie like that."

"You're totally in the dark about this, huh?"

Soames turned his palms up, arms spread wide. "Absolutely. I mean, if we'd gone out or something, and things hadn't gone well, and she wanted revenge . . . well, maybe. But it's like she planned this or something."

"What about the shirt under your seat?"

"What shirt?"

"The shirt with the Far Side cartoon on the front."

"It isn't under my seat," Soames said. "It's in my closet at the office. Sometimes I get dirty on the site, and I change clothes." The perplexed look on his face seemed genuine. "You found it under my seat?"

Tony stared, not missing a nuance of Soames's expression. "So you're saying you didn't put it there? Tell me, how do you explain the blood on it? Or the knife wrapped up in it?"

"What?" Looking astounded, Soames turned to his lawyer. "Man, I'm being framed. I noticed my knife missing from my office this afternoon. She must have taken it."

"So let me get this straight," Larry said. "You're saying that she took your shirt out of your office closet, took your knife, opened a vein to get blood all over it, then stuffed it under your car seat so that when you raped her, she'd have evidence?"

"I didn't *touch* her! She had this planned out before she even invited me to dinner. Don't you see? It's starting to make sense. I still don't know why she'd do it, but she did. Isn't it obvious to you morons?"

"It's not obvious to me," Larry said facetiously, glancing at Tony. "Is it obvious to you?"

"Sounds a little far-fetched," Tony agreed.

Soames was beginning to sweat, and he wiped his forehead with the back of his wrist. "Okay, look. If you just think about it— was the blood dry on the shirt? 'Cause if it had just happened, the blood would be wet."

Larry shook his head. "We didn't pick you up until a couple of hours after she reported it, and she didn't even call until a half hour or so after it happened. The blood would have had time to dry."

"Man, you got to believe me. I'm being set up. The woman's out to get me."

"Just like the other two were?"

Soames slammed his hand on the table. "Yes! Just like the other two. It happens, man. One person falsely accuses you, and then you're easy game for the next one who wants to get even."

"You said she didn't have anything to get even for."

"She doesn't! Hey, I don't know any more than you do what's going through her head. But I do know that she's accusing me just as falsely as the others did."

"Then I'd say you have real bad luck with women," Tony said.

The door opened, and one of the uniforms stuck his head in. "Larry, Tony, there's a call for you. Dr. Jasper. Says he's returning your call."

"I'll take it," Tony said, getting up.

Larry watched Tony leave the room, then got up himself. "We found some interesting things in your apartment, Soames. Wonder if you could explain them to us."

Soames looked uncomfortable. "I got nothing to hide."

"Right. So you have a good explanation for why there were binoculars, a camera, and a knife in a bag in your closet."

"I take them to ball games," Soames said. "I can see better with the binoculars, and I like to take pictures."

"Is that why the only pictures we found were of women who didn't know they were being photographed?"

Soames laughed then. "They were my friends. They all knew I was taking their pictures."

"Yeah? Then you won't mind giving us their names, will you, so we can talk to them."

Soames got quiet again.

"Come on, Soames," Larry said. "What are their names?"

"I'm not gonna subject my friends to your gestapo tactics."

"Do you *know* their names, Soames?"

"His friends have no relation to this case," McRae interjected.

"No, but his prey have a lot of bearing on this. And if he can't give us the names of these unsuspecting women he photographed from his car at night, then we have to make our own assumptions."

Soames turned to his attorney, beseeching him to help him out, and McRae leaned forward. "Okay, you've got your statement from him. I don't think he needs to say any more."

Tony came back in, his face glum, but before he could sit down, Larry said, "Fine, I think we've got enough. Maybe a night in jail will help him get his story straight."

"Steve," Soames pled, "can't you get the arraignment moved up? I don't want to stay in here."

"It's just one night," McRae said. "Tomorrow we can probably get you out on bond."

"I wouldn't hold my breath," Larry said. "When the judge sees the evidence and your record, he's gonna want to throw away the key. 'Course, if you came clean and told the truth, he might cut you a little slack."

"I *am* telling the truth, man!"

"Fine. Stick to your story. It's kind of a hobby of mine, shooting stories like this all to pieces."

Soames was still yelling when Larry and Tony closed the door behind them and walked through the noisy precinct. Several gang members just brought in shouted at the officer who had booked them. Across the room, an abusive husband let out a string of obscenities as he struggled to break free of his handcuffs. Somewhere a baby cried incessantly.

"So what do you think?" Tony asked.

"I think he deserves an Oscar. What do you think?"

"I don't know. I mean, yeah, the evidence is pretty clear, and his record doesn't leave much room for doubt."

"But?"

Tony hesitated, looking out over the chaos of the room. Finally, he brought his eyes back to Larry. "On the phone, that was the doctor who examined Melissa Nelson."

"Yeah, I know. What did he say?"

Tony combed his fingers through his sandy hair. "He says that, based on his examination of her, he can't confirm for certain that a rape occurred."

Larry stared at him for a moment. "Did he say it didn't?"

"No, he couldn't say that. Not for sure."

"Well, we knew that evidence was going to be flimsy because she showered. But what does he call the cut on her leg?"

"Assault, maybe, but not rape."

Larry backed up a step, glaring at his friend. "So what are you saying? Just because some doctor says he can't find evidence, it didn't happen? You *saw* the evidence in this guy's car. You saw his record. You heard what he said in there."

"That's just it," Tony said. "What if it happened just like he said?"

Larry gaped at him. "I can't believe you. You want to make this poor woman regret she ever called us."

"I just don't want to accept either one of these stories at face value," Tony said. "We might be getting a little truth from each of them. It just feels like there's something else going on here, like we're not getting the whole story."

"Well, if anybody's hiding something, we'll find out. This guy's not walking out of *this* jail on a technicality."

CHAPTER FOUR

Melissa left the hospital the next morning before the doctor had even come in. In the bright, revealing light of morning, the apartment she had left last night had a look of absurdity: tables still overturned, broken glass still scattered across the floor, the bed still rumpled and unmade.

She stood near the front door, slowly perusing the signs of struggle, the evidence laid out so distinctly, the story it all told. Stepping over the broken, overturned lamp, she went into the bathroom, where bloody towels lay crumpled on the floor. Her eyes strayed to the bathtub, then flitted away, then gravitated back again.

The memory of another bathtub flashed into her mind, and quickly she turned away, bending over the sink to splash cold water on her face. Straightening, she grabbed the hand towel and looked into the mirror. The face staring back at her was tight, as it often was, with worry, urgency, and grief. The worry was something that came and went, alternating with a death-defying courage that sometimes propelled her into decisions she had trouble carrying out. But the grief was ever present, always deep, smothering, sickening, something she could not escape. Maybe there would be an end to it now.

Turning, deliberately keeping her eyes from the bathtub that had ignited those memories, she limped into the bedroom she usually kept so neat. She found something else to wear and quickly changed, careful not to brush the cut on her leg. Then, brushing her long blonde hair with little attention to how the soft waves fell, she flipped through the phone book and found the number of the police station.

Larry Millsaps wasn't in, she learned, and neither was Tony Danks. Edward Soames was still in custody, but his bond hearing was at ten.

Fear burst through her, fear that he would somehow convince the judge that this was all a mistake, that he deserved to, at least, be released on bond. She needed to talk to someone, to find out if one of the prosecutors would be there, or if this was one of those hearings where just the defendant and his lawyer would be present. The court *had* to understand the seriousness of the crime he'd committed! Quickly, she found the number to the DA's office and asked for the attorney working on the case.

No one had even been assigned to it yet.

"But his hearing is scheduled for ten this morning! Won't anyone be there from your office? What if they release him?"

"Judges generally won't release a man charged with rape, Miss Nelson. There's really nothing to worry about."

"He'll come after me if he gets out!" she said, her voice rising. "I'd say there's very certainly something to worry about. I've seen people released on technicalities before. I've seen the justice system fumble. I don't want to be the victim of somebody's mistake!"

"I told you, we'll have someone there."

"But I need to talk to whoever it is. They need to see what he did to me, what he did to my apartment. They need to hear—"

"I'm sure we'll have the police report soon. You gave them a statement, didn't you?"

"Yes, but that's not enough! If I could just talk to someone, so you could see how important it is to keep him locked up!"

"I've got your name and number, Miss Nelson. Once the case is assigned, I'm sure they'll be contacting you. Please relax." The voice on the other end paused, then changed to a softer cadence. "Look, I know you've been through an ordeal. I have the number of a terrific counselor who specializes in rape victims. Why don't you call her this morning and talk to her?"

"I don't need a shrink!" she cried. "I need some peace of mind. I need to know it isn't going to happen again just because he managed to charm some judge into letting him go!"

"Please, Miss Nelson. I know it's hard, but you really have no alternative right now except waiting. I promise someone will contact you."

Melissa slammed the phone down and wiped at the tears forming in her eyes. She couldn't just sit here and wait. She had to go somewhere, do something. She couldn't just let it go.

She searched through the phone book for the name Millsaps, then scanned down the page until she came to Larry. Quickly, she dialed the number, then waited as it rang once, twice, three times ...

Finally, it was picked up, dropped, and then a rumbly, groggy voice said, "Hello?"

"Uh, Detective Millsaps? This is Melissa Nelson. From ... last night?"

"Yeah, Melissa," he said. "Are you all right?"

"Yes ... well, no. Look, I'm sorry I woke you. I wouldn't have, except ..."

"That's okay. Melissa, what's wrong?"

"It's the bond hearing. It's at ten this morning, and it hasn't even been assigned to anyone in the DA's office yet, and I'm worried he might get out."

Larry sighed. "He won't, Melissa. No way. They have your statement, and I stayed late last night making sure all the paperwork was in order. It's all there."

She brought a trembling hand to her forehead and shoved her bangs back. "It's just—so hard for me to trust the justice system."

His voice was waking up now, and she had the feeling he was sitting up. "I understand why you're jumpy. I probably would be, too. Are you still in the hospital?"

"No, I'm at home," she said. "You know, I'm thinking about moving. Maybe I need a new address. Maybe I just need to leave town until this comes to trial."

"That's up to you," he said, "as long as we can reach you. Are you planning to go in to work today?"

"No," she said quickly. "I don't think I can go back there. It would be too hard to face anyone. And his office is there ..."

Suddenly she realized that she was babbling like a crazy person, and she had awakened him to do it. "Look, I didn't mean to wake you up. Or, maybe I did, but I shouldn't have. I'm sorry. I'm just a little fragmented. Would you—would you call me when you get to the office today? I'd like to talk to you some more."

"Sure," he said.

"All right, good-bye." But she held the receiver in her hand for a few moments before finally setting it back in its cradle. Then, going to her favorite chair, still stained with a few drops of her blood from last night, she curled up on it and tried to think what to do next.

Larry lay in bed for a while after he hung up, wishing there was something he could do to help this distraught woman. He'd seen the way a crisis like this ate at people, how it tore at the fabric of their security and ripped away their trust in all that was good. She needed an anchor.

He rolled toward his bedside table, fighting the fatigue still clinging to him, and dialed information. Then he sat up and punched in Melissa's number.

"Hello?" Her voice was soft, apprehensive, yet hopeful. He wondered who she'd been expecting.

"Uh, Melissa? This is Larry again. Listen, I was just thinking—would you like to have breakfast somewhere? You obviously need to talk, and I've gotten all the sleep I need."

"Are you sure?"

"Well, yeah."

He could hear the relief in her voice, that someone was taking her seriously. "Yes, that would be great. When?"

"How about an hour? I don't live far from you. I could pick you up." But as quickly as he'd said that, he kicked himself. The last thing a rape victim wanted was another man coming to her apartment. "Or if you'd rather just meet somewhere—"

"No, that's fine," she said. "You can pick me up."

A little surprised, he said, "Okay. I'll see you then."

This time, she didn't sound quite as forlorn as she said good-bye.

CHAPTER FIVE

L arry wasn't sure he would have recognized her if Melissa hadn't been standing in the door of the same apartment where he'd met her the night before. Her hair had been wet and matted then, and she had been curled up in a blanket most of the time, her eyes raw and red, her skin pallid.

But today her hair, a soft baby blonde color, waved down to her shoulders. Soft bangs covered her eyebrows. The skin around her eyes was still red, but their soft blueness was striking even though she wore no makeup. Melissa Nelson wasn't a woman who needed much help from cosmetics, Larry decided. They would only cheapen the effect of the beauty she'd been gifted with.

He noticed also how small she was, no more than five-feet-five against his six-two, and he hated the image that crossed his mind of Soames overpowering her. He supposed they should be thankful that she hadn't been left dead.

"You ready?" he asked.

"Yes," she said. "Come on in. I have to get my purse."

The apartment looked just as he'd left it last night—tables overturned, glass shattered, liquid spilled and congealed on the floor. From the doorway, he could see into the bedroom; nothing had been changed on the bed. Not a pillow had been moved, not a sheet disturbed.

"I—I didn't know if the police had gotten all the evidence they needed," she explained, stepping over some glass and still favoring her left leg. "I thought I'd better leave everything alone until I was sure."

He shook his head. "We finished last night, Melissa. We have film and video of the whole scene, and we got fingerprints and a lot of other routine evidence. I don't think we missed anything."

"But are you sure? If I clean it all up, and you think of something you forgot to look for, it'll be too late."

"Have you found anything you think we missed?" he asked, confused.

"No. I'm just saying there could be something."

Gently, trying not to make her feel stupid, Larry said, "Melissa, it's really okay to start putting things back together. I could help if you want, after breakfast. You can't keep living in this mess, with all these reminders. It would drive you crazy."

"I'm willing to take that chance, if it'll ensure that he gets put away."

"I know you are. You're very brave. But you really have to start thinking of yourself. You may not even know this yet, but you've been traumatized. You need to talk to people who know how to deal with this—even some people who've been through it. It would really help you adjust."

"I'll adjust when I know for sure they aren't going to let him go," she said. She started out the door, limping slightly, and Larry followed her, locking the door behind him. Every case was different, he thought as they went down the stairs. The last rape he'd worked, the woman had not only showered before she'd called the police, but she'd cleaned up her apartment, trying to wipe away any sign that the man had ever been there. But she hadn't been able to scrub away the horrible memories, and finally, she had called the police.

It was odd that Melissa, who had also showered to clean away any bodily memory of the man who'd violated her, had chosen to keep the apartment just as he'd left it. Whether she was incredibly strong, or incredibly paranoid, he wasn't sure.

"How's your leg?" he asked.

"Fine," she said. "It really doesn't hurt much."

Incredibly strong, he decided, with a very high threshold of pain.

At the bottom of the stairs, he noticed a tiny old woman peering through the crack of her partially open door. Dismissing her as a neighbor still curious about last night, he stepped out of the building and pointed to his car parked on the street. "It's not much, but it's paid for."

She smiled, and he realized that he'd never seen that expression on her before. It changed her face, softening the lines around her mouth and eyes.

He opened the door for her, and she got in, careful not to hurt her leg.

"So what do you like to eat?"

"Anything's fine," she said. "I didn't really come to eat."

He cranked the car and pulled out into the traffic. "We'll go to this place I know a couple of blocks away. They have great omelets."

"Fine," she said.

He glanced at her occasionally as he navigated his way through the traffic. She was pretty, he thought, but he had realized that last night. Her eyes gave her face a startling softness and depth. Left alone, undisturbed, what did she think about? What did she like to do—before last night, that is. And how long would it take for her to heal?

"Do you have family around here?" he asked quietly.

She shook her head. "No. My parents live in Pensacola."

"Have you—told them?"

The turmoil in her eyes grieved him. "No, I haven't. I'm not going to. Maybe they won't hear about it."

"Well . . . if this goes to trial, it will be in the paper, and since he's had arrests in other counties, the coverage might reach across the state."

She grew quiet, and her eyes strayed out the window.

"Why don't you want them to know?"

She drew in a deep breath, then let it out slowly. "I don't think they can take it. It would kill them."

"Well, maybe you could get someone to help you tell them. Do you have brothers or sisters?"

She hesitated for a moment, and he saw the tears filling her eyes. "No," she said finally, quietly.

"Well, I could help you, if you want. I'm used to breaking bad news to people."

She brought her eyes back to him. "That must be awful."

37

He frowned and thought about it for a moment. "It used to be. I used to dread it, and wish someone else would do it for me. But then I realized that not everyone can bring bad news with any sense of compassion. I can. I finally decided that if somebody had to tell them horrible things, it might as well be me. At least I could know it was handled right."

"And what's the right way to tell a couple that their daughter has been raped?" she asked in a monotone.

"Well, I'd tell them first that you were all right. That the man is in custody. Those things should give them some peace. Then I'd let them cry and yell and cuss, if they had to. And then I'd tell them what I do in times of deep tragedy, when I don't know where to turn."

She gazed at him for a long moment. "What do you do?"

"I pray," he said. "I turn to God. And instead of asking 'why,' I ask God what he wants me to do."

Those tears resurfaced again, and she looked down at her hands. "If you've never asked why, it's because you've never experienced a tragedy so deep that it shakes the foundation of everything you've ever believed in your life. Sometimes you *have* to ask why."

"And if there are no answers?"

"Then you make some," she said.

They pulled into the parking lot of the little diner. Neither of them spoke as they got out and went inside. He was a little surprised when she ordered; he hadn't expected her to be able to eat. He was glad she could.

Finally, when the waitress brought their food, he got back to the subject they'd started in the car. "I've been thinking about what you said. About making your own answers. And I thought how convenient that would be if it were possible. But I've found that my own attempts to resolve things never work." He studied her for a moment as he sipped his coffee. "Tell me something, Melissa. Do you pray?"

Her eyes seemed to glaze over, as if she were deep in a memory from years earlier. "I used to," she said. "I used to pray all the time."

"What made you stop?"

"I don't know," she whispered. "Anger, maybe."

"Anger at what?"

She seemed to shake out of her reverie at his question, and looked at him again. "Personal things. Things that went wrong, without any reason. Things that didn't make any sense."

"And you haven't prayed since?"

She hesitated. "Some. But I don't think they were heard. Finally, I gave up."

"I can assure you they were heard."

She shrugged. "Well, maybe they were. They just weren't answered."

"Sometimes the answer is 'wait.' Sometimes we don't want to do that. Sometimes maybe we'd rather trust in our own strength."

"Maybe," she whispered. "Maybe so."

The food came to the table, and he watched as she ate, picking at her food, looking distracted.

"So do you want me to talk to your folks?"

She shook her head. "No. I appreciate it, though. If they hear about it, I guess I'll have some explaining to do. But maybe they won't hear, and then they'll never have to suffer through this. I want to protect them from this if I can."

"But you need their support, Melissa. You can't get it if they don't know."

"I'll be all right," Melissa whispered. "I can do this alone."

He shut up then, realizing that she was not only strong, she was stubborn. And she'd made up her mind.

After a few minutes, she moved her plate away and folded her arms on the table. "Detective Millsaps—"

"Larry," he interrupted. "Please, call me Larry."

"Okay, Larry. I wanted to talk to you about the evidence. What's being done with it?"

He set his fork down and leaned back. "What do you mean?"

"I mean, you're not going to just blow off the hair and fingerprints and everything, and assume that the shirt and knife in his car were enough, are you?"

Larry shook his head. "Of course not. It'll all be used in court. Every bit of it."

"And, you did have a warrant when you arrested him, didn't you?"

Larry nodded. "Search warrants, too." Her questions bothered him. He wasn't used to getting the third degree from a victim. She looked at her watch, and he knew that she was calculating how much time before Soames's bond hearing.

"Will the judge make an immediate decision about whether to release him or keep him?"

"Yes," he said. "And I guarantee he'll keep him. He'd be out of his mind to let Edward Soames back out on the streets."

"Yeah, well, I've seen judges out of their minds before. Outrageous decisions are made in court every day."

"That's one of the hardest things about being a cop. I take 'em in, and they let 'em go. But we have too much evidence on this guy. You really don't have to worry." He hoped he sounded more confident than he felt.

He paid the check, and they went back to the car. "I meant it about helping you clean up your apartment," he said. "I can help you right now."

"No," she said. "I don't want to go home."

"Where do you want to go?" he asked.

Her eyes were determined as she faced him. "I want to go with you to the police station, or you can drop me off at the courthouse."

"The courthouse? Melissa, you don't want to be there. You don't want to see this guy—"

"I have to know," she said. "I have to know that they're not releasing him. Either I can sit in the courtroom and watch the hearing, or I can wait with you until you hear something."

"Or I could take you home and call you when I hear."

"By the time you call me, he could be at my apartment banging my door down," she said. "I won't feel safe until I know for sure."

Larry sighed. "All right then. I guess you can come to the precinct. But I can't stay there all morning. I'll probably get called away."

"That's fine," she said. "I won't bother anyone. I just need a safe place, until there's a decision."

Larry moaned inwardly, anticipating what Tony would say. But he didn't have the heart to force her to go home. He'd already taken this much responsibility for her; he might as well finish what he'd started.

CHAPTER SIX

The precinct smelled like a locker room when Larry walked Melissa through, trying to find a place to put her while he worked. The waiting area was filled with what looked like a gang, no doubt waiting to post bail for one of their members. Putting her there would be like throwing a lamb to the wolves. She'd already been through enough.

So he grabbed an empty chair and dragged it around to his desk. "Here," he said.

"Thank you." Checking her watch, she sat down. Larry saw on the wall clock that it was almost ten.

He tried to recover last night's train of thought as he sifted through the paperwork he'd left on his desk. He needed more information on the other rape charges against Soames. Names of women. Circumstances. Maybe he could determine his MO, whether he only went after women he knew, or if those pictures found in his apartment were pictures of potential victims. He needed to get a job history, affiliations, a credit report, anything that would help him trace Soames's steps for the past few years. There might be other women who had been attacked and hadn't reported it—women who might come forward if they knew someone else had filed charges.

Whatever it took, he needed to make sure that the system didn't let Melissa down. She was already, for some reason, very distrustful of it.

"Hey, how're you doing?" It was Tony's voice behind him, and Larry looked up and saw that his partner was addressing Melissa.

41

"Fine."

"Is, uh, Detective Millsaps here helping you?"

Larry grinned. Tony didn't recognize her. "Tony, this is Melissa Nelson."

Tony's eyebrows shot up. "Oh. From last night?"

"Yeah," Larry said. "She's just waiting here for word about Soames's bond hearing."

"What about it?" Tony asked.

"Whether he's released on bond."

Tony almost laughed, but caught himself. "They're not letting him out."

When Melissa didn't answer, Larry spoke up. "She didn't want to wait at home, just in case. Listen, I need to talk to you about some things."

He excused himself and whisked Tony into the interrogation room.

"What's going on?" Tony asked. "Was she waiting here for us?"

"No. I picked her up."

"You what?"

"She called me this morning, all upset, worried he was going to get out and come after her. I took her to breakfast—"

"Oh, brother," Tony said, shaking his head. "You're nuts, you know that? Larry, you can't go getting involved with victims in the crimes you're investigating. That's crazy!"

"I'm not! She's just scared and paranoid right now. If sitting at my desk makes her feel better, it's fine with me."

"You can't work with her sitting there."

"Watch me." With that, Larry flung the door open and stormed through it.

"All right," Tony said, fast on his heels. "But if she's here, I'm not going to tiptoe around her. She's going to have to answer some questions."

"Ask away," he said. "She'll tell you anything you want to know."

But Tony didn't ask. Instead, he busied himself at his computer, punching the keys hard and deliberately, as if to vent some of the frustration he felt. Larry tried to ignore him, doing his own work on the computer, tracking down the work history of Edward

Pendergrast, the names of the other two alleged victims who'd pressed charges against him, and any other information he could find.

After a while, Melissa got up and wandered toward him. "Are you working on my case?" she asked.

"Yes." He gave her a distracted glance, then hit the "print" button. "It seems our man has a couple of other arrests. For the same thing."

Melissa didn't look as surprised as he'd expected. "Can that be mentioned in his hearing? Should you call the DA?"

Larry looked fully at her now, studying her face. "You didn't happen to know his background before, did you? Is that why you're so afraid of things falling through?"

She grew stiffer then, but kept her eyes clearly focused on his. "Of course not. How could I have known? I've barely had a complete conversation with him."

As she talked, Larry noticed Tony behind her. Tony stared at her, glanced back at his computer screen, then shot a look at Larry. "Excuse me a minute," Larry said. "I need to talk to Tony."

"What if your phone rings? What if someone calls about the hearing?"

"I'll hear it," he said. "Don't worry." He crossed the room to Tony's desk. "You have that look on your face," he said quietly. "Like you've got something."

Tony glanced up at him over his shoulder. "I thought I'd check out our little lady. Just to get a better take on her. Take a look at this."

Larry leaned over him and read the skeleton history he'd come up with. "She's got a degree from Florida State. Changed her major to criminal justice after her sophomore year. Graduated summa cum laude. My question is, how did a criminal justice whiz wind up here working as a secretary?"

Larry frowned. "Why would she do that?"

Tony shook his head. "Why don't we ask her?"

Larry straightened. "I will."

The phone was ringing when he got back to his desk, and he snatched it up. "Millsaps."

He listened as the secretary in the DA's office relayed the decision in the hearing. "Thanks. I appreciate it."

He hung up and leaned forward on his desk.

"Did they let him go?" Melissa asked.

He shook his head. "No bond. He's staying."

Relief washed over her, and she leaned back in her chair, finally relaxed. "I can't believe it. I was so worried."

"I know you were." He set his chin on his palm and looked at her for a moment. "Can I ask you something, Melissa?" She was smiling, and he hated to ruin it, but he had to. "We had to do a little research on you, just as a matter of routine. And we were looking at your educational background."

Her smile faded, and she fixed her eyes on him. "What about it?"

"Just seemed odd to me, that's all. You have a degree in criminal justice, of all things."

"Why is that odd?" she asked.

"Well, because you're not working in that field. In fact, I wondered why you'd take a job doing secretarial work."

She glanced away then, avoiding his eyes, and shrugged. "I worked for the FBI for three months after I graduated last spring. Three months was long enough. Now I'm a secretary, until I find something better."

"Why didn't you mention this earlier?"

Her eyebrows shot up, and she gaped at him. "I've been a little bit distracted. The subject didn't come up!" She glared at him, as if trying to determine if he was suggesting that she had covered up, then finally, she came to her feet. "Do you have any more questions for me, Detective? Like why I drive a red car instead of a green one, or why I chose exactly the apartment complex I did? I'm familiar with how a rape case often gets turned on the victim. As you pointed out, I spent a lot of time studying things like that. So go ahead! Take your best shot."

His eyes remained locked with hers, but finally, he shook his head. "I'm not trying to interrogate you, Melissa. I just have to ask about things that seem out of sync."

"And since my job is out of sync, maybe what happened to me last night is too, right?"

"I didn't say that."

"You didn't have to. Call me if you come up with anything else that's out of sync. I'll see if I can explain it to you." With that, she started to limp away from his desk.

Larry lunged out of his chair and caught her arm. "Melissa, I'll take you home. Just wait a minute."

"No, thanks," she said. "I'll get a cab."

He stood there as she hurried from the room, and it was a moment before he realized that Tony was standing next to him.

"She didn't like the question, huh?"

"No, she didn't," Larry said. "And now I feel like the kind of pond scum that makes rape victims sorry they ever report the crime."

"If she can't take the heat—"

Larry spun around, his face furious. "If she can't take the heat, what, Tony? Who really *can* take the heat? Could you? What if you were attacked on the street, and when you reported it, all of a sudden your life and your history became suspect? Would your record stand up to our kind of scrutiny? Would *you* be able to take the heat?"

Tony rolled his eyes. "Man, you've got it bad."

"Give me a break!" he shouted, and some of the others in the busy room stopped what they were doing and looked at him. "I would like to think I have a little compassion for any victim I deal with, so don't go accusing me of preferential treatment just because she's a woman!"

"What are you so hot about?" Tony flung back.

"I'm hot about putting an innocent, wounded, violated woman on the defensive, Tony! That kind of thing always gets to me! I don't know why it doesn't get to you."

"Maybe it's because my gut is telling me that things just aren't fitting into place here."

"So who are you gonna believe? A guy who's been accused of rape before, who's being accused now, who had evidence up to his ears in his car and his apartment—or a woman whose only crime is to be overqualified for her job and who had the audacity to get raped?"

Tony threw his hands up. "All right. You got me. You're right. Now can we please get back to work?"

45

Larry plopped back down into his chair and turned to his computer. This day was going from bad to worse. And he hadn't had enough sleep last night to deal with any of this.

A couple of hours later, as Larry and Tony were returning from investigating a missing persons report on two seventeen-year-old girls who had apparently run away—and for good reason, judging from the neglectful homes they'd each come from—Larry's mind wandered back to Melissa Nelson. He thought about her indignation that morning, then about their conversation at breakfast. Something had been bothering him about that, something she'd said . . .

"*. . . you're not going to just blow off the hair and fingerprints . . . and assume that the shirt and knife in his car were enough, are you?*"

The hair. That was it. How had she known that they would find follicles of Soames's hair on her bed? Just an assumption, based on what she would have looked for, had she been investigating?

He shoved the question out of his mind. Tony's suspicions—of what, he still wasn't sure—were affecting him. Rubbing his eyes, he glanced at Tony, who was driving. "Did I tell you I ordered the police file on Pendergrast from Santa Rosa County?"

Tony shook his head. "No. I was going to do it this afternoon."

"I asked them to rush it. They said it would be here by tomorrow."

"What's the rush?"

"Well, the grand jury will be hearing the case soon."

"So the DA will ask for it."

Larry breathed a laugh. "Yeah, well, you and I both know that the more we lay the case out for the DA's office, the better chance we have of conviction. I just want to make sure."

"What are you looking for?"

"I don't know," he said. "Anything I can find on the previous arrests. Who the victims were, his MO, exactly why he walked. That kind of thing."

Tony glanced over at him. "Larry, you look like a zombie. How much sleep did you get last night?"

"Couple hours," he said.

"Why don't you go on home? I'll fax the info about these runaways to some other PDs across the state and see what I can come up with. Get some sleep. You're not worth a plugged nickel when you're this tired."

"Thanks a lot." They pulled into the PD parking garage. "I think I'll take you up on it, though."

"Sure you can drive?" Tony asked with a grin.

"Hey, I've functioned with less sleep before. Remember the Barrett case?"

"Yeah. I almost killed you, man. Volunteering us to stake her place out all night after we'd been on duty for over twelve hours already."

"Hey, I did it myself."

"Yep. Another case of a lady in distress. You do dumb things for women, Larry."

"It was dumb to stake out her house?" he asked irritably. "Are you telling me there was no threat?"

Tony grinned and shook his head. "Okay, okay. But breakfast this morning? I don't think that was within the call of duty, pal."

"Just don't worry about it. I'm going home."

"Good," Tony laughed. "And don't come back until you have a better disposition. Or I just might have to kill you after all."

Larry grinned as he headed across the garage to his own car.

CHAPTER SEVEN

A knock at the door woke Larry a few hours after he'd fallen asleep. He stumbled to the door. Tony stood there, the setting sun at his back, grinning as if he enjoyed waking Larry. "Rise and shine! We've got work to do."

Larry shuffled into the kitchen, and Tony followed. "What is it?" Larry asked, measuring out some coffee for the pot.

"A witness in the Nelson case."

Larry swung around. "Really? Who?"

"A woman who lives downstairs. She gave a statement last night that she heard things crashing upstairs in Melissa's apartment. I thought we should talk to her."

"Yeah, okay. Just let me change."

A few minutes later, Larry followed Tony out to the car, wondering whether the appearance of this witness would make Tony give more credence to Melissa's story. "So what else have you been doing today?" he asked.

"Well, I interviewed the people she worked with."

"Who worked with?"

"Your friend Melissa."

Larry shot him a look. "*My* friend?"

Tony grinned. "Well, you seem to be her champion. Anyway, you're not going to like what I found out."

Larry waited. "What?"

"That bookkeeper who was still there when Soames says Melissa asked him to dinner? She confirmed it."

"That she was there?"

"No. She confirmed that Melissa asked him. She heard it. She's apparently a real busybody, and she admitted that when she saw Melissa go into his office, she listened outside the door to see what they were talking about. She heard everything."

Larry tried to absorb that. "You believe her?"

"I don't know. What do you think?"

"Well, she could have a crush on him herself, and want to help him. Maybe he paid her. Who knows?"

"Yeah, well . . . I'm just telling you what she said."

Larry stayed quiet as they approached the apartment building where they'd found Melissa last night. Things looked radically different tonight, without flashing lights everywhere and a crowd of people on the street. "Who are we going to see?"

"A Matilda Berkley," Tony said. "She lives in the first apartment as you come in the door."

"Yeah, I saw her peeking out this morning."

Larry followed Tony in. Before they had even reached her door, it opened. The little old lady Larry had seen that morning stuck her head out. "Hello, officers. I've been expecting you. Won't you come in?"

She seemed delighted to have company, and Larry couldn't help smiling. They introduced themselves, accepted the coffee and cake she'd prepared for them, and sat down, anxious to get to the point. Finally, Larry jumped in.

"Mrs. Berkley, you told the police officers last night in your statement that you heard things crashing upstairs. Could you tell us exactly what time that was?"

"It was seven-thirty, because I was baking, and the timer went off right about that time."

Larry nodded. "Did you see anyone leave the apartment after that?"

Her eyebrows shot up. "No, and I kept waiting. I had my door cracked with the chain still on it, and I was watching the stairs to see who would come down. But until you officers came, nobody came out of that apartment."

Larry frowned. "Are you sure? You didn't just miss him?"

"No. I pretty much see almost everyone who comes and goes in this building. I know everyone here, and I like to make sure the people coming and going are *supposed* to be here. Especially with Melissa—she's such a lovely girl. She's been so sweet, always checking to see if I need anything, bringing me things from the grocery store when I can't get there myself. I feel kind of protective of her. And last night, after that first gentleman left, I heard all that crashing—"

"Wait a minute," Larry said. "What gentleman?"

"Well, the one who was here to see Melissa. I opened my door and looked out when he came into the building, and he asked me which apartment was hers. He seemed like a decent young man, and I was happy that she had a date. She has so few visitors, you know."

Larry was getting impatient. "Did you or didn't you see him leave?"

"I certainly did. He came down rather quickly and slammed the door going out. I was so disappointed, because I had hoped that maybe he was a suitor. She's a very lonely girl, I think—"

Tony tried this time. "But you say you heard the crashing things *after* he left?"

"Yes. I could tell that something was wrong, and I thought someone must be up there, but I hadn't seen anyone else go up. I guess I should have called the police myself, but I just wasn't sure whether anyone was there with her. It's possible that they had come when I hadn't been listening, so I waited and waited for them to come down, so I could decide what to do. But no one ever did. Not until the police began coming. Would you like some more cake?"

"No. Uh, thanks." Larry turned his troubled eyes to Tony.

Tony sighed. "Mrs. Berkley, are you sure you didn't just get the events mixed up? I mean, maybe you heard the crashing, and *then* saw him leave."

Her chin came up with indignation. "I'm telling you the way it happened. There must have been someone else up there. That first gentleman wasn't there long enough to do anything. I'd say maybe five minutes. But if there was someone else, maybe he went up onto the roof, or got into another apartment . . ." Her eyes grew round as she imagined all the places a culprit could have hidden.

"All the other neighbors were interviewed," Tony explained. "None of them saw anything like that."

She sat back hard on her couch. "Then it doesn't make any sense, does it? It's just downright peculiar. How did he get in and out?"

Tony pulled a picture from his shirt pocket. "Mrs. Berkley, was this the man you saw coming to see Melissa last night?"

She took the picture of Soames that they'd used to identify him last night, and nodded. "Yes, that's him. Nice-looking young man, like I told you."

"And you're sure that he's the same man you saw leaving?"

"Oh, absolutely."

"Did he have anything in his hands?"

"Like what?" she asked.

"Anything at all."

The woman thought for a moment. "No. I don't think so."

"Did he look angry?"

"Well, yes, he did."

"And what did he have on?" Larry asked. "Mrs. Berkley, this is very important. Can you remember what he had on when he arrived?"

"Well, the same thing he had on when he left. One of those striped pullover shirts, like a golf shirt or something, you know? It had red and green and navy stripes that went this way . . ."

Larry glanced at Tony. The same shirt he'd been wearing when they'd picked him up.

"And you're sure he was wearing that when he left?"

"Yes," she said adamantly. "Like I told you, he wasn't up there more than five minutes. He looked just the same when he came back down."

No cartoon T-shirt, Larry thought with confusion. So where had the bloody T-shirt come from?

They finished questioning her, thanked her, and left.

As he settled in behind the steering wheel, Tony asked, "Am I the only one who notices that something is a little tilted about this case?" He pulled the car back out onto the street.

"The woman has to be eighty years old. Maybe she's imagining things," Larry said.

"Did she imagine the shirt he was wearing when we picked him up?"

"Well—" Larry sighed, looked out the window, then brought his gaze back to his partner. "Well, how do you explain the crashing *after* Soames had left? Melissa didn't tell us anyone else was involved."

Tony shook his head. "I'm not sure Melissa is telling us the truth, Larry. I know you don't want to hear that, but I'm telling you, things aren't fitting together here."

Larry couldn't deny it. "I just don't get it. What really happened?"

"There's no telling," Tony said. "But the only story we've heard that we've been able to corroborate with witnesses is Soames's story."

Larry rolled his eyes. "Oh, come on. You saw his record. You saw the things in his apartment, the pictures, the bloody shirt under his seat—"

"That's right," Tony said. "I saw them. I'm not saying that he's not a scumbag. I'm just not sure what he really did in this case."

He pulled into a parking space near Larry's apartment and let the car idle for a moment. "Look, what do you say we just sleep on it, and tackle all this fresh tomorrow?"

"Yeah, okay." Larry got out and headed back toward his apartment. But before he reached it, he turned back and walked to his own car. He couldn't just let it go; he wouldn't be able to rest haunted by the possibility that Melissa was lying. He had wanted to check on Melissa anyway, to make sure she was all right. Tony would say that he was obsessing—that if she wasn't a blonde with soulful eyes, he wouldn't be giving this case such attention. But Larry hoped that wasn't true. He'd been on the police force for nine years now, and while many of his colleagues had gotten jaded, he'd worked hard not to. He liked to think that he would always stand up for justice, fairness, and the rights of the victims—especially the more vulnerable victims who needed someone to stand up for them. As tough as Melissa's facade suggested she was, he suspected that she was as vulnerable as any victim he'd ever encountered. Even if there were things about her story that didn't make sense.

He drove back to her apartment building and tried to be quiet as he walked in, to see if anyone could get past Mrs. Berkley without being noticed. But the first stair squeaked beneath his foot, and suddenly the door peeped open, still attached with the chain lock. Mrs. Berkley peered out. He waved. "Hi, Mrs. Berkley. I'm just checking on Melissa."

She pressed the door closed, unlocked the chain, then opened it further. "Good. She's up now. She slept most of the afternoon, but I've heard her moving around up there in the last few minutes. Enjoy your visit."

He smiled uncomfortably and continued up the stairs. A television blared from one of the other apartments on the first floor, and a baby cried in another.

The walls were paper-thin, he thought. Thin enough for Mrs. Berkley to hear everyone who came and went—thin enough to know whether Melissa was alone.

He knocked on Melissa's door. He heard footsteps, then waited while, he assumed, she looked at him through the peephole. After a moment, she opened the door.

"Hi," she said.

She couldn't be lying about this, he thought. Not someone with such pure blue eyes, such porcelain skin, such fine blonde hair . . . "Thought I'd come by and check on you," he said. "See if you were all right after our questions this morning. I felt kind of responsible for making things worse for you."

She sighed wearily. "Is that an apology?"

"No. Actually, we were just doing our job," he said. "I just regret how it made you feel."

"Well, I'm fine." She stepped back and invited him in.

He looked around, and saw that the furniture had been turned upright, the toppled lamps were settled back on the tables again, and the broken glass had been swept into little piles.

"I guess I shouldn't have run out like that," she said. "It just got to me a little. If I hadn't been so tired, I probably would have realized that you had to ask. You're supposed to. I wouldn't expect either of you to just take everything at face value."

He glanced into the bedroom and saw that her bed was unmade and the covers pulled back, as if she'd been sleeping in it. "I hope I didn't wake you."

"No," she said. "I just woke up. I was trying to clean up a little. When I came home this morning, I started to, but I was so exhausted I decided to finish later. So I climbed into bed and fell asleep."

Odd, he thought. Most rape victims wouldn't have gone near the place where they'd been violated, yet Melissa had slept there all afternoon? She was tougher than he'd thought. Either that, or . . .

He tried to shove out of his mind the thought that she might not be telling it all exactly as it had happened, that she was leaving something out, or maybe making something up. Seeing the trouble in her expression, the fatigue on her face, he just couldn't believe that. She'd been traumatized. That much was clear.

"I'll help you, if you want," he said finally.

"Are you sure?"

"Sure," he said, rolling up his sleeves. "Have you eaten?"

"I was thinking of ordering a pizza."

"Great," he said. "My treat. You order it, and I'll see if I can get the rest of this up before it comes."

The misery in her expression lightened as she smiled and limped to the telephone. "You're a lifesaver, Larry. I didn't think I could tackle this myself."

It didn't take him long to scrub the stains out of the carpet and sweep up the rest of the glass, but as he did he kept remembering Mrs. Berkley's insistence that she'd heard the crashing lamps and tables *after* Soames had left.

"Melissa," he asked later, over the pizza, "did you have any other visitors last night, other than Soames?"

"No," she said. "And he wasn't exactly a visitor."

"Someone else from the apartments, maybe? Did a neighbor next door stop in? Anybody?"

"No. Nobody."

He studied the pepperoni on his slice again. "Did I tell you I met Mrs. Berkley?"

Melissa smiled. "She's a sweet lady, isn't she?"

"Tell me about her."

Melissa set her pizza down and wiped her fingers on her napkin. "She's been like a grandmother to me. It's been nice to have her around, since my parents are so far away. She's always baking me cakes and cookies, and telling me wild stories about all the neighbors."

"Wild stories? How do you mean?"

She shrugged. "Oh, you know. She doesn't really have much to do all day, so I think she spends a lot of her time imagining what everyone else is doing. And like anyone who lives in their imagination, she gets her facts mixed up. Just last week, she swore that my next-door neighbor in 2B—a forty-eight-year-old widow— had given birth to a little boy. I told her she couldn't have, that she wasn't pregnant, but Mrs. Berkley insisted. Later I found out that the niece of one of the neighbors on the first floor had a baby boy, and she's been visiting. So someone had a baby, all right; it just wasn't who Mrs. Berkley thought it was."

I knew it, Larry thought. The woman wasn't a competent witness. She was mistaken.

"So what did she tell you?" Melissa asked. "Did she see Soames last night?"

"Yeah, she saw him."

That tense look worked back over Melissa's face. "I thought so. She sees everybody."

"Yeah." He felt sorry now that he'd doubted her, that Tony's suspicions had infected him. Something definitely had happened to her. That haunted look in her eye had come from somewhere. And anyway, he couldn't believe that she would simply make up a story like this and put herself through this ordeal for no good reason. She had studied criminal justice; she had to know what this would cost her in emotional stress once it went to trial. No one would subject themselves to that unless they were telling the truth.

She ignored her pizza now, and he wished he hadn't brought the subject up again. Quiet settled over them, and that sad, grieving look in her eyes touched him. There must be some way to assuage that, he thought.

"Listen," he said, sighing. "You need to get out of this place. Just relax a little. Get your mind off things. What if I took you to a movie?"

She smiled softly. "Is that part of your job description?"

He shook his head. "Consider me off duty. This is just pleasure."

Her smile found its way to her eyes, and it was like sunshine reaching a chilled heart. "I'm assuming you aren't married, Detective?"

He shook his head. "You're assuming right."

"Then I guess it would be nice."

Mrs. Berkley was watching at the bottom of the stairs as they left. "Did you find a baby-sitter for the baby tonight?" the little woman asked her.

Melissa looked confused, then amused. "I'm not the one who had the baby, Mrs. Berkley. Remember? It was Mrs. Jasper's niece."

"That's right," the woman said. "Well, you two go on and have a nice evening, now. And be careful."

"We will," Melissa said. "And Mrs. Berkley, please keep your door locked."

"I always do," she said, though it stood wide open at the moment. "Good-bye, Detective."

Larry waved good-bye, feeling relieved that their witness's word wasn't worth much. If only he could convince Tony of that.

He could see that the movie had done her good. For two hours, she had been allowed to forget her problems, dismiss Soames from her mind, and pretend that she was someone else in another life. Now, as they flowed with the crowd toward the exit doors, he saw the shadow creeping back over her face, and how she glanced from side to side, as if expecting Soames to come out of nowhere.

Feeling protective, he reached out and took her hand. It was small, ice-cold, trembling slightly. Trying to decide what would help her right now, he asked, "Would you like to go get a cup of coffee?"

"Sounds good," she said.

He took her to a little café with lush plants spilling from windowsills and cascading down walls. A man with a goatee and a ponytail played an acoustic guitar in the corner, and they sat in a booth near the back and talked about the movie, then about favorite movies they'd seen growing up.

"My sister and I used to spend every Saturday afternoon at the movies," Melissa said. "Half our allowance went for that each week. We would laugh and cry—and when we cried, neither of us would look at the other, because we knew not to destroy the mood. Sandy was good about that."

Larry was confused. Hadn't she said she had no siblings? "Where's Sandy now?" he asked carefully.

Her smile faded, and she seemed to grow even paler. "She died. About three years ago." Tears welled in her eyes, turning the rims red as she looked away. Quickly, she changed the subject. "Do you come here a lot?"

Though she tried to look bright, the tears were still in her eyes, making her look even more fragile. "No, I don't come here much. I work a lot at night. It's nice, though."

"My father plays guitar," she said, watching the man in the corner as he strummed. "He used to play and we'd all sing with him. He taught me how to play the ukulele when I was little, but I only knew one song. I tried the guitar, but wasn't willing to practice."

Her rambling reminded him of a hamster on a treadmill, running as fast as it could without moving an inch. It was as if one moment's silence would break her completely. Even so, he listened carefully; each rambling revelation provided another clue to the woman who fascinated him.

"Do you play anything?" she asked. She had skillfully blinked back her tears by now, and she didn't look quite as forlorn. Trying to lighten things, he said, "I play softball. But no instrument."

"Softball, huh? For a team?"

"Yeah. A church team, during the summer. I can't make every game, because I have to work so much. We're not a very good team. We manage to snatch defeat from the jaws of victory pretty regularly."

She smiled—a distant, pensive smile. "I played for a while last summer, when I worked for the FBI."

The subject of her job with the FBI had seemed taboo earlier in the day when he had asked about her criminal justice degree, but now he seized the opportunity to ask the question that had been plaguing him. "Why did you quit? That sounds like an ideal job for a criminal justice major just out of college."

She breathed a laugh that said he was naive. "I was at the very bottom of the totem pole. It was drudgery. Mostly clerical work, and the pay stinks. I hated the job, and when I looked around me at the career FBI agents, I just decided that that's not what I wanted to do for the rest of my life." She looked up at him then, her eyes locked with his, and she smiled a little. "No offense, but criminal justice was a mistake for me. So I quit and took a job doing something else until I could decide what I really wanted to do. I should have just answered your question this morning, but I was upset."

"Why did you move here, though?"

She was getting tense again. "I was having trouble living in Pensacola, with all the memories—I missed my sister, okay?" Her voice cracked. "I thought if I started over someplace else . . ."

"But you graduated from Florida State, in Tallahassee. Why didn't you just stay there?"

"I wanted someplace completely new," she said. "St. Clair seemed like the perfect little town."

"It can be." He made his voice gentle and soft as he reached across the table and touched her hand. "You're not on the witness stand, Melissa."

"I know. It's just—" She smiled slightly, then brought those big eyes up to him again. "You've been so nice to me today, so I wanted to explain. I really don't know if I could have gotten through the day without you. It's weird, too. I mean, this morning, you showed up exactly when I needed you to, when I was about to lose it. And then again tonight, facing that mess—I can't believe you showed up when you did."

"I had you on my mind. I thought you could use a friend. You seemed pretty alone."

She seemed troubled by that thought. Letting go of his hand, she folded her arms across her stomach, looked away, and said, "I haven't had time to make many friends since I moved here."

"Why not?" Larry asked.

"Because . . ." Her voice quivered, and she cleared her throat and tried again. "I guess it's hard for me to get close to people."

He believed it. Melissa seemed like a loner who didn't like to be alone. Much like him.

"I've always found church to be a good place to make friends. It takes a while, but the friends I've made there will last my whole life."

She struggled against tears. "I don't belong in church. Sometimes I'm pretty sure that God is disgusted with me."

"Why?"

She wiped her eyes, smearing her tears. "What's the verse I learned when I was a kid in Bible school? 'He is of purer eyes than to even look upon iniquity.' Sometimes God turns away."

"But why would he turn away from you, Melissa? What happened last night wasn't your choice."

"I know he has, though." Struggling to fight her tears, she said, "There are things that happen, Larry. Horrible things. If God was there—if he was watching, he would stop them. When he doesn't, then I know he isn't even watching."

Larry only stared at her, feeling moisture in his own eyes as his emotions responded to hers. To tell her that she was reacting inappropriately to her own suffering would be insensitive. Who was he to say? He had never been violated in the way she had. He said nothing, unable to find words that weren't trite and pat.

"There was something that happened in my family," she whispered, covering half her face with one hand as she uncovered part of the horror that lay hidden inside her. "Something terrible. And I wanted so much to believe that God would take care of it. But he didn't."

Larry could think of no way to break the silence as he watched her struggle with her grief.

"Maybe I'm the one hiding from God," she said finally. "Maybe I've just moved too far to ever get back. There does come a point when you've moved too far."

Larry reached across the table and pushed back a strand of her hair caught in her tears. "I hope I'm around when God proves to you that you're wrong."

"I wish . . ." she started to say, but her words broke off.

She looked down at her hands as more tears fell; finally, she drew in a deep, cleansing breath. "Can we go now?"

They were quiet as they drove back to her apartment, and when they got there she was out of the car before he had even cut the engine off. Larry hopped out and caught up to her. "Let me walk you up."

She nodded and slowed her step then, and he put his arm around her and escorted her up the steps. Mrs. Berkley's door was open an inch or so as they walked by.

Melissa reached into her purse for her keys when they got to her door, but those tears were still coming, and Larry didn't know what to do for her. He took the key from her hand, opened the door, then stood in front of her for a moment, wondering what he could offer her to relieve the pain. "I know things look dark now," he whispered, "but they're going to get better. And if you need to talk, day or night, you can call me. Remember that."

She wilted as he pulled her into a crushing hug, and her arms closed around his neck. For a while, he just held her there, trying to give her support and hope and help as he felt the force of her sobs shaking her body. Some part of his heart wept with her, and his own eyes filled with tears.

When she pulled back, he touched her face. "Are you going to be all right?"

"Yes," she whispered. "Thank you for the shoulder."

"Anytime. That's what it's there for."

She drew in a long breath and looked up at him. "You make me feel safe."

"Good," he said. "That's my job."

"You do it very well." She smiled and almost laughed then, the kind of laughter that often follows weeping, and took a deep breath. "Good night."

He wanted to kiss her but knew it wouldn't be appropriate. Not the night after she was assaulted, not the moment after she'd found comfort weeping on his shoulder. Instead, he whispered, "Good night."

She went inside and closed the door, and he stood listening as she locked two bolts. He started down the stairs, then stopped and pulled one of his cards out of his wallet. It already included his extension at the precinct, so he turned it over and jotted his home and cellular phone numbers down. Then he went back to her apartment and slipped it under her door.

When he reached the bottom of the stairs, Mrs. Berkley was still peering out of a one-inch opening in her door. "Good night, Mrs. Berkley," he called.

"Good night, Detective Millsaps," she replied with perfect clarity. "Be careful driving home."

Larry frowned all the way out to his car, wondering how she'd remembered his name. Maybe she flowed in and out of confusion, sometimes getting things right, sometimes not. Still, it disturbed him.

Tony was going to hit the ceiling anyway, when he heard what Larry had done with his evening.

CHAPTER EIGHT

Y ou're losing your edge." Tony plopped into the extra chair at Larry's desk.

"What?"

"You heard me. I went by Mrs. Berkley's again today. I wanted to ask her a couple more questions, and she told me something very interesting."

Larry knew where this was going. He leaned back in his chair and waited. "Yeah? What?"

"She told me that you took Melissa Nelson out last night."

"It wasn't a date. And Mrs. Berkley is loony. She floats in and out of reality. We can't count on her story at all."

Tony wouldn't let him change the subject. "Did you or didn't you take Melissa Nelson out last night?"

He shifted uncomfortably. "I went by to see her, okay? I helped her clean up. And she needed to get out of the apartment, so I took her."

"On a date."

Larry stacked some loose papers on his desk. A telephone at the next desk rang. He wished it were his. "Call it what you want, Tony."

Tony leaned forward, fixing his eyes on his partner's. "Tell me the truth, Larry. You were disturbed by what Mrs. Berkley told us, right? And also by the stuff we found out yesterday about Melissa's job. You wanted to get to the bottom of it, and that's why you went to see her last night."

Larry dropped the papers and began rubbing his temples. "Okay, yeah. And I did get to the bottom of it. She didn't like criminal justice, once she started working in it. That happens. She decided to take a job doing clerical work until she could figure out what she wanted to do. And her sister had died, she was having trouble with the memories, and that's why she came here."

"A sister, huh?" Tony pulled a pad out of his pocket and jotted that down.

"What? Do you think she's lying about that, too?"

"Just gonna check," Tony said. "By the way, we have to testify for the grand jury day after tomorrow. Did you know that?"

"Yeah." Larry looked at him again. "And what are you gonna say, Tony? You gonna go in there and tell them that, despite what you saw that night, despite all the evidence we found, you think she's lying?"

Tony breathed a laugh. "Man, I'm telling you again. You're losing your edge. When's the last time I sat on a witness stand and told them whether I thought someone was lying or not? I'm being called to talk about the evidence, not my gut feelings."

"Good. Because your gut feelings are wrong."

A police radio on the hip of an officer nearby blared, adding to the grating noise of a teletype printing out a report.

Tony got up and looked down at his friend. "You're getting involved with her, buddy. And that's a big mistake."

"I don't do things the way you do, Tony. You've known that for a long time. I don't have to account to you or anyone else on this force for my personal life."

"Fine," Tony said. "I hope you don't have to eat those words."

Larry watched Tony go back to his desk, then stared for a while at his blank computer screen. Things had been tense between them ever since they'd met Melissa Nelson, but that wasn't his fault. Tony wanted to victimize the victim, and Larry wasn't going to let him. It was as simple as that.

Still, he thought, it probably would be better if he didn't keep seeing Melissa. Though he would never admit it to Tony, she *was* getting under his skin, and that wasn't good. Later, after the case was laid to rest, maybe he could explore those feelings again.

He got up and went into the interrogation room, the only quiet place in the building. He stared out the window at what he could see of downtown St. Clair. He watched as citizens walked by on the sidewalk, trusting the officers in this building to keep them safe.

Was Tony right? Was he slipping? Was this protective feeling toward Melissa compromising his police work?

Maybe it was, he admitted reluctantly. Starting now, he had to put it behind him. He wouldn't call Melissa Nelson again.

Melissa was trembling, two days later, as she sat on the witness stand in front of the grand jury that would decide whether Edward Soames would stand trial. Under oath, she told them her whole story—the way he'd shown up unexpectedly and shoved his way in, the struggle that had ensued as she'd tried to defend herself, the knife with which he'd cut her, his ultimate violation of her. She cried as she spoke, thankful that he wasn't in the courtroom, since defendants weren't allowed in a grand jury hearing. If he'd been sitting there, it would have been so hard . . .

But his attorney was there, and as he cross-examined her, she tried not to back up or stumble, tried not to sway at all or deviate from what she'd told them at first. When he suggested that she'd had a crush on Soames, she knew her repulsion was apparent on her face. He'd then gone on to badger her about inviting him to dinner—apparently Gretchen at work had testified before her—but his merciless bullying of her had only made him look like another monster, and her a victim suffering further abuse.

By the time they dismissed her, she was weak and exhausted. And the first person she saw outside the courtroom was Larry.

Needing his strong shoulder, she wilted into him, and he slid his arms around her and let her cry. "Are you okay?"

"Yeah," she whispered. "It was just . . . I don't know if they believed me. His lawyer was putting so many lies into their heads." She wiped her eyes and stepped back. "Will you wait with me until they give the verdict? I don't think I can stand to be by myself right now."

"Sure," he said, unable to deny her such a simple and heartfelt request. "I'll wait."

It was a couple of hours before the DA came out of the courtroom and found them sitting together. "Well, we have some good news and some bad news," he said.

Melissa looked up, bracing herself. "Was he indicted?"

"Yes, he was," he said. "But the bad news is that the judge let him out on $100,000 bond, pending trial."

Melissa sprang up. "He did *what*?"

"I'm sorry, Melissa. I tried my best to convince him that it would be dangerous to let him out, but he said that it could take a year for it to come to trial, and he didn't want to lock him up for that amount of time."

"He's getting out? When?"

"Probably today," he said.

Feeling as blindsided as she did by this, Larry stood up beside her. "Melissa," he tried, "you know he'd be crazy to come near you. He knows what the consequences would be."

"He *is* crazy! Don't you people get it? He's going to come after me!"

"No, he won't," the DA said. "The judge laid down very specific instructions. He told him he'd throw him back in jail if he so much as thought about you."

"This man doesn't care what a judge told him!" Melissa insisted, starting to cry. "I'm telling you, this is a big mistake! He could kill me the next time!" She headed back toward the courtroom. "Where's the judge? I have to talk to him!"

Larry grabbed her arm. "Melissa, you can't. There's nothing you can do. But I agree with Sid. I don't think he'll bother you."

"You don't *think*?" she shouted. "Well, what if you're wrong?"

Jerking away from him, she turned and ran toward the door that would take her into the parking garage. Helpless, Larry just let her go.

She spent the rest of the afternoon hunting for a new place to live, then packing all of her belongings and moving. The move would wipe out her savings. And she hadn't yet found another job. But it was the only way she could evade the man who would kill her if he found her.

Now, in her new apartment in a building several blocks away from her old one, she found herself still uneasy. As night had fallen and she'd made the last trip from her old apartment, she'd had the uneasy, panicky feeling that someone was watching her.

She locked the dead bolt, checked every window, then sat on the couch, her back straight, eyes darting about. It *was* safer, she told herself. Much safer. Too afraid to sleep in her bed, which sat right below a window, she tried to sleep on the couch, curled up in a fetal position.

And all night, she clutched a knife in her hand.

cross the street, in a phone booth that gave him a perfect view of the second-floor window of Melissa's new apartment, Edward Pendergrast, alias Soames, dialed the long-distance number he'd gotten from information. Keeping an eye on the window, he waited for it to ring once . . . twice . . . three times.

"Hello?"

It was the just-awakened voice of an older woman, probably in her fifties, and he got a mental picture of her right away—martyred, long-suffering, self-righteous. It pleased him to death to bring her in on this now.

"Hello?" she said again.

"Mrs. Nelson?" he asked.

"Yes."

"Is this the Mrs. Nelson who's the mother of Melissa Nelson?"

"Yes," she said tentatively. "Do you know my daughter?"

"Do I know your daughter." He chuckled then, and looked back at the window. "Yeah, I'd say I know your daughter. Listen, I need to get in touch with her. Can you help me?"

The woman hesitated. "Well, I'd be happy to give her a message for you."

"I'd rather call her myself," he said.

Again, hesitation. "Would you like to leave a message? I'll get it to her tomorrow."

He grinned. She probably didn't know that her daughter had just moved. Wouldn't she be surprised to hear why? "Yeah, okay. Give her a message. Tell her an old friend called. She'll know who it is."

"Uh—may I tell her your name?"

"Just tell her that," he said. "Tell her I've been looking for her."

"Would you like to leave a number?"

He smiled. "She knows how to reach me."

He hung up then, and laughed out loud at the conversation that was probably taking place between Melissa's parents. Her father would probably grill her mother over and over on what had been said, then convince her that it had no significance. It was just some prankster. Within minutes, they'd roll over and try to get back to sleep.

But they wouldn't get a lot of sleep tonight.

His grin faded as he stepped out of the phone booth and crossed the street. If there was a weakness in that building, he would find it. And tomorrow, he'd have a huge new surprise for her.

The phone rang again, startling Nancy Nelson awake for the second time that night. She looked over at her husband, who was squinting to read the clock. "Three A.M.," he said.

She reached for the phone. "Hello?"

"Hi. Me again."

It was the voice of the man who'd called earlier—the old friend of Melissa. Covering the phone, she whispered, "It's the same person."

Jim sat up.

"Did you give Melissa my message?" the deep voice asked.

"No," she said. "It was late. I'll tell her tomorrow."

"That's okay," he said. "I've found her."

Something about the way he said that sent chills down her spine. "What do you mean, you've found her?"

"If you talk to her, Mrs. Nelson, tell her that she can't hide."

She caught her breath, and Jim snatched the phone away. "Who is this?" he shouted. "What do you want?"

"Ask Melissa," he said. "She knows what I want."

They heard a *click*, then a dial tone.

Jim got up and turned on the lamp.

"What are you doing?" Nancy asked, getting out of bed and reaching for her robe.

"Calling Melissa," he said.

"But it's three A.M. You'll wake her."

"I don't care," he said. "Something's wrong. She needs to know about this call."

Nancy went to sit beside him on the bed, and he reached for her hand and held it in a reassuring grip as he waited for Melissa to answer.

The ringing was interrupted by three ascending tones and an operator's voice. "I'm sorry. The number you have dialed has been disconnected . . ."

He slowly lowered the receiver. "Disconnected," he said. "Where is she?"

Nancy raked her hand through her hair. "Jim, you don't think—"

Jim got up and went to the closet, flicked on the light. "Get dressed. We're driving down to St. Clair."

"But it's 400 miles!" Nancy said, reaching for the phone. "I'm calling the St. Clair police. She may need help now."

Jim nodded. "If only we knew some of her friends to call. People she works with."

He waited as she got the St. Clair police on the phone and asked them to check on Melissa. When she hung up, she was just as troubled as she had been when she'd called.

"What did they say?" he asked.

Nancy shook her head as she began to get dressed. "They said they'd go check on her and ask her to call us. And they advised us not to make the 400 mile trip until we'd tried to reach her at work. But tomorrow's Saturday, and even if she does have to work, she won't be in for another five hours. Something could happen to her before that."

Nancy threw some clothes into a suitcase while Jim closed and locked the windows. Keys in hand, Jim grabbed the suitcase. "We'll stop at a pay phone and call home every hour or so and see if the police have left a message on our machine," he said.

"Okay," Nancy agreed. Grabbing her purse, she dashed out behind him to the car.

CHAPTER TEN

The next day, tired from the fitful sleep of the night before, when she'd stirred at every noise—ever aware that she had no phone hooked up with which to call for help if he somehow found her—Melissa went to a pay phone and had the telephone at her new address hooked up with an unlisted number. They gave her the new number and told her it would be on later that day. While she was at the pay phone, she called her parents to tell them her new number.

No one was home, so she left a message, explaining that she'd gotten aggravated at her landlord because of a leaky sink, and had moved to a new apartment. She had also taken a new job, she lied—to keep them from trying to reach her at work—and she'd let them know soon what that number was.

Then she set out to make truth out of her lie, checking the want ads for a job.

It was nine o'clock when the Nelsons pulled over to a pay phone for the fifth time since leaving home and called home for messages. Jim caught his breath when he heard Melissa's voice. "It's her!" he told his wife. "Listen."

Nancy put her ear next to his and listened to their daughter's explanation. Her voice sounded calm, not troubled, and everything made sense. She would be out this morning, she told them, but would call them tonight after her phone was turned on and update them on everything.

As Jim hung up the phone, they fell into each other's arms, laughing with relief. "She's okay!" Nancy cried. "She's fine."

"Now what?" Jim asked. "We're only a couple of hours away from St. Clair. Should we go on? Maybe she needs help moving."

"She didn't leave her address," Nancy said. "We wouldn't know how to find her. Besides, there's no need to let her know how badly we overreacted. Let's just go back home and wait until she calls tonight."

Jim thought that over. "I guess you're right."

The two parents got back into their car and headed back the way they had come.

Melissa managed to find a job doing clerical work for a chemical company, a job that didn't pay very well, but which seemed to be located in a safe place. It was a plus that they would let her start Monday. The sooner, the better, she thought.

It was almost dark when she got home and checked her phone to see if it was on yet. It was, so she dialed her parents' number, then cradled the phone between her ear and shoulder as she began to unpack one of her boxes.

"Hello?" Her mother's voice was always a sweet sound.

"Mom? It's me."

"Melissa, thank heaven! It's so good to hear your voice. We tried calling you last night, but the operator said your phone had been disconnected."

"Didn't you get my message this morning?"

"Yes, but until then . . ." She let her voice trail off and sighed. "Well, we're just glad you're all right. After those phone calls, we were beside ourselves."

Melissa frowned. "What phone calls?"

"Some man called last night. He was really kind of scary. At first he said he was an old friend, but I don't think he was a friend at all."

Melissa could feel the blood draining from her face, and she slowly sat down. "Mom, who was the man?"

"'An old friend' was all he said. We were going to come down and look for you, but then we got your message this morning. Melissa, are you all right?"

She clutched the phone so tight her knuckles were turning white. "Mom, what did he say?"

"The first time, he just asked us if we knew how he could get in touch with you. He said he was an old friend, but he was a little rude, calling so late. But we wouldn't give him your number. Then he hung up, and a little later he called back and told me that he'd found you. He said to tell you you can't hide. Melissa, do you know who he is?"

Melissa swallowed hard, and her heart began to race. He knew who she really was, she thought frantically. He had called her parents.

He had figured it out.

"Melissa?"

She tried to steady her voice. "Mom, it's this guy I worked with." She stopped, tried to regroup her thoughts and manufacture the story as she went. "He kept coming onto me, and when I wouldn't go out with him, he got a little hostile." She closed her eyes and tried to stop trembling. "He's harmless, really. Just annoying. Whatever he says, just ignore it."

"So hostile that you had to change your phone number, your address, your job?"

Her hand was trembling so hard she could hardly hold the phone. Maybe her explanation had been too frightening. She'd have to tone it down. "I told you why I moved, Mom. The manager wouldn't fix my sink. And the job . . . well, it just wasn't what I wanted. None of it had anything to do with him. Mom, did he say anything else?"

"No," Nancy said. "But, Melissa, what is this about your hiding? What was he talking about?"

Dizziness washed over her, along with an overwhelming feeling that she wasn't alone. She looked around slowly, warily, as if he were in the apartment somewhere, listening to this call.

"Melissa?"

"Yeah, Mom. Uh . . ." She tried to backtrack through the conversation, to give the response her mother needed. "I don't know what he was talking about. I told you, he's just some idiot. Probably drank too much and thought he'd get a good laugh." She knew her voice was trembling, and she was giving away too much, alarming her mother.

"Melissa, are you sure you're all right? Maybe you should come home for a while."

"No, I can't, Mom. I have to stay."

Her mother was crying now, and she could hear the subtle difference in her breathing, the grainy sound to her voice. "But this is how it happened before…"

As hard as she'd tried to shelter them from this, she was causing them grief anyway.

"Melissa?" Her father had taken the phone, and Melissa knew she couldn't hide anything from him without a Herculean effort. Trying to sound upbeat, she said, "Hi, Dad."

"Honey, I want you to tell me the truth. Is something wrong? Are you in some kind of danger?"

"No," she said. "Really. Everything's fine. I just moved yesterday, so my phone was disconnected. Dad, those phone calls— they're just a guy at work." As she spoke, she broke into a sweat. Slowly, she walked into the bedroom, looked nervously around, then cautiously checked the closet. "It's really no big deal. His pride is hurt because I wouldn't go out with him…" The bedroom was empty, so she walked out of it, crossed the living room, and went into the kitchen.

"Melissa, I got a recording device today. I'm going to tape the calls from now on. Maybe you should too."

"Just relax, okay? Stop worrying. I have everything under control."

"Melissa, does this person have something to do with why you moved so suddenly?"

She hated lying to her parents, but she had no choice. "No. I told you. My sink was stopped up, and the manager wouldn't fix it. I got fed up and moved. No big deal."

The kitchen was clear, so she headed for the bathroom. "Dad, I love you. Tell Mom I love her, too. And calm down. I'm sorry about the calls, but they really don't mean anything."

"All right, honey. But if we get any more calls, we're going to…"

She stepped cautiously into the bathroom as her father continued to talk. The shower curtain was closed, and she couldn't remember closing it herself. Her heart began to palpitate, and her

73

blouse began to stick to her. Clutching the phone tighter, she grabbed the edge of the curtain and jerked it open.

Empty.

Breathing a sigh of relief, she turned slowly around and leaned against the sink. This was crazy. He couldn't know where she was. He couldn't know *who* she was. It was just a coincidence. The caller was someone else.

"Melissa, did you hear me?"

"Yes, Dad. You said if you got any more call—"

Her voice stopped cold as she looked up and saw the writing on her mirror, big red letters made with the lipstick she had left on the sink that morning. She gasped and jumped back, and her throat constricted.

"Melissa? What is it?"

She couldn't speak, couldn't breathe, couldn't think. For a moment, she only stared at the words, bold and big:

Next time for real.

In a high-pitched, breathless, wavering voice, she managed to get the words out. "Dad, I've got to go. Bathtub—overflowing—"

She turned the phone off and dropped it, then grabbed her purse and her keys and fled the apartment.

CHAPTER ELEVEN

L arry was eating a TV dinner and watching the news when a sudden banging on his door startled him. He grabbed his gun, which he'd laid on the table, and approached the door quickly but cautiously, sliding along the wall.

Through the peephole he saw Melissa and threw the door open.

Sobbing hysterically, she grabbed him and spoke so rapidly that he could barely understand her. "Help me! He was there. In my new apartment. I don't know how he found it, but he was in there. He wrote on my mirror, Larry! I'm not safe anywhere!"

He pulled her in and made her sit. Kneeling in front of her, he tried to calm her. "Tell me again. Who was there? Soames?"

"Yes!" she cried. "I moved yesterday, but he found me." She grabbed both of his arms. "He was in my apartment, Larry! He wrote in lipstick on my mirror. And he's been calling my parents! I don't know what to do. There's no place to go!"

Larry got up, pulled on his shoulder holster, slipped his gun into it, then put his windbreaker on. "All right, let's go back over there, and you can show me. What did he write?"

"He wrote, 'Next time for real.' I don't know what he means, Larry. But how could he have gotten in? Nobody knew where I was. Not even you!"

"All right. I'm gonna call Tony and have him meet us there. If we can find proof that he was in your apartment, we'll have him picked up again. This joker's going back to the slammer until his trial."

She was a wreck, Larry thought as they drove back to her building. What if he'd been in her apartment while she was home? What if he was still there now? Would he be that bold? That stupid?

Tony was waiting in his car when they drove up, and he got out and met them at the curb. Melissa was shaking and staring up at the window to her apartment.

"She says he was there," Larry said quietly. "Left a message on her mirror, in lipstick."

"Would he be that reckless?" Tony whispered.

"Looks like he was." He turned back to Melissa. "If you want to wait in the car—"

"No!" she said quickly. "I don't want to be by myself. I'm coming with you. I'll show you where it is."

They opened the door quietly and carefully—not wanting to disturb any fingerprints he might have left—pulled their guns, and went in. Melissa waited by the front door as they searched the apartment. Satisfied that he wasn't there, they came to the bathroom. "Was it in here?"

"Yes," she said, hanging back. "On the mirror."

There was a moment of silence, then Larry asked, "Did you clean it off?"

"What?" She abandoned the front door and went in to see for herself.

The mirror was clean.

"No, it was there! Right there, in big letters!" She gasped and backed out of the bathroom. "Oh, no—he was back! He came back while I was gone. Or maybe he was here all the time! Larry, you have to believe me! He's playing games with me. He was here! Dust for fingerprints! You'll see."

But she could see that Tony didn't believe a word, and Larry looked troubled and confused. "Melissa," Larry said, "are you sure you didn't clean it before you came over? You were upset. You might have—"

"No! I was on the phone with my father, and I dropped the phone. See? Here it is." She picked it up off the floor. "And then I ran out." She turned to Tony. "Please, I'm telling you—he was here. You have to pick him up. You have to get him back in jail, or he'll kill me."

"Is that what it meant—'Next time for real'?" Larry asked. "That he would kill you next time?"

"It must have," she agreed quickly. "And how did he get in here? The windows are all locked. I had the door dead-bolted. And how did he find this apartment? He must have been watching me when I moved out—stalking me."

Tony looked at the mirror again. "Is this the lipstick you said he wrote it with?"

She nodded, and Tony picked up the tube with a piece of tissue, opened it, and rolled the lipstick up. The tip was flat, as if it had been used for writing. Even so, Tony shook his head. "It doesn't make sense. Why would he risk coming back to clean it up? Why would he risk doing it in the first place, when he knows he's the first person we'd think of?"

Melissa felt herself trembling with fear and frustration. "Detective Danks, if I were lying about this, I'd have just written something on there myself, and it would still be there. And anyway, why *would* I lie about this? Why would I set myself up to look like a lunatic? I'm telling you, it happened. He came in, he wrote on my mirror, and then he came back—or maybe he was here the whole time. Only—I looked in every room before I saw the mirror. He wasn't here."

Larry left the bathroom and began looking around the apartment. After a moment, he said, "Tony, come look at this."

Tony and Melissa followed him. He stood at the far end of the hallway, pointing at a rectangular wooden door set into the ceiling. "It's an attic," Tony whispered.

Larry questioned Tony with his eyes. Could Soames be hiding there?

"Have you looked up there?" Larry whispered to Melissa.

"No. I didn't even know it was there."

"Do you have a flashlight?"

"Yes," she said, and ran to get it. When she came back, she saw that they were both preparing to open the ceiling door. "Stand back," Larry said, and pulled out his gun again. Tony did the same. Larry reached up and grabbed the hook on the door, and Tony held his gun aimed at it in one hand, the flashlight in the other.

In one rapid motion, Larry pulled the door down. They held their guns aimed for a moment, but nothing happened. Slowly, carefully, Larry reached up and unfolded the narrow ladder. Tony shone the flashlight through the black hole, revealing how small the space was.

Cautiously, Larry climbed the stairs, still aiming his gun, and stepped onto the board floor of the small crawl space. It was big enough for a man to sit in, he thought, though there was no sign that anyone had been here. He touched the floor, felt the dust, then had an idea. Stepping back onto the ladder so that only half his body intruded into the dark space, he shone the light around on the floor. A thick coating of dust covered it, but where he had just stood the dust clearly showed his footprints. He looked carefully around for any more disturbances in the dust.

There it was—the faint outline of the bottom of a sneaker. Beyond that was a wiped place, as if someone had slid across the floor.

"Tony, there's dust all over the place up here," he called down. "But in one place, it's wiped up. Like somebody was sitting there. And there's a shoe print in the dust."

"Let me see."

They traded places. "I see what you're talking about," Tony said, "but it could just be where the previous tenants had a box or something sitting."

"The edges aren't that clean," Larry said. "Looks to me like someone was sitting there."

Larry watched as Tony crawled farther into the attic, shining the light all around. After a moment, he came back to the opening. "Larry, come up here. You've got to see this."

Larry glanced at Melissa. She stood trembling at the end of the hallway, hugging herself and waiting. As Larry began to climb, she took a few steps closer to the ladder.

Tony was shining the light at a place on the attic floor. It was an opening around one of the inset lights in the ceiling of the bathroom. The plate that had been on the back was missing, as was the bulb, and they could see through the glass covering straight into Melissa's bathroom, to the sink and mirror and the area in front of them.

"Still skeptical?" Larry asked.

Tony shook his head. "He was here, all right," he said in a voice too low for her to hear, "watching her discover what he wrote on the mirror."

"Let's dust the apartment for prints."

"Okay. But what about her? He'll be back."

"She can't stay here tonight," Larry said. "I'll think of something."

They climbed back down, then both hesitated to tell her what they'd found.

"Well?" she asked.

"It looks like he might have been up there while you were here," Larry said. "He probably left because he knew you were going to get help."

The color drained from her face. "But he'll come back! He'll come back!"

"We're going to call the ID techs to come dust for prints, Melissa. As soon as we run it through the computer and make a match, we can get him."

She waited, tense and quiet, as the apartment filled up with police photographers and ID technicians. As they dusted for prints, she sat like a little child waiting to be told her fate.

"He was probably wearing gloves," Larry said. "But maybe not."

"He's smart," Melissa said in a hopeless monotone. "He knows you need evidence. He knows what kind. So as long as he doesn't leave any, he can do whatever he wants."

"We'll pick him up anyway," Larry said. "For questioning. We'll put a little scare into him."

"But can't we just tell the judge he was here? Can't we tell him Soames called my parents?"

"It wouldn't help," Larry said. "Not unless we could prove he was here with a print match."

She ran her fingers through her bangs. "I can't stay here. I don't know where to go."

Larry looked at Tony and saw the censure in his eyes, as if he knew that Larry would jump in and rescue her. Larry didn't let it stop him.

"I could take you to a hotel for the night."

She thought for a moment. "I guess so. I'm just afraid that he'll find me there, too. I can't believe he found me this time, and so soon."

"Look, we'll send someone now to pick him up for questioning. We won't move you until we have him in custody. That way we'll know that he can't follow you."

"All right," she said. "But then what? I can't come back here."

"I'll talk to the manager about letting you put your own dead bolts on the door, so that there isn't an extra key anywhere. And we'll go around and reinforce the windows, make absolutely sure that they can't be broken into. Maybe even put up burglar bars."

"I never thought I'd wind up being a prisoner in my own apartment," she whispered.

"We'll put enough fear into him that he won't come near you. I'll even tell him he's being watched."

"You said that before. But he didn't care."

"He'll care this time. And who knows? Maybe tomorow we can find a witness who saw him around here. And the pattern of that shoe print was pretty distinctive. If we can find that shoe, maybe it'll be enough evidence to convince a judge he was here."

She nodded without much hope. "I'll go pack a few things," she said, and disappeared to the back.

Larry turned back to Tony. "All right, I know what you're thinking."

"She does have to have a safe place to stay," Tony conceded. "But try not to get too involved."

"Don't worry about it." Larry picked up the phone, dialed the station, and asked to have Soames picked up for questioning.

Melissa came back out with a suitcase, her expression strained and distracted. "You know," he said quietly, "maybe you should go home to Pensacola for a while. Spend some time with your parents."

"No, I can't," she said. "I don't want to drag them into this."

"Into what?" Tony asked.

80

"Into danger. If he comes after me there—" She stopped and tried to steady her emotions. "My parents still don't know about what happened to me. I can't tell them."

"But won't they hear when it goes to trial?"

She shook her head. "I haven't thought that far in advance. All I know is that they don't have to know yet."

"But if he's calling them, they already are involved."

"I told them it was a prank. I told them my sink was stopped up, and I argued about it with the manager, so I moved. That's all they need to know."

The phone rang, and Larry answered, instead of Melissa. "Yeah? You got him already? He was home?" He shot a look at Tony. "What alibi? Well, how long did she say she'd been there? Well, have you checked *her* out?"

He sighed and rubbed his temples. "Well, take them both in for questioning. And keep them separated, so they don't compare notes. Check her out, to make sure she's not lying for him. Oh, and check to see if she has a roommate or a neighbor, anybody who can confirm how long she's been gone.

"What kind of shoes does he have on, by the way? Yeah, I thought so. Get a picture and a print of the bottom of both shoes, will you? And keep him there until we get there."

He hung up, and Melissa sank down on the couch. "He has an alibi?"

"Some woman he was with. Says he's been with her there in his apartment for the last three hours. But it looks like he's got on our shoes. Anyway, they're keeping him until we can question him, so we have some time to get you to a hotel. He can't follow you."

"All right," she said, grabbing the handle of her suitcase, but Larry took it from her.

"I'll get this," he said. "Are you sure this is all you need?"

She looked around and shivered at the thought that he might have gone through her things. "No," she said. "I'm fine. Let's go."

Larry took her key and locked the door behind them.

CHAPTER TWELVE

W e've got to let him go," the officer who had picked up Pendergrast told Tony and Larry when they got back to the precinct. "The woman he was with confirmed his alibi."

Larry glanced into the room where the woman sat. She was several years older than Pendergrast, had garishly dyed hair, and wore cheap, tight clothes. She sat flipping through a magazine, swinging her foot with bored nonchalance and popping her gum. "She's not his type," Larry said.

Tony shrugged. "His type may be anything in a skirt."

"Well, I don't think he found her at that yuppie club you like so much. My guess is he's paying her to be his alibi." He turned back to the cop. "Did you tell her he's been indicted for rape?"

"Yep. She says he's innocent. It really didn't faze her."

"And she insists that he was with her? For how long?"

"Hours."

Tony leaned against his desk and thought that over for a moment. "We don't really know what time he wrote on her mirror. Even with the alibi, he still could have done that. But if Snow White here is telling the truth, he wouldn't have been there to wipe it off while she was coming to find you."

"He's lying," Larry said. "Pendergrast—Soames—whatever his name is, he's lying. And so is the woman."

"Probably. Now prove it."

"The shoe," Larry said, turning back to the cop. "You said his shoe matched the print in the attic?"

"Yeah, but I ran it by the captain. He said it was too weak. Lots of people have that shoe. It might be different if we'd gotten a match on the fingerprints. But just between you and me—" He lowered his voice and looked around to make sure he wasn't being overheard. "That lawyer, McRae, has been raising a huge stink about the department harassing Pendergrast. Says they're thinking about a lawsuit when this is over."

Larry chuckled. "Tell him to stand in line."

"Yeah, well. If it was anybody but McRae. That brutality suit he filed for one of his low life clients a few months ago cost the city a mint."

"Come on," Larry said, disgusted. "It was bogus and McRae knew it. Our guys were trying to restrain an addict so high on PCP he had the strength of a gorilla. That was by the book."

"But besides the money, the bad press hurt. The mayor already called the chief on this, Millsaps. He said if we lock Pendergrast up, it better be on something more than his shoe."

Larry groaned and glanced toward the two-way glass of the interrogation room. "Well, at least we can put some fear into him before we let him go."

McRae and Pendergrast sat talking quietly, their heads together, as Larry and Tony walked in. Pendergrast looked up at them with a smug grin. "Is there a problem, gentlemen?"

Larry propped one foot on a chair and leaned on his knee, fixing his eyes on the man who sat waiting for them to admit defeat. "We're not fooled, Pendergrast. Your little friend in there hasn't convinced us of anything."

"Fine," he said, throwing his arms open. "Then book me. What did you say the charge was? Breaking and entering? Stalking? You do have evidence, don't you? Evidence strong enough to override my alibi?"

Larry gritted his teeth. Ignoring the questions, he said, "We're gonna let you go, Pendergrast."

"Soames," the man corrected.

Larry dropped his foot to the floor and leaned over the table, putting his face inches from Pendergrast. "*I* know who you are, *Pendergrast*. You're a slimy nocturnal rodent who preys on innocent women, and I'm gonna see you put away if it's the last thing I ever do. In the meantime, leave Melissa Nelson alone. Stay away from her, or I'll personally see to it that you regret it for what's left of your pathetic little life. Got that?"

"Is that a threat?" McRae asked.

"You bet it is."

Too disgusted to stay, Larry left the room and headed for his desk. A Federal Express package sat on top of it, its return address from the Santa Rosa County Sheriff's Department. Still seething, he tore it open and pulled out the file on Edward J. Pendergrast.

Tony came out of the interrogation room, smirking as he headed for Larry's desk. "Larry, I think you hurt Pendergrast's feelings. He was downright wounded at what you called him. By the way, are rodents really slimy? I thought they were hairy, but—"

"Take a look at this," Larry cut in, unamused. "Pendergrast's file." Sitting down, he opened it.

Tony grabbed a chair and rolled it over beside him. "Took long enough."

"Yeah, but it's all here. Look at these pictures." Larry picked up one of a young woman with blackened, swollen eyes, a broken jaw, and split, bloody lips. He often saw gruesome pictures, and saw even worse horrors face-to-face at crime scenes, but he never got used to it. And brutality to women always turned his stomach.

He began reading the report. The woman who claimed Pendergrast had raped and beaten her had positively identified him. The report said that he'd been charged and questioned, but that he'd been released due to an illegal search of his apartment.

As if he'd been directly involved in the case, Larry struggled with the indignation rising in his chest.

The next photo showed a full body shot of a woman, her face bruised and cut, her eyes blackened, her lips swollen and bloody, and slashes and bruises up and down her legs and arms. Larry handed the picture to Tony and found the report. In this case, Pendergrast had been acquitted. Despite the victim's insistence that Pendergrast was the man who'd raped and beaten her, the grand jury had felt that there wasn't enough evidence to get a conviction. Anger reddening his face, Larry tossed down the report.

"How could they acquit him? Didn't they see the pictures? She gave a positive ID. How could they ignore that?"

"Apparently there were no fingerprints, no physical evidence at all that he was the one who had done it. Plus he had an alibi," Tony said, reading the report. "The only hard evidence was her identification, but they didn't believe she got a good look at him because it was dark."

"It's the way he looks," Larry said. "He looks too prosperous, too good-looking. If he were a scruffy-looking homeless man with a tattoo, he wouldn't have been acquitted." As he spoke, Larry flipped through the file and found a picture of the girl before the rape. She was pretty and blonde, smiling at the camera, looking nothing like the abused portrait after Pendergrast had made his mark. She looked like a happy young woman with a future. She had probably never even dreamed what would happen to her one day.

"Says here she killed herself shortly after he was acquitted," Tony said matter-of-factly.

"Killed herself?" Larry grabbed back the report, read of the suicide, and felt even sicker as he turned back to her smiling portrait. "What's her name?" he asked wearily.

"Uh . . . Sandra Hayden," Tony said. "She was married, no kids. About twenty-three when it happened." He looked over Larry's shoulder and studied the photo pensively. "I wonder if she killed herself because of the rape."

"Probably," Larry whispered.

Tony flipped further, until he came to the newspaper clipping of her obituary. "Married to Jack Hayden for six months," he read. "Buried in Pensacola where she'd lived all her life."

Larry looked up from the picture. "Did you say Pensacola?" He glanced at the obituary. "That's where Melissa is from."

Tony frowned, trying to put things together. "Pendergrast came from Santa Rosa County. Isn't that near Pensacola?"

"Next county over." Larry read on, intrigued but apprehensive. "Says Sandra Hayden had just started working at a department store in a mall. Noticed the guy following her days before he made a move. He broke in one night when her husband was working the night shift. He apparently beat her and left her for dead." He hesitated, swallowed, then forced himself to go on. "But she woke up after he left, showered and cleaned

85

up everything, then passed out again from loss of blood. She never called the police. Her husband found her near death the next morning and took her to the hospital."

Tony flipped through the file, looking at the other documents. "Here's the police report of her suicide." Larry took it, scanned the contents, then shook his head and dropped it on the desk.

"What?" Tony asked.

Sometimes Larry wished he had a different job. "Her younger sister. That's who found her. She had slit her wrists in the bathtub."

"What a way to say good-bye," Tony muttered.

Larry glanced back at the room where they had interviewed Pendergrast moments ago. "We were too easy on him. He was working us. He knows the system too well."

"He must," Tony agreed. "I can't believe they let him go. We need to talk to Sandra Hayden's family. Find out anything that's not in the report. Anything about him we might need to know. Let me see the obit."

Still deep in his dismal, angry thoughts, Larry slid the newspaper clipping across the desk. "Okay," Tony said, poising his pen to jot down her parents' names. "Nancy and Jim Nelson, of Pensacola."

For a moment the name didn't sink in. It wasn't until Larry watched Tony write it that it penetrated. "Did you say Nelson?" Larry asked, reaching for the obituary.

Tony looked up, the significance of the name finally registering. "What are you thinking?" he asked.

A slow ache began at Larry's temples and spread to his forehead. He took the clipping and began to read. "Sandra was survived by both parents and her younger sister . . ." His voice broke off and the words just waited there like a live grenade.

Tony detonated it. "Melissa Nelson," he said.

Larry felt as if he'd had his body blown up from the inside out. His head throbbed, and he couldn't think.

"Oh, man," Tony said, staring at the words. "I don't believe this."

After a moment, Larry got enough control of his faculties to find his voice. "What does it mean?" he asked in a quietly desperate voice. "Pendergrast rapes and almost kills Melissa's sister. Then he comes after her?"

"Doesn't fit," Tony said, his voice growing less surprised and more excited. "*He* was here first, remember? *She* got a job working where he worked. How could he have orchestrated that?"

"Well, why would *she*?" Larry demanded. "You think a woman who'd seen her sister after she'd been left for dead by some guy would deliberately hang around with him afterward?"

Tony was in his element. This was the kind of mystery he loved to solve, the reason he had become a detective. "All right, let's look at what we've got. This happened three years ago, when Sandra Hayden was twenty-three. Melissa would have been twenty then."

"Right."

"So what *do* we know?" Tony went on, getting to his feet and pacing across the floor as he thought it all out. "We know that Melissa changed her major to criminal justice, right?"

"Yeah, so?"

"Well, maybe that was in response to the fact that the criminal justice system let her down. Or maybe it was out of anger. It's like a person with leukemia who decides to be a doctor. They want to fight the thing that has become their enemy."

Larry hated the high Tony was getting from this. And he hated even more where it was leading.

"So she gets out," Tony continued, "takes a job with the FBI, and uses the resources there to locate the guy who did that to her sister." Tony pointed at the photo.

"Now wait a minute." Larry said, resisting, getting to his feet to relieve his growing tension.

Tony shook his head. "No, listen for a minute. It's just a theory, but it fits. Let's say Melissa was obsessed with finding this guy and getting revenge. Now she knows where Pendergrast is working, what name he's using, everything. So she quits the FBI. You got to admit, that bothered us from the first."

"So you're saying she sought him out, so she could get a job working where he worked?" Larry asked angrily. "Why? To what end?"

Tony studied the picture of Melissa's beaten sister again, then brought his troubled eyes back up to Larry. "What if it was to set up another rape—one with so much evidence that he couldn't walk away from it this time?"

"You're out of your mind," Larry bit out. "She saw what he did to her sister. She would never put herself in the position of letting him do it to her."

"I didn't say she did. I said she set him up. It's the perfect revenge. He winds up getting tried for a crime that he really committed—just not to her—and gets put away. All she has to do is choreograph things a little—plant some evidence here, plant some evidence there. The truth is, this thing might have gone down just like Pendergrast said it did."

"Hold it right there." Larry leaned over his desk, seething. "Look at these pictures. This man is a monster, and you're making *her* out to be the criminal."

"Maybe they're both criminals."

"And what is her crime? Getting raped?"

"No. Lying about it." Some of the other cops were clearly listening, so Tony lowered his voice. "Look, it makes perfect sense." He got up and turned his chair backward and sat back down, but Larry kept standing. "To her, it's justice. He gets put away for something he's really done twice. She makes sure the justice system doesn't drop the ball this time. Just think about it. He probably terrorized her sister until she killed herself, and never served any time for it. Maybe Melissa wanted to set up enough evidence this time that he couldn't go free. Think about the night of the crime. She was so cooperative, so helpful. All the evidence was perfectly laid out—except for one thing. Even knowing all she knows, especially after her sister experienced all of it, she still showered before she could be examined. So that evidence was inconclusive. The doctor couldn't even say for sure there had been a rape at all!"

Larry kicked his chair, and it rolled into the desk next to his. The cop sitting there on the phone jumped. "So how do you explain the lipstick and the prints in the attic?" Larry demanded. "Do you think she set that up, too?"

Tony thought about that. "Probably not. I think Pendergrast may be after her now. If somebody set you up for something you didn't do, you'd probably want to get even, too. In fact, if he's been calling her parents, it sounds like he's put two and two together himself and figured out who she is. The 'next time for real' message could have meant that the next time, he'd really rape her. I'd say your friend is in a lot of danger right now."

Larry grabbed his chair and shoved it viciously behind his desk. "It's a theory, Tony. It's not fact. You have nothing to base it on. Just a feeling."

Tony shook his head. "I'd say, based on Melissa's relationship with one of Pendergrast's previous victims and the fact that she chose to withhold that crucial bit of information from us, I have probable cause for suspicion here. And I can get to the bottom of it, too—unless you're intent on standing in my way."

Larry clenched his jaw. "Hey, I'm in this for the same thing you are. To get to the truth."

Tony nodded. "But you're too involved with this woman. Look at you. Maybe you don't *want* to see the truth. In fact, I'd say this is disturbing you a lot."

"*You're* disturbing me!" Larry shouted. "I've never seen anyone so intent on proving the victim's the criminal. If this elaborate story of yours is anywhere close to the truth, I'll find out!"

"And how do you plan to do that?"

"I'm going to ask her," Larry said.

Tony laughed and shook his head. "Yeah. Like she's really going to confess it to you."

Larry rubbed his temples and started to pace. "I'll start with asking about her sister. She can't deny that. After that, she may tell a story that makes yours look ridiculous. Maybe it happened just like she's told us all along."

"Ask her," Tony agreed. "And then we'll measure her story against the facts, and see which one we believe."

Melissa couldn't relax or assume that Soames didn't know where she was. He seemed to know everything. He always had.

She lay in her hotel room bed, listening to the noises of people in the rooms on either side of her, their televisions blaring, their muffled exchange of voices, their footsteps going up the hall-way, the ring of the elevators. All the while, she clutched a knife in her hand—and decided to buy a gun tomorrow.

As night turned into dawn, and her numb, exhausted mind registered the sun peeking between the blinds, she asked God if he was still out there somewhere.

Her only answer was silence.

"I hope I'm around when God proves to you that you're wrong." Larry had sounded so sure when he'd said that, but Melissa knew she *wasn't* wrong. There were some crimes too despicable to atone for, some people who weren't worthy of forgiveness—and she knew herself to be one of them. Not because she was evil, but perhaps because of the way she had *responded* to evil. Now she wished she didn't believe in God at all. It made the void too deep, the expectation of his wrath too dreadful, the separation from his love too gaping.

Even before that separation, though, she had lost all faith in God's ability—or willingness—to protect her. He had failed to protect others, and he would fail her as well. She needed protection, but she wasn't sure it was to be found anywhere. She was a target now—right at the center of the bull's-eye.

CHAPTER THIRTEEN

There was no answer when Larry knocked on the hotel room door, and for a moment he felt relieved. Melissa wasn't there. Maybe he could postpone this for a while. He turned to leave, then stopped. Where was she? She'd been terrified to leave the room, knowing that Soames would be back on the streets in a matter of hours.

He glanced up and down the hall, then stepped closer to the door. "Melissa," he called quietly, knocking again. "It's me. Larry."

He heard movement then, and the door cracked open. Over the chain lock, Melissa peered out. "Oh, thank goodness. You scared me to death."

She closed the door and opened the chain lock, letting him in. "I wasn't expecting you," she said. "When you knocked, I was sure he'd found me."

"We did have to let him go," Larry said.

Her skin looked pallid, and her blonde hair was mussed, as if she hadn't given it a thought all day. She wore no makeup, and her blue eyes seemed paler, more fragile. There were shadows under her eyes, and he doubted she had slept last night. He felt drawn protectively toward her, but he held back. "Have you eaten, Melissa?"

"No," she said. "I was afraid to go out, and I didn't want to open the door for room service."

"Why don't we go get something?" he asked. "You'll be safe with me."

She sighed and shoved her hair back from her face. "Well, I guess I can't stay locked up in here forever." She went for her purse and room key, then paused and looked around. "I'm running out of money, anyway. I'll have to go home soon."

He watched soberly, pensively, as she brushed her hair, then turned back to him. She looked so young today, he thought, so delicate, like a China doll precariously balanced on the edge of a shelf.

As they stepped off the elevator, she scanned the lobby. She walked very close to him all the way to his car, then she hurried to get in.

Larry was quiet as he drove her to a little restaurant where they could have some privacy and a corner table mostly hidden from the front door. Maybe she'd be comfortable there.

After they ordered, Melissa seemed to relax; he wondered how long it would last. "You've been a lifesaver, Larry," she said, clasping and unclasping her hands in front of her. "I don't know what I'd do without you."

"I'm just doing my job," he said, wanting to emphasize that before he asked what he needed to ask.

"And it's your job to take victims out to lunch?"

"It's my job to protect them." He looked down at his own hands, then added, "And to ask them questions."

She stiffened a little. "What questions?"

Larry didn't want to ask. He wanted to make her laugh instead, ease her mind, restore to her some peace. Instead, he was going to drag up the worst part of her past and dangle it in front of her like an accusation. But he had no choice. "We got the file on Soames this morning. It seems that he has a history in the Pensacola area."

He noted instantly when she averted her eyes.

"There were two other rapes," he went on.

Melissa's big, pale eyes moved back to his and locked there, waiting. Larry knew she expected what was coming, so he forced the question out.

"Melissa, why didn't you tell me that Soames had raped your sister?"

Melissa gasped—not the reaction he'd expected. "What?"

"Sandra Hayden. She was your sister, right?"

"Yes!" Melissa's face reddened, and she stared at him. "But that wasn't Soames. That was some guy named Pendergrast!"

The waitress came to deliver their food, and Larry stayed quiet until she was gone. Neither of them touched their meal. "Melissa, Soames and Pendergrast are the same guy. Are you trying to tell me that you didn't know that?"

Tears of indignation and horror filled her eyes. "Of course I didn't know that! How could I?"

"Hadn't you seen him? Didn't you know what he looked like?"

"The defendant isn't allowed in a grand jury hearing, unless he testifies," she said in a harsh whisper. "And he didn't. I never saw him in person. I saw pictures, but he had this beard, and he was heavier . . ."

That much was true, Larry thought. The mug shots of Pendergrast had looked different. Still . . .

"There are just some questions, Melissa. Like why you quit your job with the FBI to take a job as a receptionist in an office where your sister's rapist just happened to work."

Two tears escaped and ran down her face as she gaped at him. "What do you think? That I *planned* all this?"

He looked helplessly down at his food. "I just need for you to explain to me why it happened the way it did. *How* it could happen. And why you never told me about your sister."

"Because it's not the kind of thing I like to talk about!" She looked around at the other patrons, then lowered her voice as more tears ran down her face. Her lips seemed to grow redder as she got out the words. "Have you ever found your sister dead? Have you had to make that phone call to your parents? To her husband? Have you spent years wishing you could have helped her, gotten there in time . . ."

Her voice broke off, and she covered her face with both hands. Her shoulders rolled with the force of her quiet sobs, and Larry realized it had been a mistake to bring all this up in a public place. "Look, I'm sorry. I have lousy timing."

She couldn't stop crying, and Larry felt helpless. There was nothing he could do for her in the middle of a restaurant. He motioned for the waitress and asked for take-out boxes. Then, taking the bag with the boxes in it, he ushered Melissa gently out of her seat and back to his car. He set the bag on the seat, then nodded to the park across the street. "Wanna go for a walk and talk about this?"

She was still crying, and he hated himself. Doing his job had never been enough reason, he thought, for making a woman cry. He put his arm around her as they walked, and felt her shoulders shaking as more pain flooded back through her. When they'd reached a cluster of trees that surrounded a park bench, he made her sit down next to him.

"Please believe me," she cried, wiping her face with wet hands. "I didn't know that Soames and Pendergrast were the same person. How could I have known? I left Pensacola because I couldn't stand all the memories. I wanted to get away, and I thought St. Clair was a good choice. I had heard how clean the town was, how warm and friendly, and I thought maybe I could forget here."

"How did you know about the opening at that company?" he asked gently.

"It was in the paper," she said. "I answered an ad. And when I met Pendergrast, it never for a second occurred to me that he could be the same guy. Why should it? There was no indication. Maybe—maybe *he* orchestrated it somehow. He's like that. He stalked Sandy for weeks after they let him off. He drove her completely over the edge. Maybe he was following me, too, but I didn't know it. Maybe he put the ad in to lure me."

That was a stretch, Larry thought. A big one. "You weren't a secretary, Melissa. You had a degree in criminal justice. Why would he think that you'd apply for a job like that?"

"Maybe he talked to some of my friends from school. I had told them I would take a clerical job. Maybe he knew I'd gone to a couple of employment agencies looking for clerical work. I don't know."

Larry leaned his elbows on his knees. Propping his chin on his hands, he watched two squirrels darting up the trunk of a tree. It was so far-fetched, yet there was a gut-deep part of him that wanted to believe her. "You said you were a Christian, Melissa. I want to trust your honesty. I really believe that God put me on this case because you needed someone who wouldn't shoot first and ask questions later." He sat straight and looked her in the eye. "But if you're lying, this is very serious. You wouldn't take advantage of me that way, would you?"

She hesitated a moment, and he couldn't tell whether she was struggling with the lie, or devastated that he would question her sincerity. Either way, her expression grieved him.

"I'm telling the truth, Larry," she said in a dull voice. "If I'd known Soames was Pendergrast, I would never even have come to this town. I wouldn't have gone within a hundred miles of him. I'm scared to death of him. You should have seen what he did to my sister. How he destroyed her—"

She covered her mouth then and bowed under her grief, and Larry pulled her against him. This woman had so much pain inside her, he thought, more than he could imagine. To find her only sister dead, the way she'd found her—and now this.

"Tell me about Sandra," he whispered, hoping it would be therapeutic for her. "What was she like?"

"Sandy," she corrected, laying her head on his shoulder. "She was always happy. Sweet to everyone. She had been married just a few months, and they were delirious." She thought for a moment, then laughed softly through her tears. "We didn't always get along. When we were kids, we fought like sisters do. When I started wearing makeup, I was always 'borrowing' her stuff, and she could never find what she needed. When we got to be the same size, though, she started 'borrowing' my clothes. My poor mother—she was like a referee. But we always worked it out."

"Were you in her wedding?"

She smiled again. "Maid of honor. I'll have to show you the pictures. Sandy was beautiful. I always wanted to look like her. But after Pendergrast—"

Her voice broke off again, and she shook her head dolefully. "After it happened, she never looked the same. Not just the scars. I don't think I ever saw her smile again. There was this dullness in her eyes . . . like she was already dead."

She swallowed, then looked up at him, intent on making him understand. "Her husband worked nights, and sometimes she did, too. But she got off at ten that night, at the mall, and came home. She didn't know he was following her. When she opened her front door, he put a knife to her throat and pushed his way in."

Larry tightened his arms around her.

"Rick found her the next morning when he came home from work. She was almost dead from blood loss, and she had gone into shock. He got her to the hospital."

"Tell me about the hearing," he whispered.

She got that helpless look on her face again, and she stood up, paced a few feet, then leaned back against the tree the squirrels had gone up. "I'll never forget that day they decided to acquit him. Sandy fell apart. We practically had to carry her out of the courtroom. He was out on the street again, and she was petrified. Then he started making phone calls to her, laughing about getting away with it, telling her that he was free to do it again. She was so scared she quit her job, but she still saw him following her sometimes. After a while she didn't leave her house at all, just turned it into a prison for herself. She was locked in—but she wasn't convinced that he was locked out. And she just got more and more depressed, more and more terrified, more and more paranoid . . ."

"What about her husband?"

"Wonderful guy. Totally supportive, trying to help her through it," Melissa said. "He was scared, too, and started trying to prove that Pendergrast was making those calls, that he had followed her, that sort of thing, but Pendergrast was smart. They never could catch him."

A pigeon landed at her feet, pecked a little on the ground, then fluttered away, and her eyes followed it. "Sandy was a Christian, Larry, but toward the end, instead of turning to God, she just lived in fear."

Larry watched the pigeon's progress across the sky, then brought his eyes back to her.

"The attack changed her whole personality," Melissa said. She came back to the bench and sat down, wiping her tears. "Do you think a person who commits suicide can go to heaven?"

Larry looked down at the dirt, uttering a silent prayer that he'd give her the right answer. "I don't know, Melissa. I've never seen anywhere in the Bible where Jesus said that suicide was the unpardonable sin. If Sandy really believed—in her heart, not just in her head—if she truly had faith in what Christ had done for her—"

"She did," Melissa said unequivocally. "But sometimes I lie awake at night, just praying and praying that God has her with him. That there's no more pain for her. That the wounds are all healed. That she's forgiven." She stopped and stared off with a broken look. "But he has no reason to answer my prayers."

The last words were so softly uttered that they were almost inaudible, and Larry touched her chin and made her look at him. "Why not, Melissa?"

"Because I have my own sins," she whispered.

"And you don't think you can be forgiven?"

"Not for these," she whispered, averting her eyes again. "There are criteria for forgiveness, you know. I don't think I've met them."

"Just repentance," he said. "That's all."

"That's all?" she asked, almost laughing at the complex simplicity of it. "Well, that's the problem." She looked into the trees, where the wind was lapping against the leaves, and her hair began to blow into her face. Pushing it back, she said, "When I found her, I couldn't believe she had done it. That she had let him do that to her. That I let her do it to herself."

"Melissa, you couldn't have stopped her. What could you have done?"

"I was late," she whispered, fresh tears rolling down her cheeks. "I was supposed to have been there an hour earlier. But I stopped off somewhere. I didn't go when I should have. She had left the door unlocked for me. Maybe she wanted me to find her before it was too late. Maybe she didn't really want to die. If I'd just gone straight there ..." She was sobbing now, and he pressed her head against his shoulder, wishing he could comfort her, but fearing that she would find comfort only when she was ready to receive it from God.

"Melissa, is that the sin that you think God can't forgive you for?"

"One of them," she cried. "Maybe I don't even want forgiveness. Maybe I don't even want to come close to God again. If I did ..."

As a Christian, Larry had counseled many brothers and sisters. As a cop, he'd offered comfort before. But he'd never felt more helpless than he felt right now.

He did know one thing, though. No matter where this took him, he was ready. He just might be the only one who could point Melissa back to God.

CHAPTER FOURTEEN

Tony banged a fist into the wall of the interrogation room the next morning and muttered a curse. "You're losing it, Millsaps. You're totally losing your perspective. You need to take yourself off this case now before you get any more involved!"

"What!" Larry shot back. "Just because I'm not drawing the same deductions you are, I'm losing my perspective?"

"Listen to what you're saying!" Tony shouted. "She gives you some sob story about her sister and all these horrible coincidences, and you're buying it right down to the last word. I can't believe you! You really don't think she knew that Soames and Pendergrast were the same guy? You *really* don't think she deliberately got a job there, where he worked, so she could set him up?"

"I just think we need more evidence before we draw *any* conclusions," Larry said through his teeth.

Tony headed for the door, shaking his head, then turned back before opening it. "Know what I think? I think you're stalling. You're letting your feelings for some wounded woman interfere with your professionalism."

Larry slapped his open hand on the table. "That's not true! I'm open to any facts we can find. But the key word is *facts*. So far, all you've got is speculation. You're not open to listening to her side."

"Hey, I've got all the sympathy in the world for her," Tony said. "Her sister was brutalized and driven to suicide. I can imagine how she must feel. But she sat in front of that grand jury and told them that he raped *her*. Our job is to find out: Did he, or didn't he? And man, if he didn't, if she lied in an official hearing—"

Larry dropped into a chair and rubbed his forehead. "Look, I want the truth as much as you do. And we'll find it. We're both drawing conclusions—just different ones. You're wrong, Tony. I'm not getting too close to her, I'm not losing my professionalism—"

"Then why are you spending so much time with her?"

"Because whatever Pendergrast did to her, we know that he's probably done it to others, and we know he's dangerous. She's not safe."

Tony hesitated, then nodded. "All right, I'll buy that."

After a long moment of silence, during which neither looked at the other, Tony finally shook his head. "Well, this isn't the only case we've got on our plate. We'd better get back to work."

Reluctantly, Larry got up. But he didn't want to work on any other cases right now. Melissa's was the only one that mattered.

Melissa ventured back to her apartment the next morning, propping herself up with the hope that Pendergrast wouldn't dare come back now that he knew they were on to him. But then, that was his game. That was how he had played it with Sandy. He had always gotten around the police. He always had an alibi.

She wavered from panic to determination as she stopped on the way home and tried to buy a gun, but there was a three-day waiting period. From a pay phone, she called a locksmith to meet her at the apartment and had him change her locks. Then she had him add three more locks to the door and check out the windows. And before he left, she asked him if he'd look in her attic, just to make sure she was alone.

Looking a little perplexed, as though he were dealing with a lunatic, he did as she asked, and assured her no one was there.

The bill was more than she'd counted on, and as she sat in her living room balancing her checkbook after he'd left, she realized that her funds were almost depleted. The job she was supposed to have started today was too much of a risk, so she hadn't reported to work. Since she had gotten it on the same day that Pendergrast hid in her apartment, it was possible that he had followed her to the interview, too. Now she was faced with another job hunt, and she had to find something soon.

She changed clothes, then locked all the locks on her door and rushed out of the apartment that felt so frightening, so intimidating, and so unsafe despite the measures she'd taken. Breathing freer in the fresh air, she got into her car and headed for the nearest employment agency.

CHAPTER FIFTEEN

Edward Pendergrast, alias Soames, watched from his car parked down the street as Melissa came back out of her apartment. She'd had a locksmith meet her there, as if that could deter him, and he'd laughed softly as the man had left. Did she think a new lock on the door was going to keep her safe from him, when moving to a whole different apartment hadn't worked?

She got into her car and pulled out into traffic, and he waited to let a few other cars pass, then pulled out behind her. She had gotten away from him for a couple of days, but he wouldn't let it happen again. He owed her big time.

And he always paid his debts.

CHAPTER SIXTEEN

Armed with a temporary job that started the next day, Melissa left the temporary employment agency, located in the St. Clair Mall. As she walked back through the mall toward the entrance near where she'd parked, she glanced frequently over her shoulder, feeling that someone was watching her. For a weekday, the mall was crowded. A group of teenagers—the girls dressed in black and the boys in white shirts and ties—clustered behind her, probably here to sing during the noon hour. Already, she heard another choir somewhere across the mall, singing some classical, doomsdayish song that made the hairs on her neck rise.

Determined not to let her panic drive her today as it had for the past several days, she stopped and got a hamburger, then found one of the few vacant tables and sat down to eat.

As she bit into her burger, she watched random faces in the crowd. No one seemed to be looking at her, pointing, staring. Everyone went about their own business, scurrying here and there, rushing back and forth, coming in and out.

And then she saw a man, his dark hair too familiar, his teal shirt even more familiar. She watched him walk around the food court, never looking her way. She twisted in her chair to follow him—and finally, he turned his head toward her.

Pendergrast!

Stifling the urge to scream, she grabbed her purse and pressed between the tables, toppling over a chair here and a chair there as she went, bumping into people, knocking packages out of hands. When she got to the mall exit nearest her car, she looked back.

He was gone.

She broke into a run and made it to her car. Her hands trembled as she jabbed the key into the ignition, screeched out of her parking space, and pulled back into traffic.

She searched her rearview mirror for a sign of him. Nothing.

Still, he was there, she told herself. He could see her this minute. He was nearby, somewhere, following, watching.

She headed for the police station, desperate to find Larry. Stopping in a no-parking zone, she slammed the gearshift into park and ran inside. The precinct was noisy with cops coming and going, angry prisoners, and telephones ringing on a dozen desks around the big room. She glanced toward Larry's desk but didn't see him.

Pushing to the front of the line, she asked, "Is Larry Millsaps here?"

"No," the desk officer told her. "He's out on a case."

"I have to talk to someone!" she shouted. "He's following me!"

"Who?"

"Pendergrast!" she shouted. "Or—Soames! Edward Soames. Please get in touch with Larry. He was at the mall, watching me—"

"Larry Millsaps?"

"No! Pendergrast!" She burst into tears, then, clutching her forehead, said, "Look, just ask a patrol car or someone to circle the block or something. Check out the cars in the parking lots around here. Look for his car—a dark blue Cherokee—and see if he's still following me. I'm afraid to go home."

She sat and waited for what felt like an hour. Finally, an officer told her that Pendergrast's Cherokee was parked in front of his apartment.

"Of course," she mumbled to herself as she hurried out to her car. He'd have known she'd go to the police station, so he'd have gone straight home, figuring that someone would be looking for him. But Larry would believe her.

Frantic, she drove to an electronics store and bought a caller ID device to connect to her phone, so that she'd know who was calling her before she answered. Then, from a pay phone, she called the phone company and asked them to hook her up to that service.

At least if he called her, she would have proof. If only she had access to some of the surveillance equipment they used at the FBI. But she didn't, and her money was running out.

She hurried home and locked herself inside the apartment, quickly hooked up the device, then grabbed a knife and sat on her couch facing the door, waiting for the knob to move or the floor to creak.

She had felt so relieved when the temp agency had given her a job to start tomorrow—she'd been so worried about her money running out. Now she wondered if she'd even be able to go. He was trying to terrorize her, just like he'd done Sandy. The worst part was—she was letting him.

I'm not going to let him get away with it, Sandy, she promised. *Even if it costs me everything it cost you, I'm not letting him get away with it.*

The phone rang an hour later, and Melissa checked the Caller ID and saw that the call came from the St. Clair Police Department. Quickly, she answered it. "Hello?"

"Melissa, it's Larry. I had a message that you'd been by. Are you okay?"

"He was following me," she blurted. "At the mall. I saw him."

"I talked to the officer who found his car in the parking lot of his apartment complex. It was the right car. Had his plates. And the engine was cold."

"Larry, it was him! I saw him at the food court. He's not going to leave me alone. I don't know what to do!"

"Is he still calling your parents?"

"Yes," she said. "He called a couple of times yesterday, and I keep trying to assure them that it's just a prankster. But I'm not sure they're convinced. My dad has him on tape. He express mailed the tape to me, and I should get it today. Then you'll see. Oh, and I got Caller ID. If he calls here, I'll know."

"Maybe. Caller ID can't identify calls that come from pay phones or car phones."

She sighed helplessly. "Well, what should I do? I came back here because I don't have enough money to stay in a hotel another night. I had all the locks changed. But I'm not sure that will stop him."

"He's not supernatural, Melissa. If anything happens, call me. I'll keep my cell phone with me just in case."

"Larry, I just want to lead a normal life. I have a new job to start tomorrow. It's just temporary, but it's money. If I don't get any sleep tonight . . ."

"Maybe I'll pay Pendergrast a visit. Put a little more fear into him. Let him know he's being watched."

"Can he be? Watched, I mean?"

"Off and on. But we can't spare the man-hours to put someone on him full-time."

"He knows that," she said, her voice falling to a helpless monotone. She sighed. "I'd appreciate your talking to him, Larry. It might help."

"Meanwhile, bring the tape as soon as you get it, and let me know if anything else happens."

Larry found Pendergrast's blue Cherokee in the parking lot, and he and Tony made their way up to the apartment they had searched just days before. They knocked, but no one answered.

"Now what?" Tony asked. "We can't break the door down. We don't have any evidence that he's done anything wrong."

"We have her word," Larry said.

Tony banged on the door again, waited. "He could be sleeping. Or just sitting in there refusing to answer."

"Maybe he rode somewhere with someone else. Maybe his alleged girlfriend." Larry glanced down at the Cherokee again. "Or maybe he has two cars."

"There aren't two registered to him."

Larry gave Tony a wry look. "Think that would stop him?"

Tony gave up on the door and looked back down at the parking lot. "It's possible. Maybe some of the neighbors have seen him driving something else."

"I'll take the downstairs neighbors," Larry said. "You take the ones upstairs."

Melissa hated to hear her mother cry. Worse than that, she hated to be the cause of it.

"Melissa, he's been calling over and over for the last two days. Hanging up in the wee hours of the morning, saying things like, 'Tell her I'll find her' or 'Someone has to pay.' I called the police last night, and today they found out that the calls have definitely been coming from your area. Melissa, what's going on?"

Her voice was weak when she got the words out. "Mom, he's just a jerk. I'll give him a call and tell him to stop. Maybe tell him I've given his name to the police."

"It's starting up again, isn't it? This nightmare. It's just like with Sandy. Melissa, we're worried about you. You're the only child we have left."

Melissa closed her eyes. "I know, Mom. But I'm fine. Really. I'll come home for a visit soon, and you can see for yourself."

"But you'd tell us if something was wrong, wouldn't you?"

For a moment, Melissa hesitated, wanting more than anything to share this burden with someone. But not at the cost of the pain it would cause her parents. "Of course, Mom," she lied. "Really, it's okay. Just let the machine get the phone for a while, and I'll see what I can do from this end about making him stop. Nothing to be worried about."

Her hand trembled as she hung up the phone. Edward Pendergrast had a plan, a plan that would start—and end—with her.

She went to the window and peered out at the street below, scanning the cars in the parking lot. She didn't see his Cherokee, but it could be anywhere, up the street, around the side of the building.

She checked her window locks again.

The phone rang, startling her. She checked the Caller ID, saw the words, "Out of area." Maybe it was her mother again. Her heart pounded as she picked up the phone on the second ring.

"Hello?"

"Were the windows locked nice and tight?"

She caught her breath and slammed the phone down, then looked toward the windows where she'd stood just moments before, looking down for him, checking the locks—

Trembling, she scrambled around for the note with Larry's cell phone number on it, but couldn't find it. It had to be here somewhere—

There was a sudden, metallic sound. She looked up—and saw the doorknob turning, shaking, heard the sound of some kind of gadget working in the locks. Wanting to scream but unable to find her voice, she grabbed a chair and almost leaped with it across the room, then jammed it under the doorknob. With strength she didn't know she had, not even conscious of the strain on joints and muscles, she shoved a heavy cabinet in front of the door.

Looking frantically around the room for her knife, she saw the piece of paper with Larry's number, lying where she'd been sitting. She snatched up the phone and dialed.

"Millsaps here," he said after the first ring.

"Larry, he's here," she whispered into the phone. "He's trying to get in!"

She heard the urgency in his voice. "Melissa, hang up, and call the dispatcher at 911. A squad car might make it before I can, but I'm on my way."

"All right." Melissa hung up and punched 911, but the phone went dead. Frantic, she punched some buttons and held the phone to her ear, but there was still no dial tone.

Pendergrast must have cut her telephone wire. She sat holding the phone in one hand, the knife in the other, waiting for him to come through the door.

CHAPTER SEVENTEEN

B y the time Larry and Tony made it to her apartment, there was no sign of Pendergrast. But the scratch marks around one of her dead-bolt locks made it evident that someone had tried to pick it. After hearing Melissa's story—first with the phone call, then the noise at the door, then the cut telephone wire—Larry suspected that it had all been an attempt to terrorize her. If Pendergrast had wanted her, he could have caught her at the mall. And he wouldn't have warned her with the telephone call today.

But that didn't mean he wouldn't try something more dangerous tomorrow. And Larry and Tony had discovered, when they had questioned some of Pendergrast's neighbors, that one of them remembered seeing him driving an older-model gray Toyota now and then. Which strengthened Melissa's story about seeing Pendergrast at the mall.

Larry knew, now, that he couldn't leave Melissa here alone. She was terrified, and her fears were legitimate.

He paced across her apartment, watching her sit balled up in the same chair she'd been in the first night he'd met her. She'd been terrified then, too.

"She can't stay here," he told Tony.

Tony nodded, obviously concerned—something Larry found gratifying. "Melissa, why don't you go home to your parents? Lay low for a little while?"

"Didn't you hear what I told you?" Melissa asked him. "He knows where they live. He's been calling them. I'm no safer there, and I don't want to drag my parents into danger, too."

"She's right," Larry said. "She has to go somewhere where he can't find her. At least until we can catch him doing something and get him back behind bars."

Tony got up and rubbed his neck. "Shades of the Barrett case."

"What?" Larry asked.

Tony shook his head. "It just reminds me of the Barrett case." Lynda Barrett, a lawyer, had been pursued by someone as deadly, and as sneaky, as Pendergrast. In that case, too, Larry had gone beyond the call of duty to protect a lady in distress—which, as it turned out, had been necessary to save her life. Tony was beginning to agree that it might be necessary in this case, too.

"That's it," Larry said, stopping his pacing and turning back to Tony. "Lynda Barrett. I don't know why I didn't think of it before."

Melissa looked up. "Who's Lynda Barrett?"

Larry started to answer, but Tony cut him off. "What has Lynda got to do with this?"

"Her house," Larry said. "It's perfect. And she has room. We could ask her to let Melissa stay there for a while."

"Larry, you can't be serious," Tony said. "You can't call one victim and ask her to house another victim."

"Would you please stop talking around me like I'm not here?" Melissa demanded. "Who is Lynda Barrett?"

Larry sat down. "She's a lawyer who was being stalked a few months ago. Someone sabotaged the plane she owned, and she crashed—"

"Just the first of several murder attempts," Tony said, as if this proved how foolish Larry's idea was.

"And it almost succeeded," Larry continued. "But her father had died shortly before that, and he had this great little house on a secluded dead-end street. She hid out there."

"Does she still have the house?" Tony asked.

Larry nodded. "Still lives there." He picked up the phone, remembered it was dead, then hung it back up. "I'll call her on my car phone, Melissa. We'll see if she'll take you in for a while."

"But she doesn't know me. She wouldn't just take in a stranger, would she?"

Larry nodded. "She's been where you are. And besides that, she's a Christian."

"She kind of has a hobby of taking in strays," Tony threw in.

"Stray animals?"

"No. Stray people."

Melissa didn't appreciate that label. "Is that what I am?"

Larry smiled. "He's talking about Jake, the guy who lives in her garage apartment. It's a long story." He hurried to the door, then turned back. "Stay with her while I call Lynda, will you, Tony? Meanwhile, Melissa, start packing."

"How can you be so sure she'll take me in?" Melissa asked.

"Trust me," he said. "She will."

It was just getting dark when Melissa followed Larry's car onto Lynda's street. Between Lynda's house and the next one up the street was a long stretch of woods. Larry parked on the street, and Melissa pulled in behind the car in the driveway, then waited as Larry got out and walked across the yard to her car. "This house is secluded and safe," he said as she got out. "He'll never find you here."

The stress apparent on Melissa's face told him that the last thing she needed was to be thrust into a live-in situation with a stranger.

She looked toward the house. Lynda had left the porch light on, and mosquitoes buzzed around the bulb. "You won't have to be here long, Melissa," Larry said. "Pendergrast is going to screw up, and as soon as we can prove that he violated his bond, he'll be back in jail until the trial. Then you'll be safe."

"I just feel like such an intruder," she whispered. "Complete strangers, taking me in. I may even be putting them into danger."

"That's why I thought of Lynda," Larry said. "If anyone can understand your dilemma, she can. You'll see. Come on."

He reached into the backseat for her suitcase, and the door to the garage apartment opened. A tall man stepped out, leaning on two canes.

"Hey, Jake!" Larry said, laughing. "You're walking!"

"Yeah, Lynda didn't tell you?"

Larry stepped nearer to shake his hand, then looked down at his legs. "Well, she said you were a little, but I pictured a step or two now and then. I figured you were in the wheelchair most of the time."

"Nope. Got rid of the thing. I'll be jogging around the block in another month or two." Larry turned to Melissa, who seemed small, fragile, in comparison to the tall man.

"Jake, this is Melissa Nelson. She's going to be staying with Lynda, too, for a while."

"Lynda told me," he said, taking both canes in his left hand so he could shake. "Nice to meet you, Melissa. Tough times, huh?"

"Yeah," she said quietly.

"Larry probably told you we've been through them ourselves. My legs are a result of them. There was this little plane crash."

Melissa caught her breath. "You were in it?"

"Yeah. But there must have been a team of angels surrounding us, because both Lynda and I came out of it alive. Matter of fact, I'd say we both came out of it better than before."

The back door opened, and a woman with shoulder-length brown hair stepped out. Her eyes lit up at the sight of them, as if she welcomed an old friend. "You must be Melissa," she said, bypassing Melissa's extended hand and hugging her. "I'm Lynda. I was just making up a bed for you. Gosh, it'll be good having a roommate again."

"I really appreciate your taking me in like this," Melissa said.

"Have you eaten?" Lynda asked, looking down at Melissa's small frame. "Jake made a killer stew tonight. Larry, you stay, too. There's plenty for everybody."

Before Melissa could answer, she ushered them all into the house. Supper was already on the table.

An hour later, Larry could see that Melissa was relaxing. She'd been intrigued and reassured by Lynda's own story, told over supper, of being chased by a killer. Lynda explained, too, that she had housed another young woman and her child recently, and had been lonely since they had left. Even with Jake right next door, sharing meals and conversation, Lynda said she missed having a roommate. Larry knew it all made Melissa feel like less of an intruder.

Melissa walked Larry out to his car before he left. The smell of fresh-cut grass wafted on the October breeze, conveying a sense of peace and safety. Larry looked around at the trees, whispering in the night. If any cars came up this street, it would have to be deliberate and wouldn't go unnoticed. Melissa would be safe here.

"You're a genius, Larry," Melissa whispered. "Has anyone ever told you that?"

Larry laughed softly as he leaned back against his car's fender, his hands in the pockets of his windbreaker. "No, actually. They haven't. Why am I a genius?"

"Because I think I can feel safe here. I really do."

Taking her hand, he pulled her closer. "I want you to be safe, Melissa. And I want you to trust me. I'm going to get Pendergrast."

She looked away then, and he could see the weight of worry and fear she carried. It was hard for her to believe that the nightmare would *ever* end. Sometimes, he wasn't sure he believed that himself. Pendergrast had walked before. The system didn't always work.

Her blue eyes looked paler in the moonlight as she scanned the darkness. "It's kind of funny, isn't it?" she asked. "There are times like this, when the world seems so peaceful . . . so quiet . . . You can look around, and breathe in the serenity. You can almost believe that there's nothing evil out there. Anywhere."

"But then reality always hits, doesn't it?"

She sighed. "Under these same stars, Pendergrast is sitting somewhere. Or driving around looking for me. And if not me, then some other woman who thinks there's no evil out there."

He cupped her chin and made her look up at him. "Leave the evil to me, Melissa. You concentrate on the good for a while."

She drew in a ragged breath. "I don't know if I can." When he pulled her closer, she slid her arms around him and laid her head on his shoulder.

Something about that small gesture sent his heart reeling, and he touched her hair, stroking, comforting. What a feeling. This was something he'd been missing. Something he had occasionally prayed for, without expecting it to happen.

Was he losing his perspective, as Tony suggested? Or was he gaining something important? Something God had offered him?

"The truth is," she said in a whisper, "even after this is all over, and Pendergrast is locked up forever, I don't know if I can trust goodness again. I know too much."

"No," he said. "I used to think I knew too much, too. But evil is not going to prevail. That's a promise. It's in the Bible."

"But how do you see through the evil?" she asked, looking up at him. "How do you look past a sister's suicide? How do you look past rape? How do you look past that face that wakes me up in my sleep?"

"You let God fill your life with more of himself, so that he crowds Pendergrast out. You surround yourself with his goodness. When's the last time you went to church?"

She hesitated. "I haven't been since ... since before Sandy died."

"Will you go with me?"

She stepped out of his arms and turned her back to him. "I don't know if I'm ready for that."

"Why not?" he asked. "How do you get ready? There are no prerequisites."

"It's just that—I don't have anything to wear. And I haven't gone in so long."

Frowning, he turned her around, made her look at him. "Melissa, what are you afraid of? It's just church. It's a good place. It's God's house."

Again, she turned away. He waited for an explanation as she leaned back against the fender next to him. "Larry, what do you think it means to blaspheme?"

The question surprised him. "Blaspheme? Why?"

"I just—think about it sometimes. I remember reading in the Bible somewhere that blasphemy was one of the worst kinds of sins. Maybe *the* worst. And I wonder sometimes just what it is."

He shrugged, wishing he'd come more prepared. "Well, I guess it means denying the deity of Christ. What do you think it means?"

She shook her head. "I don't know. Mocking him, maybe?"

Larry tried to imagine where she was going with this. "Well, I guess that could be a form of blasphemy. Melissa, what does this have to do with your going to church with me?"

She hugged herself and took a couple of steps farther away from him, shaking her head. "I just can't, Larry. I don't think everybody belongs in church. Some people have no business there."

"The church should be open to everyone," he said. "No one should be excluded. Melissa, if you think you're tainted in some way, that God doesn't want you anymore—"

"I can't talk about this," she said, preventing what she sensed he was about to say. "Just—just accept that I'm not ready to go back to church. I can't do it. Not yet."

He let that sink in, then finally said, "All right." The curt tone of his voice made her look up at him, and the pain on her face looked so intense, so deep, that he couldn't help reaching for her again. "Melissa, I care about you. You have the most beautiful smile I think I've ever seen. It lights up my heart every time I see it. But I haven't seen it very often. I want to help you find your smile again."

She met his eyes then as tears rolled down her cheeks, and he touched her face gently and pulled her into a kiss.

It was soft, sweet, gentle, and it tasted of her tears.

When he broke it, he pulled back and looked at her again. "This isn't about police work anymore, Melissa," he whispered. "I'm taking this case very personally."

She smiled. "I don't deserve you."

He laughed softly. "Tell me about it. You probably deserve some hunk who can give you everything."

Her smile grew wider. "That's not what I meant."

He knew what she meant, and he kissed her again, this time sliding his arms around her, holding her as he had long wanted to do, only this time it wasn't for her, for her comfort. It was for him.

"I'd better go," he said finally, dragging in a deep breath and letting her go.

She smiled and looked down at her feet. "Yeah. Thanks for bringing me here, Larry."

"You'll be safe. He doesn't know where you'll be working, and he doesn't know where you live. You can relax a little. Just be careful."

"You, too," she whispered as he got into his car.

He watched her go back into the house before he started his car.

Lynda was putting the finishing touches on the master bedroom when Melissa came back into the house. "I think you'll be comfortable here," Lynda said with a smile. "Paige was. She's the one who stayed here before you."

"But this is the master bedroom," Melissa said. "Lynda, I could just sleep on the couch."

"I don't sleep in here," Lynda said. "It was my parents' room. There are too many memories." She sat down on the bed with a sigh and ran her hand along the smooth bedspread. "My dad hasn't been gone long. Just a few months. I really miss him sometimes. Mom, too, even though she's been gone longer."

Melissa sat down across the bed from her, and looked around the room. On the dresser, there was a silver tray with a brush and comb, and an open box with a tie clip and a key ring. A tie rack hung on the closet door with her father's ties still carefully lined up. "You kept their things."

Lynda smiled. "Yeah. I haven't made myself get rid of anything yet. I used to hate this house and everything in it. I wanted more. And I got more. But when I lost it all, I started to realize how precious all my memories were. I guess I realized that *things* don't fill up your life."

"I have memories," Melissa said. "Of my family. My sister. We were so oblivious."

"Oblivious to what?" Lynda asked gently.

"To what was going to happen." She swallowed hard and cleared her throat. "Sometimes I wish I could go back and dwell on those memories. But the bad ones keep interfering. It's hard for me to be with my parents now, in their home. I keep remembering when my sister was there."

Larry had told Lynda most of Melissa's story, and she reached out and took Melissa's hand. "It's normal to grieve, Melissa. How long has it been?"

She shrugged. "About three years."

"Well, what's just happened to you has probably brought it all back. Stirred it all up." Lynda pulled her feet up beneath her on the bed and fixed her thoughtful, compassionate eyes on her. "It takes time, Melissa. Grief has a way of hanging on."

Melissa dipped her head, unable to meet Lynda's eyes with the intimacy of her tears.

"You'll never be the same," Lynda admitted softly. "The world will never be the same. You'll look back on your life before and it'll seem like some kind of surreal dream."

"It already does," Melissa said. "Like those fuzzy old reels of home movies. All laughter and no pain. Just a dream."

For a moment, there was a gentle silence between them, as if they knew each other well enough to share quiet together. "Larry brought you to Jake and me for a reason, Melissa. We've had to grieve, too. We've both had to plunge headfirst into a new era of our lives—whether we liked it or not. We've both survived."

Melissa wiped her eyes with both hands. "Maybe I'll be a survivor, too. Maybe there's hope."

Later that night, after she had gone to bed, Melissa lay awake trying to sort out all the thoughts in her mind. Why had God blessed her by bringing her here to Lynda, where she truly did feel safe, and cared for, and no longer forsaken?

The sweetness and mercy in it was almost more than she could bear, for she saw nothing in herself that merited it. God shouldn't even be able to look upon her, not after the shame of all the events that had brought her here.

In the darkness, she saw a Bible lying beside the bed, where Lynda had put it. Turning on the dim lamp on the bed table, she opened it. By memory—how long had it been since she had held an open Bible?—she turned to the Beatitudes in Matthew, a passage that had given her so much peace as a child. She had learned the whole passage in vacation Bible school once, but it had been years since she'd recited it, even longer since she'd read it.

Now her eyes fell on the one verse she needed to read tonight. "Blessed are the pure in heart, for they shall see God."

She closed the Bible, realizing how unpure her heart was, how far from seeing God she had come. Her heart had been tainted by events—many of them out of her control, true, but many of them well within it, and God could never be pleased with that.

Feeling the abyss of mourning and emptiness growing deeper inside her, she went to the door of the bedroom that opened onto the patio and gazed out into the darkness.

Lynda and Jake were sitting out there on a swing, snuggled up together, talking softly. It hadn't occurred to her that the two were a couple, but now, as she saw Jake lean over and kiss Lynda gently, she realized that something very special was happening between them.

Something she would probably never experience.

She went back to the big bed and lay staring at the tiles on the ceiling, remembering the way Larry had kissed her tonight. It was no longer just business, he had said. It was personal.

His interest in her sent a warm feeling spiraling through her, but she quickly quelled it and sent it away. She couldn't fall in love with Larry, and he couldn't fall in love with her. Nothing good could come from it. Only pain. Larry needed someone with a pure heart, someone like Lynda, who wasn't plagued with hatred and bitterness. Someone who didn't cling to her anger and injustice like an old, familiar—but lethal—friend.

When this was all over—when the trial ended and Pendergrast was behind bars for good—would she then be able to explore these feelings for Larry?

Something—that fatalistic voice that seemed to drive her these days—told her that she would never get that chance. Larry did have a pure heart, and the last thing he needed was someone like her in his life, separating him from God.

She turned over, adjusted the pillow, and tried to find sleep, but it wouldn't come. It wasn't the threat of Pendergrast that kept her awake. Tonight, it was the threat of what lurked inside herself. The threat of who she had become. How far she had strayed.

But that was why she was here. Lynda took in strays. Lynda, who loved Jake. Lynda, who missed her parents. Lynda, who had a pure heart . . .

There was something comforting in that, and finally, surrendering to her exhaustion, Melissa drifted into a troubled sleep.

CHAPTER EIGHTEEN

Edward Pendergrast watched her apartment until the wee hours of morning, then finally decided that she wasn't coming home. Like the other night, she had disappeared.

His mistake had been in trying to get in, but he hadn't been able to resist. Picturing the fear on her face when he had called to let her know he watching her had spurred him to frighten her even more.

He chuckled now at the thought. When he'd gone to her door and tried to pick the lock, she'd really gone off the deep end. He had heard her calling that cop, just before he cut the line and took off. And while he was off setting up his latest alibi, she had left the apartment to hide from him.

Despite his frustration that he couldn't find her tonight, Pendergrast at least felt the satisfaction of knowing that she was terrified of him, and that she would be constantly, exhaustingly on alert, listening for sounds, vibrations, clues that he was near. He loved these mind games. If only he could see that fear on her face. That would make it complete.

Tomorrow, he thought, heading home. He'd find her tomorrow. She wouldn't be able to hide for long.

CHAPTER NINETEEN

The red Porsche that was blocking Melissa's car in had not been in Lynda's driveway last night. Melissa was sure of it. She stood at Lynda's kitchen window, dressed and ready for work, wondering who the car belonged to. The idea of someone new being here made her a little uneasy. Besides, she had to be at her new job in half an hour, and the car was blocking her way.

"Morning, Melissa. Did you sleep well?"

Melissa turned and saw Lynda, dressed in a blue business suit that completely changed her look from soft to professional. Now she looked like a lawyer.

"Yes," she lied. "I was really comfortable, thanks. You look nice."

Lynda smiled and set her briefcase on the table. "Thanks. I have to be in court this morning. I made biscuits. Are you hungry?"

Melissa shook her head. "No, I'm not hungry." She looked out the window again. "Is someone here? I mean, besides you and Jake?"

"Oh, yeah," Lynda said. "That car belongs to Jake's mother. I don't think she'll be here long. I can get her to move it if you need me to."

Melissa turned from the window. "Jake's mother drives a red Porsche?"

"Yeah, well, it's a long story." She glanced over Melissa's shoulder to the window. "Uh-oh, here they come."

Melissa looked out the window again. Jake was coming out of his apartment with an older woman with platinum blonde hair and black roots, and a cigarette in her mouth. "Brace yourself," Lynda said with a grin as she went to the door. "Doris is never dull."

Jake winked at Lynda as they came in, then he grinned at Melissa. "Hi, Melissa. I'd like you to meet my mother, Doris Stevens."

Melissa stepped toward her, extending a hand. "How are you, Mrs. Stevens?"

The woman shook with the tips of her fingers. "Oh, for heaven's sake, call me Doris," she said in a nasal twang.

"Mama's from Texas," Jake said with a slight smile. "She came to pick up her car, and decided to stay awhile."

"It's a beautiful car," Melissa said.

"My boy gave it to me," the wiry woman said. "And I got a job here, so I may not ever go back to Slapout. That truck stop is gonna have to get used to not havin' me to kick around anymore. I can be kicked around just as good here as I can anywhere in Texas. Besides, I been workin' on my tan."

Melissa didn't know how to answer; the woman's leathery complexion looked as if it had had all the sun it could stand. "It is nice here, isn't it?"

"Hot, though," Doris said. "Well, I'd love to stay and chat, but I have to meet somebody."

"Who, Mama?"

"A customer I met at the diner last night. He's takin' me to breakfast." She tossed a wave at Melissa.

"It was nice meeting you," Melissa said.

"Pleasure," the woman returned, then bounced out to the car.

They all watched through the window as Doris cranked up the sports car and sped out of the driveway.

"What was she doing here so early?" Lynda asked Jake.

"The usual," he said. "Wanted money." He opened the refrigerator door and took out a carton of orange juice.

"And you gave it to her."

He shrugged and reached for three glasses. "She's my mother," he said.

Lynda smiled and turned back to Melissa. "A few months ago, they weren't even on speaking terms. Jake doesn't want to admit it, but that Porsche was a peace offering."

"Not a peace offering," Jake said, pouring into the glasses. "Just an opening."

Melissa smiled and took the glass of orange juice Jake offered her. "I've been seeing a change in her, though," Lynda said. "Slowly but surely. I think the change in Jake has had a lot to do with it."

"Change?" Melissa asked, glancing at Jake. "You mean, your injuries?"

Jake shook his head. "Nope. She means my change of heart. A few months ago I had a lot of bitterness toward my mother. Frankly, I didn't care what happened to her, one way or the other. Now, I can actually say I love her. Of course, it makes her real uncomfortable when I tell her."

"So he told her with the Porsche."

He laughed. "I kind of thought she'd sell it and invest the money in a house or something. But she's had the time of her life driving around town in it. Truth is, it's been kind of good for me to have her back in my life. Humbling."

Lynda couldn't help laughing. "If you knew him before the accident, you'd know what an understatement that is. Jake, there are biscuits in the oven. Melissa, are you sure you don't want any?"

Melissa watched the Porsche pull out of sight, and she set her glass in the sink. "No, I really need to get going. First day on a new job."

Both Jake's and Lynda's expressions sobered, and they glanced at each other. "Listen, you be careful, okay?" Lynda said more seriously. "If you need me . . ." She reached into her purse for a card, and handed it to Melissa. "Here's my office number. Paige Varner is my secretary, and if I'm not there, she can help you."

Jake took the card and jotted his own number on it. "Or call me here. And if I'm not here, I'll be at the hospital in physical therapy."

Melissa blinked back the tears in her eyes. "You guys are so sweet. You don't even know me."

"But we know enough about you to worry," Lynda said. "You know, if you wanted to skip this job and just stay here for a while, you don't have to worry about money. Sometimes it's best just to hide out."

It sounded tempting, but Melissa couldn't forget the bills she had piling up. "That's sweet of you, but I really do need the money," she said. "Thanks anyway. And don't worry. I'll be all right."

But as she left the house, she wasn't sure that she really felt that way.

When Larry came in that morning, running late, he found Tony on the telephone, hunched over his desk with a somber look on his face. Larry had spent the past hour driving around the neighborhood of Pendergrast's apartment. He'd found several gray Toyotas that fit the description of the second car Pendergrast's neighbor had seen him driving, and he had written down the tag number of each of them. Now he was ready to check them all out.

Larry slid into his chair and turned on his computer just as Tony hung up, then looked down at his desk, obviously deep in thought. After a moment, Tony picked up the big manila envelope on his desk, pushed his chair back, and headed for Larry's desk. "What's going on?" Larry asked.

Tony looked down at the envelope he carried. "We need to talk," he said.

"Okay, shoot."

"In private," Tony said.

Something told Larry that this was going to be another one of those conversations he would regret, but he got up and nodded toward the vacant interrogation room.

Tony followed Larry in and plunked the manila envelope down on the table. It was a hot room, kept that way on purpose so that the suspects brought here would be uncomfortable. Now, Larry wished there was a thermostat they could turn down.

"What's that?" he asked, gesturing toward the manila envelope.

Tony sat down on the mahogany tabletop and looked at his friend. "It's some stuff I found out about Melissa."

Larry stiffened. "What kind of stuff?"

When Tony didn't answer right away, Larry picked up the envelope and pulled the contents out. "Her employment file at the FBI?"

"That's right," Tony said. "And her transcript from college. I ordered them a few days ago. Just came this morning. Since then, I've been on the phone with people who knew her."

Larry's face reddened as he pulled out a chair to sit down. "All right. Sounds like you have some kind of bomb to drop."

Tony slid off the table and dropped into a chair. "She's lying, Larry. Right across the board."

Larry felt his defenses swing into place. He shook his head. "Evidence," he said. "You'll need some substantial evidence to prove it to me."

"Okay." Tony reached for her college records and consulted the notes he'd taken. "I spoke to two of her professors in criminal justice at Florida State. They both said the same thing: She had an obsession with her sister's rapist. One of the professors pulled his file on her and described some of the papers she wrote for him. Check these out: One involved how to avoid dropping the ball on search and seizures in rape cases, another one was on forensic evidence to tie rapists to the crime scene. There was one on subsequent crimes of rapists who were set free; one analyzing statistical data on repeat crimes; one on profiles of known rapists, MOs, motivations—"

"Okay, okay," Larry said, getting up and walking to the two-way mirror. He stood in front of his own reflection, but didn't see it. "If your sister was raped and the guy walked, you'd be a little obsessed, too."

"One of her professors said that she showed a lot of promise," Tony went on behind him. "He's the one who helped get her the job at the FBI, and he was surprised when she up and quit just a few months later."

"She decided she didn't like that kind of work."

"He thinks differently."

Larry didn't like where this was going. He turned back to his partner. "Okay. What does he think?"

"He thinks now, and he thought then, that she had an agenda. That she was going to find this guy somehow and catch him at something. He told me all this, and I never uttered a word to him about her rape. Excuse me—about her *alleged* rape." Larry shot him a cutting look. "I just told him that she had been a victim of a crime we were investigating, and I needed some information on her."

"Still doesn't mean anything," Larry said.

"I'm not finished." Tony turned his notes around so that Larry could read them across the table. "This guy—Mark Sullivan. He was her supervisor at the FBI. She had a real peon job—

you know, entry level. He said that if she hadn't quit when she did, she probably would have gotten fired."

"What for?"

"She was caught using one of the computer systems when someone was away from their desk. Without clearance, she broke into a program that could track people by their Social Security numbers. Sullivan says he caught her himself, and asked her what she was doing. She tore off the printout, shoved it into her pocket, and told him that she had just borrowed the computer to type something up. She tried to turn it off before he could see what she was doing, but he saw the program and stopped her. Guess who she was doing a search on?"

Larry didn't want to know. He just waited for Tony to finish.

"Edward J. Pendergrast. Mark remembered because he had an uncle named Pendergrast, so it stuck in his memory. He volunteered it before I even asked. I hadn't told him anything about the case."

Larry was beginning to feel sick. "Did she find anything on him?"

"Oh, a thing or two. Like the name he was using now, where he lived, where he worked . . ."

Larry sank back down into a chair and covered his face with his hands. A siren outside blared as a squad car sped out of the garage and past the window.

Tony's voice softened as he said, "One more thing. She said she saw the job advertised in the paper. I called her boss today, and asked him. He said he couldn't remember if he'd advertised or not. He just remembers her coming in with a resumé and asking for a job. He gave me her starting date, though, and I called the newspaper. There wasn't a job advertised for that company anywhere around the time she started working for them."

"Then how did she know there was an opening?"

"He says her resumé was so diverse that she would have fit a lot of the jobs there. It just happened that someone had just had a baby and had resigned. She fit right in. Oh, and he faxed me her resumé. Here it is."

Larry took it. It said nothing about a degree in criminal justice, or a job at the FBI. Instead, it listed bookkeeping, secretarial, and receptionist jobs in other towns. Jobs, he suspected, that could not be verified.

"You've been busy today," Larry said, looking at his partner with tired eyes.

"I felt an urgency," Tony said.

Larry sighed and shoved the papers back across the table. "And what urgency was that?"

Tony rubbed his tired face, putting off saying it. "Last night, when you were with her, worried about her, I could tell that this wasn't just any case. You've got feelings for her."

Larry couldn't meet his eyes.

"Now, I know that you're a Good Samaritan kind of guy, that you always go that extra mile. But I've never seen you so blinded by a pretty face. I've never seen a case where you haven't wanted to find the truth—but you just don't want to see the truth in this one. Not only are you buying into a lie, but you're letting her manipulate you."

Larry couldn't believe what he was hearing. "Tell me something," Larry said, finally meeting Tony's eyes. "Have you ever known me, in all the years we've been partners, to ever try to cover up anything?"

"Never," Tony said.

"And have I ever had a gut feeling about something, and been completely wrong?"

The door opened, and a lieutenant stuck his head in. Both detectives shot him scathing looks, and he shrank back. "Sorry," he said. "I thought the room was empty." He ducked out and closed the door.

Larry turned his angry eyes back to Tony.

"So what's your gut feeling here, Larry?"

Larry sighed. "That—that she's a good person. That she's been victimized. Violated."

Tony leaned forward, his eyes riveting into Larry's. "The question is: Was she raped?"

Larry hesitated again, perspiring a little. Phones rang on the other side of the wall, and printers buzzed. Another siren wailed by the window.

He wished he could be any place in the world but here. "So what do you want to do?"

Tony breathed a mirthless laugh. "What do *I* want to do? We're both go-by-the-book cops, Larry. It's not a question of what I want to do. If I had my way, I'd let Pendergrast go to jail for the rest of his life. With three rape arrests, the guy'll probably wind up there anyway, eventually. But we both know that's not the point here."

"Then what is the point?"

"The point is that perjury is a felony."

"No, it's not," Larry argued. "It's a misdemeanor."

"Not in a grand jury hearing, pal. It's a felony of the third degree. If Melissa Nelson sat on that witness stand and lied to a grand jury—"

Larry couldn't listen to the rest. "I'll find out."

"When?"

"Today!" he said. "Now."

"And what if you don't like what you hear?"

Larry shook his head helplessly, hopelessly. "I already don't like what I hear."

"Can you do the right thing, Larry? Because if you're in too deep with her, if your feelings are going to distort your thinking, I can take over from here. Completely leave you out of it."

"No," Larry said, swallowing back his emotion. "I can't be left out. I have to see this through." He looked up into Tony's eyes. "You don't have to worry about me doing the right thing."

But as he headed out of the interrogation room and back into the symphony of ringing phones, raised voices, and profanities flying from those being booked for assorted crimes, Larry had to ask himself: The right thing for whom?

And he prayed that God would enable Melissa to give him some answers that would clear all this up to both Larry's and Tony's satisfaction. Because if she didn't, he didn't think he'd be able to live with himself—regardless of what he chose to do.

CHAPTER TWENTY

The temp agency had assigned Melissa to a busy insurance company. She had been hired to collate and staple what seemed like thousands of booklets—a big step down from the jobs she was qualified to do. But she felt safe in her little cubicle at the back of the big room.

It wasn't quite eleven when her supervisor buzzed her. "There's someone here to see you, Melissa."

Clutching the phone to her ear, Melissa stood up and peered over her cubicle. "For me? Are you sure?"

"Positive," the woman said. "He's been waiting awhile because no one knew who you were. Listen, if you need to take lunch now, go ahead."

She hung up and tried to see over the cubicle again. There were too many people—she couldn't find him. But a terrifying certainty overwhelmed her as she reached for her purse.

Pendergrast had found her.

Was he waiting to surprise her in front of an office full of people? To cause her to react hysterically and to lose this new job? Was this part of his game?

She rushed out of her cubicle, looking for a back exit. Maybe there was one she didn't know about near the rest rooms. She started toward them, walking as fast as she could, rounded a corner in the hallway—and someone grabbed her arm.

She gasped and swung around.

Larry let her go as though she had burned him. "Melissa—it's me."

Tears sprang into Melissa's eyes as she fell into his arms. "Larry! I thought you were Pendergrast. I thought he had found me."

"Shhh. It's okay. How would he have found you?"

"The same way you did," she said. "How *did* you, anyway?"

"I went by your agency," he said. "But my badge carries a lot of clout. He doesn't have one."

She took in a deep breath and wiped her face. "You scared me to death."

"I can see that," he said. "I'm sorry. Come on. Let's go somewhere."

She held his hand and let him lead her back through the maze of cubicles to the front door.

The sunlight assaulted her, making her feel vulnerable and exposed. "I only have an hour for lunch," she said. "But I'm not very hungry." She looked up at Larry, and for the first time noted how sober he looked. "Is everything all right? Did something happen?"

He stared off into the breeze coming from the Gulf just a couple of blocks away. "Let's walk down to the beach."

They were both silent as they walked down the sidewalk that led from the insurance building to the park behind it. Ahead, Melissa could see the Gulf, blue-green and majestic. On the sand near the water, two little girls sat with their parents, giggling as they shared a picnic. They looked like Sandy and her, years ago, when there were still things to laugh about.

She looked up at Larry as they reached the edge of the beach and headed across the sand, their feet leaving indentations behind them. Larry took off his windbreaker and slung it over his shoulder, revealing his shoulder holster. He was pensive, squinting into the breeze coming off the water, watching the waves and the seagulls as though they might give him some peace.

"Larry, what's wrong? You didn't track me down at work for a walk on the beach."

Larry stopped then on a little hill of sand, and dropped onto it, setting his forearms over his knees. "I heard some things today. Things about you. They don't add up with what you've told me."

She didn't sit down. Instead, she stood stiffly over him, looking down with sad eyes. "What did you hear?"

He shook his head and avoided looking at her. "Melissa, Tony's a good cop. He digs. He doesn't leave any stones unturned. And he got some background on you. He talked to your college professors."

"So?"

"So, one of them said that you were obsessed with Sandy's rape. That that was the primary focus of all your studies. That all of your papers had something to do with what happened to her."

"That's true," she admitted. "I did try to apply everything I learned there to her case. It was my only point of reference. There were mistakes made in her case, and I didn't want to make those same kinds of mistakes when I got into law enforcement. I'm not trying to hide it, Larry—she was the main reason I went into criminal justice. The thought of things like that happening all the time was more than I could stand."

"Well, I can relate to that. I feel the same way. But—"

"But what?" She lowered herself onto the sand next to him.

"But that professor seems to think you had a plan. That you were going to get Pendergrast on something. That you were waiting to get even somehow."

Her gaze drifted to the waves lopping over the sand. "That was Dr. Jessup. He was worried about me. Thought I needed counseling."

"Maybe you did."

"No," she said. "I didn't need counseling."

"What did you need, then? Closure?"

The frown on her face betrayed her pain as she brought her eyes back to him. "What are you saying, Larry?"

He couldn't say it. Not yet. He looked away. "Tony also talked to your supervisor at the FBI. He said you were caught using a computer you didn't have clearance to use."

"Give me a break." She rolled her eyes and threw up her hands. "I sat at someone's desk and used their computer for a minute. I didn't break national security, for heaven's sake."

"He said you were looking up information on Pendergrast."

The indignant expression faded. "That's not true."

"Melissa, it is. Tony didn't ask him about Pendergrast. He volunteered it. He remembered the name."

For a moment she stared, incredulous, at him. "Oh, now I get it." Angry, she got up and started walking away.

Larry got to his feet and followed her.

"Melissa, I need answers! I need to know what you're doing."

"I reported a crime, Larry! And now people are digging into my past, trying to make sense of a few years there when nothing really did make any sense. I didn't do anything wrong!"

"Proffer hadn't advertised for that job, Melissa! How did you know about it?"

"I—I didn't! I put my resumé in a lot of places. He's the one who hired me."

"What other places, Melissa? Can you name them?"

"No!" she shouted. "I don't remember!"

"Why not? It's only been a few weeks."

She started to cry and began walking faster, but he kept up with her.

"Melissa, why did you leave your college degree and your FBI work off your resumé? Why did you make up all that book-keeping and receptionist and secretarial experience?"

"I didn't make them up, *Detective*," she said, spinning around to face him. "Tell your friend Tony he needs to dig a little deeper. I had several jobs in college. I included them all."

"But you didn't mention the FBI. Or your degree."

"I didn't want him to think I was overqualified!"

"But you *were* overqualified, Melissa. Why would you take a job like that in the same place where your sister's rapist worked?"

"Because I didn't know he was there!"

"According to your FBI supervisor, you did know. That's the kind of information you got off their computer."

She turned and began walking again, then, sobbing, she began to run. Larry kept up with her.

"Melissa, I have to know the truth. I've fought for you. I've defended you. I've taken care of you. Now you have to be straight with me!"

He grabbed her arm, stopping her, and she swung around to face him. Her face was raging red, and she smeared the tears on her face. "All right!" she shouted. "I did know he worked there. I did have a plan. I wanted to be where he was so I could watch him. No one else was doing it! I wanted to keep him from hurting anyone else!"

Trying to catch his breath, Larry took a step back and let her go. "Then why did you lie?"

"Because I knew what conclusions you'd jump to! I knew that you'd believe I set him up. I never dreamed he'd come after me, Larry. I thought I could take care of myself. I thought I was smarter than he was."

He remembered the classes he'd seen lined up on her transcript. "You *do* know how to defend yourself, Melissa. You don't get a law enforcement degree without that."

That guarded look returned, and more tears.

"Why didn't you use it on him?"

"He took me by surprise," she said. "I panicked. He had a knife."

Larry dropped his hands helplessly to his sides. "Melissa, someone heard you invite him over for dinner that night."

Crying harder, she turned away, shaking her head, one hand cupped against her forehead. After a moment, she turned back. "Larry, you saw me after it happened. You gathered the evidence. Are you trying to tell me you believe that I set all this up?"

"I think you could have," Larry admitted. "And I'm not sure I could even blame you. I'm not sure I wouldn't have done exactly the same thing, if I'd lost a sister because of some maniac."

"You think I'm lying."

He fought the tears coming to his own eyes, and looked out over the water again. The sun was directly overhead. "I don't know what to think, Melissa. I'm not judging you. I just have to know what really happened."

"I can't believe this!" She brought both hands to her head now, crying harder. "You're going to do it again, aren't you? You're going to let him go! It doesn't matter that he's followed me, broken into my house, threatened to kill me—you're going to let him keep walking free so that he can rape more women! How could you?"

One part of him wanted to shout that he couldn't, to pull her into his arms and hold her until her crying subsided. But that other part, that part that had been a cop for too long, that part that had sworn to uphold the law, battled with him. "Melissa," he said, his voice growing raspy with emotion, "if you set him up, you're denying his civil rights. That's a crime, too."

"As much a crime as *rape*?" she screamed. "What about *my* rights, Larry? What about my sister's rights, or the other woman he raped? Why is it that all anybody cares about is that monster's rights to go out and terrorize to his heart's content, over and over and over?" She dropped back onto the sand and covered her face with her hands, and Larry sat beside her.

After a moment of watching her cry, he put his arm around her and pulled her against him. She shook with the strength of her weeping, soaking his shirt, but he didn't care. He could understand some of what she felt. But he wasn't sure that understanding would change anything.

"Melissa, I'm not the only one asking questions," he whispered. "Tony's a good cop. A go-by-the-book detective, like me. I took a vow to uphold the law—and that means never covering up a violation of it, even when there was a good reason for it."

"So what do you want to do, Larry? See me go to jail? Is that what this is about? Put the victim in jail, so the criminal won't be harassed anymore? Some justice."

"No, of course that's not what I want. I just want the truth."

"The *truth* is that Edward Pendergrast is a malicious, brutal rapist and that he deserves to live the rest of his life in prison. That's the only truth I care about, Larry. Please don't help him get out of this."

That answer didn't satisfy him. He needed more than a rationale—he needed an honest denial. But he had pushed it as far as he could, considering that there was still a part of him that didn't want to know the truth if the truth would hurt Melissa Nelson.

"I need to go," she said, wiping her face and getting to her feet.

"We didn't eat," he said.

"I'm not hungry."

He got up then, brushing the sand off his pants. She didn't say a word as they walked back to the office.

The silence was devastating. Larry was afraid that this good thing, the thing he had thought was a gift, was fast being taken from him, and he didn't know what to do. He'd never been so confused.

When they reached the building, she went in without a word, without a backward glance. And Larry, feeling more dismal than he'd ever felt, went back to his car, trying to decide where he would go from here.

CHAPTER TWENTY-ONE

The building was hazy with smoke, and some wailing country song blared on the juke box. At the bar, several cops from Larry's precinct sat over their beers, commiserating about the day's events. Larry spotted Tony among them and wondered once again what his partner saw in this place.

He cut through the happy-hour crowd and reached Tony at the bar. The bartender looked up. "What'll you have?"

"Nothing," Larry said. "I'm not staying."

Tony glanced up at him. "Must be good, to get you in here."

"I was looking for you," Larry said. "What do you say we go have a bite? Talk."

Tony reached into his pocket, pulled out a couple of bills, and tossed on the bar. Then, bidding good-bye to some of the others, he followed Larry outside.

The fresh air washed over them, and Larry took a deep breath. "That's real similar to how I picture hell," he said.

Tony chuckled. "You know what they say. One man's heaven—"

"They don't say that," Larry said irritably. "No one ever said that."

Tony got into the passenger side of Larry's car and waited for his partner to get in. "So what's going on?" Tony asked as Larry slipped behind the wheel. "I waited for you to come back all afternoon. Where were you?"

"I had some thinking to do," Larry said. "You could have reached me if you needed to."

Tony kept his eyes on his partner. "Did you talk to her?"

Larry didn't answer right away. Instead, he cranked the car and pulled out into traffic. For a moment, he was quiet.

"Bad news?"

Larry hesitated, then said, "Just suppose—"

Tony moaned. "Larry, police work is not about supposing."

"Yes, it is. To get where we're going, we have to start somewhere. Just suppose that Melissa did lie about part of it."

"All right. Which part?"

"Well, maybe she did know that Pendergrast worked there. Maybe she deliberately got a job there so she could watch him, follow him, that kind of thing. Maybe she figured she could put her law enforcement know-how to work."

"So her job was sort of like an undercover detective?"

"Yeah. Only she was her own client."

Tony's eyes narrowed. "Is that what she told you?"

"I told you, this is supposing. Can you just suppose for a minute?"

"All right," Tony said. "I'm listening."

"Suppose it backfired, and Pendergrast came after her. She expected to be able to defend herself if that happened, but she froze. This man, who had terrorized her sister and her family, who had become this huge monster in her mind, finally came after her, and she couldn't use any of what she knew."

"She knew she shouldn't shower. But she did. How do you explain that?"

"Trauma," Larry said, his face turning red. "Maybe she was so traumatized—"

"She wasn't too traumatized to tell us details about Pendergrast, where we could find the evidence we needed, and what we needed to do to make sure he didn't get off on a technicality."

Larry got quiet again.

"Besides, Larry, when she testified before that grand jury, she didn't tell them any of what you're suggesting. She never said he was the one who had raped her sister. She never said she had hunted him down to catch him at something."

"She wasn't asked, Tony. If this is what happened, she didn't lie on the witness stand. No felony was committed."

"No, it wasn't. *If* this is what happened. But if it's not—if she wasn't really raped, if she really set out to set him up by claiming he did, then she did lie. Did you talk to her or not?"

"Of course I did."

"And?"

"And I believe in my heart that he attacked her. I believe that she is telling the truth about that. And if she only lied about the other part, I guess the question is, what difference does it make? She wasn't under oath when she talked to us about her job and how she got it. She was afraid of how it would look to us if we knew the truth. She knew how apt we were to blame the victim."

"You should start writing screenplays, man. You've got a great imagination."

Larry slammed his hand on the steering wheel. "Why *couldn't* it have happened that way? Why are you so intent on making her out to be the criminal here?"

"And why are you so dead set on defending her?"

"Because I don't think she'd lie to me, Tony. I think when it came right down to it, she couldn't do it."

"She already lied to you, Larry. More than once. How do you know this latest story is the truth? I told you she was manipulating you. What did she do, Larry? Tell you she's in love with you? Make you think that you have a future with her, if you just overlook the obvious?"

"No!" Larry shouted. "As a matter of fact, she isn't even speaking to me right now!"

"Good. Maybe you'll have time to get your head clear."

Larry turned his car around and headed back to the bar where he'd found Tony. Pulling back into the parking space in front, he waited for him to get out.

"You're not going to let this woman ruin our partnership, are you?"

Larry didn't even look at his best friend. "That's up to you, man."

Without another word, Tony got out of the car and slammed the door behind him.

Justice, Melissa thought. Everything she'd done had been done in the name of justice. She lay in her bed in Lynda Barrett's house that night, staring at the ceiling and wondering what Larry was going to do next. Would he turn her in? Would he make her out to be the criminal, just because she had tried to set things right when no one else had cared? The police had let Sandy down, and then the court system had made a mockery out of the whole ordeal. They had torn the heart out of her sister, leaving her without even the will to live.

So Melissa had taken matters into her own hands. She had tried to provide justice when no one else was offering any. But they would never understand.

She got up and went to the glass doors overlooking the patio, and stared out into the night. Lynda and Jake had gone to a movie, and they weren't home yet. They had invited her, but she'd been too upset. This was eating at her, just as it was eating at Larry.

He had wanted her to go to church with him. Was that because he knew how far she'd drifted from God?

She stared up at the stars, searching them, as though she could see God's face, angry and dark, looking down at her. Shivering, she closed the curtains and went back to bed.

But she couldn't hide from him, and her sins shone out like neon signs under God's heaven.

She'd read, many times before, "'Vengeance is mine,' saith the Lord." But she hadn't trusted his vengeance, so she'd tried to provide it herself. Now she could neither face God nor hide from him. Now, when she needed him most. Now, when she was most afraid.

She hugged herself and hunched over, crying again. There had been a time when she could pray as if Christ sat in the room next to her, and he would answer. He had always answered. But after Edward Pendergrast stalked and terrorized her sister, Melissa's prayers had been answered with "No." At least, it had seemed that way. Pendergrast had simply walked away from punishment; what kind of vengeance was that? God had not struck him dead, or made sure that he was locked up. Sandy had been the one to die, instead.

She lay back on the bed, balled up and crying into the pillow. Would God ever forgive her for not trusting him, for taking things into her own hands?

Then she heard, whispering in the back of her mind, the question that reached to the root of the problem. Was she sorry? Would she repent?

No, she thought, sitting up suddenly and wiping her tears away. No, she couldn't repent. She couldn't face the consequences of that choice.

Nor, she realized, could she face having Larry turn her in. But if she left things as they had been this afternoon, he might. She needed to do something.

Maybe, if she just explained to him what she had done and why, he would understand. Maybe he would see that she was right to do what she'd done, and that he had to keep quiet and let things run their course.

Maybe he would even protect her.

Trying to calm herself, she stumbled to the phone and dialed his number.

"Hello?" His voice was deep, quiet, distant.

"Larry?" Her voice broke, and she tried to get control. "Larry, it's Melissa. I was wondering . . . could you come over here? To Lynda's? I really need to talk to you."

He was quiet for a moment. "I'll be right over," he said finally.

She hung up and got dressed again, then sat on the edge of the bed, waiting. *Please, God, let him understand*, she prayed, but then she realized the absurdity of her prayer. Even God didn't understand. She couldn't call on him to be her ally now.

Maybe he had turned his back on her forever.

I need you, anyway, Lord, her heart cried out. *Can you forgive me if I don't repent?*

The answer was clear, inscribed deeply into her heart from years of Sunday school as a child. God only required two things of his sinners. Confession and repentance. It was a simple thing, yet it had never held such dire consequences. She couldn't confess it to God, because if she repented, Pendergrast would walk. Instead, she would confess it to Larry, hoping to make him see the necessity in what she'd done.

Tell him the truth, explain it all—since he'd already figured it out anyway—and plead with him to keep quiet. He had feelings for her, she knew, just as she had feelings for him. Maybe he would support and protect her.

Before long, she heard his car in the driveway and met him at the door. Though Lynda had stressed over and over that she wanted Melissa to make herself at home, Melissa didn't feel right bringing her own company into the home when Lynda wasn't there. So she led him back to the patio and sat down across from him, aware of the look of anticipation in his eyes, the look of hope, as if he expected her to tell him the magic words that would make this whole nasty mess go away.

"I couldn't just leave all this hanging," she said finally, looking down at her trembling hands. "Too much isn't adding up, and you're not stupid. Neither is Tony."

She saw the look of dread fall like a shadow over his face, then she looked away as she said, "You were right. I did know that Pendergrast worked at Proffer Builders. I did deliberately seek him out."

Larry opened his mouth, instinctively wanting to help her, to give her an easy out, to tell her that he believed that she had been working "undercover" to catch Pendergrast at something, and that her plan had backfired when Pendergrast came after her. There had been a rape, and she had not been able to defend herself. Those facts would mean that she hadn't lied to the grand jury, and she would be cleared. But Larry the cop couldn't suggest those facts. Because if they weren't the truth, it would offer her another lie. She had to say it on her own. *Please say it*, he thought.

"I couldn't believe it when they let him go, Larry, and he still knew where Sandy lived, and he was calling her and our parents and saying things . . . Oh, we couldn't prove it was him, but we knew. And Sandy lived in fear. She saw him in crowds, in traffic, in every public place she ever went. And at night, she'd lie awake, listening for him. I don't think she had one good night's sleep after her rape." She stopped, tried to compose herself, then went on. "I found her on a Thursday afternoon, in the bathtub. It was . . . the most awful . . . sight I've ever seen. For six months, I was a basket case. I stayed out of school for a whole year, just grieving and trying to cope with what I'd seen. It still haunts me."

She looked fully at him now, saw the mist of tears in his eyes. "Larry, I had to *do* something. I promised her that day, as I sat there holding her limp hand while I waited for the ambulance." She breathed in a sob, and tried again. "I told her that if it was the last thing I ever did, I'd see that man behind bars for the rest of his life. And I set out to do just that."

She still hadn't incriminated herself, Larry thought. It could still turn out to be what he'd suggested to Tony. It could still be something he could deal with. He waited.

"But Pendergrast disappeared. Just moved one day, and left no forwarding address. I didn't know where he'd gone, and neither did anyone else. It was time for me to go back to school, so I changed my major to the thing that interested me the most—not because of the nobility of the profession, but because it failed so often. I wanted to find out why, and how those failures could be avoided. I knew that I'd get him one day, and when I did, I wanted the system to work. I couldn't allow any mistakes."

"I can understand that," Larry said.

"So I got out, and my first order of business was to find him. I was offered the job at the FBI, and it seemed like a good opportunity to track him down. As soon as I did, I quit and came here."

"And you got a job where he worked."

"That's right," she said weakly.

"Why, Melissa? What did you hope would happen?"

"I wanted to get all the evidence I needed on him—enough to put him behind bars for good this time."

"But he was acquitted. They weren't ever going to try Sandy's case."

"Exactly. So I had to make sure there was another one."

So you followed him and watched him? he wanted to prompt her. *You tried to catch him at something, only he came after you instead?* But he couldn't ask. He couldn't give her that story. If she would just say it on her own . . .

"What did you do, Melissa?"

She got up then, unable to look at him, and walked to the edge of the patio. "I decided to make myself the sacrificial lamb."

"No," he said, his heart plummeting. She didn't mean what he thought. She couldn't.

She turned back to him. "I knew the only way I could make sure I got everything on him I needed was to be his victim." Seeing the look of horror on Larry's face, she took a step toward him. "But it's not what you think. I wasn't really going to let him touch me. I just wanted it to look like he did."

"You did set him up." The words came out in a moan, and he stood and faced her squarely. "Is that what you're telling me?"

She was crying now, and her face twisted. She covered it for a moment, then dropped her hands. "Larry, I was desperate. You have to understand. It was the only way."

"How did you do it?"

"I—did invite him over—and I was terrified. I had planned to have him come in for a while, touch some things, get his fingerprints all over the place. But I lost my nerve, and when he got there, I told him I didn't feel well, and I'd give him a rain check. He got mad and pushed his way in—"

"By force." Larry latched onto those words, thinking maybe, just maybe, Pendergrast *had* done something. Maybe she hadn't lied about all of it. Not the important part.

"Well, not for long. I had a knife, and I threatened him with it. He finally just backed off and left."

Larry's stomach sank. "But your apartment . . ."

"I did all that," she said. "I turned over tables and furniture, broke glasses to make it look like a struggle."

He turned away. "What about the cut on your leg? What about the blood on his shirt in his car?"

She waited a long time before answering that one. "He had an extra change of clothes at work. I took his shirt that day, and got the knife out of his drawer. I cut my hand and got blood all over the shirt, then wrapped the knife up in the shirt and stuck them under his seat. And I got some of the hairs out of the brush he kept in his desk, and put them on my sheets. That night, before I called the police, I cut my leg. Then I showered. In case I was examined, I knew there wouldn't be any physical evidence, and a shower would explain that. And then I called the police, and as I waited, I started to cry, deeper and harder than I had even when I found Sandy dead. I don't think I've ever been more miserable in my life, but I also felt—I don't know—justice. That, finally, something was being done."

She clutched her head as the memory came back. "It was supposed to have been easy. They were supposed to arrest him, put him in jail, take him to trial. The evidence was so conclusive that no jury could have acquitted him. But I never counted on getting involved with a cop who could see right through my story."

Larry sank down into his chair and rested his face in his hands.

"Larry, it could work! Don't you see? He's raped two women, and one of them is dead—and those are only the reported cases, the ones we know about. If he goes to jail because of this, it'll be justice—finally."

Larry looked up at her with a helpless expression. "The defense will crucify you, Melissa. He knows you lied. He knows who you are now. He'll tell them everything you did. They'll find as much evidence as we have. You'll never get away with it."

"But I might!" She sank down next to him and touched his face with her trembling hand. "They won't believe him. Even his own lawyers won't. I'm not asking you to cover up, Larry. I'm just asking you to be quiet. Just don't tell anyone what you've found. Now that I've explained it all, you must understand. Haven't you ever had a case where the end justified the means?"

His face was a study in misery as he stared at her. "Melissa, if the police force operated with that philosophy, we wouldn't even have a court system. We'd just go around shooting everybody who looked guilty. I've always gone by the book. I believe in the system."

"That's because it's never failed you!" she shouted. "Your sister didn't *die* because of it! If she had, you'd have done exactly the same thing!"

He got up again, putting some distance between them, and paced across the patio, rubbing the back of his neck. "I understand why you did it, Melissa. But it's still wrong. You can't plant evidence. You can't lie to a grand jury."

"He had already raped, Larry!" she shouted. "They let him go!"

"But he didn't rape *you!*"

Silence screamed across the night, and she looked up at him with pleading eyes. "If you turn me in, Larry, *I'll* be the one punished, and he'll walk away scot-free. Again! Is that right? You swore to get criminals off the streets. Well, I'm not the criminal, and he's still walking the streets!"

His face twisted with pain as he looked down at her, and finally he sat down next to her and cupped her chin with his hand. "Don't you understand? Even if I did keep quiet, Tony's an inch away from going to the captain with what he knows. Everyone's going to figure it out."

"No, they won't!" she cried. "They may think they've figured it out, they may suggest it in court, but they can't prove it! The jury will just think they're grasping! Another case of the victim being made to look like the criminal." She rose up on her knees and grabbed his arms, making him look at her. "Larry, it could work. The man who raped my sister and caused her to kill herself could be convicted. All I'm asking you to do is *nothing*. Just leave it alone. And get Tony off the track. Come up with a story. You can do it."

He looked at her, saw the goodness, the determination, the torture in her eyes. He had vowed to bring her smile back, but instead he was threatening to send it fleeing forever. His convictions began to wane, and he wondered what would happen if he did just what she was asking—nothing. Maybe Tony would buy the story he'd already suggested tonight. Maybe no one would ever have to know.

God will know.

That voice inside him, the one that always warned him when he began to stray, startled him.

"I'm a Christian," he said. "I don't know if that means a whole lot to you, but it does to me."

"I know," she whispered. "But God promised that he would not leave the guilty unpunished. Maybe this is his way of punishing Pendergrast."

"You know it isn't," Larry said. "God never asks us to sin to accomplish his will. God didn't tell you to lie, or to set up a crime, or to pretend that you're a victim—"

"I *am* his victim!" she cried. "The day my sister died, I became his victim. God knows that!"

"You can't hide behind God on this one, Melissa. And I can't hide this *from* him."

"I'm not asking you to. This is between God and me. Leave it at that. This doesn't have to compromise your faith. God won't blame you for it."

143

"Melissa, if you believe that," he said sadly, "you're farther from God than I thought. If I lie for you, or cover up, or even withhold information, I'll be accountable. My relationship with Christ depends on *my* heart, not yours. And if I make a choice that I know is apart from his will . . ." His voice cracked, and he couldn't go on.

She covered her mouth again and caught a sob, and she rested her forehead on his knee. He touched the back of her head, then bent down to kiss it. Misery overcame him, blinding him, scorching him, and finally, he whispered, "I've got to go. I have a lot of thinking to do."

"Yeah," she whispered, raising her head. "I guess you do."

She followed him to his car, and before he got in, he lingered there for a moment, looking at her with sad, soft eyes. He reached up and touched her wet cheek, and she set her hand on top of his, held it there for a moment. Finally, he leaned over and kissed her, sweet, long, and sad.

"I'm sorry, Larry," she whispered.

"Yeah," he said, squinting against his own tears. "Me, too."

She watched as he got into his car and pulled out of the driveway. In her heart, she knew that he would never kiss her again.

CHAPTER TWENTY-TWO

Larry sat on the edge of his bed, staring at the floor as if the facts lined up on it like ceramic tiles.

Fact. He had sworn to get criminals off the street.

Fact. Pendergrast had been charged with two other rapes.

Fact. Pendergrast had managed to beat the law and was still on the streets.

Fact. Pendergrast had broken into Melissa's apartment, called her, and stalked her.

Fact. Pendergrast had threatened to fulfill the lies she'd told about him, and his history indicated that he would do just that.

Fact. Tony knew that something wasn't right in the case.

Fact. Melissa was guilty of lying before a grand jury.

Fact. The penalty for that lie was up to five years in prison.

Fact. Larry was falling in love with her.

That final fact made him cover his eyes with his hand and fall back onto his bed. Tony had warned him. He was getting too involved, too close. He was letting her influence him. Maybe he wasn't even thinking straight.

Even so—could he honestly take the chance of sending her to prison?

He fell to his knees beside his bed and cried out to God to help him with this lose-lose decision—this choice that shouldn't be a choice at all.

He had never meant to care about her, but she had seemed so alone.

He felt God's love, radiating through him like sunlight on a July day, and he knew that love was for Melissa, too. God had a plan for her. But what if it wasn't one that Larry could live with?

"She'll go to prison if I tell what I know!" he cried out to God. "With hookers and drug addicts and thieves. She's so little— she'll never survive.

"And Pendergrast will go free—again! He'll hurt others. You know he will, Lord. That can't happen. He raped Sandy. Lord, help me understand . . ."

His prayer went on into the night, pleading with God, reasoning with him, wrestling with him. The options, both his and God's, whirled through his mind, exhausting him with choices and possibilities, absolutes and shades of gray.

And by the time dawn intruded on the room, Larry had made the choice that he knew he shouldn't make, the choice that would protect the woman he loved. The choice that would be a lie. Wearily, he cried out to God again, "Please forgive me for what I'm about to do!"

But a shadow fell over the room as he spoke, for God wasn't listening anymore. Already, there was a barrier.

Already.

Feeling empty and angry, he got to his feet, exhausted, troubled, miserable, and tried to sort out what he needed to do. He would go to the station and tell Tony that Melissa had confirmed the "supposing" he had done last night. He would say that she had worked undercover to catch Pendergrast at something, but that the tables had turned and he had come after her instead. Her plan had backfired, and she'd been made a victim.

And then he'd call in every favor Tony had ever owed him to convince him to let Larry call the shots on this case. Tony would listen. He'd have to.

Melissa would only have to answer to the DA for not telling everything from the beginning. It would look bad for her, but it wouldn't land her in jail. And any jury would believe it.

Whatever the outcome, it was better than telling the truth.

He showered and got dressed, playing the story over and over in his mind. Tony would believe him. It would make sense. And

Tony would never in a million years think that Larry would lie. Not even for a woman.

His spirits remained deflated as he went around the apartment straightening up, keeping busy so that he wouldn't think about principles, or values, or his relationship with God. And then he saw his Bible, lying open on the table where he had been reading from it yesterday. The words were suddenly threatening, whatever they were, and he couldn't bear to see them. He closed it suddenly and set it on the bookshelf where it wasn't as likely to catch his eye.

He couldn't think about what he was doing. All he could do was act—quickly—before his own convictions forced him to change his mind.

CHAPTER TWENTY-THREE

M*elissa, do you think suicide keeps you from heaven?"*

"Why would you ask something like that? Sandy, don't even think that. We're going to put this behind us. One day, it'll all be over, and he'll be in jail, and we'll be able to laugh again—"

"He's not in jail, Melissa. He's still out there. And I feel so dirty."

"You have to trust. You have to have faith."

"Sometimes I just don't have the patience for faith. Prayers take too long to be answered. Maybe I have to take things into my own hands—"

"What do you mean? Going after him? Hurting him somehow?"

No answer.

And then the dream changed scenes, and there were ambulances, police cars, interrogations, coroners, the crowd around the house just like it had been on the night of the rape . . .

Drama upon drama . . .

Then the dream flashed back to little girls on the beach, romping in frothing waves, laughing and splashing each other. It changed to a ballet recital, when Melissa, in awe, had watched Sandy as the star soloist in the spring production, then afterward, when the family had gone out for ice cream, and Sandy had laughed and talked nonstop about all the catastrophes backstage.

Then Melissa stood over a baptismal, watching as her sister gave her testimony, then was baptized—then stepped aside as Melissa, younger but just as touched by the Holy Spirit, did the same.

"Do you feel different, Sandy?" she asked as they climbed the stairs out of the baptismal.

"*I feel clean,*" *Sandy said with tears in her eyes. "Reborn. Like this is a beginning.*"

And then the dream changed again, and the baptismal was a bathtub, and it wasn't the beginning, but the end, and Sandy wasn't born; she was dead.

Melissa woke in a cold sweat, shivering from the force of emotion that had assaulted her even in the dream. Throwing the covers back, she ran to the bathroom and threw up, then sat on the floor waiting for it to happen again.

"I feel dirty, too, Sandy," she whispered. Covering her mouth, she tried to muffle her sobs so she wouldn't wake Lynda. She *was* dirty.

And she was making Larry dirty, too.

She leaned back against the wall and looked up at the ceiling, as if she could see God through it. "Why did she have to die?" she asked.

She sobbed into her knees, hugging them tightly.

After a while, she got up wearily and washed her face, dried it, and looked in the mirror. She didn't like what she saw, so she turned away.

Opening the door that went from her bedroom onto the patio, she went outside and sat on the swing, hugging her knees and looking up at the stars as if being there brought her closer to the Lord. "I've asked Larry to do something horrible," she whispered to God. She covered her face. "How could I ask him to make a choice like that? Who am I, to do that?"

Her muffled sobs came harder.

"Oh, God," she whispered. "Can you ever forgive me? Can you ever make me new again, like when I first knew you?"

Slowly, a strange peace fell over her, as though some heavenly hand were stroking her hair, whispering to her that it would be all right. And for the first time since Sandy's death, Melissa began to feel that, someday, maybe it *would* be all right.

Sliding her hands down her face, Melissa cried out, "Lord, tell me what I have to do."

She wept some more, feeling all her energy draining out of her, but into her mind crept the answer she had sought. There was only one answer.

She had to set things right—for Larry, and for herself—no matter what the consequences were. There was no one left to depend on but God. And somehow, now, she felt that she had the patience Sandy had not had to trust him. He would take care of her. He would forgive her.

She really had no choice. She had tried to do it all herself, and she had spoiled everything.

She wiped her face, tried to pull herself together, and went back into the house. Tiptoeing up the hall, she peered into Lynda's room. Lynda was in her bed, but she was sitting up, looking back at Melissa as if she'd been waiting.

"Lynda?" The word came out hoarse, raspy, on the edge of a sob. "You're awake. I hope I didn't wake you."

Lynda pulled back the covers and patted the bed for Melissa to sit down. "I thought I heard you throwing up. I went to check on you, but you were crying. Something told me you needed to be alone. But I was praying for you."

Melissa breathed a laugh. "Well, that explains it."

"Explains what?" Lynda asked softly. "Melissa, are you all right?"

Though it looked as if she wasn't, Melissa nodded her head. "I'm going to be. But I need your help."

"What do you need?" Lynda asked. "I'll do whatever I can."

"That's good," Melissa said. "Because I'm going to need a lawyer."

CHAPTER TWENTY-FOUR

Larry couldn't make himself go straight to the police station that morning. Instead, he drove by Pendergrast's apartment, looking for either of the two cars Pendergrast was known to drive. The dark blue Cherokee was in its place, and after searching the parking lot in front and back, he finally found the gray Toyota, too.

Larry put his car in park and let it idle as he stared up at the apartment where a rapist slept. Had he been out prowling all night? Was he sleeping now? Some part of him—some uncharacteristic part that he didn't recognize—made him want to kick down the man's door, grab him out of bed, and beat him to a pulp.

But he couldn't do that. He had no grounds, no warrant, no just cause.

He drove to a convenience store on the corner and found a pay phone at the end of the small building. He picked up the receiver and held it for a moment, letting his forehead rest against the phone. What would he tell Melissa? That she was off the hook? That he would lie for her?

His stomach played queasy games with him as he went over the words in his mind. Finally, he dialed Lynda's number. After a few rings, Jake answered.

"Hello?"

"Jake? Larry here. Has Melissa left for work yet?"

"Maybe," Jake said. "She and Lynda are both gone. They weren't even here when I came over for breakfast. Maybe they went out for breakfast."

Out for breakfast. His heart sank. He had been up all night, struggling with the decision to lie for her, and she had hopped out of bed and gone out to eat?

It didn't matter, he told himself. He had to stick to his decision to protect her.

His face was tired and somber when he reached the police station. As usual, it was an acoustical nightmare. Even at this hour, voices were deafening as burglary suspects and joyriders brought in hours ago waited to be booked. Printers were printing, phones were ringing. Tony's computer was on, but his chair was empty. "Where's Tony?" Larry asked one of the other officers.

The officer held a telephone between his ear and shoulder and nodded distractedly toward the interrogation room.

Larry frowned. Who would he be interrogating this early?

He walked around the wall, to the two-way mirror that allowed him to look into the room.

And his heart plummeted.

Tony sat at the table across from two women: Lynda Barrett . . . and Melissa.

"Oh, no," he whispered.

Melissa was talking nonstop, and Tony was taking notes. He saw as she turned back to look at Lynda that she was crying, and Lynda was crying, too. Lynda reached out and took her hand, and he saw her tell Melissa to go on.

She's confessing! he thought. But why? She hadn't given him the chance. Had she believed he was going to turn her in? Had she been afraid of what he might do?

He bolted around the corner and burst into the room. "What's going on here?"

Melissa averted her eyes, but Tony and Lynda looked up. "Larry, sit down," Tony said gently.

"No," he said. "I want to know what's going on."

Tony looked genuinely sorry as he got to his feet. "Melissa called me early this morning, Larry. She wanted to meet with me. She had something to say."

Finally, Melissa looked up, her red, wet eyes locking with Larry's, and he could see in her expression that she had told everything.

"I'm sorry, Larry."

He breathed out a sad, exasperated laugh. "For what?"

Floundering, she looked back at Tony. "Tony, can I have a minute alone with Larry? Just a minute?"

Tony seemed a little more humble than he had the last time Larry had seen him, and he closed his notes and took them with him.

"Do you want me to leave you alone, too, Melissa?" Lynda asked.

Melissa nodded. "It won't take long."

The two left, and for a moment Larry just stood there, staring at her. "You told him."

"I had to."

"Why?" he asked, pulling a chair to face her and dropping into it. "Last night, I told you I was going to think about it—"

"That's why. To keep you from having to."

The words came out on an overpowering wave of emotion. "But I wasn't going to!"

Her face twisted, and she touched his face as tears rolled down her cheeks.

"I never meant to put you in that position," she whispered. "God's been dealing with me, Larry."

He covered her hand with his, holding it against his cheek. "But I was going to protect you. I could have, if you'd just waited."

"And what would that have cost you?"

It had already cost him, but he didn't tell her that. "Melissa, what's it going to cost *you*?"

She tried to look stronger. "Lynda said there's a possibility that there won't be any jail time. It's my first felony, so there's a chance I could get probation, maybe some community service. And if I do get jail time, it may not be prison." Her voice cracked, and she lifted her chin. "Just the county jail for women."

He pulled her into his arms and laid his forehead on her shoulder. "I can't stand that thought," he said.

"I'll be all right," she whispered. "I have to trust God in this, like I should have from the first."

Larry wept harder, but he couldn't tell her that it was because *he* had chosen not to trust God, had in fact deliberately turned away from him, deliberately disobeyed. The fact that he hadn't actually committed the act didn't matter. He had made the choice.

"I want to thank you, Larry."

"For what?"

"For reminding me who's in control."

"But Pendergrast is still out there!" Larry cried.

"I know," she whispered. "But I finally realized last night that Pendergrast can't hide his sins from God. Anymore than I can."

Larry gazed at her, his face twisted and reddening. "You can live with that?"

"I have to," she said, wiping her eyes. "Either I believe in God's power or I don't. Sandy didn't. Maybe it wasn't her fault. Maybe she had just gotten too weak—too tired. But I do, Larry."

He crushed her against him and held her so long that he thought he might never let her go. "I love you, you know."

She smiled through her tears. "Yeah, I think I've known that for some time."

Outside the door in the noisy precinct room where people came and went, Tony leaned against the wall, a baffled look on his face. "I'm amazed," he said. "I mean, I suspected things weren't right all along, but I never dreamed she'd just walk in and confess. Why did she?"

"I suspect it had something to do with Larry," Lynda said.

"But she could have told half the truth and gotten away with it."

Lynda studied his face. "You seem almost troubled that she confessed."

"Well," he said, shaking his head. "I have to admit that I wanted to get to the bottom of it. But now, when I think that she'll be punished, and that thug is going to go free . . . It almost makes me wish I didn't know anything about the law."

Lynda sighed wearily. "I know what you mean. When she told me, I came so close to telling her to stay quiet. But that wouldn't have been right, for either of us. This is between Melissa and God. And she feels she's doing the right thing."

"You see?" Tony said, grimacing. "That's what kills me. All these things you guys do in the name of God. Does she realize she'll go to jail in the name of God?"

"She won't be going in the name of God. She'll be going because of her own wrong decisions," she whispered. "Besides, the state may decide not to prosecute."

"But if they do, she'll probably go to jail. The people in that place—" He looked around the huge room and waved his hand toward some of the criminals being charged with crimes for which they deserved punishment they probably wouldn't get. "She may not even survive it."

"She just has to trust, Tony. If she had trusted God in the beginning, instead of taking things into her own hands, none of this would have happened."

Tony had to agree with at least part of that. His gaze shifting to the interrogation room, he asked, "Did *he* know?"

Lynda shrugged. "I honestly don't know. She didn't tell me, and I didn't want to know. I don't think you really do, either. It's between them."

He moaned and looked up at the ceiling.

"But I do know this much," Lynda said. "She didn't want him to be the one to turn her in."

"Or to cover for her." Tony crossed his arms and leaned his head back against the wall. "Under normal circumstances, nothing on earth would have made Larry lie about a case. But this is different. Something about that woman. Larry hasn't been himself lately."

"Maybe he's in love with her."

"Yeah," Tony said quietly. "Maybe he is." He looked back at Lynda, who looked as tired as he felt. He wondered whether she'd gotten any sleep last night. "Sometimes I wish I'd listened to my mother and become a dentist."

She smiled. "You, too?"

The door opened, and Larry stepped out, his eyes red and glassy. Tony pushed off from the wall, and for a moment, just stood looking at his friend.

"You okay?" he asked finally.

"Yeah."

"You want me to book her, or do you want to?"

Larry struggled with the emotion so clear on his face and rubbed his jaw with rough fingertips. "You do it. But go easy, okay? Don't make a spectacle out of her."

"You know I won't, buddy."

Larry touched Lynda's arm, making her look up at him. "Do what you can for her, Lynda. Don't let her go to jail."

"I'll do my very best."

His face was losing its battle with the feelings coursing through him, so he started briskly across the room.

"Larry?"

Larry turned at Tony's call. "Yeah?"

"Where are you going?"

His mouth trembled as he tried to get the words out. "Out. Something I need to take care of. I'll be back."

"All right, buddy."

And Tony and Lynda watched as Larry fairly ran through the precinct and out the back door.

CHAPTER TWENTY-FIVE

The pain raging inside Larry was inescapable and constant. His habitual instinct to turn to God for help, for peace, seemed foreign to him now. He was angry, and there was nowhere to turn.

The bell warning that his gas tank was dangerously low kept ringing until he finally pulled over into a small parking area along a beach. He didn't know how long he'd been driving, but he figured he was somewhere in St. Petersburg. The beach was bare, for the day was overcast, just as his heart seemed to be. He left his car and walked across the sand, staring furiously out at the clouds billowing over the farthest reaches of the Gulf.

She won't survive jail, his mind railed. *She'll never make it. She doesn't know what she's doing.*

He reached a long pier that stretched over the water and started walking toward the seagulls perched on the railing at the end.

It's too much—she'll be punished, and he'll go free.

He walked faster, his sneakers making little sound on the wooden planks. The cool wind whipped harshly through his hair and flapped at his jacket. Overhead, he heard the rustle of wings as a flock of egrets settled on the railing behind him.

He reached the end of the pier, scattering the seagulls, and looked across the water to the clouds beyond. It was majestic, beautiful, but it looked like anger coming home to settle on the water.

God's anger.

Larry's anger.

He began to weep, hard and loud, his anguish catching on the wind and flying off to some unknown place where it wouldn't be heeded. "Why?" he shouted. "Why?"

But there was no answer, just the loud drumming of the waves against the shore, and the ruthless *caw* of the seagulls soaring overhead.

He ran back down the pier, across the sand, and back to the car. He slammed the door and collapsed against the wheel, his head resting on his arms.

Forsaken. That was the word. He had been forsaken. His refuge was gone, and his peace had been shattered. He was alone, by his own choice.

Gritting his teeth against the rage that it had come to this, he started the car and pulled out into traffic, pushing his car to the speed limit and beyond.

But it would never be fast enough.

CHAPTER TWENTY-SIX

It was no surprise that the state decided to prosecute, nor was it a surprise that Melissa appeared for her arraignment that afternoon with a guilty plea. The judge wasn't interested, at this point, in why she'd done what she had done. All that mattered was that a crime had been committed. He ordered a presentence investigation by the Department of Corrections, then set the sentencing for a little over two weeks away.

All of the charges against Pendergrast were dropped.

As Melissa rode home from the arraignment with Lynda, she was quiet, preoccupied. "What are you thinking?" Lynda asked. "You're not having regrets, are you?"

Melissa thought that over for a moment. "Not about confessing. But I wish I'd found another way to get him." Her eyes strayed out the window as they drove through downtown, past the Ritz cinema and the hardware store and the newspaper office, all part of the town she had never really gotten a chance to know. "He's out there. He's going to hurt more women. Maybe even kill somebody."

"You're scared, aren't you?"

She moved her eyes back to Lynda. "Wouldn't you be?"

"Absolutely," Lynda said. She reached across the seat and patted Melissa's hand. "I've been there, remember?"

"Yeah." She sighed. "I just keep thinking how much rage he must feel toward me, knowing I lied about him and set him up. A man like him—he won't just sit still for that. He'll get revenge somehow."

"Well, you're more than welcome to stay with me as long as you want. Maybe he'll just let the court system get revenge."

"The court system," she muttered. "I'll go to jail, won't I?"

"Not if there's any way I can convince the judge not to send you there. But I have to tell you. This judge, L. B. Summerfield, is the toughest one I've ever dealt with. When the DOC interviews you for the presentence investigation, you need to tell them everything. Everything about Sandy's rape, how he continued to terrorize her, how he terrorized your family—"

"Does any of that really matter?" Melissa asked. "Everybody acts like it's only what I've done that matters." She looked thoughtfully at Lynda. "Won't the fact that I recanted and confessed have any bearing on his decision? Wouldn't he be more lenient because of that?"

Lynda sighed. "I wish I could say he would. But by law, you can't use recantation as a defense—at least, not in your case. There are some cases where you can—like if you recant during the same official proceeding where you lied—but it won't work for us now. The best we can hope is that your story will be enough."

"Will the DOC be interviewing Pendergrast, too?"

"Yes, thank God. And if they have any sense at all, they'll see him for what he is."

"No, they won't," Melissa said quietly, looking out the window again. "He's too smart. Too convincing. He'll make them think he's the victim."

"They'll look at more than his story, Melissa. They'll look at his history, too. You just have to have faith." She glanced at Melissa as they rounded a corner. "Are you going to call your parents?"

For a moment, Melissa couldn't answer. "I don't know. I guess I'll have to. I mean, I can't very well go to jail and keep it from them. Part of me wants to just wait and see how the hearing comes out. But if I'm sentenced to jail time, I might not get the chance to explain it all to them, to make them understand . . ."

"Tell them before the hearing," Lynda said. "Don't leave them out of this. You're their only child. They need to know."

Melissa wiped her tears away. "I'll think about it."

"Good." They reached the outskirts of her neighborhood. "Are you going to see Larry tonight?"

Melissa's mouth twisted, and she shrugged. "I doubt I'll be seeing him anymore. I mean, I don't blame him. It's not real good for a cop's reputation to be involved with a known felon."

"Melissa, the man cares about you. He's not just going to cut you off because of this. You saw how upset he was this morning."

"Exactly my point."

"Well, if I were a gambler, I'd bet that you're wrong about him. If I know Larry Millsaps, this isn't the end."

She turned down her long street, past the two houses on the corner. When her house, set alone at the end of the dead-end street, came into view, there was a small black Chevy parked in the driveway, and Lynda smiled slowly. "As a matter of fact . . ."

Melissa only frowned, afraid to get her hopes up as they pulled into the driveway next to Larry's car. She got out, looking for him, and in a moment, the door to Jake's apartment opened, and the two men walked out.

It had been a hard day for Larry, Melissa thought. His eyes were red, like hers, and she knew he hadn't gotten much sleep last night. He'd probably been up all night struggling with the decision she had given him to make. And this afternoon, in the courtroom, he had seemed to be in worse shape than she was.

She hated herself for putting him through this. If he'd never met her, if she'd never lied, he'd still be out there doing his job, arresting people and locking them up, going to his church, and enjoying his friends—rather than suffering because of something she had done. Yes, she hated herself.

But Larry cut across the driveway without a word and pulled her into a hug that crushed life back into her.

"It'll be all right," he whispered. "Somehow, it's gonna be all right."

She began to cry against his shoulder, and she saw Lynda and Jake disappear into the house, leaving them alone.

"We have to talk," she said finally, looking up at him. "See— you don't owe me anything. What I deserve is to have you just forget you ever knew me. I would be all right. Really."

He stepped back, framed her face with his hands, and gazed intently into her eyes. "Melissa, that's not going to happen. I'm going through this with you."

"But I don't want you to," she cried. "I don't want you to have to suffer."

"But I am suffering," he said. "I'm suffering because you are. I wish I could move the clock back three years and stop what happened to Sandy, for your sake, but I can't. All I can do is be here with you now. And you have to let me."

She wilted in his arms then, allowing herself to feel the peace and comfort and sustenance he offered, the support she didn't deserve, the grace she hadn't earned. Just like God's love, she thought. For she saw Larry as a gift, sent as a light in the darkness her life had become.

They spent as much time together as they could for the next two weeks, avoiding the subject of the hearing coming up, avoiding mention of the names Soames or Pendergrast, avoiding the topic of jail or hearings, avoiding the media, who had latched onto her story like hungry dogs to a bone. Because notice of her arraignment had appeared in the local paper, Melissa lost her job with the temporary agency. That was part curse and part blessing, Larry decided, since her mind wasn't on work right now, anyway, and she needed this time to prepare. Besides, her interview with the DOC had lasted for two whole days, and it had taken a few days after that for her mental and physical exhaustion from rehashing the whole story to fade.

Larry, too, was interviewed, along with Tony and some of the other cops who'd answered her call that first night. It was apparent to him that they were trying to determine just how much damage had been done with her lie, and how calculated it was. Melissa never asked what he had told them, and when he'd tried to tell her, she'd refused to listen. He didn't owe her an explanation, she told him. But whether they spoke of it or not, the clock was ticking.

He took some vacation days the week of her sentencing, and on that Tuesday, drove her to the beach. They took off their shoes and rolled up their jeans and walked barefoot through the gentle waves at high tide. The sun was just beginning to set, and a cool breeze swept in from the Gulf, whispering through Melissa's hair, the pink-golden rays of the sun making her hair look even lighter.

She slowed her step and kicked at a wave as it frothed around her ankles, then turned toward the breeze and watched the sunset fill the sky with a brilliant array of pinks and golds and yellows. "It's beautiful," she whispered. "Look, Larry. Isn't it beautiful?"

He put his hands on her shoulders and stood behind her, watching the sky. She felt so small beneath his hands. Her head barely reached the indentation of his neck. "Yes," he whispered, kissing the top of her head. "It's beautiful."

"Let's just sit here for a while," she said. "Let's watch it until it goes down."

She sat in the white, dry sand, and he sat beside her, holding her against him as the sun made its grand finale of the day. It took over an hour for it to disappear below the horizon, and in all that time, they didn't utter a word.

Finally, when the pinks and golds had given way to a grayish blue, Melissa scooped up some sand in her hand and watched it fall through her fingers. "I have to call my parents," she said.

"Good. I hoped you would."

"It's not going to be easy," she said, still watching the sand. "In fact, I can't tell them this over the phone. I need to do it in person."

"I'm sure they'll come."

She swallowed and looked up at him. "Will you help me, Larry? Help me tell them, I mean?"

"Of course. I'll tell them *for* you if you want."

"No," she said. "They have to hear it from me. But I'm just not sure I'm strong enough. And I'm not sure they are." Her voice broke off, and Larry pulled her against him.

When she finally pulled herself together and sat up straight again, she drew in a deep, rugged breath. "Let's go. I want to call them now. Maybe they can come tomorrow, and I can spend a few days with them before the hearing."

CHAPTER TWENTY-SEVEN

Melissa had trouble getting the words out over the telephone, but she managed to tell her parents that she was in trouble and she needed them. They were already frantic after not being able to reach her since her last vague, evasive phone calls, and the cursory note she'd sent them telling them not to worry hadn't helped. When she tried to tell them where she'd been, she couldn't go on. She handed the phone to Larry.

"Mrs. Nelson?" Larry asked. "This is Larry Millsaps. I'm a friend of Melissa's."

"Is she all right?" Nancy Nelson asked with a quiver in her voice.

"What's going on there?" Jim Nelson threw in from the extension.

"Well, she'd rather talk to you in person. I gathered from her end of the conversation that you're coming tomorrow?"

"Yes. We'll get the earliest flight. We can come tonight if she needs us to."

"No. Tomorrow will be fine."

"Mr. Millsaps, tell us—has she been hurt? Is she sick?"

"No, ma'am. She's not hurt or sick. She's fine."

"But she said she was in trouble!" her mother said.

"Does this have anything to do with—Edward Pendergrast?" her father asked.

Larry looked at Melissa, then closed his eyes. "Why would you ask that?"

"Because of the phone calls. The threats. The way she's been evading our questions. All the secrecy! It's so much like it was with Sandy. Does this have anything to do with him?"

Her mother was crying now. "We've just had a feeling all this time. When that man called us . . . I kept thinking I knew that voice."

Larry put his hand over the phone and whispered, "They want to know if it has anything to do with Pendergrast."

"Oh, no." She took back the phone. "Mom, Dad? Please. This is real important, and I need to talk to you in person. All I can tell you right now is that no one has hurt me. Can you just accept that and wait until we can talk?"

"All right, sweetheart." Her father's voice cracked. "All right. If that's how it has to be."

"Will you be all right until morning?" her mother asked.

"Yes, Mom. I'm in really good hands. I'm staying with a terrific person, a new friend. And Larry's watching over me, too. I didn't mean to scare you. This is not like it was with Sandy. My trouble is of my own making."

Perplexed, her parents were silent for a moment, then finally, her father said, "We'll see you early in the morning. Will you be at the airport?"

She wished she could say yes, but the airport was in Tampa, and she had been ordered not to leave St. Clair until her hearing. "Larry will be meeting you," she said. "He'll bring you to where I'm staying. He's a tall man, about six-two, with dark brown hair . . . good-looking . . ." She smiled slightly, and Larry couldn't help returning it. "You'll like him, Mom."

"Is he someone you're seeing?"

"Yes," she said.

"Well, why haven't you mentioned him?"

"I'll explain everything tomorrow, Mom."

Her mother didn't answer for a moment. "Melissa, I'm so worried about you."

"Please try not to worry, Mom. I'll see you both tomorrow."

Larry had made it a point to drive by Pendergrast's apartment several times a day to check for both cars. If one was missing, he would call Melissa and make sure everything was all right. It didn't appear that Pendergrast had yet figured out where she was staying. Larry had found Pendergrast's car parked at Proffer Builders for the past two days, so he assumed that he had gotten his job back. Everything was back to normal for him, Larry thought bitterly. Meanwhile, Melissa had to tell her parents that she might be going to jail.

Satisfied that Pendergrast was nowhere near Melissa, he drove an hour to the Tampa airport and walked the long walk to the gate where the Nelsons would be coming in. Melissa had described them to him, but somehow he felt that he would know them anyway the moment he saw them.

The plane was just landing as he reached the gate, and he stood by the window, watching, praying silently that they'd manage to take this well. It wouldn't be easy dealing with a jail sentence for their only daughter. God certainly knew it wasn't easy for him.

He watched the passengers come out of the tunnel, searching their faces. And then he saw them. The woman's blonde hair was pulled back in a bun, revealing a little gray around the temples, but it was clear from her blue eyes and the shape of her mouth that she was Melissa's mother.

They both looked younger than he had expected, probably in their late forties, and their eyes were troubled as they scanned the crowd for him.

Slowly, Larry worked his way to them. "Mr. and Mrs. Nelson?" he asked.

"Larry?" Jim Nelson returned.

Larry smiled and shook his hand. "It's nice to finally meet you. Do you need to go to the baggage claim?"

"No," her father said. "It's all in our carry-ons."

"All right. My car's this way."

They walked in silence for a moment. Larry glanced over at them. "Did you have a good flight, Mr. Nelson?"

"Jim," he said. "Call me Jim."

"And call me Nancy," Melissa's mother said. "You're obviously important to our daughter. There's no point in formalities. Have you known her long?"

"Only a few weeks," he said.

"Oh. From what she said last night, I thought it had been longer."

"It seems like longer," he agreed. They came to the escalator, and he stood back and allowed both of them to precede him.

Not much more was said as he led them to his car. When they were on their way, with Jim in front and Nancy in back, Larry could sense Jim studying him. "I know Melissa has something to tell us, and she wants to do it herself, but can you at least tell us where she's living? She has an apartment, doesn't she? Why isn't she in it?"

"She's just been spending a couple of weeks with friends," he said. "It wasn't a good time for her to be alone."

Her mother leaned forward on the seat. "Is she living with you?"

He glanced in the rearview mirror. "No, ma'am. Absolutely not. She's staying with a friend named Lynda Barrett."

Jim looked him over again. "What do you do for a living, Larry?"

Larry hesitated to tell him. "I'm a police officer."

Jim let the words sink in for a moment, then glanced back at his wife.

"How did you two meet?" her mother asked in a voice that was growing more raspy.

He swallowed. "I'll let her tell you about that, if you don't mind."

For the rest of the hour's drive to St. Clair, no one spoke. There was nothing more he could tell them, after all, without treading on Melissa's ground.

Lynda was at work and Jake was at physical therapy when Larry brought the Nelsons to Melissa.

Her parents looked apprehensive as they got out of the car and looked around at the modest little house. The side door to the house opened, and Melissa came out. "Mom. Dad." She ran into their arms, and for a moment, Larry stood back, feeling like an outsider. But he had promised her he would stay.

When the family hug broke, she led them all into the house, and into the living room. Her mother and father huddled together on the couch, waiting for the bomb to drop. "What did you want to tell us, Melissa?" her father asked gently. "Please don't make us wait any longer."

Melissa took Larry's hand and sat down across from them. "All right." She took a deep breath, and looked up at Larry, struggling to find the words. She'd practiced all night and all morning, but now that the time had come, all her scripted words escaped her. How would she tell them?

Mom, Dad, I may be going to jail.

No, she couldn't tell them that yet. She had to start at the beginning.

She cleared her throat. "You know when I quit my job at the FBI, and you were all upset and confused?"

"Yes," her mother said.

"I quit because I'd managed to locate Edward Pendergrast." Her mother gasped, and her father's frown grew deeper. "He was working here in St. Clair under another name," she went on.

"Oh, no," her mother cried, sitting back hard on the couch. "You came here to find him? Why? You should have stayed as far away from him as you could!"

Melissa blinked back the tears in her eyes. "I got a job working where he did."

"What?" her father asked in horror.

"I wanted to set him up," she said. She got to her feet, paced across the living room, and turned back to them. "I thought if I made it look like I'd been his next victim, then this time he'd get convicted. I'd make sure that there were no loose ends. That he wouldn't get off on a technicality this time. That he'd go to prison, where he belongs."

Her father stood slowly. "Are you telling us that you pretended he'd raped you?"

"Yes," she said. "That's exactly what I did. Larry was one of the detectives assigned to the case. He's a good cop."

Her mother was starting to cry. "Melissa, how could you do that? It could have gotten you killed! No wonder Pendergrast started calling us. He was looking for you!"

"Yes, he was," Larry agreed, "and they didn't keep him in jail after his indictment. He was out pending trial."

"Oh, Melissa! Is that why you kept moving?"

Melissa shoved her hair behind her ear. Her hand was trembling. "Yes. I caught him following me a couple of times. And he broke in."

"He was in your house?" her mother whispered.

Melissa nodded. "Nothing happened. I think he was just trying to scare me."

"I brought her here because I knew he wouldn't find her here," Larry cut in. "Lynda's a friend of mine."

"But—you lied, Melissa," her father said. "Is he in on this?" he asked, pointing to Larry.

"No, Dad. The thing is, I confessed two weeks ago."

Larry braced his elbows on his knees and propped his chin on his fist. Melissa kept her eyes on her parents.

"Why?" her father asked.

"Because it wasn't right. I had lied. And lying to a grand jury is a felony."

Jim's face paled, and he sank back down onto the couch. Her mother took his hand. "A felony?" she whispered.

"The actual charge is 'perjury in an official proceeding.' I could get up to five years."

"In prison?" her father asked in horror.

Her mother's face reddened. She covered her mouth, then asked, "What about him? What about that monster?"

Larry saw how Melissa struggled with that answer, so he spoke up. "They dropped all charges against him. They couldn't try him for something that hadn't happened."

"So he's still out there?" her mother asked on a sob. "And *Melissa's* the one who might go to jail?"

Larry nodded. "Unless the judge decides to go easy on her. The sentencing is Friday."

"Only two days from now?" Nancy gasped.

"Lynda's my lawyer," Melissa managed to say in a higher pitched voice. "She's hopeful that I won't have to serve any jail time. But there's no way to know for sure until we get into court. The judge will read all the testimony in the presentencing investigation, and he'll make his decision. All we can do is pray."

Melissa watched the pain distorting her parents' faces, and she broke into a sob. "I wanted you to hear it from me. I wanted you to be here."

Both of her parents got up and drew her into a hug. They all wept as Larry sat alone, wishing he could ease their pain.

CHAPTER TWENTY-EIGHT

Thursday dawned with harsh finality—the last day of life as she'd always known it. Tomorrow was Melissa's hearing; tomorrow she would find out if she had a future. She had hoped to sleep late, but she woke just after dawn and lay awake staring at the ceiling.

Tomorrow she could be going to jail.

She closed her eyes and prayed for deliverance, but even as she did, she felt the shame of deserving what she was getting.

The funny thing about God's forgiveness was that the consequences still had to be paid. Not because God necessarily required payment—but because the state did.

Not for the first time, she longed to turn back time, to forget her obsession with making Pendergrast pay. If only she had put him out of her mind and gone on with her life, tried to forget. But such a big part of her hadn't wanted to forget. Feeding her vengeful hatred had somehow sustained her. Now it was doing her in.

Tears rolled down her temples and into her hair as she stared up at the ceiling. The image of Gethsemane flashed through her mind—Jesus weeping the night before his own arrest—the disciples sleeping through it all as Larry and Lynda and Jake all probably were. She closed her eyes and thought of Christ's prayer for deliverance. She, too, had asked for deliverance—had pleaded and bargained for it. But she feared that the price of her disobedience would still have to be paid.

Getting out of bed, she pulled on her robe and went barefoot down the hall. A light was already on in the kitchen, and quietly, she stepped into the doorway. Lynda was sitting at the table reading her Bible. In her white cotton nightgown with little blue flowers, Lynda looked like a little girl, rather than a successful attorney. "Hi," Melissa whispered.

Lynda looked up. "Did I wake you?"

"No. I thought you were still asleep. You don't have to be at the office for two hours, do you?"

"No." Lynda closed her Bible and pulled her knees up under her gown as Melissa sat down. "I'm thinking about taking the morning off."

"Why?"

"Because I'm ready for court tomorrow, and I think somebody needs to get your mind off things."

"I'm okay, really."

Lynda set her chin on her palm. "I'm not sure I am."

"This puts a lot of pressure on you, doesn't it? You're worried."

"I want to do my best for you," Lynda said. "I just don't know—"

Melissa touched her hand to silence her. "It's okay, Lynda. I know you'll do your best, and if things don't work out just right, it's not your fault. It's mine."

Lynda sighed. "I know how scared you are, Melissa."

Melissa couldn't argue.

"I've been scared, too," Lynda went on. "I was just thinking about it, trying to put myself in your place. The sense of dread, of uncertainty. And I kept going back to that morning when Jake was test-flying my plane, about to buy it, and we realized the landing gear wouldn't go down. We had forty minutes to burn fuel before we landed. That gave the airport time to prepare for a crash landing, and it cut down on the fire hazard. But it was the longest forty minutes of my life."

"I can imagine."

"I haven't flown since. It's weird, because I used to fly every day. The fact that I don't have a plane anymore has something to do with that, but I had planned to rent one every now and then and get back up there. It's just been kind of hard to get back in the saddle."

"How about Jake? Has he flown yet?"

"No, not yet," she said. "He hasn't been able to get a medical release yet. He still has a way to go before his legs are a hundred percent. But I don't think he's afraid of it. I think he misses it. Just the feeling of being up there in the clouds, looking down over the world . . . you can forget everything."

"Well, maybe when you're ready, you can take him up."

Lynda looked at her for a moment, and a slow smile dawned across her face. "I just had a wonderful idea."

"What?"

"What if we all went up today? I could rent a plane, if Mike— my friend who runs the St. Clair airport—has one available. It would be a great treat for Jake, and it would help distract you and Larry."

The thought didn't appeal to Melissa. "No, you and Jake go ahead. This should probably be a private moment for the two of you."

Lynda shook her head. "The more, the merrier. Come on. Let's make a memory today." When Melissa still hesitated, Lynda leaned forward, her eyes wide, as if a thought had just occurred to her. "Unless you're scared. Maybe you don't want to go up with me after what happened the last time I flew."

Melissa laughed softly. "I trust you, Lynda. Even in a plane. I'm not afraid."

"Great. Then let's do it. I'll go call Paige and tell her to cancel my appointments for the morning."

"Are you sure?"

"Absolutely. I'll be in the shower. If Jake comes over, don't tell him what we're planning. I want to surprise him."

"What if he doesn't want to go?"

"He will," Lynda was certain. "He's been chomping at the bit to get back in the sky. Even if he's not the one flying."

The morning air was brisk for Florida, and Jake thought maybe there was hope that he'd experience an autumn here, after all. This time of year, especially during his short morning walks, he missed Texas. He'd never thought much, before, about the colors the leaves turned, the piles of leaves in the yards, the way the wind felt sweeping through the stands at football games. He'd taken a lot for granted before, including his ability to walk without thinking about every step. But he was grateful he could walk at all. Not so long ago, he'd believed that part of his life was over.

Now he started each day with a walk up Lynda's street and around a couple of blocks. It took a long time, for he had to walk slowly, but lately he'd been relying on his canes less and less. His legs were getting stronger, and it was just a matter of time before he'd be a hundred percent. Already he'd come so far since the crash—and he'd come a lot further mentally and spiritually than he had physically.

He wished he could make Melissa see that this tragedy about to reach culmination in her life could be a beginning. That tragedies weren't always a curse. Sometimes they were a blessing. Through human eyes, they could look like the end of the world. But through God's eyes, there were forces at work, plans aligning, miracles taking place.

His breathing grew heavier as he passed the small church not too far from Lynda's street, then the house beside it with a bicycle and a pair of skates in the yard. He should get a bike, he thought, and try riding it for exercise. It would get him farther and help him to build up his legs more. Then maybe, finally, he'd be able to get his medical release and fly again.

His eyes strayed to the sky, clear blue and cloudless, and once again he found that melancholy sweeping over him. Yes, his tragedy had been a blessing. Yes, he realized God's sovereignty in all of it. Yes, he'd been given wonderful gifts as a result of his fall. He had met the woman God had chosen for him—the only woman he'd ever given serious thought to spending the rest of his life with—and that only because he couldn't stand to spend a single moment without her. But Lynda understood the emptiness that still ached inside him whenever he thought of flying. Would he never fly again? Or was God going to give that back to him someday?

He made his way up the street to Lynda's driveway, thankful that he could sit down for a while before he went to physical therapy. He wondered if Melissa was up yet. For her sake, he hoped she slept late, so she wouldn't have to deal with the unmitigated fear she must feel at the idea of what could happen to her in court tomorrow. He'd felt that way the weekend before they'd taken the bandages off of his face. In a way, he had feared prison, too. The prison of living the rest of his life with only one eye, with harsh scarring down his face that would frighten children. But now he could see that even that had carried with it blessings.

He saw Larry's car as he approached Lynda's driveway, and the cop came out of the house, dressed in a pair of jeans and sneakers and a pullover shirt—minus the windbreaker he wore to hide his weapon when he was on duty.

"Hey, Larry," Jake said, reaching for his hand.

Larry looked pale and tired as he shook, and Jake wished he would get some sleep. "How's it going, Jake?"

"Great. You take the day off again?"

"Yeah," Larry said. "I wanted to try to take Melissa's mind off things, but I'm afraid we're just going to feed each other's anxiety. Hey, you wouldn't happen to know what those two are cooking up today, would you?"

Jake glanced toward the window, and saw Lynda looking out. She smiled at him, something that never failed to brighten his day. "What do you mean?"

"I mean, Lynda's taking the morning off, and she's walking around the house like she's about to burst with excitement. She said it was a surprise."

Jake's breathing was returning to normal now. "Oh, yeah? Think it has to do with Melissa's case?"

"No, that was my first question, too. They just said it was a diversion."

"A diversion, huh?" He glanced back toward Lynda again in the window. "Then we're going somewhere?"

"As soon as Melissa finishes showering." Larry lowered his voice. "I told them I wasn't really in the mood for much—and frankly, Melissa doesn't seem to be, either. She's pretty down. But Lynda insisted that it wouldn't take more than a couple of hours."

Jake started for Lynda's door. "Well, I don't know what it could be, but I do know this. When that woman sets her mind to something, you might as well sit back and enjoy wherever it takes you."

An hour later, Jake still seemed confused at where, exactly, Lynda's enthusiasm had carried them. When they pulled into a parking space at the small St. Clair airport, Jake gave Lynda an uncomfortable look. He hadn't been back here since the crash, and it occurred to her that he might not be ready to see where his life had almost ended.

"What's going on?" he asked quietly.

Lynda squeezed his hand. "I was trying to think of a way to get Melissa and Larry's minds off tomorrow, something that would make a memory, and I thought of this." She leaned toward him on the seat, her eyes big, beseeching. "What do you think, Jake? Are you ready to get back into the sky again?"

For a moment, he stared at her, quiet, expressionless. Finally, he asked, "You rented a plane?"

"Just for the morning. Melissa needs to spend some time with her parents this afternoon. But I thought it was time."

Jake looked out over the tarmac, at the planes lined up, just as they had been the morning of their crash. He had driven his Porsche out onto the tarmac and parked beside the plane he wanted to buy, as if that Porsche gave him privileges that everyone else didn't have, never dreaming how final that short drive would be.

The wind had been blowing hard that day, just as it was today, only that day had been warmer. He remembered Lynda mentioning her concerns about the crosswind, but he'd assured her that he could handle it. He was a commercial pilot, after all. But no amount of training or experience could have prepared him for what happened that day. Now, looking back, he felt like Nebuchadnezzar, proud of how high he'd climbed, arrogant about his own status, believing he was invincible. God had showed them both, he and Nebuchadnezzar, just how dependent on him they were.

He looked at Lynda, remembering the conversation in the cockpit as they'd prepared to land that day. She had been trembling. He took her hand now, and felt the slight tremor again. "Are you sure you can do this? You're not afraid?"

She smiled with only a tinge of uncertainty. "I don't think anybody's out to kill me this time, Jake," she said, referring to the man who had sabotaged her plane. "I've really been wanting to do

176

this. And I've wanted to take you. I can't forget that look you had in your eyes that morning when you were hotdogging in the sky like a Thunderbird."

"You hated me then. You thought I was the most obnoxious man you'd ever met."

"I was right. You were."

Jake grinned and looked at the two in the backseat, who listened with mild amusement. "She called me a psychopath."

"I sure did," she said proudly. "He was really being a jerk, showing off with all these loops and dips. But we had one thing in common. We both loved to fly." She squeezed Jake's hand. "And neither of us has done it since the crash."

Jake's hesitation diminished. Raising his eyebrows at the two in the backseat, he grinned. "Are you guys game?"

Larry shifted uneasily and peered out at a plane that was just taking off on runway 3, where he'd seen the jumbled, charred mass of Lynda's plane after the crash. "I don't know."

Melissa took his hand. "Come on, it'll be fun."

"Really?" he asked. "You want to do this?"

"Sure. It's better than moping around all day and playing all the different scenarios of tomorrow over and over in my mind. This might be my last day as a free woman. I might as well soar a little."

The shadows on Larry's face returned. "Melissa, don't say that. Lynda's a good lawyer."

Her eyes turning serious again, she touched Larry's mouth with her fingertips to hush him. "Anything could happen, Larry. I've cried until my eyes are raw, I've prayed until I've run out of words, and I've had so many regrets . . . I can't do anything about tomorrow right now. So let's just take advantage of today."

He leaned wearily back on the seat. "All right," he said without much enthusiasm. "Let's go fly."

Even though the flight was supposed to be relaxing, Lynda's hands trembled as she waited for Mike Morgan—the airport manager who served as air traffic controller in the small concessionlike booth inside the airport—to clear her to take off.

177

"Take it easy, now," Jake said, his eyes scanning the controls with some discomfort of his own. "We did a real good preflight check. Everything looked good. There's nothing to worry about."

"I know," she said. "I'm not scared to fly. I was just remembering . . ."

The radio crackled, and Mike gave them the go-ahead. The cabin was quiet except for the changing pitch of the engine as she accelerated down the runway.

The moment the wheels left the ground, Jake began to laugh like a little boy on his first Ferris wheel. "This is great!" he said. "Look how clear the sky is! Oh, man, I've missed this."

"I have too." Lynda relaxed as they gained altitude. She glanced to the backseat where Larry and Melissa sat close together, gazing out the window. "You two okay?"

"Yeah, we're fine," Melissa said quietly.

"As soon as I get my medical release—" Jake started to say, then stopped before he could get the rest out.

Lynda looked over at him, grinning. "That's the first time I've heard you say it so positively, Jake. Till now, you've seemed a little unsure if you ever would."

"I will," he said without question. "And when I do, we're buying another plane."

She looked over at him, her amused eyes searching his face. "We?"

"Yes," he said, returning her grin. "We."

Melissa grinned and winked at Larry. She had known Lynda and Jake were getting serious, but she hadn't known if they had discussed marriage. Judging by the pink flush across Lynda's cheekbones, and the smile on her face as she moved her eyes to the window, this may have been the first time they had.

Beginnings, she thought with a sigh as her smile faded and her eyes drifted back to Larry. Other people had beginnings. She had endings.

Larry noted the sadness that had fallen over her like a thick fog, so he slid his arm around her and pulled her tightly against him. She laid her head on his shoulder, wishing there could be a future for her with him. But that was too much to ask.

If they'd just met under different circumstances . . . If she'd just been more worthy of him . . .

But she knew that, if she had to go to jail, her relationship with Larry would be over. Cops didn't associate with convicts. He would forget about her; she almost hoped he would. He deserved happiness, and she would only bring him sorrow.

A tear dropped to her cheek and she quickly wiped it away. Larry saw her do it, and tipped her face up to his. She saw the trouble in his expression, the despair, the heartache. And she hated herself for putting it there.

Lord, please comfort him. Let him forget quickly. Let him find the person who can make him happy.

But it was hard to imagine any happiness replacing the sorrow in his eyes.

"You know, you were right, that morning we went up," Jake said softly to Lynda, breaking the silence in the plane. "This is a sanctuary. As reverent as a church."

"You have a different perspective now, don't you, Jake?" Lynda asked.

"Yeah," he said. "I thank God every day for that crash. Life has been a struggle since then, but I wouldn't trade a minute of it. Sometimes, you just have to go through hell to find heaven."

Was there a lesson there for her? Melissa wondered. She let the words sink in and tried to find comfort in them as her gaze drifted back out the window. Would there be a life after all this was over? Would there be a heaven at the end of her hell?

She knew that her life would go on, ultimately—but first, she would have to pay for her crime. She had to trust, she told herself. Like Jake, she had to believe that good would come out of it all.

She looked up and met Larry's eyes. He was going through a hell of his own, she thought. She was dragging him through it with her. Slowly, she began to withdraw. She lifted her head from his shoulder and sat straighter.

She saw his confusion as he loosened his hold on her, but he was demanding nothing from her today. He was here to give, and she received.

Thank you for letting him be here now, she prayed silently. Even if it was temporary . . . even if he forgot her . . . it was okay. God had given her this little interlude as a memory to take with her.

It was a memory that would remind her that she hadn't been forgotten or forsaken. God still loved her, in spite of herself. And he would see her through this, whatever happened tomorrow.

CHAPTER TWENTY-NINE

T he harsh rap of the gavel intensified the headache that had plagued Larry since he woke in the early hours of the morning. Melissa, too, looked as though she hadn't slept. He sat next to her, gripping her hand.

Around them in the courtroom, others with criminal charges waited to be called—some who looked as nervous as she, others who'd walked this path many times before. In the midst of it all, Melissa looked like the lady she was. She held her head up, as if she'd come prepared to accept whatever the court decided, and Larry hoped the judge would see into her heart and give her a second chance. The agony of waiting until her case number was called was almost more than he could stand.

He had sat through many days in court in his career, waiting to testify in a case against someone he'd arrested, but it wasn't until now that he realized how coldly impersonal it was. There should be privacy when someone's future was being decided, he thought. There should be quiet, reverence. He thought of the injustice of Melissa's having to sit through all the ugliness, like one of these thugs who deserved what they were going to get.

He looked up as the doors opened, and saw Melissa's parents come into the room. Melissa got to her feet instantly and stepped past Lynda and Jake.

She placed her parents between herself and Lynda with whispered introductions, and Larry could feel the agony these two people felt. They had lost one daughter already, and now, in an attempt to set that right, their only remaining daughter had broken the law. It would kill them if she went to jail, he thought. The brutal injustice of what continued to happen to their family was devastating.

The judge ordered a recess of fifteen minutes, and they all stood up. Melissa's parents embraced her tightly for a small eternity, weeping out their hearts. Larry stood back, feeling out of place, not sure where he fit in this circle of tears.

He tried to avert his eyes, tried not to watch the quiet display of emotion. The courtroom doors opened as people quietly came and went. Idly, Larry scanned the faces, wondering what their stories were, whether they were lawbreakers or hurting family members. A man came in alone and stood in the aisle with his back to them, looking for a seat. Slowly, he turned around.

It took a moment for the face to register in Larry's mind, but suddenly he recognized the one man he'd never considered might be here.

Edward Pendergrast.

Some cross of rage and anguish burst inside Larry's mind.

Pendergrast grinned as their eyes made contact, then, one by one, he regarded the faces in their row until he came to Melissa with her parents, the same parents he'd terrorized before.

Instead of taking a seat, he stood still at the end of their row, that smug grin on his face, that victorious expression of hardened pride, of invincible evil.

Melissa was stunned at the sight of him. Her parents slowly turned and saw him.

Pendergrast lifted his hand in a wave, as if they were all old friends, then slid into a seat across the aisle from them.

Larry's teeth clenched, and his breathing grew heavy. He bolted out of his seat and stepped around Melissa and her parents. Pushing out of the row, he headed toward Pendergrast. But Melissa caught his arm. "Larry, don't. Please—just stay here."

"I can't," he bit out, and kept going.

Pendergrast was enjoying this, and he beamed up at Larry as he approached. "Well, if it isn't ole gullible Detective Millsaps. Believer of beautiful women. Swallows their stories hook, line, and sinker. But all's forgiven, man. There is justice, after all." He held out his hand to shake, but ignoring it, Larry leaned over until his face was square with Pendergrast's.

"Don't talk to me about justice," he said through clenched teeth. "You don't have any business in here."

"*Au contraire*," Pendergrast said with a laugh. "As the victim of her little fantasy, I'd say I belong here even more than you do. I might even have something to say to the judge."

Larry's face paled, and he glanced back over at Melissa. She'd shown unbelievable composure until now, but since Pendergrast had entered her face had reddened and was twisted into a fragile, on-the-verge expression that made his heart ache. Her parents, too, looked as if they might come undone.

Larry pointed a finger in Pendergrast's face. "I want you to know something, Pendergrast."

"Soames. The name is Soames."

Larry wasn't daunted at his coolness. "I'm going to get you, *Pendergrast*," he said. "One of these days, I'm going to get you."

"I don't think so, Millsaps. Better men than you have tried."

"Watch me," Larry said. He stepped back across the aisle and bent down to Lynda's ear. "He says he's going to say something. Can he do that?"

She gave Pendergrast a troubled look. "I'm afraid so. The judge will listen to anyone who has something to say about this. The wronged party always has the right to speak."

"Then let me speak," Larry said. "I'll tell them what a good person she is, that she had good reason—"

"No," Lynda said, touching his hand. "I'm sorry, Larry, but I don't think it would help. You're the cop she originally lied to. It would be better if you stayed seated. Melissa does plan to address the court herself. I think that'll be enough."

"But you'll tell the judge about his past record, won't you? You'll tell him about Sandy?"

"It's all in the PSI, Larry. The judge has reviewed all of it."

"But maybe he hasn't made up his mind yet!"

She looked to the front of the room, and swallowed. "I'm going to do what I can, Larry. Please, just try to keep Melissa calm."

Miserably, he pushed further down the row, past her parents, and sat on the other side of Melissa.

Melissa was trembling worse now, and her palms were sweating. He didn't know how she would make it through this. Or how he would. "What did he say?" she asked.

"He's just trying to scare you," he said. "It's intimidation. Just ignore him."

Slipping his arm around her shoulders, Larry pulled her against him and pressed his mouth into her hair. Quietly, he prayed for her, not in words she could hear, but he knew that she knew what he was doing.

The gavel banged twice, making her jump, and the bailiff called out the case code. "Pinellas County versus Melissa Nelson."

Melissa got up, wobbling slightly, and Lynda slipped out of her seat with her files and led her to the judge.

Slipping into the seat she had previously occupied, Larry took her mother's hand, squeezed it. And then Jim Nelson, her father, reached over and took both of theirs. They drew strength from each other's touch as they watched Melissa take a seat at the table in the front of the courtroom.

"Is she going to say anything?" Jim asked him in a whisper.

Larry shook his head. "She wasn't sure when we talked about it, but Lynda wants her to, I think." He glanced over at Pendergrast, who had sat up straighter, as if preparing to go forward himself. Every muscle in Larry's body tightened.

The state attorney addressed the court in routine legalese concerning the findings of the presentencing investigation. When he recommended that the judge give Melissa at least two years in the state penitentiary, Larry closed his eyes.

"Your honor, before you rule on this, there's someone here who would like to address the court."

"Fine," the judge said. "Go ahead."

The state attorney turned back and nodded to Pendergrast. With a solemn look on his face—the look of a fine, upstanding citizen who has been deeply wronged—he made his way to the front of the room.

Melissa started to rise in protest, but Lynda made her sit back down and whispered to her as Melissa's face reddened and her eyes filled with tears.

"Your Honor," Pendergrast said, "I'm Edward Soames, the person this woman accused of raping her. I just wanted to say a few words before you decide on her sentence."

"All right," the judge said, taking off his glasses and fixing his full attention on Pendergrast.

Pendergrast cleared his throat and looked at his feet, looking for all the world like a clean-cut professional man who was nervous coming before the judge. "One day I was a successful architect with a lot of friends, just living life and not bothering anybody, and the next day, because of one lie that someone told about me, I'm branded a rapist, I lost my job, my friends won't talk to me—" His voice seemed to catch, and he stopped, swallowed, and started again. "You see, this all started because I didn't return her interest in me."

Across the room, Melissa's muffled cry interrupted, and the judge glanced at her. Lynda quieted her.

"So she got even," Pendergrast went on. "Now I have to live the rest of my life with this stigma following me around. Even though the charges have been dropped, my friends are still suspicious. She made a mess out of my life, and I didn't do a thing to deserve it." He seemed to get emotional, stopped, and pinched the bridge of his nose. After a moment, he looked up at the judge. "That's—that's all I have to say, Your Honor. Just think about that before you decide on her sentence. Women shouldn't be allowed to just go around ruining people's lives. They shouldn't get away with it."

The judge seemed moved. "Thank you, Mr. Soames."

As Pendergrast turned around to go back to his seat, he got that grin on his face again and glanced back at Larry. He was proud of himself.

Lynda stood up. "Your honor, my client would like to address the court herself. That is, if she can still manage to speak after that classic performance."

"All right," the judge said. "Proceed."

Melissa stood up, her knees shaking. She couldn't stop the sobs still overtaking her. "His name is not Soames," she said. "It's Pendergrast, and he's a liar. He killed my sister—"

The judge, looking disgusted, slapped his hand on the table. "Unless you have a murder conviction to back that up, Miss Nelson,

I suggest that you rephrase it. Otherwise I might be led to believe that you haven't learned your lesson."

She covered her mouth and tried to pull herself together. Finally, attempting to speak again, she said, "He caused my sister's suicide. He's a rapist, Your Honor. She wasn't the only one."

He shook his head and began taking notes, as if he'd already dismissed her for making false accusations again.

"Your Honor, I know what I did was wrong. I shouldn't have done it. But I was trying to right things. The court system let my family down, and he was still out there—you just don't know how desperate you can get, when you find your only sister dead in a bathtub, and the guy who ruined her life is still walking the streets, working, living like a normal person—"

She broke down then, covering her face, and collapsed back into her chair, unable to go on.

The judge looked up, waiting for her to go on. It was impossible to tell from his expression whether he was disgusted or sympathetic. "Do you have anything else to say, Miss Nelson?" he asked.

Melissa couldn't answer. She only shook her head and tried to muffle her sobs.

Lynda stood up, obviously shaken that Melissa's speech hadn't been more eloquent, and that she hadn't been able to finish what she'd tried so hard to say. "No, You Honor. She doesn't."

"Anyone else?"

She hesitated, then turned and glanced back at the three people huddled together in the back. "Yes," she said finally. "One more. Detective Larry Millsaps."

Larry sat still for a moment, not sure he had heard correctly. Finally, prying his hands away from Melissa's mother, he got up and headed to the bench.

Because it was an informal hearing, he stood in front of the judge and began speaking without preamble. "Uh . . . Your Honor," he said, "I've seen a lot of criminals in my day. I deal with them day in and day out. Melissa Nelson is not a criminal. She's an innocent young woman who's been deeply wounded by her sister's rape and suicide. I saw the pictures after Sandy's rape, your honor. They were brutal. And I saw Pendergrast's rap sheet. The very reason he changed his name is that he had these other arrests on his record. Yes, there was a stigma. There always is when one is charged with rape—not once, but twice. Yes, this third charge was false, but if you had lived through what Melissa and her family have lived through, and knew that a rapist was still out on the streets, waiting to terrorize more women, your state of mind wouldn't be the best in the world, either. As a police officer, I can say that Melissa is no threat to anyone. But if you send her to prison—" His voice cracked, and he looked up at the judge, his eyes pleading. "—with people who have committed horrible crimes for which they deserve that kind of punishment, I'm just not sure she can handle it, Your Honor. I'm not sure she'll survive it."

He looked at Melissa, still lost in her pain and grief, then brought his eyes back to the judge. "Look at her, Your Honor. How do *you* think she'll fare in prison? Will any justice really be served by sending her there?"

Unable to think of anything other than getting down on his knees and begging, he uttered, "Thank you," and went back to his seat.

The judge put his glasses back on and began to study his notes again. He scribbled something, frowned, then looked back up at Melissa. Setting his pencil down, he steepled his hands in front of his face.

"Well, we have two drastically different stories from three different people. While I do understand the emotional nature of this case, and perhaps even the reasons behind her actions, I can't condone anyone's calling the police on someone they don't like, for something that that party may or may not have done years ago to someone else. I can't condone anyone sitting before a grand jury and lying. Miss Nelson, this man has not been convicted of a crime. Citizens cannot pin crimes on innocent people, no matter what they may think they deserve, and get away with it. There has to be a punishment for that. I think six months in the Pinellas County Correctional Facility for Women should be enough of an example to anyone else who ever thinks of doing such a thing."

Despite her mother's muffled scream and Melissa's guttural sob, he banged his gavel again.

CHAPTER THIRTY

Six months. The words took a moment to penetrate into Larry's mind and sink down into his heart.

Had the judge really given her six months in jail?

Melissa sat stiff, stunned, as the judge continued reading his decision. He heard her mother's muffled, strangled cry. Across the aisle, Pendergrast was laughing.

The rapist was free. Melissa was going to jail.

It didn't compute, wouldn't sink in, and Larry found himself coming to his feet as the bailiffs came to take her away. They weren't giving her time to say good-bye, or to break down and cry, or to prepare for where she was going. She looked quickly back at her parents, then at Lynda, her eyes brimming with apology and remorse. Then her wet eyes connected with Larry's.

It can't be right, his eyes told her. *It's not over!*

But they all knew it was over, as the bailiffs ushered her out of the room.

Stepping on the feet of the people next to him, Larry hurried out of the row, then ran out of the courtroom and around through the back door where she would come out. His breathing came too hard, and he felt light-headed, as if he might pass out. He leaned back against the wall, his mind racing as he tried to find something that made sense.

The rapist free . . . Melissa in jail . . .

A sheriff's car drove up and idled at the door, and in a moment, the door opened. The two bailiffs came out with Melissa between them.

Fortunately, he knew one of them. "Al, let me talk to her for a minute. Just for a minute. What would it hurt?"

His friend glanced around at the sheriff and the others, and they all shrugged. "All right, Larry, but just a minute."

Larry looked at her for a moment, aware of the people standing around them. She was struggling to hold back her tears, but her chin trembled with the effort. Finally, he pulled her into a smothering embrace. "It's okay, Larry," she whispered in a fragile, broken voice. "Really, it is. I expected this."

"But Melissa—"

Her face changed, and her eyes fixed on some point across the street. Larry followed her startled gaze to the man standing there alone, leaning against the building opposite them, grinning and rubbing her nose in his freedom.

Something exploded inside him, and he almost launched across the street with his hands poised to grab Pendergrast by the throat. But Melissa stopped him. "Watch him for me, Larry. Catch him on something, okay? Something real."

He turned back to her. "I promise," he whispered. "And I'll come visit you. First visiting day. I'll be there."

"No, don't," she said. "I don't want you to."

"Why not?"

"Because—I don't want you to see me that way. You don't owe me anything." The bailiffs ushered her toward the back door of the car.

"I'm coming anyway," he said. When she didn't answer, he looked around one of the bailiffs at her car door. "Did you hear me, Melissa? I'll be there!"

She slid in and they slammed the door, and she looked at him through the window. Tears streamed down her face as they got into the front. As the car drove away, she looked down at her hands.

When the car was out of sight, Larry started to cross the street.

Pendergrast was gone, but it felt as if the evil lingered in his wake.

"I'll get him for you, Melissa," Larry whispered, looking up and down the sidewalk for a sign of him. "If it's the last thing I ever do."

CHAPTER THIRTY-ONE

T he Pinellas County Correctional Facility for Women in Clearwater had been finished—after a flood of controversy over how much money the separate facility was costing the state—just six months before, not far from the jail that had housed both men and women for so long. Legislators had insisted that it was needed, due to the growing number of women being convicted of crimes. In her wildest dreams, Melissa had never guessed that it would be her home for six months.

The building still smelled like paint, and the floor down the long hall was polished, but she knew that that appearance of clean comfort was deceiving. Within these air-conditioned walls were other women who had committed crimes. Drug dealers, prostitutes, child abusers, thieves—the reports she'd read about the women imprisoned here had seemed like fantastic stories to her then, stories of dangerous women who'd surrendered to evil in their lives. Now Melissa was one of them.

The corrections officer who oriented her didn't care that hers had not been a violent crime, or that it had been designed to bring justice to someone who deserved it. To her, Melissa was only a number: 6324655. A faceless, nameless, colorless member of the inmate population, to be treated no differently from the women who'd been sent here for acts she couldn't even imagine.

Wearing her prison-issued orange jumpsuit with the words PINELLAS COUNTY CORRECTIONAL FACILITY in black block letters on the back, and carrying an armload of provisions— sheets, a thin pillow, a blanket, and the few things she had been allowed to bring from home in a small paper sack, which had been carefully searched—she followed the CO through the maze of locking doors and meandering hallways. They came to a wall of yellow iron bars. The guard pushed a few buttons, and the wall began to rise.

"You'll be in cellblock C," the big woman said, leading her into the cellblock. "We're putting you with Chloe."

"Chloe?"

"Yeah." The guard gave a cursory glance back at her. "If you start trouble, you'll be put in isolation. Trust me, you won't like it. If she—or anybody else for that matter—makes trouble with you, call a guard. Chloe likes to fight."

Melissa swallowed her terror and tried desperately to keep tears from filling her eyes. "Isn't there someone else, then?"

The woman seemed amused. "What are you looking for? A welcoming committee? Sorry, but our Welcome Wagon has four flat tires. Truth is, the other prisoners usually do harass the new ones, especially when they look as scared as you do."

With a loud bang that reverberated through Melissa's body and made her jump, the doors to cellblock C slammed shut behind them. "The cellblock doors are open certain hours during the mornings and at night, so people can get to their jobs in other parts of the facility. Most of the time, the cell doors are open, too, so inmates are allowed to go in and out of each other's cells. They're locked down at night, and if you want your cell locked during the day when you're in it, you can ask the CO. I wouldn't recommend locking Chloe out, though. She holds grudges."

Melissa followed her down a long hall with metal doors on either side, not at all like the cells with bars she had expected. Women she assumed were prisoners milled around the cellblock, smoking cigarettes and watching her make her way up the hallway.

"Most of the gals are working right now," the guard said. "They'll be back in a couple of hours. Some of them go early and get off early. Some of them play sick every day so they don't have to lift a finger. They get time added onto their sentence when they miss, but that doesn't matter to them, I guess."

Two women standing beside one of the cells turned to see the new addition to the block, and Melissa averted her eyes. Her arms were trembling, and she almost dropped her load. Stopping, she tried to get a better grip, but the CO looked back. "Hurry up, will you?"

She fell back into step behind the CO, breathing heavily and beginning to perspire. The guard stopped at a closed door, opened it, and peered in. A huge black woman who could have played linebacker for the Miami Dolphins lay on the lower bunk, and she turned to look at them as Melissa came in.

"Chloe, this is Melissa," the CO said brusquely. "She's your new cellmate."

"Hi," Melissa said, wishing the corners of her lips would stop trembling.

"I told you I don't want no cellmate."

"Well, you may have noticed that you don't call the shots around here, Chloe," the guard said. She pointed to the small table where Melissa could set her load, but Melissa only stood motionless, paralyzed.

"Oh, I've called some shots," Chloe smarted back. She gave Melissa the once-over, then sat up. "And you can't have the bottom bunk. This is my bunk."

"That's fine," Melissa whispered. "The top's fine." She turned back to the CO, her eyes beseeching her to reconsider and find her a smaller, more compatible cellmate, one who didn't terrify her.

But this was not a college dorm, and no one cared whether they got along or not.

The CO barked off a few final instructions that seemed to bounce around and echo in Melissa's head as she tried to take it all in—the bunk bed that was bolted to the floor, the small sink and toilet on the other side of a half wall, a wooden chair, two metal lockboxes. Beside the bed was a nightstand, also made of metal, with a small drawer. In one corner, Chloe had stacked some boxes that she used for shelves. Torn magazines lay crumpled on them, and a radio, and a little vase with some dead flowers.

"Well, do you?" the CO asked, breaking into her thoughts.

Melissa turned back to the woman. "Uh—beg your pardon?"

The woman smirked. "I asked if you had any questions."

"Uh . . ." She struggled to find some just to keep the CO from leaving her alone with Chloe, but her mind was drawing a blank. "No. I guess not."

The CO left, and Chloe lay back down, ignoring her. Melissa set her things down on the dirty floor, slowly, quietly, carefully, then turned back to Chloe. What did one say to one's prison cellmate? *What're you in for?*

Though it was a pressing question on her mind, she didn't feel free to ask it. It might make Chloe mad, and she might take time to show Melissa how she got her fighting reputation.

"So what're you in for?" the big woman barked.

Melissa tried to think. "Uh—perjury."

"Do *what*? You didn't shoot nobody? Didn't rob nobody? Didn't steal nothin'?"

"No."

"And they put you in *jail*?"

"That's right."

"Abomination!" the big woman said in a voice so gruff it made her jump. "They really are tryin' to fill up this joint, aren't they?"

She turned over then, as if to go to sleep, effectively dismissing Melissa.

Quietly, Melissa got her sheets, pillow, and blanket and threw them on top of the bed, then grabbing her bag, she climbed up the steps at the end of the bed and sat down on her bunk, pulling her knees to her chest and hugging them with her trembling arms.

Tears started to flow immediately, but she bit back her sobs. *Sandy, I can't believe this is happening . . .*

And then she looked up at the ceiling, beseeching the Savior who had seemed so forgiving just a few days earlier, when she had decided to confess, when that feeling of peace had flooded her spirit. Had he left her now? Could he even find her here?

If there was good for her in this, or for anyone, she couldn't think what it was just now. Quietly, she opened her bag and pulled out her Bible. It had been dusty when she'd found it under the seat of her car, where she'd left it the last time she'd been to church. She'd have plenty of time now to catch up for all the years that she hadn't been reading it.

She heard the noise of the cellblock door opening down the hall. Voices echoed up the hall, voices of women coming back from their jobs and heading for their cells. She glanced at the open door, wishing she could close it. But it would make noise, and that might

193

disturb Chloe, and she didn't want to have to deal with that just now. She didn't have the courage.

So she sat still, wiping her face and hunched like a little doll on her bunk, waiting for the next shoe to drop, for the next act in this nightmare she had written.

An alarm sounded when it was time to convene in the prison dining room. Melissa felt the bed shake as Chloe awakened and pulled herself up. As the woman stood, Melissa realized she had to be over six feet tall and weighed probably over 230 pounds.

Chloe gave her a cursory glance. "That's supper," she said.

Melissa glanced out the open door and saw the other women ambling by amid shouts, laughs, profane insults. "Uh . . . I'm not really hungry."

"So what you gon' do? Starve? Take it from me, honey. You gon' need your strength."

She felt nauseous at the thought of eating in this atmosphere. That would be all she needed, she thought, to throw up in front of everyone her first day here. If that wouldn't make her look vulnerable, she didn't know what would.

"Do I have to go?" she asked in a raspy voice. "I mean, is it required?"

"No, it ain't required. You can eat in your room, if you have something. But I don't see no food."

"Where—where are you supposed to get it?"

"Your family can bring it. Up to thirty-five pounds every two weeks. Or you can buy some things from the commissary, if you got money." Chloe went to the sink, bent over it, and tossed some water on her face. Drying it on her sleeve, she went on. "There's one hot plate per cellblock, and you got to stand in a long line for it. Ain't worth it, you ask me. I like my meals hot. You know, if you don't eat, you won't sleep tonight. You'll probably keep me up all night blubberin'."

It was true, Melissa realized. It was going to be hard enough to sleep tonight as it was. She hadn't eaten much in the last few days, and she would need her strength here.

Quietly acquiescing, she slid down from the bunk. Chloe stood a good head and shoulders taller, and the look in her eye revealed impatience and a low level of tolerance for Melissa's fragile state.

"So what'd you lie about?"

"What?"

"You said you were here for perjury."

"Oh. I kind of—I set someone up for a crime they didn't commit."

"Who was it? An old boyfriend? Dumped you, so you got him back?"

"No," she said. "It was someone who really had committed that crime earlier. He got off, and I just—I wanted him back in jail."

"Hmmm," Chloe said in that gruff voice. "Too bad you got caught."

"I didn't get caught," she said. "I confessed."

"Say *what?* You mean to tell me you in here because you confessed to somethin' you hadn't even been caught doin'?"

"Yeah, basically."

"Man, I thought I was dumb. How long you got?"

"Six months," she said.

"It'll be the longest six months of your life." She went to the doorway, then looked back, as if waiting.

Melissa looked beyond Chloe to the women streaming by. The looks in their eyes frightened her, and she wondered if they would be able to see her fear.

Chloe stepped out into the stream of women heading for the door, and suddenly Melissa felt even more vulnerable, even more afraid. Following, she stayed as close as she could to Chloe all the way to the dining room.

CHAPTER THIRTY-TWO

L arry didn't want to hear the doorbell ring that night. He didn't feel like company. He had sat alone in his apartment, with the shades drawn and the lights out, until dusk had fallen. Now it was almost dark in the apartment, but he didn't care.

The bell rang again, and he got up and headed slowly for the door. It was probably Tony, he thought, with some lame invitation to go get a pizza, trying to pick up Larry's spirits. But when he opened the door, Lynda and Jake stood there.

"We just wanted to make sure you're all right," Lynda said.

"Me?" he asked, turning his back on them and going back to his living room. They closed the door and followed him in. "It's Melissa who's not all right."

"She is, Larry," Lynda said. "I checked on her this afternoon. She's okay."

Tears came to his eyes, and he covered his face with his hand and plopped into his chair. Jake went to the couch and sat down, leaning his cane against the arm, but Lynda kept standing.

"Every time I picture her there, I just . . ."

"I know," Lynda whispered. "I'm so sorry. I did everything I could."

"I know, I know," Larry said, cutting her off. "Tony and I didn't help a whole lot. I keep going over and over the things I told the DOC, wondering if something I said tipped the scales, if I could have worded things differently. Maybe I could have said something better, different, at the sentencing. Maybe I didn't plead hard enough."

"You did the best you could, Larry. And as for the DOC, you didn't have a choice. You told them the truth. That's all Melissa wanted you to do. Nothing you said would have made that much difference."

He sighed, then leaned his elbows on his knees and looked down at his feet. "Sometimes it's just so hard to understand. I prayed and prayed, with all my heart. I felt God listening."

"He *was* listening."

"Then why did this happen?" he said through gritted teeth, getting to his feet. He walked to his window, pulled back the blinds, and looked down on the parking lot. The streetlights were on, making it seem even darker in the apartment, but he didn't care. "Why didn't God answer this prayer?"

Jake got up and went to stand behind Larry. With his hand on Larry's shoulder, he said, "I've asked that question myself, buddy. More than once. I'm not smart enough to answer it."

"I don't get it," Larry said. "Why wouldn't God intervene? What purpose could it possibly serve to have Melissa in jail?"

Jake's eyes misted. "I've never been to jail, Larry, but after the crash, when I lay flat on my back, not able to move from my waist down, that was as close to prison as I ever want to get. I lost my job, my friends, my looks . . ."

Larry glanced up at the scar on Jake's cheek. He hardly noticed it anymore.

"I asked over and over what purpose there could have been in that. For the life of me, I couldn't see any good in it. But there was a purpose, Larry. A big one."

"But she's in *jail*. There's *not* a purpose in that!" Larry cried, turning sharply away from Jake and marching to the darkest corner of the room.

Lynda and Jake said nothing. Finally, Larry shrank a little, as if the anger were draining out of him. He turned on the lamp and dropped back into his chair.

After a long silence he said, "I'm sorry, guys. I didn't mean to yell at you. It's just—you're the only ones here to yell at."

"Yell away," Lynda said softly. "It's okay."

He wiped his eyes, then looked at Jake. "I wish I could believe it'll all work out. That good will come of it. That there's a reason.

That it makes sense, somehow." He leaned back, studying the ceiling. "See, when I think about it, I do trust God. I do know that he's in control. It's just that sometimes it seems like things are so *out* of control. How can anything good come out of all this?"

"He's God," Lynda said. "He made order out of chaos. He created the universe. He also created Melissa, Larry. He'll take care of her."

Lynda saw Larry's Bible lying on a nearby shelf, picked it up, and flipped through it. "There's a verse in Psalms that I quote to myself, whenever I watch a battered wife go back to her husband, or whenever I have a client who winds up serving time. I didn't know this verse when I was going through all my trouble, but it's important to me now." She found the page, then handed the Bible to Larry. "There it is. Psalm 91. Read the whole chapter when you get time, but for now, just verses 11 and 12."

Larry looked down at the verses. "For he will command his angels concerning you to guard you in all your ways; they will lift you up in their hands, so that you will not strike your foot against a stone."

"That's what he'll do with Melissa, Larry," she whispered.

"Do you think so?" he asked, his pain arguing against this simple expression of faith.

"I know it. She's there because she decided to tell the truth. To right a wrong. God will honor that."

He studied the verses again, and slowly felt his tension and bitterness easing a bit, leaving him only bone tired. "Thanks," he whispered. "I'll hold onto that. I really don't have any choice."

They sat still for a moment, then finally, Lynda stood up. "Would you like to come over and watch a movie with us or something? I could make popcorn."

Larry shook his head. "No, thanks. I have something else I have to do. But I really appreciate you guys. You're good friends."

Lynda hugged him quickly, and then they were gone.

Quiet settled over the house. Returning to his seat, Larry read the whole psalm again, feeling the peace that it held. But behind that peace was a growing sense of guilt. Who was he to feel peace while Melissa was where she was? It was Melissa who deserved to feel peace, not him—not after the decisions he'd made.

He set his Bible back on the shelf, grabbed his keys, and headed out the door.

He hadn't lied to Lynda and Jake. He really did have plans. He was going to watch Pendergrast. As he had promised Melissa, he was going to catch him at something. And he didn't care if he had to give up sleep for the next six months to do it. Somehow, Pendergrast was going to pay.

With God's help—if he still had any right to expect God's help—Larry would be the one to *make* him pay.

CHAPTER THIRTY-THREE

The women spoke in low tones and sat where they were supposed to sit at dinner, unwilling to start trouble—and no wonder; guards were everywhere. Still, Melissa felt the eyes of some of the inmates on her, assessing her, testing her for that look of fear she knew she wore like a banner. Chloe sat next to her, saying little to those around her, just scarfing down her meal with a zest that Melissa had not seen in many others.

The food was bland but nutritious, so she ate. She thought back over the meals she'd eaten with Larry, when they had shared deep heart-to-hearts, with Melissa sharing parts of her truths with him and Larry probing for more. The memories of time wasted and time lost brought tears to her eyes, but she blinked them back, desperate not to let anyone here see her crying.

When she'd eaten all she could, she set her napkin back on the tray and waited to be told where to go next.

"They give you an assignment yet?" Chloe asked after she'd polished off her plate.

"Laundry," Melissa said.

"It's hot in there," Chloe said. "They got me in there, too."

Melissa looked over at her roommate. She was a brooding woman, and she still sounded gruff, angry, frightening. But she had made a stab at conversation; that was a hopeful sign.

"You watch TV? You can go to the TV room after dinner."

"No. I'll just stay in the room and read." She couldn't bring herself to call it a cell.

"Look," Chloe said, as if growing weary of the timid act. "Your best bet is to get a look at as much as you can this first day in. See what you're up against. Besides, if you stay in the cell by yourself, I can't promise you'll be safe."

"Well, I can lock it, can't I?"

Chloe grinned and breathed a laugh. "You *are* dumb. Girl, these doors lock from the outside—not the inside."

"Oh." She looked around, noted that more inmates had spotted her. A group across the room to her right were staring at her and whispering among themselves, and to her left others were wrenching their neck to see her. "Then I guess I'll go."

Chloe shook her head at her idiocy, and again Melissa stared down at her food, unable to make eye contact with any of the threatening eyes around her.

The TV room was a big room full of couches and game tables, and a television sat up high in the corner, in a metal box that kept anyone from vandalizing it. The biggest, most ominous inmates among them controlled the station selection, and the others sat around in clusters, talking.

Melissa watched two women get up as soon as they saw Chloe come in, and Chloe ambled over to the chairs they had abandoned and sat down, as if they were understood to be hers.

Melissa hung back at the door, trying not to attract any attention. But it was too late. Two of the women standing near her turned toward her, amused. "You new?"

"Yes," she said quietly.

"Hey, everybody!" one of them shouted. "Check this out!"

All eyes in the room turned to her, and Melissa shrank back against the wall.

"So what's your name, honey?" one of the women, with a pasty complexion and greasy red hair, asked.

"Melissa," she choked out.

"Melissa!" the redhead shouted. "Aw, ain't that pretty!"

"Look, I don't want any trouble." But that was the wrong thing to say. She watched as the COs turned their backs, allowing the harassment to continue, as if she somehow deserved it.

"She don't want no trouble!" the redhead said. "I'll bet a sweet thing like you never expected to end up here. Can't believe a jury would convict you, with that soft hair—" She grabbed a handful of Melissa's hair, but Melissa jerked back. "And them big eyes."

"It wasn't a jury," Melissa choked out.

"Not a jury? A judge then. Didn't you bat them eyes at him and tell him that you were just too delicate to be in here with all us criminal types? So what'd you do, anyway?"

Melissa didn't answer.

"Honey, I asked you a question," the redheaded woman asked, growing more agitated. "I don't sense a lot of respect from you. Didn't you hear what I asked?"

"She's in for child abuse, Red," one woman on the couch piped up. "I heard about her last week on the news. She left her children in the house, then burned it down."

"No, I didn't!" Melissa cried.

"I saw it, honey. That was you."

"Child abuse? Murder? Arson?" the redhead taunted. "No wonder even that soft blonde hair didn't save you."

Tears were coming to her eyes, despite her efforts to hold them back. "It's not true," she whispered. "Please."

Another woman grabbed a handful of her hair and jerked her head back so she was looking up at the ceiling. "Please what?"

"Let me go!" Melissa shouted through her teeth. "I haven't done anything to you!"

"We're just welcomin' you, honey," Red said. "Like we do all the girls." A round of laughter erupted over the room as others got up and started toward her.

"SHUT UP!" Chloe's voice cut like a chain saw through the room, and breath-held silence fell over them as the big woman rose to her full height. "Can't you see I'm tryin' to watch *Wheel of Fortune*?" she belted out. "Let her go so she'll shut up! I been listenin' to her whimperin' all day as it is!"

The inmate dropped her hair, and Melissa rubbed the roots where it had started to tear out of her scalp. She looked at Chloe, waiting for her wrath to fall.

The women scattered slowly, so as not to appear frightened by the big woman, but they left Melissa alone.

Melissa stood at the door a while longer, trying to catch her breath, trying not to cry, not knowing whether to go right or left. Finally, she sat down in an empty chair and fixed her eyes on the television, trying not to provoke anyone else, holding her hands clasped to keep their trembling from showing.

She hadn't expected God to protect her through Chloe, but it seemed he had. The next hurdle, she thought, was to stop being so terrified of her protector. Chloe had rescued her from the others, but she didn't know who would rescue her from Chloe. Maybe she could learn not to make Chloe mad, she thought. Maybe she'd be lucky enough not to be around when someone else did. Maybe she was just going to have to get used to living in abject fear.

Maybe not every day of her six months would pass as slowly as this first day was.

The noises of the jail kept Melissa awake that night, though Chloe had fallen asleep the moment her head hit the pillow. Melissa lay in her cell, staring at the ceiling, listening as doors opened and closed for reasons she didn't know and didn't want to know. Now and then, COs spoke to each other without lowering their voices, and the sounds of hard shoes clicked on the floor.

Somewhere, she heard the sound of someone crying, a sound that was sometimes audible, then muffled, then loud again. She wondered how many inmates lay awake as she was tonight, nursing broken hearts, missing family members, bitterly regretting their mistakes.

She wondered about the dead flowers Chloe kept in the vase on the cardboard shelf.

Her own tears couldn't be held back any longer, and she covered her mouth to keep from giving in to the despair. She didn't want anyone to hear her crying. She didn't want to incite the wrath of the guards, or of Chloe.

She wondered if Pendergrast was laughing at her, rejoicing at the way things had turned out. His crime against Sandy was still being played out, the ripples still rippling. He was still raping their family, and Melissa was one of the victims.

Bitterness swelled within her. Her hands trembling, she reached for the Bible that she'd put under her pillow and clutched it tightly against her chest, like a shield that would keep her from her wayward thoughts. There was someone in the world she hated, and before this ordeal was over, there might be many others.

She couldn't forgive—not yet. It was too hard.

Help me, Lord. Help me to do what I'm supposed to do.

Chloe's heavy breathing ceased for a moment at the gasping sound of her tears, and Melissa turned over and buried her face in her pillow.

"You cryin' up there, ain't you?" Chloe barked.

Melissa didn't answer.

"I told you I didn't want to hear no blubberin'."

"I'm sorry," she whispered. "I was trying to be quiet."

She waited, bracing herself, for Chloe to get up, but the woman didn't move.

"Least you ain't makin' all the racket that other one is. You'd think she lost her best friend. Probably killed her herself."

Melissa didn't answer.

"I find out who that is, she'll have a *reason* to cry tomorrow."

Melissa sat stone still, holding her breath to keep from agitating the big woman.

After a moment, Chloe's deep, heavy breathing returned.

She was asleep for now, and Melissa would do well to let her stay that way.

Lying as still as a log, and just as rigid, Melissa waited for the night to pass.

CHAPTER THIRTY-FOUR

Larry ate dinner in his car the next night. The minute he'd gotten off work, he had headed for Pendergrast's apartment complex. The man's Cherokee wasn't there, so he tried Pendergrast's office. The Cherokee was still sitting there on the gravel parking lot.

He parked behind a low-hanging willow tree and rolled down his window. A heat wave had come through, making temperatures hotter than usual for October, and now, as the sun went down, it seemed hotter than it had been all day. As he bit into the hot dog he'd brought with him, he tried to imagine what Melissa had eaten tonight. Was she still terrified? Was she able to eat at all?

His appetite left him, and he tossed the hot dog back into the bag it had come in and sipped on the drink that was now watery from melted ice.

Please Lord, let me catch him at something tonight.

It wouldn't get Melissa out of jail, but at least he would be able to see some justice being served.

He saw the front door to the office building open, and Pendergrast came out and got into his car.

Larry waited until Pendergrast was a block away and had turned right onto the main road before he cranked his Chevy. Staying back in traffic, he followed him across town to Highland Drive, a brand-new, just-paved road near the mall.

Pendergrast pulled into a site where a building was going up; men were still there working. Pendergrast got out, cut across the dirt, and shouted a few orders to the men around him.

Larry waited about twenty minutes for Pendergrast to go back to his car as the other construction workers split up and headed for their own cars. Larry let three trucks pull between him and Pendergrast, then followed them back to the main road. He trailed as Pendergrast went home, locked his car, and trotted up the steps to his apartment door.

Larry waited.

His cellular phone rang, startling him. He reached for it and clicked it on. "Hello?"

"I knew you were in your car." It was Tony, and Larry braced himself.

"Yeah? So?"

"Did you even go home?"

"I had things to do, okay?"

"Yeah, well, I just wanted to see if you'd want to go get a bite to eat."

"I've already eaten."

"Where are you, man?"

"What difference does it make?"

Pause. "You're at his place, aren't you? You're staking out Pendergrast."

Larry glanced up at the apartment. "I'm off duty. I don't have to account for my time."

"Look—let's go eat, and talk, and then you can go back there if you have to."

"No," Larry said. "I'm staying right here."

"He knows you're gonna be on him, Larry. He's not going to do anything this first couple of weeks. He'd be nuts."

"He *is* nuts."

"Man, you're asking for trouble. You're obsessing. You need to let yourself off the hook, man. Melissa doesn't expect this. She wouldn't want you to suffer just because she's in jail."

Larry rubbed his forehead. "Tony, if you don't have anything more constructive to say, I have to go."

"Look, just be careful, will you? I don't want to break in a new partner."

Larry clicked the phone and tossed it on the seat. Maybe Tony was right. Maybe nothing was going to happen tonight. But one of these days it would, and when it did, he would be there.

An hour or so later, Pendergrast came back out, got into his Cherokee, and pulled out. Larry followed, not optimistic that Pendergrast would commit a crime tonight, since Pendergrast seemed to do his prowling in the other car. Still, he followed him to the bar where they'd first arrested him.

He knew it was going to be a long wait as Pendergrast ambled in. To keep busy, he pulled Pendergrast's rap sheet and file out from under the seat. The two rapes they'd known about had happened very late at night, when the women were alone. It was clear that Pendergrast had known they would be alone, because both had been married, and in both cases he'd come on a night when their husbands had been working. Which meant he'd been watching them for some time. Then, on exactly the right night, he had broken into their homes and overpowered them.

Maybe there's someone he's watching now, he thought.

It was nearing midnight when Larry saw Pendergrast strutting out of the bar with a woman under his arm. Quickly, he cranked the car.

He watched as Pendergrast got behind the wheel and started the car, and thought how he'd love to slap a DUI charge on him. But that wouldn't help. That would keep him behind bars for about an hour.

He followed him to a neighborhood with small stucco houses, and hung back, several houses down with his lights off, as Pendergrast and the woman went inside.

Larry checked his watch. Maybe he should just go on home. This wasn't Pendergrast's typical MO. He didn't date the girls he raped. It was all done anonymously, cruelly, without any warning. He doubted this girl was in any danger.

On the other hand, he couldn't take the chance of leaving, just in case Pendergrast did hurt her.

He almost fell asleep several times, but shook himself awake, forcing himself to stay alert. It was almost three when Pendergrast came back out of the woman's house. He watched the man get into his car and drive off, and then he saw lights being turned off throughout the house. She was all right.

Cranking his car, he followed Pendergrast back to his apartment. It was nearing 3:30 when Pendergrast walked slowly back inside. Larry sat watching for a long moment, waiting for Pendergrast's lights to go off. When they did, at around four, he realized that the man was in for the night and wasn't likely to go out again.

Wearily, he headed for home and fell into his bed, praying that he'd be able to function the next day.

He fell into a troubled sleep, filled with dreams of Melissa being stalked and hounded by inmates and prison guards, being hurt or abused.

When the clock woke him at six A.M., he was soaked with sweat. He sat up abruptly. *God, help her*, he cried in his heart. *Please protect her.*

But the troubled feeling wouldn't leave him as he got ready for church—then changed his mind and decided to resume his stakeout instead. The obsessions he'd been accused of kept growing—more and more intense.

CHAPTER THIRTY-FIVE

Larry's eyes were getting tired as he wove between cars on the interstate, trying to keep up with Pendergrast in the inconspicuous gray Toyota. He had followed Pendergrast home from work again tonight—as he had last night—watched as he went into a fast-food restaurant for dinner, then home. And just after nine, when Pendergrast had come out again and gotten into the gray Toyota, Larry's adrenaline had begun pumping. Maybe this was what he'd been waiting for.

He almost gave up when he saw Pendergrast turn into the mall parking lot and park outside a Dillards store. Was he going shopping just before closing time?

But Pendergrast didn't get out. Larry parked a few rows away and reached for the infrared binoculars he'd laid on the seat next to him. From where he sat, he had a terrific view of Pendergrast. The man made no move to get out. He was waiting for someone. And it didn't seem likely that he'd have brought the gray Toyota to pick up a girlfriend.

Larry watched as several families spilled out of the store near closing time, and he saw the manager of Dillards lock all but one of the doors as they prepared to close.

Group by group, employees walked out, escorted by a security guard, then dispersed in the parking lot, heading to their separate cars.

Pendergrast sat straighter now. He brought something to his face—binoculars? A camera?

Yes, it was a camera, Larry realized. Probably the camera they'd gotten from his apartment. He had, of course, gotten all of his confiscated things back after the charges against him had been dropped. The camera had a long lens on the front, and Larry guessed it was a night lens. He was taking pictures of the employees coming out. Larry moved his binoculars in the direction Pendergrast was shooting, and saw a young woman who looked about twenty, with long, flowing blonde hair a lot like Melissa's. She passed Pendergrast's car, unaware that she was being watched, and got into her own, which was two spaces down from his. By reflex, Larry reached for his gun and waited for Pendergrast to make a move.

The girl got into her car. The lights came on as she cranked it. Pendergrast did nothing as she pulled out of her space. The moment she was far enough across the parking lot not to see him, Pendergrast's lights came on and he pulled out in the same direction.

Larry followed, keeping his lights off, as his mind reeled. Pendergrast had targeted that young woman as his next victim. Larry's heart pumped triple-time as he followed both cars out into the light stream of traffic.

The young woman took an unfortunate route home—Highland Drive, the newly paved road where new construction was in progress during the day. The same road where Pendergrast had construction projects under way. Now, at night, the road was deserted.

From this distance, Larry couldn't read her tag number. He reached for his night binoculars again and held them to his eyes. Mumbling the numbers back to himself, he pulled the pen out of his pocket and scribbled the numbers on his arm. Tomorrow he could look it up, if it wasn't too late.

He followed as they came to an area of new housing at the end of the long road, and she pulled into an apartment complex only a couple of months old. He held his breath, waiting to see if Pendergrast was going to make a move. Pendergrast, too, pulled into the complex but continued on around the parking area, appearing to be just one more resident looking for his parking space. Larry pulled in near the young woman's car and cut his engine, waiting.

She got out and locked her door. Clutching her purse, she started toward her apartment.

Pendergrast's car came slowly around now, and pulled into a space. Larry watched him as Pendergrast watched her go up the steps and around to her apartment door.

"What are you doing?" Larry whispered as Pendergrast just sat there. Was he going to wait until the lights went off, then break in somehow and attack her? Or was he just watching, planning, for some other time?

After about twenty minutes, Pendergrast cranked his car and pulled out again.

Larry sat still for a moment before following. Then, staying far enough back not to be seen, he followed him back across town to Pendergrast's apartments. Pendergrast parked the Toyota at the far end of the parking lot, locked it, and walked over to his Cherokee. He pulled out, and Larry followed him to the bar where they'd arrested him. Was he done with the woman for tonight? Was he going back later?

Not willing to take the chance of missing whatever Pendergrast was up to, and risking the life of that young woman in the process, Larry decided he could make it the rest of the night without falling asleep. He had to.

Pendergrast was getting ready to make a move, and when he did, Larry would be there to catch him.

Larry's eyes were raw by the time he made it to the police station the next day. Pendergrast hadn't made a move; instead, he'd left the bar well after midnight with some other woman, and Larry had sat outside that house, waiting for some sign that there was trouble inside. At nearly four A.M., Pendergrast had driven home.

"You look like death warmed over," Tony said as Larry approached his desk. "Have you been sleeping?"

"Not much." Larry sat down and flicked on his computer.

"Are you sick, man?"

"No," Larry said irritably. He punched in the tag number of the car he'd seen the young woman driving last night, and waited.

"What are you doing?"

"He's stalking somebody."

211

Tony pulled up a chair and straddled it, looking over Larry's shoulder to the computer screen. "Who is?"

"Pendergrast. I followed him last night. He's stalking a woman who works at the mall."

Tony looked confused. "What do you mean, he's stalking her?"

"He's been watching her. He knows when she gets off work, what kind of car she drives, where she lives. He follows her home, and watches her go in."

"Well—does *he* go in?"

"No. He waits and watches, and then he just drives away."

Tony thought that over. "Are you sure he's not just pulling your string? I mean, maybe he realizes you've been following him. Maybe he's just trying to give you something to chew on."

"He doesn't know I'm there."

"How do you know? You've been watching him every night. How do you know he doesn't see you?"

"Because I've been careful, okay?" The name came up on the screen, and Larry sat back in his chair. "Her name is Karen Anderson. She's twenty-one. That's her, all right."

"What are you planning, Larry?"

"To get the captain to put somebody on her twenty-four hours. Maybe warn her what's going on."

"Larry, we can't spare that kind of man-hours. We have work to do."

Larry banged his fist on the desk and swiveled around in his chair. "That *is* our work, man! Keeping a woman from getting raped is just as much a part of our job as it is to clean up the mess afterward. Personally, I'd rather do it before."

Tony backed away slightly and lowered his voice. "But look at the logic, Larry. We know at least a dozen dangerous guys out there right now who are likely to commit a crime at any given time. It doesn't mean we can follow them around every minute of the day just to catch them at it."

"Then this whole system is twisted! If we can't prevent crimes, we might as well not even be here!"

Tony got up. "Look at you, Larry," he said, an edge of anger in his voice. "You're going to drop from exhaustion, and nothing's going to be accomplished. As a matter of fact, you'll probably make some terrible mistake and get yourself killed, just because you're not alert."

"I'm plenty alert."

"Oh, yeah? Your eyes look as bloodshot as a drunk's on Monday morning. And you haven't shaved."

Larry rubbed his jaw. He'd forgotten. "I'm growing a beard."

"In honor of Melissa? Have you taken a vow of self-deprivation until she serves her time?"

Ignoring him, Larry got up and kicked his chair out of his way. "I'm going to talk to the captain," he said.

Tony gave the chair a kick of his own as he went back to his desk.

Sam Richter was a no-nonsense captain who hated wasted time more than anything else in the world. He hated meetings and conferences and telephone calls that took him away from his work. Today, he was in a particularly bad mood because of a frustrating new case. And he was in no mood to listen to Larry's pleas to go off on some wild goose chase to get revenge for his convict girlfriend. The thought thoroughly disgusted him.

"Come on, Captain. I know he's about to strike. I have the name of the victim. We need to put a twenty-four-hour watch on her."

Sam looked at the ceiling, as if trying to find some patience there. "Millsaps, tell me something. When's the last time you slept? Or shaved, for that matter? Or took a bath?"

Larry thought of pleading the fifth, but instead he chose to remain silent.

"That's what I thought. It hasn't been recent." He leaned forward on his desk, his big hand propping up his chin. "Millsaps, I'm going to tell you this one time. Leave that man alone. You've caused him enough trouble. If you keep at it, you're going to get this police department slapped with another lawsuit, and I'm not in the mood to negotiate with that ambulance-chaser of a lawyer again."

"But Captain, you can't ignore what I saw! He's going to strike—I know he is. We can keep another girl from being raped."

"*Another* girl?" Sam asked on a laugh. "Millsaps, there wasn't a *first* rape. At least, not one that we can prove."

Larry burst out of his seat. "You're not buying into that innocence story, are you? How many times have you seen a suspect admit to what he's done? He's pretending he's innocent!"

"He may not be pretending." The captain stood up dismissively and took a file over to his file cabinet. "Millsaps, I know your girlfriend's going to jail really knocked you for a loop. Everybody in the precinct's talking about it."

Larry rolled his eyes and peered out the window to all the activity beyond it. "I should have known."

"But I don't have time to coddle you, man. I don't have any man-hours to devote to making you feel better. About fifteen minutes ago a jogger discovered a body washed up on Peretta Beach, and it turns out she was one of those two seventeen-year-old runaways from St. Clair. Now, I only have two detectives. You and Danks. I need you working on this, not going off on some hunch."

Larry couldn't accept that. "We can do both, Captain. Work on both cases. We can follow the girl, and—"

The captain leaned over his desk. "What part of 'no' don't you understand, Millsaps?"

Larry slapped at the chair he'd been sitting in, knocking it over.

The captain straightened with a look of quiet rage in his eye. "One more word—one more outburst—one more *anything* from you, Millsaps, and you're on suspension. Matter of fact, I just might put you on it, anyway. You're losing your edge, Detective. You're cracking up. I've never seen you behave this way in all the years I've known you. If you come in here like this tomorrow, you can look forward to a long vacation."

Not honoring that with a reply, Larry turned and slammed out of the office. As he bolted across the room, Tony looked up. "Hey, Larry. Wait!"

Larry didn't answer. He fled from the building as fast as he could.

CHAPTER THIRTY-SIX

Though the prison was air-conditioned, the huge room where they worked on the laundry was sweltering. Tiny vents at the top of the big warehouselike room blew cool air in, but the heat from the irons and the dryers and the steam from the washing machines all filled the room with a humid heat.

Melissa had been there only an hour, and already her hair was soaked with perspiration. Her clothes were sopping wet and sticking to her, and she began to feel dizzy, as if she might faint from the heat.

Behind her, women cursed at each other, but guards who had the misfortune of being assigned to this location didn't bat an eye. They were used to the foul moods and foul mouths of the women who worked here day after day.

She grabbed the next jumpsuit in her basket, laid it on the ironing board, and quickly reached for the iron. Her fingers brushed the hot metal, scalding her flesh, and she jumped back, knocking the iron over.

A CO was at her side in an instant, not to help, but to warn her against wasting time.

Quickly, she picked the iron back up, fighting back the tears in her eyes as her skin began to blister.

Where was the peace she was supposed to feel? Where was the comfort that would chase away the paralyzing, stomach-knotting fear? All she felt was the terror of messing up, the horror of making the wrong person mad, the fear of getting killed in this abyss where they had sent her to teach her not to lie.

She looked across the room and saw her big roommate, Chloe, folding towels with a slow, methodical rhythm. Each night, she lay awake, listening to the rhythm of Chloe's breathing, waiting for the woman to snap and decide that she was angry enough at Melissa to attack her.

But she hadn't. Chloe was a mystery. One minute, she was leering at Melissa as if she could snap her in two, and the next she was leering at the others who looked as if they might like to try. She couldn't decide if the woman was tormentor or protector.

She longed for ice to put on the burn to relieve the pain, but she kept working. She tried to shift her mind away from the pain by wondering where Larry was, whether he was working today, whether he would be coming to visit tomorrow.

She wouldn't be crushed if he didn't come, she told herself. It was best if he didn't. She didn't want him to see her this way.

Her parents would come, and that would probably be all the emotional upheaval she could stand for one day. That she had ever put them in the position of having to visit their child in prison gave her such shame that she wanted to die.

Her mind counted the hours she had been here already. Five days. That meant there were only 177 days to go. 4,248 hours. 254,880 minutes.

Only three days before she'd earn her first visitation privileges.

She needed something more constructive to occupy her mind and wished that she had memorized Scripture so that she could call on it now when she felt such despair. Maybe that's what she would start doing during her free time in her cell. Maybe it would get her mind off Chloe's bad moods—and her fears that the next moment she might explode like a ticking bomb.

CHAPTER THIRTY-SEVEN

The back door to his church was open, as it always was during the week, and Larry stepped into the big corridor, avoiding the choir director and minister of education who were conversing in the hall just outside their offices. Hurrying, he made his way to the small private prayer room at the back of the building and slipped inside.

It was dark, except for two dim little bulbs at the front of the room. There were four pews, and he slipped into the back one and looked at the small podium on which a big Bible lay open. His sister had gotten married here—it had been a quiet wedding, with just the families in attendance. Katie was shy, and she hadn't wanted a big production made out of something she considered so personal.

That had been a joyous occasion, an occasion when Larry had felt the Holy Spirit's presence so keenly that he'd felt he could reach out and touch his Savior. Now, it seemed like ages since he'd felt that.

He sank into the pew, covering his face, letting out the deep, dark misery on his heart. "Everything's out of control," he whispered to his Creator. "I can't help. I can't change anything. And now I can't even come to you."

The barren loneliness in those words hit him harder than anything else had that day, and he wept into his hands, desperate for some word that would somehow restore him. But there was a wall there—between him and God—a wall he had constructed himself. And he had made no move to break it down. Like Melissa, he'd decided that he wasn't worthy, that his own choices had rendered him unacceptable in God's eyes.

"I was going to lie for her," he whispered, propping his elbows on his knees and looking down at his feet. "You took it out of my hands. I didn't have to do it. But I would have. And I'm just as guilty as if I had."

He wondered whether he'd have felt repentant and remorseful if Melissa hadn't come forward and if he'd gone through with his plan to cover for her—

Yes, he thought unequivocally. He had been miserable about the choice even before he'd made it. It would have eaten at him, just as it did now. That was God's curse—as well as God's blessing.

He looked up at the ceiling, as if he could see God sitting there, judging him. "I don't even know what to say," he cried. "I want to pray for her, plead with you to change things somehow, to get her out of jail, to put Pendergrast away—but how can you hear my prayers when I've turned away?"

He leaned his arms on the pew in front of him and rested his head on them. "Nothing makes sense, Lord. He's going to do it again. To another innocent girl. And it's Melissa in jail instead of him. Help me to understand!"

A verse like an admonition came into his mind:

You do not have in mind the things of God, but the things of men.

He looked up, his face wet and twisted, and wondered why that verse, of all others, had spoken to him just now. It couldn't work to God's glory, he thought, for a beautiful, sweet, broken woman to be in jail. Or for Pendergrast to ruin another life. Those couldn't be "things of God."

Again, the verse played like a chant through his mind, and finally, he broke down and got to his knees. Maybe that *was* God's answer—that Larry *didn't* understand it, and that in fact it wasn't up to him to understand. Who was he to question the mind of God?

Suddenly, an overwhelming remorse fell over him, so deep and heavy that it almost flattened him. He had done exactly as Melissa had done. He had trusted his own solutions rather than God's. He had taken things out of his Father's hands, and with his own limited vision, had decided how things should go. "Please forgive me, Lord. Forgive me for not trusting you. Forgive me for making a decision to lie and cheat, for turning away."

He wept until he was exhausted. Finally, he got up again and sat on the pew, listening, waiting, hearing. His eyes fell on the open Bible, and he slowly got up and went toward it.

The book was open to Luke 22. Aloud, in a trembling voice, he read Jesus' words.

"Simon, Simon, Satan has asked to sift you as wheat. But I have prayed for you, Simon, that your faith may not fail. And when you have turned back, strengthen your brothers."

But he replied, "Lord, I am ready to go with you to prison and to death."

Jesus answered, "I tell you, Peter, before the rooster crows today, you will deny three times that you know me."

Jesus had known that Peter would turn away, that he would lie, and cheat, and run. And even knowing that, he had assured him that his relationship with God would not be ruined. *When* you turn back, Jesus had said. He had known he would. Just as he had known Larry would.

Larry felt that same forgiveness washing over him, cleansing him, filling him with the strength he would need to get through the days ahead. They were no worse than Peter's future had been—no more frightening, no more uncertain. But this was *his* future . . . and Melissa's. And he would need God to get him through it.

He sat back down, amazed and awestruck at the way the Lord had ministered to him, even when he hadn't deserved it—but then he realized that he had *never* deserved it. That was the beauty of grace. God was not dwelling on his past sin. God was looking ahead to how he wanted to use Larry.

"Strengthen your brothers."

Melissa would need strengthening. And he would be there for her.

"Peace I leave with you; my peace I give you. I do not give to you as the world gives. Do not let your hearts be troubled and do not be afraid."

More Scripture he'd memorized, never realizing how much he would need it one day. Now it came to him like an old friend, holding his hand, propping him up.

He sat there for a while longer, in his own private Gethsemane, soaking in the peace of God's love and forgiveness and hope.

And knowing that whatever was to happen in the next few hours and days, it was all in the hands of the Almighty God.

An hour later, as Larry and Tony drove in silence in their unmarked car to the beach where the runaway's body had washed up, Tony looked at him. "I took it from the way you burst out of the building a little while ago that the captain nixed your idea."

"He said what you said. Not enough manpower."

"I figured."

"So meanwhile, another girl is going to end up a victim before we act."

"Maybe not."

Larry was bone tired and didn't feel like arguing. But he couldn't let that go. "He's a rapist, Tony. We know it. And now he's stalking another woman. How long before we realize what's going on? What'll it take? Why is everybody so dead set on proving that Pendergrast is a saint?"

"History," Tony said. "We thought he'd done something before, and it turned out he didn't. Nobody else wants egg on their face." Tony looked over at his friend, as if deciding whether to say what was on his mind. "Larry, there are people on the force who think you're losing your edge. They think you snapped when Melissa went to jail. They don't give a lot of credence to your ideas right now."

Larry sat still for a moment, letting it all sink in. Too emotionally exhausted to fight back, he said, "I've been on this force for twelve years, Tony. I've always done my job with a clear head and all the energy and commitment I could give it."

"We know that, Larry. But look at you. You haven't shaved in days, you haven't slept, you're probably not even eating—it's hard to put a lot of stock in what you say when you look like you're about to go over the edge."

"Then ride with me," Larry entreated. "Ride with me tonight, after we're off duty. You'll see. I'll show you."

"Larry, you saw him stake her out once. That doesn't mean he does it every night."

"He might," Larry said. "Ride with me. Just come once and you'll see."

"Man, I need my sleep. So do you."

"All right. Just until the mall closes. Just give me that long, and I'll take you home."

"So what do you hope to accomplish? I mean, even if I come, and he stalks her tonight—"

"Back me up with the captain. Tell him I'm not losing it. Talk him into putting a tail on the girl."

Tony sighed. "I don't even know if he'd listen to me."

"That's my problem. Just come with me. Let me show you."

Tony moaned. "But it's Friday night, man. I have a date."

"Cancel it. Look at the irony here, Tony. We're heading out to the beach to investigate this girl's death—and at the same time, *another* girl's life is in danger, and we won't do anything to stop it."

The look in Larry's eyes was so haunted, so weary, so determined, that Tony found himself agreeing.

"No matter what we find, the girl on the beach is dead. We're not going to bring her back. But what if we had seen somebody preparing to kill her before she died? What if we could have stopped it? Would we have turned our heads and gone on with our other cases?"

Tony thought that over for a long moment. "All right, Larry," he said finally. "But just tonight. And that's only if we're finished with the work on this case by then. After the news reports on this girl's death come out, we might get some call-in leads on the girl who ran away with her. But if we don't have any strong leads on this case, I'll go with you."

The girl who'd been found on the beach was a young blonde who had apparently been raped and beaten to death before she'd been dumped into the Gulf. Larry and Tony hadn't spent much time at the site where she'd washed up; there was little evidence there to collect. Instead, they spent the afternoon talking to her shocked family members and friends. Her best friend, Lisa, who had run away with her and still hadn't been located, had been known to abuse drugs with her. The coroner said that the girl may have been dead for two weeks.

The trail of her killer was cold, and Larry suspected that it would take them out of their jurisdiction. She had probably been thrown in from a boat somewhere out at sea, and it had probably taken several days for her to wash up. They had already spent entire days searching for leads on the girls' whereabouts, and Larry suspected that they would have just as much trouble piecing together the facts surrounding her death.

Since they had no leads, and little information about what had happened to the girls since their disappearance, Tony agreed to ride with Larry that night.

They followed Pendergrast home from work, then ate their own cold burgers in the car, waiting for him to come back out. "I thought of going into the mall and finding her," Larry said. "Telling her to be on her guard."

"That would be a mistake at this point, Larry. You can't alert every girl Pendergrast looks at. The man has never been convicted of anything. If you start going around telling people to look out for this guy because he's a rapist and he's after them, you'll wind up losing your job."

The door to Pendergrast's apartment opened, and he came out into the darkness and headed quietly down the steps.

"He's going to the Toyota," Larry said quietly. "He thinks he's covering his tracks with his Cherokee parked at home."

He cranked the engine, and pulled out without turning on the lights. Across the parking lot, they saw the lights come on in the gray Toyota, and Pendergrast pulled out.

"What do you think?" Larry asked, pulling into traffic several cars behind him. "You want to go to the mall?"

Tony was silent as they followed. "Isn't it a little early? The mall doesn't close for another hour."

"I don't know. Let's see."

"He's turning."

"Going to the mall," Larry said victoriously.

They followed him down the streets that would take them to the mall, and Larry pointed to the Dillards store. "He'll go there," he said. "Watch him."

They watched as he pulled into a parking space not far from the Dillards entrance. Larry and Tony pulled in several aisles over.

"Now what?" Tony asked. "Does he just sit there?"

"Did last night. Just sat there watching and waiting."

Tony absorbed it for a moment. "Maybe it's not just her he's after. Maybe he's just waiting for anybody who looks vulnerable."

"Maybe," Larry said. "He was taking pictures. Looked like he had some kind of night lens on his camera."

"He took pictures of her?"

Larry nodded.

"Hmmm." The light came on in Pendergrast's car, and Tony leaned forward. "Is he getting out?"

"Looks like it." Larry grabbed the handle of his car door. "He's going in. I'll follow him. You stay here in case I lose him and he comes back out."

Tony nodded, and Larry got out and quietly mashed the door shut behind him. He walked several yards behind Pendergrast, several rows over, and waited to let him get inside before he made it to the door.

The lights of the department store assaulted him as he stepped inside, and he looked around to find Pendergrast. He was up ahead, walking through the cosmetics section.

Larry skirted the area, then rode the escalator upstairs. As soon as he got off, he went around to the rail that looked down on the cosmetics area in the center of the store. From here he had a perfect view, and Pendergrast wasn't likely to look up and see him.

He watched as Pendergrast seemed to be studying the men's cologne. After a moment, the girl he'd followed home last night finished with her customer and waited on him.

She was pretty, Larry thought, and younger than she'd seemed last night. She looked just the way Pendergrast liked them: blonde, small, delicate—like Melissa and Sandy.

Larry's stomach tightened into a knot as Pendergrast leaned on the counter, with that charming, drop-your-guard grin that was so deceiving. She was enjoying him, he thought. She was laughing at his flirtations.

After a moment, he paid for the cologne and, with one last comment that made her laugh again, he sauntered away.

What is he doing? Larry asked himself as he watched Pendergrast head back out the door. Did he ask her out? Was this whole thing nothing more than a man getting interested in a woman and pursuing her?

He waited until Pendergrast was gone, then rode the escalator back down and went to the same counter. He saw the display of men's cologne that Pendergrast had purchased and picked up a bottle, himself.

"May I help you?"

He knew by the information in the computer about her, based on her car registration, that she was only twenty. She looked even younger. "Yeah, I was just trying to decide if I wanted this. That guy who was here a minute ago, he bought some, didn't he?"

She smiled. "Yeah. He did."

"Is he a regular customer?"

She shrugged. "I've never seen him before, but he said the scent caught his attention. I tried to interest him in the bath products and shaving cream, too. I'll bet he comes back."

"Why?"

"They usually do. They get one product and they fall in love with it. Or they get such a response from their girlfriends that they can't help wanting all the rest."

Larry smiled. "Do you get many of them hassling you for dates?"

She giggled. "Occupational hazard when you sell men's cosmetics. Here, you want to try some?"

She sprayed the cologne on his arm, rubbed it in, then offered him the back of his wrist to smell.

He nodded. "I like it. But I don't generally wear cologne."

"Your girl will like it."

His grin faded slightly. "She likes me without it."

"Then buy *her* some. I sell women's cologne, too. Over here. You can try some of it—"

He held up his hand to stem her sales pitch, and leaned on the counter. "No, I don't need any today. But just tell me one thing. That guy who was here. Did he ask you out?"

She looked confused at the question. "No. Why?"

"I was just curious. He looked a little old for you."

She was irritated now. "I really don't think that is any of your business. Now, if you'll excuse me, I'm a little busy."

As she walked to the other side of the counter, he thought about telling her that the man who'd just bought cologne from her was a known rapist, that he was stalking her, trying to build trust, but that she couldn't trust him. The phone rang, and as she answered it, Tony's cautions raced through his mind. He couldn't panic her now. Not without more cause.

Sighing, he headed for a different entrance from the one he'd used coming in, and circled through the dark parking lot back to the car, praying Pendergrast would be watching the doors he was closest to and not see him.

The light didn't come on when he opened the door. The mechanics at the precinct had long ago wired his car to keep that from happening. He slid into the driver's seat.

"Where have you been, man?" Tony asked. "He came out ten minutes ago."

"Talking to the girl."

"Oh, no. You didn't."

"He bought something from her. Didn't ask her out, though. He's still sitting there?"

"Yeah. Getting close to closing time. Larry, you didn't tell her who you are, or who he is, did you?"

"Nope."

Tony breathed a sigh of relief.

"We just have to watch," Larry said. "Get a little more to go on. He's trying to establish her trust. Maybe so she'll go with him later."

"But that isn't his normal MO, is it? I mean, he didn't attack women who knew him. He uses the element of surprise, breaks into their homes—"

"Those are just the ones we know about. Besides, they identified him, didn't they? Maybe they had seen him before."

Tony grew quiet.

Customers began leaving, going to their cars, as a security car patrolled the parking lot.

They waited quietly for the employees to scatter.

"Here she comes," Larry said as the young woman came out of the building, along with several other women and a security guard. "Funny how they all have such a sense of security being

225

with that guard, but the minute they pull out of the parking lot they're on their own."

"She has us," Tony said.

"Yeah. Tonight she does."

They watched her car start up, and just as Larry had expected, Pendergrast's lights came on, too. "Time to go," Larry said.

Keeping his lights off, Larry waited until she had pulled to the parking lot's exit. Pendergrast followed.

As they drove down the deserted street, Tony shook his head. "Unfortunate route home."

"Tell me about it. 'Course it depends on your perspective. From his, it's the perfect route."

After a few minutes, they reached the end of the road and she turned into her parking lot. Pendergrast followed, but Larry didn't pull in. This time, he stayed way back, on the side of the street, watching.

Tony brought his infrared binoculars to his eyes and watched her trot up to her apartment. Pendergrast stayed in his car, watching.

Her light was on for several minutes when Pendergrast pulled out of the parking lot and headed back the way he had come.

Larry's heart sank.

"Guess he's not doing anything tonight," Tony said.

"No. He's not ready yet. But I don't think he'll wait a whole lot longer."

Larry started the car but headed in the opposite direction from Pendergrast.

"Where we going?" Tony asked.

"Home," Larry said. "That was the deal. After the mall closes, I take you home."

Tony was quiet for a moment. "You're coming back, aren't you?"

Larry didn't answer.

"Larry, are you gonna stay up all night again watching him?"

"What do you want me to do, Tony? He raped Sandy at three A.M. What if I go home and get some sleep in my nice warm bed, and tomorrow morning the headline in the paper is that a nice, young, innocent blonde woman was raped by an unknown assailant during the night."

"Larry, you can't stay up all night and work all day."

"Then back me up on this," Larry said. "Tell the captain we need to be on this case for a while—then we can just work nights. Tell him what we saw tonight. Tell him I'm not crazy."

Tony sighed. "I'll try. But with this other case—"

"There's no case more important than this one," he said. "Not to me. There's a rapist walking the streets of St. Clair. You tell me what's more important."

Tony didn't answer.

CHAPTER THIRTY-EIGHT

T he captain didn't come in the next day; he had meetings with the mayor all day long. Larry found himself torn between hurrying through his other cases to get back to Pendergrast and haunting City Hall, hoping to run into the captain. Giving up, he resolved to sacrifice another night's sleep to follow Pendergrast, just in case. Tony, afraid that Larry was about to reach the point of exhaustion, agreed to keep watch with him.

Pendergrast was getting bolder. Tonight, as Larry and Tony watched from across the dark mall parking lot, Pendergrast went into Dillards again. This time they both followed, watching him from two separate vantage points in the department store.

Pendergrast didn't go near the young blonde woman; instead, he watched her from a distance across the store. His fascination with her was clear. He watched her wait on customers, watched her clean the counter, watched her restock merchandise.

When she took a break and walked out into the mall, Pendergrast followed her, with Larry not far behind. She went to the food court and bought some French fries and a drink, then joined some friends at one of the tables. Pendergrast blended into the crowd at one of the vendors, continuing to watch her.

Tonight, Larry thought. *He's going to do something tonight.*

One by one, her friends left to go back to their jobs, leaving the woman alone at the table, and Larry held his breath, waiting, wondering if Pendergrast would approach her now. But he didn't. It wasn't his style. He had shown himself to her only once, so that he would be familiar to her, but not recognizable. He probably didn't want to be identified later.

Two women had identified him already. He had probably learned from those mistakes.

Finally, she threw away her bags and her drink and headed into the ladies' rest room.

Pendergrast followed.

The long hall leading to the rest rooms was dimly lit. Larry had long been aware of it because so many crimes had happened right there, and he had once tried to convince the management to either put an armed guard there or else to close the facility altogether and put a rest room out near the mainstream of mall traffic. But so far they hadn't listened.

Now, he felt helpless as Pendergrast gave her a head start to reach the ladies' room around the corner of the long hall, then started down it himself. Larry couldn't follow without being seen. All he could do was wait, and listen, and pray.

Five minutes later, he saw the woman coming back up the hall. Breathing a sigh of relief, Larry backed into the crowd, becoming invisible. After a few seconds, Pendergrast came back up the hall, his eyes intense as he followed her all the way back to her store. When she was behind her counter again, he headed back to his car.

Tony was already in the car when Larry made his way back. "See anything?" Tony asked.

Larry reached for his infrared binoculars. "He followed her to the bathroom. I thought he was going to act then, but he didn't."

"He's getting hungry," Tony said. "No question. Something's about to happen."

"Poor girl is walking right into this." Larry watched as Pendergrast settled back in his seat, watching the door. "So what did you see?"

Tony shrugged. "Same thing you did. When I saw you following them out of the store, though, I figured you had it under control. So I took the opportunity to take a look in that car of his. The door wasn't locked."

Larry dropped the binoculars and looked at him. "Find anything?"

"Nothing in the front. But when I clicked the release on the trunk, it came open. I found a shovel and a jumbo-sized garbage bag."

Larry's face went pale.

"Doesn't mean anything," Tony went on. "He could have been taking them to clean up a construction site or something. Just because it was big enough to put a body in—"

"You think he's a killer?" Larry asked.

Tony shook his head. "I didn't say that. We can't jump to conclusions."

But Larry already had. "Tony, we know that he's got an obsession. We know he's raped twice before, and my bet is that he's done it more than that. We don't know how many times, or how bad. He almost killed Melissa's sister. Could be that he's stopped someone from talking before." He brought the binoculars back to his eyes. "He broke into Melissa's apartment, wrote on her mirror, hid in her attic. He was probably going to kill her, too."

Tony peered toward the man sitting so inconspicuously in his car. "Yeah, well, you should probably be glad she's locked up. She's probably in the only place she could be safe from him. Hey, if somebody set me up for something I didn't do, I'd want to get even. Put that revenge in the mind of a man who's a maniac already, and you don't know what he's capable of."

"Then you're admitting it," Larry said. "He's a maniac."

Tony didn't answer, but he didn't need to. Larry knew Tony was convinced.

"As it stands," Larry whispered, "he's just going along with business as usual. Setting up his target, moving in for the kill ..."

"Well, if you're right, he won't get away with it this time." Tony looked at his watch. "Mall closes in an hour."

They waited, watching, as Pendergrast waited, watching.

An hour later, when the employees began to come out, they saw Karen Anderson among them. This time, however, she wasn't alone as she separated from the group and headed for her car. There was a man with her. They watched as she got into her car, and the man got in on the other side.

"She's giving this guy a ride home," Tony said, cranking the car but leaving the lights off. "What's Pendergrast doing?"

"He's cranking up," Larry said, watching him through the binoculars. "He's going to follow, anyway."

They followed quietly as she took her usual route home. Pendergrast drove about a quarter of a mile behind her, and Larry and Tony, with their lights still off, followed a good distance behind him. When they reached her apartments, they parked on the street again. The man got out with her, and the two of them headed up to her apartment.

Pendergrast didn't wait. As if angry, he sped back out of the parking lot and headed back up the way they had come, past the construction sites. Larry and Tony struggled to keep him in their view as they turned the car around and followed. Halfway up Highland Drive, Pendergrast turned onto a dirt road and disappeared among the trees. Tony stepped on the brakes.

"Where's he going? Should I follow him?"

"No. We don't know where that road goes. Besides, there's only room for one car. If he turns around and comes back, he'll see us. Let's just wait."

So they waited, holding their breath, for Pendergrast to return. After about twenty minutes, he did.

They followed him back to his apartment. When his lights went off after twenty minutes, they assumed that he'd gone to bed. Quickly they drove back to the dirt road down which he had disappeared earlier. Tony started to turn the car into the little dirt road, but Larry stopped him. "Not a good idea," he said. "Let's park and walk. If he sees our tire tracks tomorrow, he'll know someone's on to him."

Tony pulled the car to the side of the road. They got out and hiked up the long, dirt road, shining their flashlights as they went, not knowing what they were looking for, but hoping they'd know when they saw it. They followed the tiny, broken road all the way to the end, about a mile into the woods, then around a curve and further into the trees.

"Do you think this is where he was going to take her?" Tony asked.

Tony nodded. "Has to be. But it's too dark to see anything tonight. We'll have to come back tomorrow when the sun comes up."

Larry agreed. "Even if we don't find anything, at least we can get familiar with it in case we have to come this way again." He gave Tony a pensive look. "It won't be much longer now," he whispered. "He's ready. I'm just worried about the girl."

"Well, we could tell her and stop the whole thing. She could quit her job, never go home alone again, move. It would divert this attack, all right, but it wouldn't stop him from the next one."

"I want to get him," Larry whispered. "I want to get him for good."

"Then this is the only way. She'll be traumatized and terrified, but she'll be alive. We won't let him hurt her."

Larry thought about that for a long moment. "I just wish I could be sure of that."

CHAPTER THIRTY-NINE

I t was nearly nine in the morning by the time Tony and Larry made it back to the dirt road they had seen Pendergrast turn down the night before. They had watched his apartment for most of the night, then gone home for a little sleep before getting up and getting started again. Today, fatigued but determined, they made sure that Pendergrast was engaged at a construction site in another area before they checked out the road.

In the daylight, Highland Drive looked less threatening. Construction was going up in various places along the road, and the curb was lined with the trucks of men working. But the dirt road to which they'd followed Pendergrast last night was at least half a mile from the nearest construction site.

Again, they left the car on the street and followed the road on foot. After walking for twenty minutes or so, Tony asked, "How far do you think we've come?"

"A mile, at least," Larry said. "I didn't even know the woods back here were this thick. Where do you think it goes?"

"Nowhere," Tony said. "The next road is close to the interstate, but that's several miles from here. Listen." He slowed his step. "Do you hear that?"

Larry listened for a moment. "Water. Do you think there's a pond or something? Maybe people fish here?"

"Now that I think about it, there's a little canal that feeds into the Gulf. The road Highland runs into crosses it. It must cut through these woods."

They followed the road until they came to the canal. The Toyota's tire tracks turned onto a clearing there, and Larry muttered, "Bingo."

"This is where he came last night, anyway," Tony said, stepping into the clearing and looking around. "Well, one thing's for sure. If he's planning to bring her here at night, it's far enough back that nobody would hear her scream."

"And if he left her here, it's not likely that anybody would find her for a while, either."

He set his hands on his hips and looked around. The canopy of trees was so thick that little sun got through. It was hot, too, for little wind was able to sweep through the thick brush. He wondered how Pendergrast had found this place to begin with, then realized that the guy probably knew the land around here intimately, since his company contracted the clearing of it for new construction sites. Proffer Builders might even own it.

"What's this?"

Tony was across the small clearing, stepping through bushes and trees, getting closer to the water.

"What?" Larry asked.

"Oh, man." Tony turned back. "You've got to see this."

Larry hurried across the clearing and stepped through the brush. His breath caught in his chest when he saw what Tony was standing over. "Unbelievable."

It was a round hole about six feet deep, but the diameter of the hole was no more than three feet. The dirt that had been dug out of the hole was piled next to it, ready to be shoved back in.

Larry got down on his knees and peered into the hole. "Well, there goes the possibility that it's preparation for clearing the land. That shovel and bag you saw last night?"

Tony looked in and saw them at the bottom of the hole. "He's planning to kill her."

"Yep."

"He would have buried her here, and nobody would have found her. He could bury her in five minutes, kick a few leaves over the dirt . . ."

Larry sat down on the ground, resting his arms on his knees. "He might have buried Melissa here."

"Do you think he'll go after Karen Anderson tonight?"

"Could be. We have to be ready. Somehow, he's going to have to get her into his car, so he can get her here." Larry was beginning to look pale. "What if we don't make it in time, Tony? What if we get there too late?"

"We won't."

Larry rubbed his face. "This poor kid. She has no idea what's about to happen to her."

"We'll stop him before he hurts her, Larry."

"We *hope* we will." He looked at Tony, playing possible scenarios over in his mind. "What if we used a decoy?"

"We can't," Tony said. "Not if we want to catch him on something that'll stick. You can't really think he's going to drag some woman off and rape her without looking at her face."

"We have to catch him," Larry said. "But there has to be some other way."

"There isn't, man. She'll be all right. We'll be right there, and the minute something happens, we'll have handcuffs on that guy so fast he won't know what hit him."

"I don't like it."

"What do you mean, you don't like it? This is your case! You started the whole thing!"

"But this is somebody's life, Tony!"

"Hey, if it weren't for you, we wouldn't know anything happened until her mother reported her missing. You're saving her life, not risking it!"

"But there's a way to be more sure. First, we have to tell the captain, and get his support on this."

"Yeah, I'm with you. And then?"

Larry looked up at him. "And then we have to tell her. Maybe she can help us."

Despite Larry's absolute exhaustion, his adrenaline was pumping as he went back to the station. He was about to catch Pendergrast, and that was enough to keep him going.

It was midmorning when he and Tony finally were able to get in to talk to the captain about taking the Pendergrast case full-time until they caught him. Tony backed up what Larry had already said—adding credence to the story with his clear-headed, emotionless recitation of the things they'd observed—and the captain paced in his usual way, turning the facts over in his mind.

"Okay, I'll buy it—something's about to happen," he said. "And since we don't have any leads at the moment on the girl on the beach, I guess you can work on this for a couple of days. But if nothing happens in the very near future, I'm gonna have to take you off of it again."

Larry's relief was apparent, but he pressed on to the next question. "Thanks, man," Larry said, getting to his feet. "But there's one more thing. I want to let the woman in on it. See if we can convince her to cooperate with us."

Sam considered that for a moment. "You might blow the whole thing if she says no."

"I'll convince her."

"How?"

"I don't know," Larry said, leaning over the desk. "But her life is at risk here. If we tell her, arm her, let her know what's about to come down, she might be willing to go through with it. It's the only way we can be sure to stop it when it happens. Otherwise, something could go wrong, and she could get raped, or even killed."

The captain sat slowly down at his desk. Clasping his hands in front of his face, he gazed at Tony. "What do you think?"

Tony wasn't sure. "I'd hate to have her balk and run. Then we might never catch him. On the other hand, if anybody can convince her, Larry can."

"It might work," the captain said. "We can do a lot more to prepare if she's with us."

"All right," Larry said. "Then we'll go talk to her. But we're going to have to make some promises. Give her a sense of security. Let her know we won't abandon her."

"Let me know what you need," the captain said. "I'll make sure you get it."

Tony shook the captain's hand and started to the door, but when Larry reached for his hand, the captain held it a beat longer than necessary. "Sorry about the other day, Millsaps. I may have been too hard on you. I was a little stressed, what with this body washing up, and the mayor breathing down my neck about the drug problem."

"Don't worry about it, Captain. I have a tough skin."

"You must," he said. "How long've you been working around the clock now? A week?"

"I'll sleep when we get that jerk in jail."

"So will I," the captain said. "So will I."

CHAPTER FORTY

The crowd of inmates walking from the dining hall to cellblock C threaded into a single-file line that followed the yellow line down the hall and back to their cells. Melissa watched a group of correctional officers coming toward them, walking side by side. She had never realized how much she would miss the freedom to walk the way she wanted, where she wanted. Now, every step, every thought, every activity was monitored and controlled.

Some of the women talked as they walked behind each other, but most were quiet, for one never knew when the wrath of one of the "bosses" might be stirred. It didn't take much. One woman had been caught looking too long at a male officer, and it had made one of his jealous coworkers angry. She had dragged that woman out of line and put her in isolation for three days. So Melissa walked with her eyes downcast, never straying from that yellow line, for fear that she'd be cited for bad behavior and have even one extra day added to her sentence.

As they drew closer to the doors to their cellblock, instead of crossing diagonally toward it, they had to follow the yellow line to its corner, turn ninety degrees, and then follow another line toward the doors. It was degrading, humiliating.

As soon as they were in their cellblock, however, they were free to leave the line and mill about their floor. Melissa hurried toward her cell.

Something tripped her, and she stumbled, then quickly recovered her balance. She turned around. The redhead who had harassed her on her first day was walking behind her, grinning.

Melissa compressed her lips, determined not to be drawn into a fight. But when she turned to walk on, the woman tripped her again. This time, Melissa swung around. "What do you want?" she demanded.

Red shoved her then, and Melissa lashed out to defend herself. Before she knew what had happened, the woman flung herself away from Melissa across the concrete floor, slammed herself into the opposite wall, and screamed. She came up with her knee bleeding. "I'll kill you!" she shouted.

Realizing that she was watching an award-winning performance, Melissa backed away, hands raised, as the COs rushed toward them. "I didn't touch her," she said. "She was harassing me, and then she flung herself across the hall—"

"She's lying!" Red screamed. "She knocked me across the hall! Look at my knee! I think it's dislocated. I won't be able to work tomorrow because of her."

"All right," one of the COs said, grabbing Melissa's arm roughly. "I'm writing you up. You can spend a night in isolation, and see if you still want to fight tomorrow."

"But I didn't do anything! She set me up!"

But the CO didn't care. He dragged Melissa out of the cellblock and down to the isolation cell she had heard about but never seen. It was six feet by four feet; everything was metal and welded down. There were no sheets on the bed, just a two-inch-thick pad that served as a mattress on the metal bed frame. A metal sink and a metal toilet were welded to one wall. The room was sweltering.

"Listen to me, please," she told the CO. "I'm telling you—"

But the huge, sliding metal door slid shut behind him, and she was locked in.

"I didn't do it," she whispered, sitting down on the edge of the bed. "I didn't do it."

She sat there for hours, waiting for someone to come so that she could plead her case, but no one came. Unable to tell what time it was, but guessing that it was nearing midnight, she finally stretched out on the miserable excuse for a mattress and tried to sleep. Red was probably sleeping soundly in her cell, with her knee bandaged up from her self-inflicted wound, and laughing that she'd escaped a day of work at Melissa's expense.

Fantasies of revenge floated through Melissa's mind—fantasies of *really* dislocating the woman's knee—but in the wee hours of morning, she realized that she'd tried that before. That's what had landed her here. She wasn't going to become like the others here, she told herself. Even if it killed her, she would resist.

Tears ran down her temples and into her hair. *Help me to forgive them, Lord. I'm not very good at that.*

And as she finally drifted into a fitful sleep, she knew that she could trust God to answer that prayer, in his own time.

CHAPTER FORTY-ONE

arry and Tony made sure that Pendergrast was working away in his office before they went to Karen Anderson's apartment. They had already learned from her license tag information her address, her name, and her age. Now all they needed was her trust.

They tried to be quiet and inconspicuous as they made their way up the stairs to her door. Larry knocked. After a moment, they heard footsteps.

"Who is it?" a woman asked through the door.

"Larry Millsaps, St. Clair Police Department. Can we talk to you for a moment?"

The door cracked open, and Karen peered beneath the chain lock. "What about?"

Larry glanced at Tony, and he stepped forward, flashing his badge. "We're detectives with the St. Clair P.D. Are you Karen Anderson?"

"Yes." She reached through the crack in the door and took both badges, read them, then peered up at the two detectives.

"We need to talk to you in private. It's very important."

Reluctantly, she closed her door, unlocked the chain, and opened it again. "You were in the store the other night," she said to Larry as they came in. "You didn't tell me you were a detective."

"No," he said. "I was hoping it wouldn't be necessary." He closed the door and glanced around the small apartment. "Could we sit down?"

She led them into the small living room furnished with old furniture that had seen better days. A pair of shoes lay in the middle of the floor, and books and papers were scattered all over the couch and coffee table. "Excuse the apartment. I've been studying."

"You're in school?" Tony asked.

"Yes," she said. "I go to Jones College in the mornings."

Larry moved some library books out of a chair and sat down. "Don't clean up on our account. You probably have everything right where you need it. We just need to talk to you."

She stopped straightening and swept her hair behind her ears. "What's going on?"

Larry gestured for her to sit down, and finally, she did. "Miss Anderson, we're here because you're in danger. In the course of an investigation that we've been doing, it's come to our attention that you're being stalked. Were you aware of this?"

She frowned and looked from one cop to the other. "Stalked? What do you mean?"

"You're being followed by a man who has been arrested before on rape charges. He's been watching you. We believe he has every intention of making you his next victim. And soon."

"What?" The word came out in an astonished whisper, and she sprang up and went to the window. Peering out, she asked, "Is he out there now?"

"No," Larry said. "We made sure he was someplace else before we came here."

She kept staring out the window. "Why haven't you arrested him?"

"Because he hasn't done anything yet. Twice before he was arrested and got off on technicalities. We have to wait until we can catch him at something substantial enough to get him put away for a long time."

"How do you know he's following me? Maybe it's some-one else."

"No, you're his target," Larry said. "He goes into the store, watches you. He's approached you once that we know of."

"Who? Who was he?"

"The one I asked you about that night. Do you remember?"

She came back to the couch, trying to remember. "No. I waited on a lot of men that night. I can't remember . . ."

"Well, that's just as well. He also parks out in the parking lot and waits for you to come out. For at least the past three nights he's followed you home."

Terror crossed her face, and she rushed to the door and turned the dead bolt, then hurried to the living-room window to see if it was locked. Desperately, she turned back to them. "The phone calls. Could he be the one making them?"

"What phone calls?"

"I've been getting a lot of hang-up calls. Like someone's just trying to see if I'm home. At all hours, day and night."

"It's him," Tony said, glancing at Larry. "Has anything else happened?"

"Well—no. I didn't know anyone was following me. I can't believe I didn't see him." She hurried around the apartment as she spoke, frantically checking window locks. "I've been taking the shortcut home, driving down Highland Drive all by myself. My mother warned me to take another route—" She swung around, confronting them. "What are you going to do about this?"

"We're going to catch him. But we need your help."

"*My* help? Are you kidding?"

"You're the only one who *can* help us right now," Larry said.

"But how? What can I do?"

"You can cooperate with us. Help us catch him."

She went back to her seat and sat on the edge. "By doing what?"

"Just what you've been doing," Tony said. "Keep going to work, driving the same way home, letting him follow you."

"Until what? He rapes me?"

"He won't rape you. We can protect you. We need for him to think everything is normal. But if you help us plan this out, we can trap him."

"So I'm the bait? Dangle me under his nose, and he'll strike?"

Larry looked down at his shoes. "I'm afraid you're the bait, anyway. We're just trying to protect you."

"No!" Beginning to cry, she shot up again. "I can't do this. I'll—I'll move. I'll go back and live with my mother."

"What about your job? School? Don't you think he'll find you?"

She thought about that for a moment. "There's a law. A stalking law, isn't there? You could arrest him just for following me."

"It wouldn't hold him any amount of time," Larry said, "if it stuck at all. He's smart. He's gotten off twice. We have to make sure that what we get him on is substantial enough to lock him up for a long time."

She shook her head again and began to pace. "Maybe—maybe he'll get discouraged if he can't find me. I mean, why is he after me, anyway?"

"He's sick. He's picked you out, Karen. He likes blondes. He's obsessed with you. If you change what you're doing, you could throw him off for a few days, but there's no guarantee that he wouldn't catch up to you eventually. By then he'll just be more desperate."

"I can't believe this!" she shouted. "I haven't done anything to anybody. All I do is go to school, work, and study. Why would this happen to me?"

Larry got up and took a couple of steps toward her. "You can turn it around, Karen. Go from being the victim to being in control."

She wiped her wet face with a trembling hand. "What would you do for me, if I did?"

"We'd have someone watching you twenty-four hours a day. We'd never let you out of our sight. When we think he's about to strike, we could wire you with a microphone so we would know what was happening every minute."

"But how far would things have to go before you arrested him?"

"At least far enough that there's no question that he was going to do you bodily harm."

Terror flooded her face as she shook her head violently. "I can't do it. You're asking too much."

"We realize it's asking a lot," Tony said. "But there's no other way."

"Karen, he's a threat to countless women out there," Larry said, getting face-to-face with her. "One woman is dead because of him. He broke into her house and brutally raped her. Almost killed her. She wound up killing herself. I don't even know how many others he's raped. But he's smart, so he's still out there on the street. We need to get him, Karen. Right now, you're the only one who can help us."

Her breath caught on a sob. "I'm twenty-one years old. I weigh 105 pounds. I can't fight him."

"We'll fight him. All you have to do is bait him."

"But I'm scared!" she cried. "Let somebody else do it, a policewoman or something."

"And what will you do?" Tony asked. "Move out of this apartment? Quit your job? Give up school? Are you going to let a maniac like this control your life?"

"I don't want to."

"Even if you did, would you ever know for sure that he wasn't stalking you again? As long as he's out there, he could come after you. He might find you, before we ever had the chance to catch him again."

"I can't do it!" she cried. "You'll have to find another way. I'll hide, if I have to. But I can't do this!"

"Then what *are* you going to do?" Tony asked.

She thought about that as she looked frantically around the apartment. "I guess I'll pack a few things and leave." She ran back to her bedroom, pulled a suitcase out of the closet.

Larry came to the door of the bedroom. "Karen, just trust us. We'll be there. We won't let anything happen to you."

"How can I know that?" she screamed. "It's my life that's at stake, not yours. If you mess up, let me down, it's no skin off your nose! I—can't— do it!"

Larry glanced over his shoulder to Tony. The look his partner gave him said this was hopeless. She was going to run, and Pendergrast would be thrown off. Sam would get impatient and close the case. On his own, Larry would have to haunt him night after night, waiting for another chance. Who knew when that would come?

Meanwhile, Melissa was sitting in jail, and Pendergrast was free, and the injustice of it all was overwhelming.

Larry leaned his forehead against the door casing as Karen ran around, grabbing the things she would take with her.

"Karen, this really good friend of mine—a woman I care a lot about—her sister was the woman who was raped and then killed herself."

Karen slowed her packing and looked up at him.

245

A tear stole out of Larry's eye, and he wiped it away. "He got away with it. Walked scot-free. My friend, Melissa, she's sitting in jail right now because she tried to set it up to look like he'd raped her. She figured she'd have all the evidence they needed this time. He'd never walk free again. That's desperation, Karen. She put herself in jeopardy, could have been raped or killed, to catch him. But it didn't work out, and she finally wound up confessing. She's in jail, Karen, and he's out there somewhere, terrorizing women like you. He's dangerous, and nobody's going to stop him."

She covered her face with both hands, and her shoulders shook with the force of her despair.

"If Melissa were here, she'd cooperate. She'd do anything, because she wouldn't want even one more woman to be stalked and raped like her sister was. Melissa loved Sandy. She was pretty and blonde, like you. She had a new husband, and everything was going great for her. And one night, when she didn't expect it, this man broke in and ruined her life. She couldn't live with it. And she's not the only one, Karen."

"I scream when I see a roach," Karen bit out as the tears soaked her face. "When the wind blows hard, I have nightmares. You're not looking at a brave person."

Larry took a few more steps into the room, his eyes beseeching. "Karen, the terror's not going away just because you run. Wouldn't you feel safer knowing that we're with you? Watching you?"

"No," she said, closing her suitcase and snapping it shut. "No, I wouldn't feel safer. I have to get out of here." She grabbed the suitcase up off the bed and dragged it into the living room. Leaving it at the door, she started gathering her schoolbooks. As she stacked the last one, she broke down. For a moment, she stood there with her books clutched in her arms, her eyes squeezed shut, and her shoulders rolling with the force of her sobs.

Larry touched her shoulder, but words escaped him.

"I don't want to quit school!" she cried. "I'm almost finished. It's not fair!"

"No, it isn't," he whispered.

"I like my job, and I like living here. How come he gets to ruin everything?"

"He doesn't," Larry said. "We don't have to let him."

She hesitated and looked up at him, and for a moment, Larry thought she might give in.

But instead, she opened the door and grabbed her suitcase. "I'm sorry," she said.

Tony and Larry followed her out, watched her lock the dead bolt with her key, and Larry carried her suitcase down the steps to her car.

She was still crying when she got behind the wheel and looked up at him. "I'm sorry. Call me a wimp. I just can't do it."

"I understand," Larry said. "Just be careful, okay?" He pulled a card out of his pocket. "If you need to get in touch with me, call these numbers. You'll catch me at one of them."

She took the card, looked down at it, then nodded and sucked in another sob. "I have to go," she said.

Larry backed up, and she closed the door.

She backed out of the parking space, and sped out into the street, leaving them standing there alone.

"Now what?" Tony asked.

Larry shook his head and sighed. "I don't know. I honestly have no idea."

"Maybe she'll change her mind."

Larry thought about that for a moment. Somehow, he didn't think so.

Slowly, he walked back to the car without saying a word.

CHAPTER FORTY-TWO

Larry was one of the first ones to show up Saturday for visitors' day. He waited outside for the group to be let in, and let his eyes sweep over the other family members and friends who were waiting to see loved ones. A young woman who looked no older than seventeen stood with a baby on her hip, a toddler at her knees, and a hyperactive three-year-old running up and down the sidewalk, refusing to heed her warnings to stay by her side. Larry wondered if she was the children's mother, or just keeping them while their mother served time.

A man who looked as if he'd just crawled out of bed sat on a step of the jail with two little girls—one on each side of him, holding his hands. Had they come to see their mother?

And then came a small, quiet man alone; and two women together; and more children.

Did they all feel as forlorn as he did, coming here to see what the justice system had done to the person they loved? Ironic, he thought, that he would feel like this, when he was often the one putting them behind bars. But he had never seen the pain from the other side.

The doors opened, and they all filed in. One by one, they were searched for items that were against the rules. Larry set the bag of books he'd brought Melissa on the table. As he waited for them to search him, his heart recalled the despair he'd felt yesterday when he had searched the stores for something that he could bring her—something that would lift her up, give her strength, help her to feel God's mercy and grace. He had sat in his car and wept because he'd been unable to find anything other than books—so impersonal, so benign.

"All right," the guard said, shoving the bag of books back across the table. "These are fine. Just go that way into the rec room."

Larry followed the flow of people into the big room. Since this wasn't a maximum security state penitentiary, there were no glass booths to talk through. They could sit at the same table, touch, hold hands, and he could hold her if she cried.

That, he supposed, was something he should be thankful for.

He waited with sweaty palms as one of the guards ran down a list of rules for visiting.

Most of these people were regulars, like he would be, he thought. Even the small children knew the rules and the routine.

The doors opened, and one by one the prisoners came in, some with hugs, others with cross words, others with a dull expression that said they didn't care who visited, because no one really mattered. He watched hopefully, expectantly, each time the door opened, and when Melissa didn't come right away, he began to wonder if she was going to refuse to see him. She had told him not to come. What if she'd really meant it?

His heart was sinking lower when twenty or more inmates had been brought in, and Melissa still wasn't among them. Abandoning his bag of books on the table, he walked over to the guard.

"If she didn't want to see me, would they come tell me, or would they just let me sit here and wonder?"

The guard's eyes fell on the door, and he asked, "Is that who you're looking for?"

Larry turned around and saw her at the door. She was wearing her orange jumpsuit and looking timidly around for him. He started toward her, noting how pale she was, how tired she looked. Her hair was pulled back in a ponytail and she wore no makeup— as some of the other inmates did. She looked like a fragile sixteen-year-old rather than the gutsy twenty-three-year-old who'd almost beaten Edward Pendergrast. But he'd never seen a more beautiful sight in his life.

She saw him and started toward him, and he met her halfway and threw his arms around her.

For a moment, he just held her and felt her body shaking as she began to cry. Then, quickly pulling herself together, she let him go.

"Let's go sit down," she whispered.

He led her to their table and set the books on the floor. Taking her hand, he looked into her eyes to see what he could read there. "You look great," he whispered.

"I'm okay," she said. "Really. It's not so bad."

"Are you getting along okay? With the others, I mean?"

She took in a deep, ragged breath. "Yeah."

She was holding back, he thought. She wasn't going to share much. "Do you have a cellmate?"

She nodded and looked around. Chloe was across the room with a man who must be almost six feet, but still shorter than Chloe. They were standing and talking quietly. "See that woman over there? She's my cellmate."

Larry's heart plummeted again. She looked like a linebacker—a linebacker in a bad mood. "Do you two get along okay?"

Melissa looked down at the woodgrain on the table. "I stay out of her way. Try not to make too much noise."

He was getting alarmed, and he cupped her chin and made her look at him. "Melissa, has she been harassing you?"

There was honesty in her eyes when she answered. "No. Thankfully, she's kind of left me alone."

"What about everybody else?"

Her eyes teared up, and she looked down at the wood again and tried to rub off a spot. "Well, I haven't met Miss Congeniality yet. I'm still looking for her. This isn't the best place to make friends."

He watched as she clasped her hands, and he saw the burn across her fingers. "What's this?" he asked.

She covered the burn and withdrew her hand. "I burnt myself on an iron. I work in the laundry. It's no big deal. I did it myself."

He wasn't sure she was leveling with him; carefully, he took her hand and examined the blisters. "Have you put anything on it?"

"I told you, I'm fine," she said. "Now, can we change the subject? Let's talk about you. You look tired. Are you sleeping?"

"Of course," he lied, though he couldn't remember the last time he'd had more than two hours' sleep at a time. Even though Karen had disappeared yesterday, Larry had followed Pendergrast last night to see what he would do. He had sat outside her apartment most of the night, waiting for her to come home. When she never did, Pendergrast had finally given up.

He rubbed his hand across his jaw and told himself he should have shaved for her. He had been so anxious to see her that he had only taken time to shower.

"Are you growing a beard?"

He tried to smile. "Looks like it."

She wasn't buying his "everything's fine" routine any more than he was. "Larry, tell me what's going on."

He sighed and decided there was no point in hiding the truth. "I've been following Pendergrast. Watching him."

Behind them, an inmate and her lover became embroiled in an argument, and their profanities were gaining volume. Melissa seemed not to notice. "Really? You're watching him?"

"Yeah." He lowered his voice. "He's been stalking another girl. I'm afraid to let my guard down for a minute."

"So what are you doing? Following him around the clock?"

"Something like that," he said, glancing over his shoulder at the loud couple. "But I'm thinking that may change pretty soon. The girl's onto him now, so she's kind of disappeared. As soon as he realizes it, he'll give up and look for somebody else."

"How do you know she's onto him?"

"I told her. I wanted her cooperation, so we could catch him, but she balked and ran."

Across the room a baby in a carrier wailed, and its tired mother ignored it. "What if you used somebody else?" Melissa asked. "Put another girl in her place."

"The problem is that it's a little touchy. He's watching her. We can't replace her at work, because he'll know. We could pull a switch as she gets into her car, but even then, the minute he gets close enough to see her, he could back off. I can't catch him and get enough to convict him until he does something. And if he balks and cans the whole thing, I may not be around the next time he tries this. No, the only way was to get her cooperation. Now I'm almost wishing I hadn't told her."

"You had to. You couldn't let her walk into this blindly."

"That's how I felt yesterday. Today, I'm not so sure." He looked up at her with a half-smile. "I was really hoping I could bring some good news in here today. I wanted so much to tell you he was in jail."

"Larry, I want him caught too. But I don't want you killing yourself to do it. You're exhausted." She folded both arms on the table and fixed her troubled eyes on him. "Don't let anything happen to you, okay?"

He nodded his promise.

The CO crossed the room and reprimanded the angry couple behind them. Melissa swallowed and looked around at the other inmates interacting with families she didn't know they had. The room was quickly filling up with cigarette smoke and more crying babies, and she wished she and Larry could go outside together, breathe the fresh air, feel the sunshine. But that wasn't possible. She moved her troubled, timid eyes back to his. "You know, I really didn't expect you to come today. I knew my parents were coming this afternoon, but you were a surprise."

"Why? Didn't I tell you I would?"

"I told you not to."

"Well, I had to."

"Why?" she asked.

He took her hand again and seemed to study the shape of her fingers. "Because I miss you like crazy. I've worried about you day and night. I can't stand the thought of you here."

Her lip began to tremble, and she struggled with her tears again. He hated himself for making her cry.

"I don't know how all this happened," she whispered, bending her head down to hide the tears. "I did something wrong to try and right things, and I wound up hurting so many people. I didn't want to hurt you, Larry, and the last thing I want is for you to keep coming here out of obligation. Six months is a long time. You'll forget about me. I hate to get used to having you come, and then start noticing that you're coming less and less. I hate for you to feel guilty about having fun when I'm in here, like you owe me some debt."

"That's not going to happen," he assured her. "Melissa, look at me."

She looked up, her eyes red and wet.

"I love you. It's not something I chose to do, but it happened. I really mean it. I've never felt like this about any other woman."

She sucked in a sob and covered her mouth. "I love you, too," she whispered. "But I'm so worried about you."

"*You're* worried about *me*? Why?"

"Because you're out there, and he's out there. And you're trying to catch him at something all by yourself. Larry, I've tried that. It didn't work."

"There's a difference. I'm a cop. I know what I'm doing."

"I knew what I was doing, too."

"But you manipulated what happened with you. I'm not manipulating anything. I'm just watching."

"Please don't get so tired that you get sloppy and let him see you. He might kill you, Larry. He's a vicious, violent man."

"I'm going to get him off the street. But I'm going to come and visit you on every visitors' day, too. Got that?"

She sat gazing at him for a moment, wiping her tears as fast as they came. "I have a lot to be thankful for."

"What?" he asked. "Tell me."

She tried to think. "Well, I have you. Not everybody in here has somebody. And I'm safe from Pendergrast. He can't get to me in here."

Larry smiled. "That's right. That's what Tony said. Thank God for small favors."

"That's a big one," she admitted, "and I do thank him. I thank him for other things, too. Like the fact that I'm learning to depend on God. Completely. Being this low makes me realize how high he is. But he's still here, too, even in this place. I feel him."

"I feel him, too," Larry whispered. "Sometimes when I think of you being here, and I get such dread, I feel his comfort. But I don't think I want to be comforted. I guess in a way I feel I'm doing some kind of penance by worrying myself sick about you."

"We have to have faith, Larry," she whispered. "This morning, I was reading the book of James. He said life wouldn't always be easy. He said to let your trials strengthen you. I intend to do that."

"Then I will, too," he said.

As the noise grew around them, and the chaos in the room continued, they put aside their doubts and fears, their worries and anxieties, their remorse and regrets, and lost themselves in the world they had in common.

But that night, as Larry sat in his car in the parking lot across the street from Pendergrast's, waiting for him to come out of his apartment, Larry began to worry again. Melissa had looked so tired. The burn on her hand might not have come from the iron at all. And that cellmate of hers would instill fear into the toughest of men.

He had a long talk with God, pleading with him to find her another cellmate, pleading with him to protect her with his angels, pleading with him to let something good come of all this.

And then he pleaded that he would be able to catch Pendergrast at something soon, so that he could lock him away.

But it wasn't going to happen tonight. Pendergrast didn't go out. Larry wondered if he'd realized he'd been found out.

He gave up around four A.M. and went home to get a couple of hours' sleep before he had to be at church. He needed to worship today, he thought. He needed to feel God's glory. He sure hadn't seen enough of it in that rec room at the Pinellas County Correctional Facility for Women.

CHAPTER FORTY-THREE

T he prison chapel was filled with more women than Melissa had expected that Sunday morning. She had hoped it would be a sanctuary—a safe place in the midst of all this madness. But as she went in, she saw the red-haired woman who had harassed her sitting at the back, and some of the others that she feared scattered around the room.

Had they come to worship, she wondered, or had they come to break the monotony of their lives?

It didn't matter, she told herself. What really mattered was that she had the opportunity to worship here, and she was going to.

Her heart felt lighter as one of the women from the prison ministry began to play the piano and direct the inmates in some praise songs. Most of the women didn't sing, she noted, but some of them did, Melissa among them.

Next to her sat a tiny Hispanic woman with dark circles under her eyes, singing in a lovely, lilting voice, with tears running down her face. Melissa could easily picture the woman in a small evangelical church, with a cotton, flower-print dress on, and maybe a hat with a bow. Instead, she sat here in her prison-issue jumpsuit looking as out of place as Melissa felt.

The chaplain who gave his time to come here on Sunday mornings was a young man in his early twenties, probably someone who had never had a church of his own. His name was Doug Manning.

"If you have a Bible with you, please turn to John, chapter 4."

Melissa opened her Bible to John, and noticed that the woman next to her did as well. Few others had Bibles with them.

It was the passage about the woman at the well, and as he launched into his sermon about the woman with a past, the woman who stood before Christ with all her sins exposed, and was offered forgiveness freely and without cost, Melissa felt a renewal of hope.

After the sermon, the chaplain entreated the women to stay for a prayer time, but one by one, most of the women filed out. Only the woman sitting next to her, and four others in different parts of the room, stayed behind.

Melissa sat quietly, waiting for the pastor to lead them.

He looked disappointed that so many had gone. "Well—since there aren't many of us, why don't we come up to the front here, and sort of put our chairs in a circle?" As they came, he asked, "Do you all know each other?"

Melissa looked around. A couple of them knew each other, but she knew none of them. "No. I'm new."

"Then let's introduce ourselves. I'm Doug, and this is my wife, Tina."

The woman who had been sitting next to Melissa offered her a timid smile. "I'm Sonja. I'm in cellblock C. I haven't been here long, either."

The next woman, a heavyset, jolly-looking woman, spoke up. "I'm Betty. I used to be a choir director in a little mission church we belonged to."

The next one, a black woman whose Bible looked worn and used, nodded to Melissa. "I'm Keisha. In cellblock A."

And after her, the last one, another black woman with huge, almond-shaped eyes who looked like model material, said, "I'm Simone. Cellblock B."

Doug smiled, pleased, then looked at Melissa. "And you are?"

"Melissa," she said quietly.

"Do any of you have any specific prayer requests?" he asked.

Sonja spoke up as tears filled her eyes, and she groped for the tissue she carried in her pocket. "I need prayers," she said. "I don't belong here. I didn't do what they said I did."

Doug looked as if he'd heard that before, but he didn't voice it.

"I didn't know my husband was selling drugs," she went on in her heavy accent. "When he got arrested, they arrested me, too, because they had seen me driving him places and dropping him off

256

at places where he was making deals." Her face reddened, and she covered her face. "But I didn't know what he was doing." She stopped, sniffed, and tried to steady her voice. "I have three small children. Two, three, and five. I have to serve a year, but that's an eternity to them. They'll forget all about me."

The horror of that situation gripped Melissa, and by instinct, she reached out and took Sonja's hand.

"All right," Doug said. "We'll pray about that. Anyone else?"

"Yes," Betty said. "I'm due to get out in four weeks. I need prayers that nothing happens to mess up my release."

"All right." Doug looked around, waiting, for anyone else to speak up. "Anyone else?"

"Yes," Melissa said, almost in a whisper. "I'm not like Sonja. I did something wrong to come here. But I need prayers for strength. I need to see some sense in all of this."

"You may not ever," Doug warned her. "Sometimes you just have to trust God's sovereignty."

She breathed a laugh. "I'm beginning to realize that."

"Well, let's pray for these particular requests, and then I'll pray for each of you, that you'll be safe here, and that you'll be lights in this dark place. You know, a lot of those women who walked out of here just now are hurting. They need some Christian influence here. And you may not have noticed just now, but each of the cellblocks is represented in this little group. That's no coincidence. Each one of you has the power to change this whole facility."

"I don't feel very powerful," Keisha said.

"Me, either," Betty added.

"Well, neither did the disciples after Jesus died. But they didn't understand what was ahead. God saw their future, even when they didn't. He saw the reason, and all the purpose. Maybe you're here to work on the women in this prison."

"It's hard to care about them," Sonja said. "Some of them are hateful and wicked."

"Maybe they've never known any better."

"Maybe that's just an excuse," Sonja said. She brought her remorseful eyes up to Doug's. "I'm sorry. I just haven't been feeling much love for my fellowman—or woman—lately."

"Then we'll pray about that, too."

They held hands and prayed, earnestly, openly, with tender, broken hearts, and in doing so they created a bond that Melissa hadn't felt in years. She wanted to feel it more than once a week, she thought.

When the prayer was over, she felt empowered. "We need a Bible study," she said. "More than just once a week. Would that be allowed?"

"Of course it would," he said. "But I'm in seminary during the week, about three hours from here. I can only get here on Sundays. Would you be willing to lead it?"

Melissa's eyes widened. "Me?"

"Sure, why not?"

She looked around, surprised, and saw that everyone was looking expectantly at her. "Well, the truth is—I'm not real well educated on the Bible. I haven't really been walking with God for the last few years."

"Great opportunity to learn more," he said. "Just be available, pray about it, and God will lead you."

She hesitated and looked from one woman to another. "Would you come, if we had one? Say, three times a week?"

To a woman, they all agreed that they would.

"From this core group, other women can be reached," Doug said. "One by one, you'll bring them into the group, and it'll grow. I've seen it happen before."

"When?" Sonja asked. "You're too young to have seen much."

Doug only smiled. "My mother was in prison for several years when I was a boy," he said. "She was a battered wife, and she killed my father to keep him from killing me. That's why I feel such a burden to keep this prison ministry going."

"How many years was she in?" Sonja asked.

"Seven," he said. "But I had a loving grandmother who brought me to see my mother every time she could. My mother became a light in the prison. She built up a Bible study that started with three women and grew to about 200. And Sonja, I can tell you that, even from prison, my mother had a strong influence on me. I saw her making the best of the worst situation, and I saw her taking what had been given to her, and still being available for God to use. She wrote me a lot of letters, and read

258

me books over the telephone at night, and rocked me when I visited. It wasn't the best situation, but she made it good."

"Wow. And look how you turned out," Sonja whispered. "Maybe my babies will be all right, too."

"And so will you. You know, some of these women were drug addicts when they came in here. Now that they're clean, they're different women. Regular human beings, with feelings, and regrets, and loneliness. Think of them as being like you, even the ones who act like monsters, and love them, anyway."

He knew, Melissa thought. He understood. And she felt so blessed that God had sent him to them.

As she went back to her cell, she felt called to be the light that God had sent for this dark corridor. And she decided that Chloe needed to be the first to see that light.

That afternoon, Larry came to visit again, and this time, Melissa was brighter. As they sat and talked and watched the other inmates with their families and friends, she noted Sonja in the corner with her children. The two babies were in her lap, and she was rocking them, while the five-year-old performed some little songs she'd memorized from a videotape she had at her grandmother's.

And then she saw Chloe again with her husband. The soft look on the woman's face made her look like a different person.

Later, when they were back in their cells, Melissa tried to make conversation as she straightened her things. "Your husband seems nice, Chloe."

"Yeah. He's a prince. He's stuck by me, too. Through thick and through thin. He'll be there when I get out. And you can bet I won't wind up back in here. This is my last time. I ain't like those other women, who don't know no better than to keep doin' stupid stuff—killin' and prostitutin' and sellin' and shootin' at folks. Man, if you could get the chair for havin' the stupids, they'd be killin' ninety percent of the women in this jail."

Something about that struck Melissa as funny, and quietly, she began to laugh.

"What's so funny?" Chloe asked.

Melissa covered her mouth with her hand and tried to stop.

She heard Chloe laughing on the bunk beneath her, and felt the bed shaking with it.

"Well, it's true," Chloe said. "You can laugh, but these girls—they ain't like you and me, with our little namby-pamby crimes. Some of these women did some bad things."

Melissa came to the end of her laughter and took a deep breath. The laughter had cleansed her, relaxed her. "What did you do, Chloe?"

The woman's voice got deeper and more serious. "You won't tell nobody?"

"Of course not."

"I'm in for forgery. Forged some checks. They belonged to the woman I worked for. It was stealin', but I never shot nobody. And I never shot *up* neither. I was clean, except for forgin' checks. Never thought I'd get caught. She had plenty of money. Didn't think she'd notice if a little of it was missin'. It was what they call a victimless crime. I never hurt nobody."

That was something to be proud of, in a place like this, Melissa thought. One person's sins were worse than another's. There was always someone whose sins were worse than yours. She supposed that was why the other inmates had tried to pin child abuse and murder on her, so they could all hold her up as an example of how far they would never go.

The thing was, she wasn't sure there was a big difference in God's eyes.

"Why don't you want me to tell?" she asked.

"'Cause," Chloe said. "Some o' them might have the impression that I'm in for murder. I might have given 'em that impression."

Melissa began to laugh again. "Why, Chloe?"

"It helps for them to be scared of you."

Melissa sighed. "You have an advantage."

"You got that right. Ain't nobody much who wants to cross me here."

They were quiet for a moment, as Melissa contemplated her size.

"You married to that honey who keeps comin' to see you?" Chloe asked.

"No," Melissa said. "How long have you been married?"

"Herman and me got married three years ago. He's my man."

Something about that made Chloe seem more human. "Does Herman come often?"

"Every weekend. Never misses a one."

Melissa turned over on her back and studied the dark ceiling again. "At first I didn't want Larry to come. I didn't want him to see me like this."

"You may not have a bunch of makeup, but you don't need none. You look fine. He'll probably just be glad to see you're in one piece."

"Will I stay that way, Chloe? In one piece, I mean."

Chloe didn't answer for a while. "It ain't gon' be easy, sister, but I'll do what I can."

After a few minutes, she heard Chloe's deep, heavy breathing on the rhythmic edge of a snore, and she knew she'd gone to sleep.

CHAPTER FORTY-FOUR

Karen Anderson sat up abruptly in bed in her mother's guest room, and listened . . .

She could have sworn she heard a noise. But the trees outside the window were rustling too loudly, and the wind was blowing too hard—

What if he was out there?

She hadn't slept a full night since the two detectives had dropped their bomb on her. All night she heard things, and expected things, and imagined things.

She got out of bed, went to the window, and peered out into the night. There was no one there. At least, no one that she could see.

She thought of waking her mother and asking her to keep her company, but her mother would only think she was crazy. Karen hadn't been able to tell her mother about the man who was stalking her. She didn't want her to be afraid, so she'd just said that she'd had her heart broken and she didn't want to be alone. But now, in the middle of the night, listening for any and every sound, the loneliness and fear were overwhelming.

When would she stop listening? When would she be able to go back to school, or work, or anywhere, without looking over her shoulder?

Not until the man was caught, Larry had said. And he wouldn't be caught if Karen didn't help. Not until he picked another girl to attack—assuming that the police hadn't given up trying to catch him by then.

She went into her mother's room and stood in the doorway, feeling like a little girl who'd had a nightmare and needed her mother. Only the nightmare wasn't a dream—it was real. And her mother couldn't help her.

She thought of the woman who was in jail because she'd tried to get this man put away. And she thought of the woman who had killed herself. She could almost understand getting that desperate.

She went back to bed, climbed under the covers, and tried hard to go to sleep. But even with her eyes closed she saw the shadowy, mystic figure of a man who wanted to hurt her. He was still out there, even if he couldn't find her. One of these days, if he wanted to badly enough, he would. And then, just as she let her guard down, just as the police did, he would make his move. And there wouldn't be anywhere to turn.

Feeling sick, she closed her eyes and tried to sleep. But it was impossible to sleep when you were listening, waiting . . .

CHAPTER FORTY-FIVE

The steam of the showers hung in the air, wetting the concrete floor. Still in her stall, Melissa dressed quickly, her jumpsuit clinging to her damp skin. The thought of dressing in front of some of these violent women didn't appeal to her, so she tolerated a little discomfort for her privacy.

Hanging her towel over her arm, she pulled back the curtain and stepped out, her flip-flops squeaking as they slipped across the floor. She couldn't get out fast enough, she thought. Even though the showers were closely guarded, this was the most threatening room in the prison. She'd seen two fights break out here, for which several inmates—even the ones who'd been victims—had gotten isolation. It seemed that the high temperatures and the steam added up to boiling tempers.

She had just dropped her towel in its designated tub and headed for the door when she heard someone running toward her from behind. Before she could turn around, something walloped the back of her head, knocking her to the floor, facedown. Someone was on her instantly, her weight crushing her. She screamed as someone wrenched her arm behind her back, threatening to break it. The other inmates began to laugh and shout encouragement. "Let me go!" Melissa screamed.

"Not until you learn who's in charge around here."

"What do you want?" Melissa asked through her teeth.

"Respect. And I ain't been sensin' any from you."

The woman lifted Melissa's head by her hair, then banged it back into the concrete, bloodying Melissa's nose and scraping the skin off her forehead. She yelled again, but the guards weren't there.

She heard another set of footsteps coming, and suddenly the weight of the woman was jerked off of her.

She turned over, wiping the blood from her nose. Chloe was holding Red against the wall with her hand at her throat. Other inmates stood around, suddenly quiet.

"This is my cellmate, understand?" the big woman asked each of them. "*Nobody* touches her, or they answer to me. Any questions?" She looked around at each face in the room. When no one protested, she shook Red. "And you—I'd take great pleasure in cleanin' out the toilets with your head. If there's somethin' about what I'm sayin' that you don't understand, feel free to speak up any time."

Red didn't answer. It was clear that she feared Chloe.

Chloe let her go. "Get out of here now!" The woman leered at Melissa, silently promising to get her later, and headed out of the room.

When Chloe was satisfied that no one was going to attempt anything else, she turned on the water in the sink and began to brush her teeth, ignoring Melissa, who still lay on the floor. Melissa got to her feet and looked around at the others who were staring at her. Some of them snickered quietly. Others found other things to do. No one wanted to be the target of Chloe's wrath.

Bending over one of the sinks, Melissa washed the blood off of her nose. She fought back the tears as she looked up in the mirror. Chloe stood next to her, drying her mouth. "Thank you, Chloe," she whispered.

Chloe grunted and handed her a towel to stop the bleeding. "If it don't stop, you could go to the infirmary. Get out of a day's work."

"No, it's okay."

As she washed the rest of the blood off of her face, she wondered if God had provided this huge hulk of a woman to be the guardian angel who would protect her.

His grace amazed her. As she went back to her cell, she thanked him for disguised blessings like Chloe.

CHAPTER FORTY-SIX

The light on his answering machine was blinking when Larry got home at four o'clock Tuesday morning, exhausted and agitated from watching Pendergrast watch Karen Anderson's empty apartment. A couple of times he'd seen another petite blonde get out of her car and trot up to another apartment, and he'd tensed up, expecting Pendergrast to go after her. But it seemed that he was waiting for Karen. For now, no one else would do.

Pendergrast had finally given up and gone back to his apartment at about 3:30. How he existed on as little sleep as he was getting, Larry couldn't imagine. He knew it was killing him.

He pulled off his shoes, sat down on the bed, and punched the button on the machine.

"Uh, Larry, this is Mrs. Nelson—Melissa's mother? We just wanted to talk to you and see how you think Melissa is doing. Please call us tomorrow if you get time."

He fell back on the bed in frustration as it beeped. What would he tell them? They wanted reassurances that she was all right, but he wasn't sure himself.

As a message from one of the guys at his church played, he tried to remember what day it was. Tuesday, he thought. Wednesday was the midweek visitation day at the jail. He could see Melissa tomorrow night. But first he had to make it through this day and the next.

The line beeped again, and the third message began to play. "Detective Millsaps," a woman's voice said. "This is Karen. Karen Anderson."

Larry sat up and lunged for the machine to turn it up.

"I—I need to talk to you. I've changed my mind. Please—no matter what time it is, call me at this number."

He grabbed the phone and dialed as she called it out. She answered on the first ring.

"Hello?"

"Karen? This is Larry Millsaps."

"Thank goodness." She breathed out a heavy sigh of relief. "I've been so scared."

"Why? Has something happened?"

"No," she said. "But I keep thinking something's going to. I can't sleep, I can't eat . . . If I help you, if I do what you ask, will this all be over soon? Will I be able to go back to my life?"

"Yes," he said. "Karen, it's really the only way to put this all to rest."

"All right, then," she whispered. "What do I have to do?"

CHAPTER FORTY-SEVEN

It was the first time Melissa had found the pay phone in her cellblock not in use, and she hurried to it, jabbed her quarter in, and quickly dialed Larry's number.

His machine answered, and she left a tentative message that she was sorry she'd missed him, then hung up, feeling like an idiot. What made me think he'd be at home? she asked herself. Did I really believe he'd just sit around grieving over me?

Feeling that old anxiety and despair creeping in, she pulled another quarter out of her pocket and dialed the operator. "Collect to Pensacola," she said. "James Nelson. From Melissa." She wondered if the operator could tell that the call was coming from jail, if she was judging her . . .

Her mother answered the phone and accepted the call, and Melissa felt instant relief. Just to touch base with someone she loved, just to hear the voice of someone who loved her.

Her mother was telling her about the prayer chain she'd started, when Red rushed around the corner, making a beeline for the phone.

"Get off," she said. "Now!"

Melissa hesitated. Chloe wasn't around, and she knew better than to cross the woman without her. But her mother was talking, and she didn't want to frighten her by hanging up suddenly. Trying to compromise, she raised one finger, promising to get off in a minute, but Red didn't back down.

"It's an emergency," Red said. "I have to call my kid."

Melissa doubted that there was an emergency, even though she had seen emergency messages occasionally brought to the inmates. Still, there was an anxiety in Red's eyes that she didn't want to provoke. "Uh—Mom? I'll call you back in a few minutes, okay? Somebody needs to use the phone."

Melissa hung up, retrieved the quarter that had come back after the operator connected them, and turned around.

Red shoved her away from the phone, almost knocking her down, and grabbed the phone. "Give me a quarter," she said.

"I only have one," Melissa said. "I need to use it."

"I said give me the quarter!" she shouted. "Now!"

Gritting her teeth, Melissa handed her the quarter.

Red snatched it and shoved it into the machine, and Melissa thought about leaving. But something, some stoic, stubborn pride, made her stay. Maybe she was making a collect call, too, she thought, and the quarter would come back. Maybe she could still get it and call her mother back.

"This is Jean," the woman barked into the phone. "I got a message to call. Where's Johnny?"

She waited, then said, "I don't care. I want to talk to him. No, I don't want to talk to Carol. Where's my kid?"

Again, she waited, and her face began to redden. "What do you mean, an accident? Put Carol on the phone. Now!"

Something was wrong. Melissa looked up at her.

"Carol, where's Johnny?" Red yelled louder. "I want to talk to him! Put him on the phone!"

She cursed, then kicked the brick wall behind the phone, and let another curse fly. "You're lying. This is just some sick joke, isn't it? Put my kid on the phone!"

Melissa took a step forward. Red's face was twisted, and tears came to her eyes.

"He wouldn't do that! He knows to look both ways. I did teach him that!" Her voice broke and she began to sob. Letting go of the phone, she slid down the wall. The receiver dangled on its cord as Red buried her face in her knees and wailed.

Melissa stooped down next to her and took the phone. "Uh . . . they're still talking. Do you want to . . ."

Red just shook her head. "Hang up!" she sobbed. "They're liars."

Melissa slowly brought the phone to her ear. "Hello?"

"Where's Jean?" a brusque woman's voice asked.

"She's—she can't talk. She asked me to hang up."

"She thinks I'm lyin'," the woman said. "But I wouldn't lie about a thing like this. Her kid's dead. She's got to accept it."

"Dead?" Melissa looked back at the woman sitting huddled on the floor. "What happened?"

"He ran out in front of a car. It was bound to happen. He never listened to nobody. Wouldn't do nothin' I said. It wasn't my fault. And I can't pay for no funeral."

"I'll tell her to call you back when she's able." She hung up the phone, heard the quarter roll into the coin-return slot. Sitting down on the floor beside her, she tried to find the words to help her. It was strange, she thought, that until now she hadn't even known the woman's name.

"That witch. I never should have let her keep him. I should have let the state take him! He's not dead. She's a liar. Always has been."

Melissa looked around, wishing someone would come and rescue her from having to extend any compassion at all. But she was the only one here. Finally, as the woman's sobs grew deeper, she touched her shoulder. "You could have the warden find out for sure."

"No," she said. "I don't want to know. I don't want to know." Her voice got higher in pitch as she went on, until it was just a hoarse squeak.

"How old is Johnny?"

"Seven," she cried. "He's just seven. He can't be dead. He wouldn't be dead."

"If it is true, you could probably get out to go to the funeral."

"There's not gonna be any funeral for my baby!" she cried, getting to her feet. "He's not dead!" She looked at Melissa suspiciously. "You'd like it, though, wouldn't you, if he was! You'd think I deserved that!"

"No, I wouldn't," Melissa said. "I wouldn't wish that on anybody."

"Well, he's not! He's probably asleep in bed, and my sister just got drunk and thought she'd see if she could pull my string. He's a weapon she uses against me. She's always been like that."

She wanted to ask why Red was crying so hard, if that was what she believed. Instead, she watched as the woman ran back to her cell and closed herself in.

Melissa heard the soulful wailing late into the night, and when Chloe asked if she knew who it was, she didn't tell. Even Red deserved a chance to grieve her dead son.

By the next morning, word around the cellblock was that the news was true: Red was getting out that afternoon for the funeral but would be brought back right afterward.

Before she went to work that morning, Melissa wrote her a note and slipped it under her door. It said, "Please let me know if there's anything I can do for you. I'm so sorry about your son. Melissa."

Red didn't respond.

Melissa prayed for her all that day as she worked, and that evening, when Red came back to her cell, she saw the red swelling in her eyes, the purple tint to her lips, the pale cast to her cheeks. Her heart ached for her.

Again, before supper, she stuck a note under her door. "We're having a Bible study tomorrow at 4:00 in the chapel. Please come. It may be comforting to you. Melissa."

All that night, she listened to Red's wailing again, but the next morning, when she encountered the redhead at breakfast, she did nothing to acknowledge either of the notes she'd sent. Instead, she sat with the group of malcontents she usually sat with, her eyes cast down at her plate. She ate little and didn't speak at all.

That afternoon, when Melissa started to leave her cell to go to the chapel, Chloe looked up from a letter she was reading. "Where you goin'?"

"To the chapel. We've started a Bible study group. It meets at four."

"You gon' miss visitation?"

"No," Melissa said. "It'll be over by five."

"You ain't goin' by yourself, are you?"

"Well, there's another woman, Sonja, who's going from our cellblock."

"Sonja?" Chloe asked, astounded. "Goin' with her is like hangin' a rib-eye steak around your neck to swim through a school of sharks. They'll eat you alive."

"I'm going anyway," Melissa said.

Groaning, Chloe pulled her big body off the bunk. "Well, then, I guess I'll have to go with you. If I don't, you'll wind up mincemeat and I'll be stuck with another roommate. Probably one who's worse than you."

Melissa smiled. "You're welcome to come, Chloe, for whatever reason."

"I ain't got no Bible, though."

"You can look on with me."

"Whatever."

The woman followed Melissa out into the corridor, past the bubble—which wasn't really a bubble, but a booth where the guards sat—out of the cellblock and toward the chapel.

There were already three others waiting when they got there.

One of them was Red, sitting slouched in a chair with her arms crossed across her stomach.

Chloe took one look at her and said, "I'll handle this."

Melissa stopped her. "No, Chloe. I invited her."

"What? Are you crazy?"

"Her son died. She's in pain. I told her to come."

"Well, you're gon' be the one in pain, if you don't watch out. Abomination, it's a good thing I came."

Red looked up as they walked in, then quickly averted her eyes.

Both she and Chloe sat stiff and disinterested, not offering anything to the conversation about the book of John. But the group went on, each of the core members aware that a witness was being made here, that the two women, each here for different reasons, were hearing at least some of what was being said.

Red left before the meeting had entirely broken up, but as Melissa and Chloe went back to their cell, Melissa silently thanked God that progress had been made. She didn't fear the red-haired woman anymore. She'd had a glimpse into her heart, seen a little of her pain. Now she had compassion for her, and she knew that was a miracle. But she expected more miracles.

The next time she was able to get to the phone, Larry still wasn't home, and this time she left a message that she had called to see if he was coming to visitation tonight.

It was frustrating hanging up without talking to him, and she wondered again where he was. Was he still following Pendergrast? Was he getting any rest at all? Had anything happened?

When she started back to her cell, she saw Red hovering in the corridor. She tensed, wondering if Red had overcome her grief enough to go back to her old, threatening ways. Was she waiting for an opportunity?

Melissa kept walking until she was a few feet away from her. "I need to talk to you."

Red's words were clipped and angry, and Melissa was apprehensive. Choking back her fear, she said, "Okay."

Red stepped back into her cell, and Melissa tentatively followed, wishing Chloe were nearby, instead of in the TV room. She stayed near the door, but watched as Red sat down on her bunk.

"What's wrong?"

Red just looked down at her feet and shook her head. "I was just thinkin'. You know, about hell. Wonderin' if there's one for little kids."

Suddenly all the fear rushed away, and Melissa sat down next to her. "Oh, Jean." It was the first time she'd used her name and it felt strange, but she went on. "Little children don't go to hell. They're too small for God to hold them accountable for their mistakes."

The woman looked hopefully up at her. "Then Johnny's in heaven, you think?"

"I'm sure of it. Jesus had a special place in his heart for the children."

Red pinched the bridge of her nose, fighting her tears. "I never really thought much about heaven or hell before. I pretty much assumed I'd go to hell when I died, if there was one. But Johnny—I never counted on takin' him there with me, or sendin' him ahead of me." Her stoic face cracked. "I didn't take him to church even once. What he knew about God, he never learned from me."

Melissa took her hand, squeezed it.

"I just wish . . . that the last time he visited here . . . about a month ago . . . I wish I'd known I was never gonna see him again. I'd have read him that book he likes a few more times. He wanted me to, but I got tired of it and wouldn't. I coulda read it twenty times and he wouldn't have got tired. I should have read it just one more time." She dropped her face in her hand and wept harder. "I can't believe I'll never see him again."

Melissa touched her hair, stroked it, and began to cry herself. "You can see him again, Jean. You just have to make sure you go to heaven, too."

"Too late for me," Jean said. "Some things you can't take back. I done too much."

"God can forgive anything."

"Not what I've done."

"Try him."

Jean looked up at her and saw Melissa's tears. Frowning, she asked, "What are you cryin' about?"

Melissa sniffed. "The same thing you are. I'm just so sorry."

"Why?" Red asked suspiciously. "I would have beat you to a pulp the other day if Chloe hadn't stopped me. How do you know I still won't?"

"You might," Melissa acknowledged. "I realize that."

"Then why would you cry over my baby?"

Melissa wasn't sure, but she gave it her best shot. "Because I know how I would feel if I were in your place."

They stared at each other for an eloquent moment, a moment in which anything could happen. Then Red looked away, as if uncomfortable with the thought of truly connecting with anyone.

"What did a debutante like you do to get put in here, anyway?"

The question, designed to break the intimacy and put Melissa on the defensive again, didn't daunt her. "I lied to a grand jury."

"About what?"

"I told them I'd been raped when I hadn't."

Red began to laugh. "What was it? Revenge on some guy for dumpin' you?"

Melissa looked at her feet. "Yes, it was revenge. But I was never involved with him. It's a long story."

"Looks like the joke turned out to be on you."

She felt the blow, knowing it was aimed to hurt, but she didn't let it. "You're right. It backfired. But God's forgiven me."

Red thought that over for a minute. "Bet you never thought you'd wind up in here with us losers when you were sippin' wine with all your elite little friends, plannin' out your lives and doin' lunch."

Melissa realized where this was all going, so she got slowly, sadly to her feet. "Look, if you need to talk again, I mean if you really need to talk, instead of just flinging insults, you know where I am."

Red's eyes got a dull, thoughtful gleam as she watched Melissa leave.

CHAPTER FORTY-EIGHT

Karen Anderson's hands trembled as she buttoned her blouse back over the microphone and wires taped to her chest. "Are you sure they'll be able to hear me?" she asked Pam Darby, the lieutenant who was helping her.

"Positive. They'll hear every word."

"But couldn't I have some kind of ear phone so I could hear them?"

Pam shook her head. "Sorry. It might be too obvious. But as long as you're at work, they can reach you by phone."

"It's not the part at work that I'm worried about," Karen said. "It's the part where he approaches me." She raked her fingers through her hair. "See, I just can't believe that they could get to me soon enough. I mean, what if he has a gun? What if he has a knife? What if by the time they hear him hurting me, it's too late?"

"These are good cops, Karen. You have to trust them."

"Right," Karen said, flinging her hair back over her shoulder and leveling her eyes on the cop. "So you're telling me that you wouldn't be scared to death to walk into a maniac's hands like this?"

"Of course I would. It takes courage. Lots of it. You're a hero, Karen."

Karen wasn't buying it. To her, it just sounded like flattery to get her to cooperate. "Not yet, I'm not. And if I wind up getting killed in the process, am I just going to be one more statistic?"

"You're stopping the statistics, Karen," Pam said evenly. "That's why we need you."

Karen went to the window and peered out to the street, where cars passed by in a steady stream and pedestrians hurried to and from their offices. She wondered what she had ever done to wind up attracting Edward Pendergrast. Was it something she'd worn? The way she acted? Maybe it was her hair. He liked blondes, they'd said. Maybe she should dye hers after this was all over.

If she survived it.

Beginning to feel sick, she turned back to Pam. "Those other women he raped . . . do you have pictures of them?"

She thought for a moment. "Well, yeah. In his file."

Karen lifted her chin. "I want to see them."

"Why?" Pam asked.

Karen's eyes filled with tears as her face reddened. "I want to see what he did to them. I want to see what I have to expect."

Pam shook her head. "Karen, nothing like what happened to them is going to happen to you. Trust me. You don't want to see those pictures."

"That's what I thought," Karen said. "That bad." Her stomach roiled, and she set her hand on it. "I think I'm gonna be sick."

"Just take some deep breaths," Pam said, getting face-to-face with her. "In . . . out . . . in . . . out . . ."

But Karen only shoved her out of the way and headed for the bathroom. She bent over the toilet and wretched, making the tape on her chest pull with the effort, reminding her that someone was probably listening to every sound. She flushed, left the stall, and rushed to the sink. Cupping her hands, she caught some water, drank, then caught more and splashed it on her face. She looked up into the mirror, at the wet, pretty face that had caused her so much confusion over the last few years. She was too pretty to be taken seriously, and she'd fought that since high school. A woman who worked full-time and put herself through college deserved a little respect, she'd always thought. Now, that prettiness was more than a stumbling block. It was her enemy.

She began to cry as she stared past that face, to her hair, vowing to cut it off the moment this was all over, so that it wouldn't attract any more attention from sick rapists.

Pam poked her head into the bathroom. "Are you okay?" she asked. "I could get you something to settle your stomach."

Karen nodded. "Anything you have." She watched as the cop left her alone, then looked back into the mirror and began to sob. She would never make it. She would get sick the moment he spoke to her. She would throw up, ruining everything. She would slip up somehow, and he'd kill her.

Quickly, she began to unbutton her blouse, her trembling hands making it almost impossible to function. She grabbed the end of the tape with her fingertips and started to jerk it back, tear the microphone off . . .

But then what? Would she go back into hiding? Would she have to keep waiting?

She slammed both fists against the mirror, then spun around, trying to calm herself. She had to do this. She had no choice. It was the only way to find peace again.

She tried to breathe as Pam had told her . . . in . . . out . . . and slowly, she began to button her blouse again.

The door swung open, and Pam came back in. "Here's some Pepto-Bismol. Captain Richter keeps two or three bottles in his desk all the time. He has ulcers on his ulcers. Why don't you take it in your purse in case you need it while you're at work?"

Karen nodded and took it, opened the bottle, and guzzled a mouthful down. Then she shoved it into her purse.

"Do you think you're ready?" Pam asked.

Karen closed her eyes and tried to summon her strength. "I guess so," she whispered. "Ready as I'll ever be."

Is there anything we've forgotten?" Larry peered at Tony and the captain across the table in the interrogation room.

"I don't think so," Tony said. "I think we've covered every-thing. As soon as she's ready, we are."

"What if she loses her nerve?"

"She can't. We've gone over and over it."

The captain stood up and peered out the window. "The van's ready. And we have enough men on the case. We can't afford to do this again. We have to bring this to a head tonight."

"I think it would have come to a head without us, Captain," Larry said. "There's a hole dug with a body bag just waiting for her. I don't think he plans to waste any time."

The door opened and Karen came in, followed by Pam Darby. Karen looked pale and more fragile than usual, but she'd dressed as she usually did for work.

"Ready?" Larry asked.

She pulled in a shaky breath. "I guess so." Her hand trembled as she ran it through her hair. "You're not going to let me down, are you? You'll be close by the whole time?"

"I promise," Larry said. "And we'll be calling you in the store every step of the way, letting you know if he's waiting, where we are, everything. And when things start happening, we'll hear every word you say."

She closed her eyes. "This is the worst thing I've ever been through in my life."

"It could have been a lot worse," the captain said.

She wasn't sure about that. "So what do I do now?"

"Get in your car," Larry told her, "go by your apartment, take your suitcase in like you just got back from a trip, just in case he's watching. We need to let him know that you're home—that things are back to normal. Then come back out, head to work. I don't think he'll strike this early. The risk is too great. He'll wait until you get off work."

"I'm gonna be sick again."

"Can't," Tony said. "There's no time."

They started out of the room, but Larry hung back. "You guys go test her mike. I'll be there in a minute."

He waited until Tony, Karen, and the captain were gone, and then he sat back down and stared at the wood grain of the table. *This is it, Lord,* he thought. *Please help us. Don't let anybody get hurt.*

He wished he'd been able to talk to Melissa when she'd called earlier, to tell her to pray for them tonight. But she hadn't called back, and now he wouldn't be able to make visitation. She would wonder where he was and convince herself that he had already lost interest. It would be Saturday before he'd be able to tell her differently.

Maybe he'd have good news.

He felt a little sick himself as he pulled up from the table and started for the door. In all his years of police work, he'd never wanted to catch anyone so much. And he'd never been more afraid that something could go wrong.

CHAPTER FORTY-NINE

Melissa tried to look her best with what she had to work with as she waited to be called to the rec room for visitation. Chloe had gone over half an hour ago, as had many of the women from her cellblock, but Melissa's name hadn't been called yet. She tried to read while she waited, tried to straighten up her cell, but no one called.

Finally, she ventured out of the cell and went to the bubble at the end of the block, where two guards sat doing paperwork.

"Excuse me," she said. "No one's called me, but I'm pretty sure I was going to get a visitor tonight. Could you check the list and make sure there's no one out there for me?"

The CO scanned the list. "Sorry, honey. No enchilada."

Her heart fell, and she started back to her cell. There were still two hours left. Maybe he was just running late.

She climbed up on the top bunk and curled up into a ball. Whatever the reason he wasn't here, whatever it meant, it was his happiness that mattered. Not hers.

Closing her eyes, she began to pray for him, that whatever he was doing, God was with him. She prayed that he wouldn't feel guilty for skipping this visit, that he wouldn't be distracted from whatever he was doing or whomever he was with—that if God had another plan for him that didn't include her, that she could accept it.

But even as she prayed, despair washed over her. Loneliness as smothering as a gas seemed to suffocate her, and she began to cry. She cried for the next two hours, until Chloe came back.

"He didn't come?" Chloe asked.

"No," Melissa whispered. "He's a busy man. I'm sure he would have come if he could."

"Yeah, right." Chloe changed clothes and plopped onto the bed. "It's not a lot to ask, you know. That they come and spend a hour with us, just to break up the time."

Melissa didn't want to talk about it anymore. "I'm okay," she whispered. "Good night."

"Yeah," Chloe said.

The big woman was snoring long before Melissa fell off to sleep.

CHAPTER FIFTY

The surveillance van was an old purple van with no back windows, in which they had a wealth of equipment that could monitor everything that Karen said in the store, and everything that was said to her. She was nervous. Her conversations at the counter were short, brief, clipped. One of her coworkers asked her why she was in such a bad mood, and she told her she had a headache. When she spilled two bottles of cologne, then knocked another one off the counter while trying to clean them up, Larry and Tony began to wonder if she could go through with this at all.

Two rows away, they saw Pendergrast, waiting as usual for the mall to close. It was only fifteen minutes until closing time. Karen's voice was shaky, and her coworker suggested that she sit down and drink a glass of water. But she refused and tried to finish doing her job.

Tony sat in the front seat, watching with infrared binoculars through the windshield. "He's reaching for something in the backseat," he said. "What's he doing?"

Larry abandoned the tape recorder to John Hampton, their surveillance expert, who sat with headphones on in front of the tape equipment.

"He's getting out!"

Larry came to the window and watched as Pendergrast got out, looked both ways to make sure no one saw him, then sauntered over to Karen's car.

Larry grabbed his camera with the night lens and focused it. "He's got something in his hand." He clicked. "What is it?"

"Can't tell," Tony said. "He's bending over."

Larry snapped the camera again as Pendergrast stabbed something into Karen's tire, then hurried back to his car.

"Okay, this is it." Larry's heart beat wildly as he hurried back to the telephone. "I'll let her know. Tonight's definitely the night." He dialed the number for the men's cologne counter.

Through the binoculars, Tony tried to determine whether the tire was flat yet. It was hard to tell. "He's either going to try to get her into his car right here in this parking lot, or he's expecting her to drive off and not realize anything's wrong for a block or so."

"It's too risky to get her here," Larry said. "Too much could go wrong." He held up a hand to stem Tony's reply as Karen picked up the phone.

"Men's Cologne."

"Karen, it's Larry. You okay?"

"Yeah. We're getting ready to come out. I'm just waiting for the security guard who usually escorts us."

"Okay. Now, listen. He just did something to your front left tire. Looks like he punctured it—not real bad, so I don't think it's flat yet."

"What's he gonna do?" she whispered.

"We don't know yet. But get in your car like normal, and pull out, like you would if you didn't know. Stop a quarter of a mile down the road, and get out to see the tire."

"And then what?" she whispered viciously.

"He'll probably pull up behind you and approach you."

Dead silence, then in a high-pitched squeak, she said, "I can't do this."

Larry glanced back at Tony, who could hear her through the tape recorder. "Look, we're right behind you, Karen. We're not going to let anything happen to you."

"Where will he take me? What if he loses you? What if something happens before you can get to me?"

"You have to trust us, Karen. Now, just act normal."

He could tell she was crying. "The guard's coming. We're about to go."

"We're ready, Karen. Are you?"

"No, but that doesn't really matter, does it?"

Larry glanced at Tony again. "Karen, we can hear every word that's said. Remember, you're not alone. It's going to be all right."

"Here goes," she whispered, and hung up the phone.

Tony slipped into the driver's seat, keeping the binoculars to his eyes. Already, some of the employees were being escorted out. Pendergrast was sitting at attention, watching, waiting, for Karen to come through those doors.

Larry grabbed the radio mike. "All right, guys," he said into it. "We're almost to liftoff. Stand by."

The three men in the van held their breath as they watched the front door open again. Karen and a group of employees spilled out. Karen stayed with the security guard until she was almost to her car, then ventured out, as stiff as a board, and tried to jab her key into the door lock.

She dropped her keys, reached down to pick them up, then seemed to have trouble getting the car key into the keyhole in the door.

"She's shaking like a leaf," Tony muttered, watching through the binoculars.

She got the door open, then quickly slid in and locked it again. It took a moment for her to start the engine, turn on the lights, and pull out of her space.

"Is it flat?" Larry asked.

"It looks low," Tony said. "Won't last much longer, but it'll at least get her out of the parking lot."

"Here he comes." Pendergrast had cranked his car and turned on his lights like any of the other employees who'd just come out. Pulling out of his space, he took another parking lot exit, as if trying to be far enough away from Karen that she wouldn't know she was being followed. He waited until she'd pulled out, then slowly began to follow her to the barren road where he would carry out his plan.

The van pulled out as soon as he was far enough away not to see them.

"All right. She's having trouble," Tony said. "Looks like the tire's completely flat now."

"She's not stopping," Larry said as he slowed to stay far enough back to be invisible in the darkness. "When's she gonna stop?"

"She's riding on the rim," John Hampton said from behind them. "She's scared to stop."

"Well, she'll have to sooner or later. Pendergrast is getting closer."

They watched as her brake lights came on, and she pulled to the side of the road. "You guys had better be back there," she said in a hoarse voice.

"We are, baby, we are," Tony answered, though she couldn't hear him. "All right, he's pulling in behind her. Stop the van."

They stopped, and Tony watched with the binoculars as John monitored the tape. Larry began to sweat.

They heard the car door open, and saw Karen get out as Pendergrast approached.

"Hi." It was Pendergrast's voice. "You having some trouble?"

"Yeah," she said, so quietly they had to turn up the monitor to hear. "My tire's flat. Do you happen to have a jack?"

He took a look at the tire and whistled. "No, I sure don't. But I'd be happy to give you a ride somewhere."

She hesitated. "Do you have a car phone? Maybe you could just call someone for me, and I could wait."

He chuckled like anybody's big brother. "Sorry. Look, I don't want to leave a woman out on this road by herself. I wouldn't be able to sleep tonight. You never know who might come along. Let me just take you up to the nearest gas station, and you can call."

Again, hesitation.

"Come on, Karen," Larry whispered.

"Okay," she said finally. "Let me just lock it up."

She was stalling, and Larry looked over at Tony. He was sweating, too.

She locked the doors, then walked slowly back to Pendergrast's car and got in the passenger side.

Larry began to inch the van forward as he pulled the mike off its hook. "All right, boys," he told the cops who'd been planted at various spots in the woods where Pendergrast had dug the hole. "He's got her. Everybody in place. Let's not drop the ball now."

Pendergrast's car pulled slowly back onto the road.

"I can't believe it's flat," Karen said. "That tire was new."

"You probably ran over something." His voice had changed.

"I'm glad you were coming by. It sure would have been scary to stand out there alone. I've been meaning to get a car phone, but—"

From the van, they saw Pendergrast turn onto the dirt road. "Where are we going?"

"Shortcut," he said.

Larry punched the accelerator, and the van flew toward the dirt road, its lights still off.

"On a dirt road?" she asked. "I don't think so. Look, stop the car. I'm getting out."

"You're not going anywhere," he said calmly.

The van reached the dirt road, and Larry pulled over to the curb.

"You can't go up in here with your lights off," Tony said. "Road's too rough. You'll get stuck."

Larry drew his gun and opened the van door. "I'll go the rest of the way on foot. Radio the others. Tell them not to make a move until I give them the word. As soon as you hear them get out of the car, pull in, and hurry."

Bolting out of the van, Larry took off on foot, following the dirt road. His heart pounded faster with every step, and he uttered a prayer under his breath that nothing would go wrong. He ran for what seemed an eternity, following the dirt road. He heard the water and knew he was getting close to the clearing.

A car door slammed, and he heard a blood-curdling scream, propelling him faster.

The road curved, and he saw the clearing. The Toyota was parked there.

Karen screamed again, but he didn't see her or Pendergrast. Holding his pistol out in front of him, he scanned the trees, but couldn't see where they had gone. Frantic, he followed the sound as fast as he could, into the thick brush. It was too dark to see where he was going, so he pulled his flashlight out of his pocket and almost turned it on. But he knew Pendergrast would see him.

He heard Karen pleading and crying, and he ran faster, pushing through bushes and around trees, feeling his way as he gripped the pistol in one hand and the flashlight in the other, while he groped for his radio to tell someone to intervene.

His foot sank into a hole, and he tripped and dropped both the radio and the flashlight. He reached for them frantically, feeling through leaves and dirt, but couldn't find them. She screamed again, so he left them and went on as fast as he could. He was getting closer—he could hear Pendergrast's voice, and Karen's screams were louder . . .

Karen struggled to free herself from Pendergrast's arms as he dragged her through the brush, branches and twigs tearing her clothes and scraping her skin as they went. With all her might she screamed, but he wasn't afraid. They were too isolated out here, and he knew they couldn't be heard.

It wasn't supposed to go this far! They were supposed to stop things before Pendergrast got her out of the car, she thought on a wave of terror. But here he was, dragging her off where no one could get to her, and she was going to be dead before anyone stopped him. Was catching him all they cared about? Did they need a dead body to get the conviction they wanted?

They reached another clearing where the moonlight shone through, and she could see more clearly now. If she could just break away—maybe she could run—

He grabbed her hair and flung her to the ground, and she screamed out again. They weren't going to come, she thought desperately. She looked up at him, saw the crazy look in his eye as he pulled a scarf out of his pocket and wrapped the ends around his hands. Was he going to strangle her?

Deciding her allegiance to the case wasn't as important as her life, she used the only weapon she had. "The police know you're doing this! They're all over this place! They followed us here!"

Pendergrast seemed amused by that. He grabbed her hair again, pulling her up, his fist in her hair almost drawing blood at her scalp. He crammed the scarf into her mouth, then wound it around her head until it cut into the sides of her lips, choking and cutting her at the same time. She tried to scream, but couldn't, as he knocked her to the ground again.

As the van made its way down the dark road, silence screamed through the headphones. Tony cursed. "Something happened. He must have found the wire."

"I don't know," John said, listening carefully on the headphones. "I still hear the struggle. Maybe he gagged her."

"Where's Larry? He should be there by now. He should have sent the others in."

John shook his head and clutched the headphones, as if it would help him to hear better. "Stop the van, Tony. We're getting too close. He'll hear us and we'll have a hostage situation. Maybe that's why Larry hasn't signaled us yet."

"We *already* have a hostage situation!" Tony said, continuing to drive. But as he reached the clearing, he saw the Toyota and realized he was going to have to go the rest of the way on foot anyway. "All right," he told John. "I'm going in. Get up here so you can drive if you need to."

"Negative," John said. "I can't monitor the tapes and drive the van at the same time. We need the tapes for evidence!"

"Well, we don't need a dead girl!" Tony hissed. "Or a dead cop. I'm going!"

Before John could stop him, he took off down the dirt road, desperately hoping that it wasn't too late.

Larry tried not to make a sound as he pushed through the brush toward the scuffling sounds he could still hear. He came to the end of the brush, at the clearing where they'd found the hole yesterday.

He saw the opening in the trees overhead, and moonlight shone down on a circle of ground.

Karen was on the ground in that circle, kicking and fighting with all her might, though she was gagged and couldn't scream.

Pendergrast's back was to Larry, and Larry inched closer as Pendergrast fought, struggling to grab Karen's hands to restrain her.

Larry lunged forward and shoved the barrel of his 9 mm to the back of Pendergrast's head. "Freeze!" he shouted. "Let go of the girl, step back, and put your hands behind your head!"

Stunned, Pendergrast froze, and as he let Karen go, she slid across the dirt out of his reach.

Pendergrast spun around, trying to knock the gun out of Larry's hand. He kept his grip, but Pendergrast lunged at him, trying to wrestle it from his hands.

The gun fired.

With a yelp, Pendergrast dropped, clutching his shoulder with one hand. With the other, he reached into his boot and drew his own small pistol.

"Don't even try it," Larry said through his teeth, pointing his gun between Pendergrast's eyes. "Drop the gun. Drop it! Now!"

Pendergrast looked up at him, evaluating him, testing him. Slowly, he raised the gun, holding it between his thumb and forefinger as if he were about to toss it toward Larry. But he didn't.

Instead, he flipped it up until his finger was over the trigger, and aiming it at Larry's forehead, he cocked the hammer.

"Drop—the—gun," Larry uttered through his teeth. "I'm giving you to the count of three."

Pendergrast smiled.

"One . . ."

He wasn't moving.

"Two . . ."

A *whack* split the night, and Pendergrast fell over. Behind him stood Karen, still gagged, but holding a fat branch. Pendergrast twisted on the ground, grabbed her legs, and pulled her down, shoving the barrel of his gun against her ear. "You put the gun down, Millsaps," he choked out. "Drop the gun, or she's dead."

"Killing her won't keep me from killing you, Pendergrast," Larry said. "I'll bury you in that grave you dug."

Karen bucked and twisted with all her might, making it hard for Pendergrast to keep the gun against her head. Grabbing a fistful of hair, Pendergrast slammed her head down.

He tried again. "The gun, Millsaps. Drop it, and nobody has to get hurt."

Out of the corner of his eye, Larry saw Tony stealing through the brush, the same way he had come. He knew that, by now, at least five other cops were hiding in the shadows. Slowly, he lowered his gun and dropped it on the dirt.

Pendergrast laughed out loud, letting Karen go long enough to turn the pistol on Larry.

The gunshot shrieked through the air, but it wasn't Larry who was hit. The bullet from Tony's gun hit Pendergrast in the hand that clutched the pistol.

He let out a high-pitched yell, and the gun went flying.

Larry dove for his own gun, but Pendergrast went for it, too, fighting for his life with his one good hand. His fist flew across Larry's jaw, splitting the skin, but Larry struggled to grab the pistol. Pendergrast reached it first, and Larry clamped his hand over Pendergrast's. On their knees now, each of them reached for the hammer, and both fingers grabbed for the trigger.

When the gunshot rang out this time, they both dropped to the ground, still entangled.

"Larry!" Tony shouted, and burst forward.

Sirens blared as a convoy of squad cars reached the clearing, shining their headlights into the trees.

Only then could Tony tell which one of them had survived.

Larry pushed Pendergrast off him and slowly stood up.

Tony rushed forward to the limp body lying on the ground. Turning him over, he felt his neck for a pulse. "He's dead."

Larry looked down at the gun as if it were a foreign thing. Opening his fingers, he let it fall to the ground. Then he went to Karen and untied her gag.

She was sobbing as he got it off, and she fell against him, weak and hysterical. As he held her, he looked back at the body.

Cops swarmed out of the trees, lighting the area with flashlights and headlights.

But the victory was hollow. Larry had wanted the man in jail. He had wanted him exposed, tried, locked away in a prison where he would endure the torment he deserved. He hadn't wanted him dead. That was too easy. That was too quick.

Shaking, Larry helped Karen up and walked her to one of the squad cars. Helping her in, he told one of the cops, "Get her to a hospital. Make sure she's all right."

He stood back, watching, as the car pulled away.

When it was out of his sight, he went to the hole Pendergrast had dug to hide Karen in. The shovel and bag were still there, as was the pile of dirt waiting to be pushed back in. He reached for his flashlight to better see the contents of the makeshift grave, but remembered he had dropped it, along with his radio.

The lights from the headlights made it easier for him to find his way back through the brush, and he spotted the flashlight. He reached for it, and his foot sank again, just as it had when he'd been running through earlier.

Turning the flashlight on, he shone it down on the circle of sinking dirt. It was loose and thinly covered with leaves. He stooped and brushed the leaves away.

It looked as if the dirt had been put there to fill a hole, and he scooped a handful out, then another, and another.

"Tony!" he shouted. "Over here!"

In seconds, Tony was beside him. "Get a load of this," he said. "Looks like we have another hole. Question is, what's it burying?"

They got a shovel and centered all their efforts around digging, until the beams of the flashlights revealed what was hidden there.

"Oh, no," Larry said. "It's a woman."

They pulled the dirt-encrusted body out and shone the light in her face.

"Ten to one this is Lisa," Tony said. "Our other runaway."

Larry dropped wearily down to the dirt. "So Pendergrast killed her. That means he killed the girl on the beach, too."

"Yeah," Tony said. "He must have dumped her in that canal."

"Her and who else? We might find others."

As the others photographed the hole and the body, and recorded all of the evidence they would need to close the case, Larry began to feel bone tired, sick with exhaustion. He got up and started to walk away. Tony followed him. "Look, man. I owe you an apology."

"For what?" Larry asked.

"For not taking all this as seriously as I could have. I mean, I did at the end, but in the beginning—it never crossed my mind that he was a killer—or that he had anything to do with the girl on the beach."

"Didn't cross mine, either," Larry said. He stopped and looked off into the night. "I just keep thinking. That could have been Melissa in that hole. He might have killed her, too."

"He didn't. And he didn't kill Karen Anderson. She was roughed up and traumatized, but she's in one piece. It could have been a lot worse. Karen and Melissa are both going to be fine."

"Yeah," he said. "You're right."

He walked back to the van and leaned on the hood as the flurry of activity went on around the bodies. He wanted to hold Melissa, and listen to her breathe, and thank God that it hadn't been her in one of those holes, covered with dirt . . .

Tony walked up behind him and slid his hand across his back. "Why don't you go home, buddy? It's all over. We can take it from here."

"No," Larry said. "The evidence. We have to make sure—"

"He's dead," Tony reminded him. "The evidence won't matter much now."

Larry realized wearily that Tony was right. There would be a rush of news reports, and friends and acquaintances of Edward Pendergrast would come out of the woodwork, providing glimpses of the dark side of the killer. Maybe even more bodies would be found.

But there wouldn't be a trial. Pendergrast had already been convicted. And he wasn't going to find a way to squirm out of this one.

"Come on, buddy," Tony said. "Go home. Get some sleep."

Larry didn't have the energy to argue as he got back in the van.

he depression that Melissa had gone to bed with had kept her awake for most of the night. She tried to tell herself that it didn't matter that Larry had skipped that visit, that she'd expected as much, that it was inevitable. But the bottom line was that she was already in love with him, and the worst part of her incarceration was that she was going to lose him.

Had God really forsaken her?

She forced herself out of bed early the next morning, dressed in the orange jumpsuit that she was beginning to hate with all her heart, and got her Bible. Chloe woke up as she opened the door that the CO had unlocked just moments before.

"Where you goin' so early?"

"Bible study," Melissa said. "We decided it would be a good way to start our day."

Chloe cursed and pulled out of bed. "Well, I guess I have to go, too, if you are."

"No, you don't. You can sleep some more."

"And let you get pulverized walkin' to the chapel?"

"Chloe, everyone's still asleep. Nobody's going to hurt me."

Chloe ignored her as she stepped into her jumpsuit. "Your blood ain't gon' be on my head."

Quietly, they started down the long hall to the door of their cellblock.

It was midmorning when one of the officers came to get her. "Put your stuff up," she said. "You have a visit from your lawyer."

"Lynda?" she asked, turning off her iron and taking off her apron. "Why?"

"Do I look like I know all the answers?" the woman barked. "She's waitin' in room B."

Sweeping her bangs back from her perspiring forehead, Melissa followed the officer out.

But it wasn't just Lynda who waited for her. It was Larry, too.

Her face lit up, and when he reached for her, she threw her arms around him.

"I missed you last night," she whispered.

"I missed you, too," he said. "But you know I wouldn't have skipped if I didn't have to, don't you? You knew that, didn't you?"

She let him go, and he saw from the look on her face that she hadn't had that faith at all.

"Melissa, something happened last night. Something really important. And Lynda agreed to get you out for an attorney's conference today so I could talk to you. She pulled a few strings to get me in."

Melissa gave Lynda a half-smile. "Thanks, Lynda." She realized then that she had no makeup on and was damp with perspiration. Her hair was pulled back in a ponytail, and she felt like a frump. But before she could apologize for her appearance, she saw the bruised cut on Larry's jaw.

"What's this?" she asked, touching his face gently. "Were you injured?"

"Melissa, Edward Pendergrast is dead."

She stared at him. "What do you mean, he's dead?"

"We were able to catch him trying to rape a woman—"

She caught her breath. "That one you told me about?"

"Yes. She cooperated with us, and we had everything we needed on him. I wanted to get him in jail, make him rot there. But things took a turn . . . and now . . ."

Lynda stood up. "There was a struggle over a gun, and—"

"And I shot him," Larry said.

She could see that they weren't easy words for Larry to utter.

"He's really dead?" she asked.

"Yes," Larry said. "He can't hurt you anymore."

She threw her arms around his neck, holding him for dear life. Together, they began to weep.

"I prayed he'd get caught and convicted," Melissa whispered. "Sometimes I didn't think God was going to answer."

"He did," Larry whispered. "He was caught *and* convicted. It just wasn't our court he was judged in."

"He's really gone," she whispered, awestruck. "When I get out, I don't have to be afraid."

"He's really gone."

Lynda smiled. "I've sent a plea to the governor, Melissa, as well as the judge who sentenced you. I've asked them to pardon you, or at least consider reducing your sentence to probation, given the circumstances surrounding Pendergrast's death. Now that the story's going to be all over the news, I think we may be able to get something done."

Melissa considered that for a moment. "When?"

"I don't know. It might be a few days. Maybe even a couple of weeks. But I'm doing all I can."

"Good," Melissa said, letting go of Larry. "I need a couple of weeks, at least."

Larry shot Lynda a look, and they both looked at Melissa as if she'd lost her mind. "For what?"

She wiped her eyes and smiled, the first genuine smile Larry had seen on her in a long time. "I'm not here by accident," she said. "God needed me here. We've got this Bible study going . . . and some of the people I was terrified of . . . they're coming now, and they're listening. If you get me out, I'm coming back as often as I can, to keep the group going."

Lynda's eyes grew tearful as she began to smile. "That's one of the most amazing things I've ever heard."

Dismissing that, Melissa looked at Larry again and wiped the tears on her face. "The girl—is she all right?"

"She was pretty shaken up last night," Larry admitted.

"Can I see her when I get out?" she asked.

"I'm sure it can be arranged. Until then, you could write her a letter. I'd take it to her."

"All right," Melissa said. "I want to thank her. For myself . . . and for Sandy."

CHAPTER FIFTY-TWO

Karen Anderson sat in her apartment the next day, curled up in her favorite chair with a blanket over her that covered the scrapes and bruises on her legs. The ones on her arms and face were more apparent . . . but it was the ones on her heart that she worried most about.

She had spent the first night in the hospital on a sedative, and though she knew that Pendergrast was dead, she'd been afraid to come home. Her mother had threatened to sue the police department for involving her in such a dangerous situation, and Karen hadn't known whether to support the suit or discourage it. Finally, she had forced herself to return to the apartment where he'd watched her, and try to get on with her life.

She had almost refused to let Larry in when he'd shown up at her door, but when he told her that he had something to give her from his girlfriend who was in jail, she had reluctantly opened the door. She'd had little to say to him, and he had left quickly, but not before telling her that she was his idea of a true hero, a gift sent from God, and that he would do anything he could to help her heal from her trauma.

Now that he was gone, she opened the manila envelope and emptied out the contents. There was a letter there, and several pictures of a beautiful woman, with blonde hair and bright blue eyes. Beneath the snapshots was a smaller envelope.

She unfolded the letter first and began to read.

Dear Karen,

I started this letter several times, trying to find the right words, but there just aren't any. How can I tell you how much it means to me that you would risk your life to save the lives of so many potential victims? How can I explain the closure I feel at knowing that he won't be waiting when I get out of here? How can I describe my gratitude to you?

There aren't words to do it, Karen, so I decided to send you pictures. Meet Sandy, my sister . . . at her graduation, and her wedding . . . with me, and with our parents. Losing her caused pain so deep in us that we thought it would never go away. But what you did has helped to relieve that pain so much.

Thank you, Karen, and if you feel up to it when I get out, I'd love to meet you and shake the hand of the brave woman who helped me wake up from my nightmare.

God bless you,
Melissa

Karen wiped her eyes and looked at the pictures again. The beautiful, happy eyes of the woman who had killed herself smiled out at her. In comparison, what had happened to Karen seemed mild.

She picked up the smaller envelope, and opened it. It was another stack of pictures, but this time, a note from Larry was stuck to the top of the stack.

Karen,

I thought you might like to see the two women we know Pendergrast killed, and some of the other women whose lives you may have saved. Some of these were pictures we recovered from Pendergrast's apartment.

Larry

She saw the two women on top, the one who'd washed up on the beach, and the one he had buried. She flipped further through them and saw the random snapshots of women who didn't know they were being photographed. Women coming out of their homes, getting out of their cars, coming out of stores . . .

She leaned her head back on the chair and looked up at the ceiling for a moment. What she'd done was a good thing. Maybe it hadn't been so terrible, after all. It could have been so much worse. For her. For all of them.

The telephone rang, but she didn't move. The machine picked it up, and she kept looking through the pictures as her voice played its message. It beeped, and a voice said, "Miss Anderson, this is Chip Logan with the *St. Clair News*. We'd like to do a feature story on you for our paper . . ."

She smiled softly then, but didn't pick up. She wasn't ready for that just yet. But maybe later, she thought. Maybe soon.

This hero stuff was just going to take a little time to sink in.

EPILOGUE

After the phone call from the governor the following week, and the *20/20* interview with Melissa about the Pendergrast case, Judge L. B. Summerfield, who'd sentenced Melissa, agreed to release her on probation.

She had a final Bible study with her group that morning, including Chloe, who had begun to read her Bible each day so she could "argue" intelligently with the others in the circle. Melissa promised them she would be coming back with Doug to worship on Sunday mornings, and that she'd start work immediately to get permission to continue meeting with the Bible study group as part of her personal prison ministry.

Before she left her cell, she sat down on the bunk next to Chloe. "You know something, Chloe?" she asked.

Chloe grunted.

"For most of the time that I've been in here, I've considered you my personal angel, sent by God. Did you even realize you were being used by God?"

"Me? God ain't *never* used me."

"He did, Chloe. Before I came in here, my lawyer, who's also a good friend, gave me a verse of Scripture that meant a lot to me. It said that God would protect me. And it was so true. God protected me through you. Thank you . . . for being there."

Chloe smiled one of her rare smiles. "So you think God was really usin' me?"

"I sure do."

She chuckled slightly. "I'll be. Didn't even know God knew I was here."

"He does."

"Thank ya, Melissa."

"Are you going to keep coming to the Bible studies, even if you're not having to protect me?"

Chloe shrugged. "Might."

Melissa stood up and looked around the cell. "Would you like to keep all these books?"

Chloe's eyes widened. "I never been much of a reader. But I have been a little interested. Maybe I will read 'em."

"All right. They're yours. And I'm going to visit you Saturday and bring you some groceries. How's that sound? I'll bring you a box of Snickers."

Chloe laughed. "Girl, you're a saint."

She leaned over and kissed Chloe on the cheek, and the woman looked embarrassed. "Thanks, Chloe. For everything."

Then, quietly, she left the cell for the last time.

Red was lurking in the hallway, leaning against the wall. "I knew you wouldn't be here long. What did you do? Flap those blonde locks in the judge's face? Promise him somethin'?"

Melissa just looked at her. "You know what happened, Jean. You saw it on the news just like everyone else."

"Yeah, but I know what goes on behind the scenes."

"And you know me." She extended her hand to the bitter woman, but Red only slid her hands into her jumpsuit pockets and started to walk away. "I'm coming back," Melissa said to her back. "For the Bible studies."

"Right. I'll believe it when I see it."

Melissa smiled. "You've got a deal." She watched until Red had gone back into her cell, then left cellblock C for the final time.

Larry was waiting for her at the warden's office. She ran into his arms, laughing and crying. "Am I really free?"

"Completely," he whispered against her ear, holding her as if she could be snatched from him at any time. "Free to do anything you want," he whispered. "Free to go back to the life you had before. Or free to go in a new direction."

"I didn't have much of a life before," she said, looking up at him. "For the last three years, everything has revolved around my obsession to get Pendergrast."

"Then it's time for you to start over," he whispered. He handed her the bouquet of roses he'd laid on the table, and as she buried her face in them, he added, "And maybe that new beginning could include me."

She looked up at him, her eyes soft with anticipation. "What do you mean, Larry?"

"I mean that I love you," he whispered. "And I want you to be my wife."

The fragile joy and hope in her eyes slowly faded. "What will your friends say? I'm an ex-con. You're a cop."

"They'll say, 'Congratulations, Larry. She's the prettiest ex-con we've ever seen.'"

A soft smile broke through her turmoil. "No, really. What on earth will you tell them?"

He thought for a moment, then framed her face with his hands and looked into her eyes. "I'll tell them that when God shows me a treasure, I'm going to take it every time."

She wiped her tears and stared up at him with soft eyes that seemed so innocent, but she'd experienced more than she'd ever wanted to. Larry was a gift from God, something she hadn't earned, but she wouldn't refuse, either.

Throwing her arms around him, she said, "Of course I'll marry you!"

He whisked her up in his arms then, holding her in a crushing hug. Melissa laughed out loud, and he joined her, and they each realized what a new, magical lilting sound the mingling of their joy produced. It sounded like grace.

And Melissa knew why they called it amazing.

AFTERWORD

I often think my life is much like that of a mouse in a maze. There's a plan and a path which is perfect for me, and it's not so hard to find. But I can convince myself that I have a better way—a shortcut, or a more interesting route to where I'm going. Sometimes, I even think the destination I choose is better than what has been ordained for me.

I picture God standing above that maze, urging me to take the turns and twists he's planned for me, luring me this way and that, showing me open doors and nudging me past the closed ones … but so often I ignore him and go in my own direction. Sometimes I kick down the doors that would keep me out of trouble, and I forge headfirst into what lies behind them. Those are the times when God groans and slaps his forehead in frustration. But then—always—he says, "I can still work with this," and moves to Plan B, C, or D, making another path for me. It might be less wonderful, because of my own careless choices, and it might be less useful to him, but he doesn't give up. He continues to work with me and guide me away from the dead ends in my life, and he opens the doors that will lead me to what he wants me to have. I have never strayed so far that he couldn't guide me back.

That's grace. That's the grace of a father who loved me—a poor, ignorant, rebellious, vagabond mouse—enough to send his Son to die so that I could get out of that maze once and for all. With my eyes on the cross, I don't have to bump into walls and turn in circles and backtrack through the corridors of my life. All I have to do is follow him. And trust.

Abundant life? You bet it is.

That's why they call that grace *amazing*.

Terri Blackstock

OTHER FAVORITES FROM TERRI BLACKSTOCK

Seasons Under Heaven
SOFTCOVER 0-310-22137-4

NEWPOINTE 911 SERIES

Coming Soon! October 1999

Shadow of Doubt
SOFTCOVER 0-310-21758-X

Private Justice
SOFTCOVER 0-310-21757-1

Word of Honor
SOFTCOVER 0-310-21759-8